D1554153

THE

HOOD

TWISTED KINGDOMS

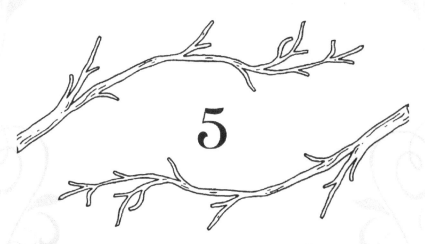

5

FROST KAY

Copyright

Also By Frost Kay

TWISTED KINGDOMS
(Fairytale Retelling)

The Hunt

The Rook

The Heir

The Beast

The Hood

The Wolf

DRAGON ISLE WARS
(Fantasy Romance)

Court of Dragons

Queen of Legends

THE AERMIAN FEUDS
(Dark Fantasy Romance)

Rebel's Blade

Crown's Shield

Siren's Lure

Enemy's Queen

King's Warrior

Warlord's Shadow

Spy's Mask

Court's Fool

Prince's Poison

THE AERMIAN FEUDS COLLECTION
(Dark Fantasy Romance)

Kingdom of Rebels and Thorns

Queen of Monsters and Madness

Reign of Blood and Poison

HEIMSERYA

Dedication

This is for those who have felt downtrodden and lesser
because of societal expectations.
You're special and I see you.

Prologue

13 Years Ago

"Papa, it's not fair," Robyn complained, pushing back her long, black hair away from her face. It always fell in her eyes, but her mama wouldn't let her cut it. "I want to be Lord Lochslee, too!" She glared at her twin who smiled at her from his bed. "I'm older than John!"

Her father picked her up and kissed her on the cheek, his beard tickling her face before he tucked her into her own bed. "I know, darling, but the law is very clear. The land and the keep go to the eldest male heir."

"The law is stupid," she huffed, crossing her arms. Girls were just as good as boys.

"You're not wrong," her father murmured. "Although, don't let your mum hear you use such language."

Robyn nodded and pulled her blanket up to her chin as her father moved to John's bed and tucked him in as well. He kissed her brother on his pale forehead. John was *always* sick.

"Papa, why do we obey the laws if they're not nice to

people like Sissy?" John asked.

Her father sighed and sat on the edge of John's bed. He glanced toward Robyn and then back to her brother. "This is important, dear ones, so listen closely."

Robyn rolled onto her side and widened her eyes. Was he going to tell them a secret?

"Do you know why we have Robyn dress up in your clothes, John?" he asked.

"Because the people need to see a healthy boy, so they can have confidence that our land is secure and—" John scrunched up his nose, like he was trying to remember the rest. "And so they can trust in our leadership."

"But why is that necessary?"

"Because the bad men will try to take our land," John whispered.

"That's right, my love. This is the world you two were born into. Equality between men and women only exists in *this* home. The kingdom in which we live does not agree with our beliefs. A man is believed to have more worth than a woman."

"That's just silly," Robyn piped in. "John and I both came from Mama."

Her father smiled. "How astute you are. You are both equally precious in our eyes, but most don't think that way."

"Then they're stupid," John muttered.

"Language," their father chastised softly.

"Sorry, Papa."

"It's okay, my son." He patted John's leg. "It's important that we treat all with respect and love. That's how our creator would have wanted it. No person is better than another."

"Why do people think girls aren't as good as boys, Papa?" Robyn asked.

"Most have been taught that lie from infancy, and so they believe it to be the truth." His solemn gaze locked on to Robyn. "Do you know why I have you train in the yard with swords?"

"Because sometimes John can't," Robyn said. She knew her mama hated it when she sparred.

"That's not the reason, love. I can't take away the prejudice against your sex. I wish I could. Life will always be harder for you than for John. It's not right, and I'm sorry for it. But what I can do is that I will prepare you to be tougher, smarter, and stronger than anyone who crosses your path."

"I can be tough, Papa," Robyn chirped.

"I know you can." He glanced back at John. "You both must look out for each other. You only have one sibling. When your mother and I are gone from this world, you'll only have each other."

"Yes, Papa," both twins replied.

"I love you both so very much. Good night." He rose from the bed and blew out the candle that had been burning on the dresser near the boy. "Sleep sweet." He closed the door.

Robyn heard John turn onto his side. Only a slip of moonlight shone through a crack in the curtains, lighting his face, which was now turned toward her.

"I'm sorry you can't be Lord Lochslee," he murmured.

"S'okay. It's not your fault."

"This is a big land, though, and a big house. Even when Papa and Mama are gone, I don't want you to leave. You can help me with our people, and we can always share a room!"

She smiled at her brother. "Promise?" she said, leaning

out of bed, holding her pinky finger out.

John grinned and wrapped his pinky finger around hers. "Promise."

But he lied.

Life was never that fair.

Chapter One

The Sheriff

Present Day

Men in love were fools.

At least it worked in his favor.

The lovesick monster Luca had raced from his keep the moment he had healed, and, along with him, the annoying green dragon that had plagued the place for weeks.

Gustav hadn't been able to make a single move until the beast had vacated the premises. It was a bloody miracle the sheriff had survived after the blasted dragon had attacked him.

Gustav limped through the halls of the monster's castle in the dead of night. The flower he'd been tasked to procure—wrapped carefully, root and all—was in the satchel at his hip. A shiver ran down his spine, and he gritted his teeth, not slowing his pace. There was something about this place that bothered him. Maybe it was the torn paintings, the broken mirrors, or creepy gargoyles that seemed to glare at him from above.

It was too quiet.

Gustav had been raised in Lord Merjeri's keep. The place was never silent. This castle seemed like the stones held the bloody secrets of the past.

The hair at the nape of his neck rose as he finally crept from the castle that resembled more of a crypt. Someone was watching him.

It's your imagination.

He pushed against the keep and scanned the moonlit meadow for several moments. No one was in sight.

Unease roiled in his belly, and he broke out in a sweat. He needed to leave now. His lord had been waiting far too long for the flowers as it was.

The sheriff straightened and hustled toward the ledge that crossed the river. No matter where Gustav turned, he was in danger. He'd take his chances with his lord. At least he wouldn't tear him apart with his bare hands.

Don't count it out.

That was the thing about the heir to the Merjeri province. Ruslan was a brute, a knave, and a viper, which Gustav enjoyed as long as it wasn't directed at him. But there always was the chance that he could turn on you.

One part exciting, one part terrifying.

Which is why, at a very young age, Gustav had made sure to become invaluable to the heir. Had he committed despicable acts? Yes. Had he received power beyond anyone else in his station? Yes.

In the end, it was worth it.

Because the fact of the matter was, Gustav was lowborn with the smallest traces of Talagan blood flowing through his veins. If anyone knew, he'd have been in the fields with the rest of the shifters. Instead, he had power, gold, land, *and* the support of the most powerful province.

And to a wily gutter rat?

It was *everything.*

Chapter Two

Robyn

The sun had barely risen, and already Robyn was fleeing through the woods for her life.

Her wound pulled, and she winced. Of course, she was injured while making a run for it. Everything about Robyn's situation was wrong, wrong, wrong. In truth, it had been for years now. Her mother's sickness, her father's apathy, and her brother's death had changed everything. Sometimes, the pain and loss of her twin was so much to bear that she wished for a different life where she was an only child, if only it would give her a moment's reprieve from the aching loss that haunted her each day.

But none of that mattered anymore.

All that mattered was getting away from her attackers before she collapsed to the forest floor. Blood seeped from her shoulder, and the world wavered. She stumbled but caught herself. If she fell now, she worried she'd never get up again.

It's too soon for you to die. Push.

She had gone through so much to get to where she was, and she had so much left to do. She hadn't fought successfully in her dead brother's place in the war to die like this. It couldn't possibly be a coincidence that nobody in Robyn's regiment had caught on to the fact she was a woman, posing as her brother so that her aging father did not have to fight in her stead. A wave of hot, burning shame turned Robyn's already flushed face crimson. What would her papa say when he saw her again? Would he cast her out? Had she brought shame upon their family?

She glanced up, catching a glimpse of the lightening sky through the trees above. Her breath stuttered out in clouds of cold air.

If he sees you again.

Robyn shook her head and pushed through the pain in her shoulder to outrun her would-be attackers. There was no 'if' about it. Robyn *had* to see her father again. She had to get home.

It wouldn't only be the end of *her* life if she failed to return.

The captain of Robyn's regiment believed her to have fallen in battle, meaning her family, their land, and everything they held dear was now vulnerable. He was too much of a sadistic lout of misery not to pass on the terrible news.

Robyn couldn't have that. She had to protect her family. She had no other choice but to survive and push on. For her family, her people, and herself.

When the sound of the men pursuing Robyn abated somewhat, she took the opportunity to pause by a gnarled oak tree. She bent low over her knees, heaving in a breath that stabbed through her lungs like a thousand knives. Winter's bite, it hurt.

She squeezed her eyes closed and coughed, feeling liquid wet her lips. Her eyes snapped open, and she cringed at the sight of her blood on the forest floor. The last year of warring and fighting had not cured her fear of blood. It still sickened her. Bile burned the back of her throat, and she retched, pulling her shoulder wound again.

Agony speared her, and she fought the urge to pass out. Blood coming from her lungs was bad, and Robyn knew it. It meant the festering wound on her shoulder was no longer merely skin-deep. She needed help.

And soon.

She heard the rhythmic sound of running and lurched away from the tree. Her attackers were catching up.

Gritting her teeth, she pushed through the pain wracking her body and surged through the shadowy trees. If she didn't manage to lose track of them soon, the sun would be fully up, giving her pursuers an advantage in spotting her. She needed to reach a part of the forest that the weak winter sun could not touch. She was smaller and lighter on her feet than the men pursuing her; all she needed to do was burrow through a space they could never reach, then she would be safe.

For now. Until her injury forced her out of the woods once more.

Just one more step.

Robyn's body heaved with the effort it took to remain upright, moving, and conscious.

One more step, then another, then another. Just one more.

Just—

She slipped on a layer of thick winter mud, and it took every ounce of her strength to bite back the scream that her lungs longed to let loose. In her injured, delirious state, she couldn't right herself and lost her balance, pitching forward. She slid down a steep verge through the forest. A groan of pain escaped her lips as she tumbled down the ravine. The trees and snow swirled around her, and pain became her companion. Just as she thought she couldn't survive much more, she slowed, and her body slid to a stop as she reached level ground.

Shivers wracked her body, and black spots ran over her vision. Had she died? No. She hurt too much. Was she dying? Probably. Her teeth chattered, and she sucked in a freezing breath that caused her teeth to ache.

Robyn gingerly lifted her head. Arrows were scattered around the area, but her bow had survived the journey. It laid just out of her reach, a little beat up but no worse for wear. A sharp pain stabbed her in the temple, and she immediately lay back down, closing her eyes as the world lurched around her. She reached out her right hand and curled her fingers around one of the arrows. The touch helped ground her amid the pain. If she stayed and napped where she was, like her body wanted, it meant sure death.

Get up. You can do this. Don't give up. Fight.

Two tears slid down her frozen cheeks as she forced her eyes open and took stock of her body. Her shoulder was screaming, but other than that, nothing seemed to be broken, which was a bloody miracle. Something to be thankful for. She huffed out a wry chuckle—it was that or sob. If John were still alive, he wouldn't be able to accuse her of being a pessimist anymore.

You're not dead. Get moving.

The sharp pain in her shoulder and lungs, and the dull throb of every muscle in her body, told Robyn that she was very much still alive and could stay that way if she was smart. She closed her eyes and focused on listening to her surroundings.

Everything around her was still. Silent.

No one was coming after her.

Robyn almost laughed at this turn of events. The fall should have been fatal—she had been too startled to fall *properly*—but the thick mud beneath her had softened her tumble. Aside from some cuts and grazes from the thorns, and no doubt several new bruises that would bloom on her skin over the next few hours, she was no worse for wear than she had been before the fall.

A snort escaped her, causing her head to throb.

What were a few bruises compared to her lung injury and possible concussion?

Also, on the bright side, she had lost the men following her.

She should almost be thankful for her mistake.

On legs heavily protesting against supporting her weight, she got to her feet and struggled to pick up her arrows and toss them into her battered quiver. She yanked her bow from a nasty looking thorn bush and really took in her surroundings. It was a far darker, colder part of the forest than she had ever found herself in. She took a limping step toward the ravine, and her vision went hazy, intermittently red, white, then black.

Lovely. No doubt she'd concussed herself, too.

Just before Robyn's vision went entirely, her hands touched upon the hulking carcass of a dead redwood tree. It was hollowed out on one side; she would find no better shelter than this. In any case, she lacked the strength to continue looking for anything better, so she stepped into the apparent safety of the tree's gargantuan trunk.

Cuddling into her cloak, she leaned against the wall of her new shelter. Slowly, the pressure in her skull lessened. The cold seeped in, and she registered the damp fabric of her tunic. Carefully, she lifted her cloak and cursed. Her shoulder had begun bleeding in earnest again. She touched her shaking fingers to the dirty wound, a shiver traveling down her spine and a lurching feeling filling her stomach at the dark, poisonous color of her own blood.

Robyn's legs buckled, and she fell to her knees. She was unconscious before her head hit the forest floor.

Chapter Three

Robyn

5 Days Earlier

Robyn wandered through the forest just outside town. Stars, she was tired. It was a thankless job protecting the people of the small northern village they were currently encamped at. Every time she stuck up for the locals was another strike against her. The bullying had gotten worse over the last few weeks. If it hadn't been for Madam and her girls, Robyn knew she would have been seriously hurt.

Kicking a stone, she leaned against a nearby tree and savored the small shaft of sun that poured down and warmed her face. It was times like these that she missed her family so keenly that her heart felt like it was bleeding. How were her mother and father fairing?

"No! Stop it!" a woman screamed.

Robyn's eyes popped open, and she turned toward the sound. Quietly, she pulled an arrow from her quiver and crept in the direction of the commotion. She crested a hill and spotted three soldiers surrounding a washerwoman. They cackled and tore at her dress as she desperately tried to fight them.

An ugly rage ignited in her gut. No one had the right over someone else's body. *No one.*

Robyn kept to the trees, her pulse pounding in her ears as she closed the distance between her and the group. The tallest of the men—her captain—grabbed the woman and licked the side of her face.

That was enough.

Robyn loosed an arrow and pierced him in the shoulder. He screamed and dropped the woman. Robyn ducked behind the tree and steadied her breathing. If she was discovered, she'd be dead by nightfall.

Wound them and get out unseen.

"I knew he'd come. He just can't help himself." A pause. "Robyn, we know you're out there. Why don't you come say hello?"

She smiled despite the ice trickling down her spine. At least they hadn't found out her secret. Was this all a set-up?

She scanned the trees around her and spotted an archer to her left. Robyn moved just as an arrow embedded itself in the tree trunk where she'd been standing. She took off running up the hill, shouts ringing out behind her. Hopefully, this would give the washerwoman a chance to escape.

Robyn's arms and legs pumped as she reached the crest of the hill, and she cried out as she was hit in the chest. She gasped and stared at the arrow protruding from her shoulder. Another archer.

She stumbled into the thicker trees, pain almost blinding

her.

Don't stop running. If you stop, you're dead.

Twigs slapped against her face and tore at her clothes, but she kept going.

"I hit him. He can't be far," snarled a familiar voice. Desmond, their second captain. "Find him!"

Their voices sounded farther away, but she wasn't sure if that was because she had gained enough ground or because she was about to pass out from blood loss.

Find a hiding spot.

She tripped on a root and crashed to her knees. She grunted, and tears ran down her face as pain ricocheted through her body. Panting, she glanced around, her gaze snagging on a tree whose roots rose enough that they created a door of sorts. Robyn crawled to this entrance and stared at the dark hole that led to some creature's burrow.

The captain or a badger?

The badger.

She spun around and painfully brushed away any evidence of her tracks and backed into the large burrow. Her heart pounded as she entered the dark, dank hole. It was bigger than she expected and blessedly empty of any critters as her back met the farthest wall of the burrow. Robyn curled in a ball and whimpered. She wrapped her hand around the arrow and tried to breathe through the pain.

Footsteps pounded in her direction, and she tried to hold her breath as they slowed near the burrow. She pressed her spine against the side of the hole and prayed they didn't look inside.

"Any sign of him?" Desmond demanded.

"He couldn't have made it much farther," Nemron crowed.

"I pierced him in the heart." Blessedly, he had not. "He's as good as dead."

Desmond laughed, the sound sinister. "Our lord will be happy to hear the news. Finally, the heir to the Lochslee estate is dead. Come on, let's go and celebrate."

The captain had planned on murdering her. The Lord of Merjeri had planned it. The greedy lout just wanted her family's land.

Tears of pain trickled down her face as she put pressure on her wound, and their voices faded away. Robyn swallowed hard and stared at the roots of the tree as stars began to dance across her vision.

If it was the last thing she did, Robyn would bring down the crooked, greedy Merjeri lords. They thought they'd disposed of the heir to Lochslee, but little did they know that a betrayed woman was infinitely more dangerous than a soldier.

She smiled as her eyes closed.

They'd all pay.

Chapter Four

Tempest

5 Days Earlier

Winter's bite, her bloody back hurt.

Tempest rubbed her lower spine with both hands as the crisp winter breeze ruffled her loose periwinkle hair. She inhaled slowly and pushed the unruly waves from her face, her fur cloak keeping her warm. Spring would be coming soon. She took another step across the outer balcony of the mountain palace, the chill from the stone floor seeping through her heavy socks. She should go back inside and warm herself by the generous fire her husband and mate—Pyre—had built for her before he'd stormed out a few hours prior, but Tempest couldn't make herself budge from her spot.

Each time she stood on the balcony, it felt surreal. She'd never imagined a future outside of the palace, where she wouldn't be a lapdog and glorified assassin for the Crown. Tempest had never contemplated marriage. It was out of the question for a Hound—one of the elite warriors—to wed. Their devotion belonged to the monarchy. Plus, after everything she went through to be the first woman to join the ranks? A husband, hearth, and home hadn't been in the cards for her. Luckily, she had a mind of her own and a wily kitsune shifter husband who defied all rules.

Her uncle Malcom told her he'd always known she was destined for great love, but the man was too romantic for his own good. It was pure luck and a ridiculous amount of evil that had thrown Tempest into her mate's path. It was a miracle in and of itself that Pyre hadn't executed her on the spot or that she hadn't crept into his room in the night and smothered him to death.

A slow smile lifted her lips.

Some days she was tempted to do just that.

The man was all sorts of gray, crooked, and devious. But he was hers, and she wouldn't have it any other way. Pyre might have painted himself as the villain for years as the Dark Court's lord, but he was the farthest thing from it. To his chagrin, he had a bit too much honor, gallantry, and mercy to live to be the bad guy he had pretended to be for years in order to overthrow the former corrupt king. Tempest liked to think she had a hand in helping her husband turn over a new leaf. Despite the changes they'd both made for each other, they were still themselves.

If only he'd stop wearing his garish clothes.

Tempest snorted and tucked her hands beneath her fur cloak. Stars above, Pyre owned more pairs of shoes and hats than she did. Being trained as a spy and assassin had taught Tempest one vital truth: never draw attention.

That meant dressing in clothing that blended—earthy,

dark, common colors were her favorites. But not her mate. He wore jewel tones, brocades, gold and silver. She leaned against the balustrade. For Dotae's sake, he was more interested in jewels and shiny things than she'd ever been. If it hadn't been for his dark-red kitsune ears that sat atop his head, Tempest would have suspected her husband of being a crow shifter.

She sighed and pushed away from the parapet and moved back inside, her fur cloak trailing behind her. She closed the glass doors and padded across the thick gaudy rug and stood before the fire, holding her hands out to warm them. While she was accustomed to the frigid temperatures of her kingdom, living in a palace carved into the northern Dread Mountains was a cold affair. She was literally surrounded by icy stone walls fifty percent of the time.

Her jaw clenched.

Tempest wished it was more. The Dark Court was her home, but she missed being out on the road. Being the queen's spy mistress was more paperwork than what she was used to. An evil smile spread across her face. Which is why she'd snuck some of her paperwork onto Pyre's desk last night, a fact he'd discovered this morning. He'd promised payback before he kissed her silly and then stormed from the room, muttering about conniving, sexy females.

Sweet poison, she loved needling her mate.

She caught a whisper of sound a second before the double doors to their personal study slammed open, cracking against the walls with a little too much force. Tempest rolled her eyes but didn't look in Pyre's direction. Someone had tickled his temper.

"Did you kill anyone?" she asked.

"Not yet, but I plan to."

It wasn't her husband.

Tempest turned around and eyed the cracked plaster. Pyre wasn't going to appreciate that. She arched a brow at Damien, the Dragon King. "Was that really necessary?"

Damien's emerald eyes snapped to the wall and then back to her face. "My apologies."

"It can be fixed." She scrutinized her friend, noting his labored breathing and the fury radiating from him. "Obviously, something is bothering you. What is on your mind?"

The dragon huffed, lacing his arms across his bare chest. At least, he'd worn pants this time. He had no shame, and she'd seen more of him than she'd ever desired to.

Damien's jaw worked, and he glanced away from her, staying silent. Oh, boy. That wasn't good. Her smile dropped and she stared hard at him. "Tell me."

He gritted his teeth and growled, "I lost him."

Tempest blinked slowly and schooled her expression. She knew exactly who he was talking about. The sheriff was what he called himself, and the only thing she had to go on was Thorn's word that he was somehow connected to the province of Merjeri. Tempest had sent out spies to gather more information on the man who'd attacked Damien's cousin Luca and somehow survived his encounter with Damien. The problem was that all had been silent which irked her. Silence meant mischief in her line of work. And when it came to the Duke of Merjeri and his heir, they were always up to nothing good. Merjeri was known to be a thorn in the monarchy's side, now more than ever since the princess had been coronated months prior.

"What can I do to help?" she asked briskly. Damien was the type of person who liked to get right to the point. No sense in beating around the bush. The proud dragon wouldn't have come to her if he didn't need her assistance.

"I need to find him," Damien snapped, his dark tone not fazing her in the least. He may be a big, scary dragon king, but she'd faced down far greater foes.

"I understand. I sent my spies out as soon as you notified me that the sheriff had escaped. It's a long journey from here. I doubt they've been able to gather much so soon."

Damien snarled and pulled at his green hair, breathing hard. "He's got away!"

Tempest was at his side in an instant and laid a hand on his bicep. "That's not true. We'll find him."

"Humans crawl across this kingdom like ants. Finding him will be almost impossible."

"Come now. You know me better than that," Tempest murmured softly. "Give it some time."

He dropped his hands and stared down at her, some of his anger leeching away from his face. "Time is against us. You know as well as I do that once the trail has gone cold, the person is long gone."

"But I know something you don't."

Damien's gaze sharpened. "Do tell."

She stepped away from him and grinned. "The diamonds."

His brows slashed together. "The diamonds?"

"Despite the Merjeris' best attempts to keep everyone out of their province, they can't hide their excessive spending. They love to flaunt their wealth."

"All men in power like spending their hoard."

"You're not wrong," she said, strolling to the fireplace. She stirred the embers and added two more logs to the fire. "But the Duke of Merjeri was almost bankrupt within the last ten years."

"Interesting. So where is the gold coming from?"

Tempest pointed the fire poker at Damien as he dropped into Pyre's wingback chair. "That's what my husband wanted to know."

"The land is fertile and the forest full of game and lumber," her friend pointed out.

"True, but the forest is Lochslee land. Plus, with all the civil unrest in the province, many fields have been burned. Last year's crops were poor, and this year doesn't look much better. The duke is taxing the life out of the people, but it still doesn't add up to what he is spending."

Damien waved his hand. "Get to the point, woman. I think you've been spending too much time with your mate. You're waxing on about all the little details I don't care about."

"The details matter," she countered, setting the fire poker down on the hearth. "I reached out to an old friend of Pyre's..."

"A criminal, no doubt."

She smiled. "A merchant. It seems that the duke has gotten his hands on diamonds."

"The mountains east of Merjeri don't have gems. I would know."

"Exactly." She moved to her chair and plopped down, pulling her fur cloak over her lap. "They are getting diamonds from somewhere."

"And nothing is free," Damien tacked on with a wicked smile.

"That's right." She steepled her fingers as the dragon took on a contemplative expression. "So, what exactly are they exchanging for these diamonds?"

"Slaves?"

She shook her head. "The duke would be out of his mind to try something like that with Ansette on the throne. Plus, he's more subtle than that."

"So, drugs," Damien said flatly.

"That's our guess as well. Now," she rubbed her hands together, "it's time for the diamonds. There are rumors that there are unsanctioned diamond mines in Betraz."

Damien sucked in a sharp breath. "Old Mother's territory?"

Tempest nodded solemnly. "Indeed."

The dragon leaned forward in his chair. "You need to tread carefully, Tempest. She is not to be trifled with. Old Mother has been around for many years. No one quite knows *what* she is, only that she rules her wolves with an iron fist. After her last marriage, she rules the duchy through her stepdaughter. Everything is under her control. She's one of the strongest alphas in history."

"I know, but I go where the intel takes me." She sighed and ran a hand down her face. "I think it would be easier to sneak around in her territory than Merjeri at this point."

"And yet, you send spies there." A pause. "For me."

Tempest held Damien's gaze. "Yes. You're my friend. When someone hurts you, they hurt me. Family sticks together."

A slow smile worked its way across Damien's handsome face. "Are you sure you don't want to leave that kitsune and come with me?" he teased, breaking the tension.

"Never. As I've told you before, *things* do not please me."

"Peculiar female," he mumbled before slapping his hands against his thighs. "Who have you sent to Betraz? Brine?"

"No."

Damien cocked his head, losing his smile. "Have you informed him of the situation?"

Tempest glanced away, staring at the dancing flames. "No, I have not."

"Why? He is your best asset for this situation."

"I will not send him back into that purgatory," she snapped, staring Damien down. "You know what they did to him. He barely made it out alive. Sending him back would be a death sentence."

"Don't keep this from him."

"I won't, but I'm not sending him in. I'm not going to risk his life." Old Mother would never sink her claws into Brine again.

"So, who are you going to send in?"

She arched a brow. "Who do you think?"

Damien bared his teeth in a vicious smile. "Me."

"You. If you're willing. The sheriff has a connection to Old Mother. That's where you'll find your trail."

The dragon pushed out of his chair and towered over her for a moment before he took her hand in his and kissed the back of it. "Your wish is my command."

"If only," she retorted. He dropped her hand and strode toward the exit. "Keep in contact. Keep a low profile. I want information only, no bodies."

"No promises."

Tempest rolled her eyes before she scowled at her hand. "You left your scent on me," she accused.

Damien released a deep belly laugh. "A gift for your mate."

Lovely.

Bloody men.

Chapter Five

Robyn

Present Day

Robyn blinked back into consciousness. Her eyelids were heavy and sore as she registered the sun filtering through cracks in the hollowed-out trunk. How long had she been out? Five or six hours? Longer? Going by the grogginess in her head, she reasoned she could very well have slept for a day and a half. But if she had done so, with no fire to warm her body, then she surely would never have woken up, instead falling prey to the deepest, darkest sleep of all?

She peeked at her wound. It was grisly, but at least the bleeding had stopped. She closed her eyes and took stock of her body. Her entire being was stiff and pain-riddled. She wiggled her cold fingers and grimaced. Even that was difficult. Tears filled her eyes as she shifted, the wound in her shoulder aching so intensely that she bit her bottom lip in an effort not to cry. She couldn't afford weakness right now or she'd die.

Get up.

With the taste of iron on her tongue, she forced herself to sit up.

Her stomach revolted, and she leaned over to heave. Bile filled her mouth but nothing else. When was the last time she'd eaten? Yesterday? The day before? Stars, she didn't even know what day it was.

Wiping her mouth, she pressed her back against the curved wall of the fallen tree trunk and eyed the open end. Light danced on the snow in small shafts, and large dark trees stood silent like sentinels. That was at least something. If she'd strayed too far from her path and into the dark wood, there wouldn't have been any light at all. Or maybe she'd run far enough that she had reached the other side.

Doubtful though.

Robyn was in poor shape. There was no way she would make it through the dark wood unscathed by carnivorous creatures or vagrants. A puff of laughter escaped her cracked lips. For all she knew, she had barely managed to skirt into the trees before deliriously circling back around. That was where the danger lay. Losing one's way in the woods was deadly.

You need to discover the position of the sun and find a landmark. A sign of the direction. A stream. A region-specific moss. Anything.

Her joints throbbed as she tried to massage the feeling back into her fingers. It wasn't helping. In fact, Robyn could not feel her hands or her feet—save for a burning, like knives, in her extremities that told her she was freezing. A shiver wracked her body, and her teeth began to chatter.

That was something, at least. If she could still feel the cold and move her extremities, then she had not been asleep that long. If she got moving, she'd warm up and could find some firewood in the process to prepare for the night. There was little sense in not using the failing light of the afternoon to first work out where she was as she worked.

Exhaustion plagued her something fierce, but she gritted her teeth and forced herself first to her knees and then to her feet. She swayed and stumbled out of her shelter, snow and mud squelching beneath her boots. Tilting her head back, Robyn savored the winter sun on her face and strained to hear anything. Relief followed as she heard the soft babble of a brook.

Water and food.

With slow steps, she moved toward the sound. Hopefully, she'd find fish and watercress.

To her luck she did not have to go far. Picking up her pace, she soon found a small but blessedly clean snake of water crossing right in front of her. She crouched and forced some of the freezing liquid down her throat, the icy water burning her fingers as she cupped her hand and drew the liquid to her lips. Cursing her lack of a waterskin or bottle, she stood up to take in her surroundings.

The slant of the sun suggested it would set within the next two hours. She eyed the tip of the Dread Mountains just visible over the tree and then how the stream flowed in the opposite direction. A flutter of hope took flight in her chest. Lochslee Keep couldn't be more than two days away in her current shape. Although, if her memory served her correctly, she'd wandered just inside the border of Betraz. She pulled a face and sighed. Just when she thought things couldn't be worse. Betraz was a province known for its ruthlessness, outlaws, and bandits. Everyone knew that the duke's marriage and subsequent death was a product of Old Mother's plotting. Now she lorded over not just the woods and their inhabitants, but the duchy as well. Robyn shivered. It was best that she got out of there as soon as possible.

She placed the back of her icy hand against her forehead and winced. Her fever was raging—a sign that an infection had taken root. Another shiver wracked her body.

Heat. Robyn needed heat. She had to get a fire going.

Now that she knew where she was, she would continue traveling in the morning. The failing afternoon light was better spent gathering wood, tending to her wounds, and not freezing to death before the night was through. Good thing she'd become an expert at such things.

She peeled the bark from a dead, standing tree and moved back to her shelter. She tossed it on the floor and worked through her pain and sickness.

Focus on something positive.

Despite the bad apples, Robyn had made friends among the soldiers. Comrades. They had looked out for one another. Her friend had been a big, burly man almost two entire feet taller than her, named Borris. When he had become sick after a wound in his leg festered, Robyn had been the one to help him. In turn, when Borris grew well once more, he ensured she'd gotten extra rations whenever mealtime came around. It was a give-and-take relationship that she understood and appreciated: if you looked after your people, your people looked after you.

Now she had only herself to rely on.

"You can do this," she whispered to herself.

Robyn painstakingly collected some Grandfather's Beard from the closest trees, along with sap, and carefully placed it atop of her bark pieces. Next, she focused on gathering winter herbs for a poultice. It was a good thing she knew what the plants around her were and what they could do. If she could just get a fire going then she could grind several of them with snow into a bitter, unappetizing paste mixture and force it down her gullet. That would help the infection, and some more of the paste slathered over her shoulder would help seal the wound. She would then be subjected to a painful, unsettled sleep, but in the morning, she should feel better.

She was so close to home. The thought of her family hurt more than all the physical aches and pains riddling her body. Had the news that she'd died in the war been brought back to her family? It didn't matter. Soon enough, they'd know the truth. She had to soldier on for just a little longer.

Robyn tossed her handful of herbs onto the snow near her shelter and added some fresh pine needles. That would have to do for now.

Next, she moved up and through the hollowed-out tree trunk until the top of the trunk was just inches from her head. She grinned when she found a recess in the ground where the tree had rotted away. It would act as an ideal spot to protect a fire and hide her from prying eyes. Peering up, she looked away as she punched a hole in the top of her shelter and prayed it wouldn't crash down around her ears. When it didn't collapse, she moved away, satisfied with her smoke hole.

She hobbled outside the shelter and walked around it, scrutinizing the woods. She looked for any blind spots that might prevent her from keeping track of her surroundings while she was there and found none. Though she was quite certain she had lost her attackers by now, she couldn't take any chances. Using a nearby bough, she tried to cover her trail to the fallen tree trunk.

Satisfied, Robyn got to work, collecting the driest wood she could find on the forest floor, thanking the gods above that the hard tumble through the woods had not caused her to part with the small satchel tied around her waist. It contained two daggers, the thinnest of blankets, a wooden bowl and, most importantly, flint and steel.

Her fingers were so cold, they were turning blue, and tremors seized her as she set up the fire. Her hands shook as she tried and failed three times in a row to light the Grandfather's Beard.

"Come on," she whispered, licking her lips. She tucked her hands into her armpits and rocked in place. She had to get the fire going. *Had to.* Robyn tried again and cursed when she dropped her flint. "Dotae be g-good," she bit out through her gritted teeth—she'd uttered the curse before she could stop herself. Her mum would be appalled if she knew how colorful Robyn's language had become in her time with the regiment. She picked the flint up and struck it again. "Just w-w-work. *Work!*"

With her exclamation finally came the successful strike. Robyn cupped her hands around the miraculous flame as it began eating up the sap, dry pine needles, and Grandfather's Beard. She reveled in the burst of life she had created and the heat it carved through her frozen flesh, then she ever-so-carefully fed it more kindling. When the kindling in front of her was safely lit, she moved to the opposite side of the circle of wood.

As her fingers heated up, Robyn winced in pain but fought her way through it to spark several more flames to set the firewood alight in multiple places. Only once the fire was in no danger whatsoever of burning out did Robyn dare collapse beside the warmth of the flames.

For a long moment, she simply lay there, taking in the sight of the orange, red and yellow flames as they cracked and blackened the wood that fueled it. If she had it her way, Robyn would have fallen asleep there and then, but she knew that would be the death of her. So, with a shudder she collected herself, staggered back to her feet and out of the tree trunk and forced herself to grab a few stones from the edge of the stream.

Between the failing light and Robyn's feverish, aching state, her search was slow going. She straightened and blinked slowly as she spotted a group of small purple flowers growing along the water. Her breath caught. It couldn't be. Robyn stumbled forward and dropped to her knees, leaving her stones behind. With care, she touched one soft purple petal and almost cried.

A mimkia plant.

Robyn plucked two of the four flowers and quickly said a little prayer of thanks. It still boggled her mind that something that looked so delicate could survive the harsh winters of Heimserya. She tucked the blossoms into her cloak pocket and went back to retrieve the stones she'd dropped. What little light the afternoon had afforded was well and truly gone by the time she returned to her fire.

With some effort, she sat down by the warmth and fished out her wooden bowl from her satchel. It had been cracked *before* her fall; now that crack had spread through the polished wood at an alarming rate. Robyn knew it would not last another fall, but if she was lucky, it would not need to. In two days' time, she would be home, and she could trade in her wooden bowl for one made of jade. She set her rocks along the fire's edge. They would feel amazing tucked inside her cloak once they heated up.

Her fingers protested against being used for something as complicated as ripping and shredding herbs into the little bowl, but like with every other trial she had faced, Robyn persisted. Once done, she reached outside her shelter and added a handful of snow into the bowl. The flames quickly melted the snow, and she mixed the contents with her fingers to form paste. Lastly, she dropped one mimkia blossom into the mixture and let it simmer until the paste was hot but not scalding. She pulled it from the fire and brought it to her lips. The smell of its contents turned her stomach.

Here goes nothing.

Pinching her nose, she gulped the stuff down, gagging, and the sludge coated her teeth and tongue. As expected, sharp, lurching pain filled her body, and she had to force back a swallow to keep her stomach from upending its contents.

She focused on her breathing. In, out. In, out. Again and again and again, until she was sure nothing would come out of her mouth but air when she opened it once more. Next, she heated more snow and pulled away part of her tunic and the old bandage. She blanched from the smell but managed not to vomit. Cup after cup, she poured warm water over the wound, despite the pain, to clean it and flush out any debris. Finally, she concocted another thicker paste. Robyn blew out a heavy breath and braced herself for what came next.

Dipping her fingers into the paste, she pressed it into her wound. Robyn yelped and stars crossed her vision, but she didn't pass out. Just barely. With unsteady hands, she finished up. She tore strips of her blanket to make bandages and covered the wound. With that done, she wiped out the bowl with the edge of her cloak. She tossed more snow into it as well as fresh pine needles for tea.

She'd done it.

Her eyes dropped, and she fought against sleep. Needing something to do with her hands, she checked her quiver. Though her fall that morning had not damaged her bow, Robyn *had* lost a few arrows. Not all of them—not even half of them—but enough for her to come to the conclusion that if anything attacked, each of her arrows would have to fly true in order for her to beat them.

It was a good thing Robyn was the best archer in Merjeri. And in her regiment in the army. She wasn't a boaster, but from the time she was a young girl, it had come to her naturally. She was yet to meet anyone who could best her with a bow. Even in the state she was in, with a good line of sight and a stable place from which to let loose arrows, she could more than hold her own. With her bow, she'd managed to provide meat for her family and her people on more than one occasion. It had also saved her life in the army.

It was only after counting her arrows, cleaning her daggers, and stoking the fire that Robyn flung out what remained of her insubstantial blanket around her and relaxed one shoulder against the trunk's wall, hands and feet stretched out toward the fire. She had done all she could. Though she was hungry, and there were fish in the brook, food would have to wait until tomorrow. Some sleep and some warmth would do more for Robyn than fishing in the dark ever could.

She closed her eyes.

It felt as if barely a second passed before Robyn jerked awake. The hair at the nape of her neck rose, and she strained to figure out what had woken her. Her fingers curled around her bow as she struggled to quietly sit up. Was it an animal?

The barest crunching of snow and twigs beneath a heavy boot caused her heart to drop. Most definitely human. She steadied her breathing and focused on the sounds of the forest like her father had taught her. Someone was stalking closer and to her left. Then, to her right, she heard a rustling through the trees.

So much for losing her attackers that morning.

Hardly daring to breathe, Robyn used her glimmering firelight to locate her quiver, and notched her bow in silence.

She stood, muffling her groan as she tucked the daggers into her belt and crept to the opening of her shelter. If Robyn got out of this alive, it would be a miracle.

But Robyn had no miracles. She had no one at all.

She only had herself.

Chapter Six

Robyn

The bandits knew Robyn was here, and she knew they were there.

The time for surprises was over.

"Now, now boys," she shouted. "It's not nice attending a party you weren't invited to." Adrenaline rushed through her system, and her pain dulled to almost nothing. She eyed the shadows moving between the trees. She was outnumbered and outmatched.

"You cheated us, girlie," a man growled to her left.

"No. I did not. I paid fairly." She had. They'd grown snoopy and greedy. "Plus, you have a bag full of diamonds. What do you need me for?"

"That was before we knew you was a woman impersonating a soldier. What kind of reward would we get for such information, Cas?" one man rumbled.

"I reckon heaps of gold," Cas, the weasel-faced bandit replied.

She kept her fear and panic from her face. "Leave, and I'll forget about this."

A chilling chuckle cracked through the air. "I'll be the one making demands, girlie."

Blearily, Robyn counted five—no, six—assailants heading toward her. "If that's how you want it," she whispered.

She released an arrow from her bow before she had time to process it, and one of her attackers fell to the forest floor with a heavy thump. The rest of the men ducked beneath the underbrush and trees, preventing Robyn from seeing them, and she cursed.

So, they know you're good with a bow, which means they will try to get around you and stick to the shadows. That was bad. That was really, really bad.

Her skin crawled as they crept through the forest. She knocked another man down.

Two down. Four to go.

She gritted her teeth and pulled a dagger from her belt, preparing to fight to the death once her arrows were rendered well and truly useless. Hand-to-hand combat was her weakness. Robyn hissed when Cas lunged from the trees to her right. She barely had a chance to knock him over the head with her bow before he jabbed at her with his short sword. Robyn darted out of the way, and he growled, turning on the spot to avoid a second hit from her bow. He attempted to grab her cloak, but Robyn stumbled, her delirious state saving her, just this once. Cas glared at his empty hands and pushed his greasy blond hair from his face.

"Come here, you little—" Cas roared and leapt for her, infuriated by Robyn's successful dodge. She braced herself and thrust her dagger upward. His curses turned into a spluttering cry, and she jerked back as he toppled to the ground, holding his belly.

"I'm sorry," she murmured. Robyn didn't want this.

She kicked away his short sword and swung around with her bow in one hand and dagger in the other, looking for a hint of the other three assailants. But the forest was worryingly silent and still. *Just where have the other men gone?*

Robyn's silent question was answered when a shadow leaped from above and crashed into her, knocking her straight to the ground. Lying face-first in the mud and snow, her mouth full of the stuff, she spat and hollered. Robyn bucked and scratched her attacker's hand with her dagger. She yelped and managed to roll away, spots dotting her vision, but before she could get her bearings or get to her feet, they grabbed her ankle.

"Get—get *off*!" she cried, kicking desperately at the man's face. He grunted heavily, and only let Robyn go when she aimed another kick at his teeth. With tremendous effort, she snaked away from him on her belly, then used the bow to help her stagger to her feet.

An agonizing bolt of pain lanced down Robyn's shoulder when she put her weight on the bow. She just barely managed to stay standing, wielding her bow as if it were a sword until her vision cleared enough for her to take aim at the man on the ground and fire an arrow.

Four down, two to go.

She panted heavily and growled at the mud that covered her. So much for cleaning her wound. Her legs shook as Borris approached with another man—sick, twisted grins full of certain victory plastered to their faces. Betrayal shook her. This was all a game to them. They were just trying to tire her out. The joke was on them. She was exhausted before they even began.

Slinging the bow over her back, she pulled her second dagger from her belt and angled herself into a fighting stance. Robyn bared her teeth. "That all you got? I've had rougher scrapes with my baby brother."

The world wavered for a moment, and she blinked hard to focus back on Borris and his last standing companion. They smirked but didn't attack. Her brows furrowed as she caught a small sound behind her.

Except there weren't two men.

There were *three.*

In her fevered state, Robyn had miscounted six attackers in the beginning when in fact there had been seven, and now that unaccounted-for man grabbed Robyn's injured shoulder and shoved his thumb straight into her wound.

Robyn screamed.

The world swirled around her. For a moment, Robyn couldn't even breathe. The pain was worse than anything she had felt so far in her entire life. Then her assailant pushed his thumb in even farther and she could do nothing but black out for a few, precious seconds. By the time she was coming to, Robyn heard the man shift a blade into his hand—how was it she could hear that when she could neither see nor breathe?—and she let out a low moan.

This was the end.

How pitiful. John would be disappointed.

Her vision came back in a spurt of hazy, dark flashes. She cried out as he tossed her to the ground, and she braced for the flash of pain that would signal her life being extinguished.

And waited.

And waited.

When no such strike came, she became uncomfortably aware of the fact that everything around her had gone silent. Blinking furiously to try and regain her vision further, she lifted her head and realized she had fallen to her hands and knees once more on the forest floor. With a strength she knew would not last once the adrenaline left her system, she forced herself to turn and look at her attacker.

His eyes widened and he gurgled, clutching his chest.

She gaped at him. What in the blazes was this deviltry? Had she accidently stabbed him? No, the wound was much too high. That wasn't her handiwork. Robyn only wounded, never murdered.

One of the other attackers hurt him?

She shook her head and tried to make sense of the body. The seven men had gone at her in a coordinated strike; there were no traitors in their midst. Her assailant collapsed onto his side as heavy and lifeless as a bag of grain, and she only narrowly managed to avoid being flattened beneath him. She backpaddled—crying out in agony—with a mere moment to spare. Robyn knew she wouldn't have possessed the energy to haul the man's corpse off her, and she breathed a shaky sigh of relief that he was down for the count and had not fallen on her.

"Sweet poison! Someone else wants our bounty! Get him!" Borris roared.

She needed to move and now. Whoever had taken care of her assailant could be just as much of a threat. Her head spun as she tried to focus beyond the din. She climbed to her feet and wavered as she stumbled into the hollowed-out tree.

Goosebumps ran down her arms, and then all at once, noise erupted around Robyn, finally breaking the eerie silence that preceded it. Her other assailants were clearly outraged at the fact their partner had been felled. Their victory had been so assured, after all. Their shouts and crashes through the forest were all aimed in the direction of the one who'd murdered their comrade. She pressed against her shelter as Borris and his companion rushed into the woods, her legs giving out.

Get up. Move.

Robyn staggered to her feet and then back inside her shelter. There was only one entrance and exit. Sure, she was cornered, but at least it was warm. There was something calm about the state she was in, despite the adrenaline in her system, the pain surging through her shoulder and down her body, and the screams of death around her. She was in danger—imminently so. Yet, for whatever reason, Robyn could not find it in herself to *feel* in danger.

A dull ringing began in her ears, and she kept her gaze locked on the darkness just outside her fire. Her pulse thundered in her veins as the screams fell silent and the forest seemed to still and hold its breath. Whoever had taken down Borris and his men was coming for her. She could feel it.

Ice trickled down her spine as she felt eyes on her. Even though she couldn't see them, she knew he was there all the same. She gripped her daggers with far less strength than she would have liked, steeling herself for whatever was waiting for her.

"Are you just going to stand outside or are you going to

come in and say hello?" she rasped, nerves strung tightly. She waited, and nothing. "Don't be—"

Robyn gasped as a naked man stepped from the shadows. A very tall, broad, naked man. To Robyn's out-of-focus vision, it almost looked as if his skin was...shimmering. Did he have scales?

You're delirious.

She blinked, and the man took a step forward. Another blink, another step. On the third blink-and-step combination, instinct kicked in and she threw her dagger. Her jaw dropped when he snatched it from the air, blade-first, with his bare hand. She was going to die.

Not like this. On your own terms.

He stepped into her shelter and past her fire, and Robyn lashed out with her dagger and tried to let out a scream, though it came out as more of a wheeze of pain. She collapsed back to her hands and knees, no longer able to bear standing.

"Come any closer and I'll end you," she rasped.

His ankle came into view, and she weakly swiped at him, but he stepped out of range. Black dots edged her vision.

"Oh, darling, I have much bigger plans than killing you."

Right before she passed out, Robyn took one last look at the man as he knelt before her and bent low by her side. Those were scales on his naked skin, she was sure of it. She smiled at what her addled brain had conjured. Dying before a handsome man wasn't the worst way to go.

She toppled forward and he caught her, turning Robyn in his arms. He watched her just as oblivion welcomed her.

And she could have sworn his pupils were slits, too.

Chapter Seven

Damien

It was Damien's first official assignment for Tempest, and already he had caused a girl to faint. A smile quirked his lips. Not that women hadn't fainted in his presence in the past, but this time it was different. He'd have laughed at the sight of said girl if it weren't for how gravely injured she was. He could scent the putrefaction of her wound from where he stood.

Damien sighed and glanced outside the makeshift shelter at the fallen bandits. Only one of them was dead by his hands—the rest were merely mildly maimed and unconscious...though, going by the way they'd screamed at his presence, Damien would have thought he'd pulled their innards out through their mouths. Part of him was tempted by the thought. He'd witnessed enough depravity to last him a lifetime. His lip curled, and Damien spat on the ground. Maybe he should just dispose of the rubbish right now...

"Don't bring attention to yourself," Tempest's warning

echoed in his ears.

A snort escaped him. If she wanted someone stealthier, she shouldn't have asked him. Dragons hid from no man.

His attention moved back to the unconscious girl in his arms, her dirty black hair hanging over his arm as limply as she was in his embrace. Her chest moved slowly, and her breaths sounded wet. She had liquid in her lungs, and even though he ran hot because of his Talagan heritage, he could feel heat pouring from her abused body. His lips thinned. Dragons never suffered fevers, but he knew they were dangerous for humans. She needed care. But what intrigued him the most was how she'd fought despite her condition.

"What a resilient creature you are," he murmured.

His gaze ran down her filthy face and body—a very petite body. She'd held her own. Even with her nasty wound and while clearly sick, she'd managed to dispatch four men twice her size. It intrigued him. Humans were predictable most of the time, and their females, while alluring at times, usually showed a penchant for hiding behind their men. Some males enjoyed that, but Damien's tastes...ran a bit wilder. He liked a spirited soul in his companions. And despite this female's tiny stature, she was powerful—and he would know. He'd been following her for the last day.

It hadn't been intentional.

He'd stopped for a drink right before the sun had set the prior night and happened to spot the female running through the forest with the men hot on her heels. Her scent had then reached him. Beneath the infected blood and sweat, was the faintest scent of something *alluring*. Damien hadn't quite been able to put his finger on it, but it had caused enough curiosity that he'd began following her. Each time she had fallen down, she had gotten back up. The female was clever in disguising her tracks. If it hadn't been for the large group tracking her, she would have escaped easily.

Damien pushed back her soiled cloak, and his lip curled. Her bandage was covered in mud. With a claw, he nudged the linen out of the way and inhaled. The wound was diseased to be sure, but he caught whiffs of sage, peppermint, dandelion, and mimkia. His brows rose as he scanned the shelter. She didn't have any supplies with her, it seemed, so had she foraged the herbs? Interesting. Brave *and* smart. It was a rare combination.

A cough rattled her chest, and he frowned. If he did nothing to help her, the girl would surely die. Decisions, decisions... Damien really hated involving himself in human affairs, but he'd already attacked the men.

In for a penny, in for a pound.

Plus, he had a soft spot for females. Especially feisty ones.

With a gentleness that his huge stature belied, Damien cuddled her closer to his chest and placed her closer to the decent campfire she had managed to construct despite her gravely injured state. He frowned when her body was wracked by a violent shudder.

Tonight was going to be a long night of caretaking.

He ducked out of the hollowed-out tree trunk and yanked a cloak from one of the fallen men. Damien shook it out and placed it over her slight figure. He crouched next to her and examined her features through the layer of mud on her face. He couldn't tell much, other than she had a heart-shaped face with a widow's peak. One of the men groaned outside, and Damien pushed to his feet. The little female would be okay while he learned exactly why these bandits had been attacking her in the first place.

Prowling outside, he glared at the men who grunted and groaned, halfway to wakefulness, as he dragged them into the shadows before unceremoniously throwing them against the trunk of an ancient, gnarled oak tree and tying them to it. The ringleader—Borris, if he remembered correctly—cursed, his older face red with rage.

"You'll pay for this!" Borris growled, one eye swollen shut. Damien bared his teeth and growled, causing Borris to flinch and lean back against the tree. "What are you?" he whispered.

"Your reckoning," Damien remarked with a smile.

He inhaled deeply and scented poison on the old man— the same poison he scented in the girl's blood. Why was she their target? Had she stolen something? Even then, he believed no harm should come to females. Sure, they should be accountable for their actions but not physically harmed. It was wrong.

With a blunt kick to the ringleader's knee, Damien leaned against a nearby tree and crossed his arms. "Hello, Borris," he purred. "I have a few questions to ask you which you will answer. Do you understand me?" His tone brooked no argument. "What are you doing chasing a lone girl through the forest like this?" It was disgusting, really. Robbing someone was one thing but poisoning them and pursuing them like a fox through the forest for a few days was quite another. "What could she possibly have of value that you need this badly?"

Borris shook but stayed silent.

Damien held his hand out and examined the claws that tipped his fingers. "I *hate* repeating myself."

The bandit paled. "You—you are—"

"A dragon, yes," Damien cut in, impatient with the man's spluttering. He rolled his neck. Questioning criminals was so tiresome at times. "Answer my question."

"The boy had a fair face," the man said, too terrified for his life to lie. "Wealthy features. We were desperate. We—"

"Boy? She's obviously female," Damien cut in, pointing toward the small, sleeping heap beside the fire, the girl's head just barely visible above the cloak. Strands of sweat-soaked ebony hair were plastered to her dirty forehead, her mouth twisting in unconscious pain. Damien supposed that she may well be having a nightmare.

"We would never—we thought she was a boy! That bow he—she—has. That's expensive wood, and well-made! We thought surely she must have other expensive items in her bag. We're just trying to feed our families, sir. There is naught to be done in these woods now but steal. The duke himself does so with his taxes. He robs us blind!"

Damien tsked and narrowed his eyes. "You think to lie to me?"

Borris shook his head. "I—"

"Think carefully about your words," Damien sang.

"We didn't know she was female *at first*. She bought a few things from us. We did notice how fine her bow was and it would have fetched a high price, but then one of my men went to steal it and he noticed her changing her bandage and he saw that she was female." A pause. "But she's wearing a soldier's uniform."

"And?" Damien drawled.

"A lady impersonating a soldier? We would have been rich men if we turned her in. Our families would be set for the rest of their lives."

"So, your solution was to poison the girl? To kill her?"

Borris shook his head miserably. "Things went too far. We didn't know she'd fight so much. We only meant to slow her down. We were going to heal her, but she was vicious."

Damien clicked his tongue. "How noble of you." He eyed Borris and his rag-tag group of men. "You've been causing problems in this area."

"We've only stolen from those who are wealthy, and we haven't shed innocent blood. We've left that life behind."

"Oh?" Damien drawled. "Did the old witch let you go that easily?"

Borris blanched. "The Alpha never lets anyone truly go. We're not as young as we used to be, though, so she doesn't rely on us much anymore."

Interesting. The old wench was going to make enemies that way. He filed it away to think upon later. Damien focused back on the rag-tag group of men.

Their methods had been terrible, and Damien was not sure the girl would make it through everything she'd experienced, but all things considered, his disgust washed away as he stared at the pitiful men in front of him. He could respect doing anything for one's kin. Plus, he could scent the truth on Borris. Damien knew only too well the state of the kingdom right now. It was one of the reasons he was working with Tempest on behalf of Queen Ansette. Although he was the Dragon King and bowed to no one, sometimes his goals lined up with other monarchs' work.

Tempest, Pyre, and Luca needed him to help sort out Heimserya, to weed out the corrupted individuals who sought to profit from turning the population into mimkia-addled drug addicts. The country needed a fresh start—and that began with treating the smallfolk fairly, for once. Plus, he held a fondness for the female Hound. She had more sway over him than he would ever admit.

"Are you going to kill us?" Borris croaked.

"No." It was probably a mistake, but Damien was experiencing too many pesky emotions tonight. Plus, Tempest wouldn't be happy with a bunch of dead bodies.

He strode into the darkened forest and picked up his pack that he'd thrown to the ground earlier. He riffled through it for a few seconds, then located a drawstring pouch full of gold coins. He tossed them at the ringleader. It hit Borris in the chest and fell to the ground, some coins falling onto the snow.

Damien pointed to the gold. "That will be enough to take care of all of your families for years to come. I suggest you make good use of that fortune."

"Sir!" Borris exclaimed, his eyes wide. It was clear he couldn't believe his luck. "Thank you! Thank you so—"

"If you do not change your ways, I will find you. Believe me when I say Old Mother has nothing on my rage and vengeance," Damien warned. "Clean up your act and stop stealing. Trust me... I know your scent. I know your faces." He sliced his claws through the rope and held his hand out. "The antidote and then you may go."

The bandit quickly handed over a small bottle of blue liquid and then scooped up the coins.

"Wake your men and take your dead with you. I don't want the female to be disturbed when she wakes."

Borris didn't need to be told twice. He shook all his men awake, and the moment they were all free from their bonds, they scattered away on limping legs and nursing broken arms. Only when Damien could no longer scent them did he drop his head and scowl at the blood-stained snow. A twinge of sympathy passed through him—they had been mere desperate villagers. People always assumed dragons were bloodthirsty, but the truth was they felt things more deeply than the average person. It was part of the reason he preferred to be solitary. It made things easier. Emotions were messy. Damien didn't like messy.

He sighed and ran a hand through his emerald-colored hair.

They brought their deaths upon themselves. The girl defended herself, as was her right. It is their fault they targeted someone with a will to cling onto life far stronger than their own.

Time to deal with the female.

Damien strode back to her side and lifted the cloak from her shoulder, taking stock of her body. Looking at her not from a distance, but within reach of touching her face, Damien realized the girl was more of a woman; though she was short and slim, she had most definitely left her childhood years behind, if her unbound chest was anything to go by. Damien realized the bandits had spoken true; she had fine features, clearly of a noble line, visible even beneath the mud. His gaze darted to her bow. It *was* finely—expensively—made. A prize indeed.

"What are you doing out here alone, little dove?" Damien wondered aloud. He knew he couldn't leave her alone. His lips thinned. Didn't *want* to leave her alone, all things considered. But they couldn't stay here. If she didn't get medical care soon, the woman was likely to die. She also needed a bath and new clothing.

Besides, Damien could smell the rain, and he hated the rain. He unstoppered the bottle, sniffed it once to make sure it wasn't poison, and then proceeded to painstakingly feed it to her. With that done, he scooped up her meager belongings before retrieving his bag and stowing them with his things. He eyed the woman and sighed. She was a delay he didn't want, but she was now his to care for, whether he liked it or not.

Without another thought, he picked the woman up and held her close to his chest, stamped out the fire and left for one of his dens nearby. There, she could recuperate and tell him who she was.

And he for one looked forward to hearing the woman's story when she woke.

Chapter Eight

Damien

Despite the grime on her skin, the muck in her hair, and her general unwashed state, to Damien the unconscious woman he'd saved still smelled...intriguing. He'd spent time with other females over the years but none of them held the promise of something more—even Tempest's scent paled in comparison to the tiny woman in his arms. Tempest, who was clearly Pyre's mate, but for a moment long ago, Damien had thought she could be his—but it wasn't to be. Now, he glanced at this woman's dirty face, and his heart clenched as he took in another breath of her essence.

A mate. She smelled like a *mate*.

Well. Kind of. There was something off about her scent. It didn't smell bad...just muted, perhaps?

He ignored it and made a beeline for his closest haunt. These days, he rarely had the desire to visit Betraz. Despite his long absence, it wasn't difficult to find with his scent marking the area. A smile curled his lips as he approached one of his homes. Ancient, twisted trees and black-green vines obscured the entrance, making it easy to overlook. Normally, he would have chosen a cavern higher in the mountains, more protected, but he liked the secrecy of the place.

He pushed through the vines, and some of the tension leaked from his shoulders. He was home. The cave was cavernous—large enough even for Damien to use it in his dragon form—but despite its size, it was not easy to locate from the outside, thus, perfect for Damien to use to store things precious to him.

With dusk on the horizon, the inside of the cave was shrouded in darkness; now, in winter, it was blacker than black within its walls. But Damien's sight was sharp and his footsteps sure; he easily located an ideal spot to place the woman: far from the bitter air seeping in from the entrance, but not too deep in the cave to be consumed by darkness not even a flame could ignite. Gently, he laid her down, making sure her cloak covered her shivering form.

He eyed the sleeping female as she twitched, her face scrunching up. What was she dreaming about? Damien shook his head. It didn't matter, but her health did. A dragon never let down those in his charge.

Damien immediately set about creating a fire using the stock of timber he always kept freshly topped up within the cave via one very well-paid, trusted servant. He smiled at how quickly the wood took and he made a note to give his man a raise when he spotted newly stocked food, blankets, clothing, and herbs.

Once the fire was crackling merrily and filling the room with flickering light and heat, he took it upon himself to inspect the girl. Well...woman. He was careful to touch his ward with the utmost of care. While he was capable of mass destruction, he tried his best to be gentle when possible. Most had no understanding of what it meant to be capable of such softness when they could easily snap a human in two. It took more power, more resolve. He wasn't some mindless beast out to devour virgin flesh like the stories of old said. Although... He grinned, remembering a time when villagers left their daughters out as prizes for dragons in order to protect their herds. It had been an...indulgent time. The dragon clans had grown in the mountains with the influx of mates. If the humans had wanted to throw away their precious females, well...the clans would take them off their hands and care for them the way they deserved in the first place.

The woman sighed, bringing Damien out of his memories. He pushed back the cloak and frowned at the boyish uniform covering her figure. Why would she cover herself in such a manner? Sure, one could dress the way they wanted, but it was unflattering. Plus, trousers were so troublesome to get off. He eyed her shoulder wound. There was no way he'd be able to lift the tunic above her head to get it off.

With a sigh, he extended one claw and pulled the fabric away from her right side. He cut the tattered fabric from the armhole to the hem and did the same on her other side. Next, he sliced the linen sleeves off her undershirt and cut through both garments from shoulder to neckline. Damien tossed the sleeves into the fire and pulled down the necklines of her clothes until the garments rested above her breasts. It would have been easier to strip her, but those from Heimserya were finicky about nudity, the silly creatures. He doubted she would have liked her body bared to him when she was so vulnerable.

He inspected the wound and sniffed it.

The poison from the bandits had wound its way through the woman's bloodstream. But it was poorly made and weak; if it hadn't been for her general state of exhaustion and the other injuries she had sustained—Damien concluded that she had been on the run long before the bandits set their sights on her—the woman's body would have likely purged the poison on its own. As it was, the antidote was working its magic. What worried him the most was the infection. Infections were nasty critters that tended to stay longer than one liked.

He stood and fetched his pot from the shelf which was carved in the back of the cave and went outside to fill it with snow. Once done, he placed it in the fire and strode to the rear of the cave. He smiled as he spotted his prey. Mimkia plants grew out of the cracks in the walls and draped down in beautiful white and purple garlands. He plucked a few blossoms from one of the plants and moved back to his shelves and workbench. Damien made quick work of the flowers, forming a paste with them.

Grabbing a few clean linens from the wall, he padded back to the woman and set the supplies on the cloak. The water began to steam, and he pulled the pot from the fire and set it next to the rest of the supplies. He pursed his lips and dropped to his knees. Her whole body needed to be cleansed before he could do anything about the wound. As fast as possible, he stripped her of the rest of her clothing except for the tunic, making sure to preserve her modesty.

Her skin was soft beneath his calloused hands, and he washed the dirt from her ivory skin. He frowned at all the bruises dotting her delicate flesh. They had no right to be there. For such a petite thing, she was *strong*. Her slender legs were muscular, as were her arms, and she had callouses on her palms. Damien was absolutely delighted when he cleaned the mud from her face and neck. His female was stunning. Her eyes turned up at the corners in a delicate way, and her lips seemed to hold a constant pout. He traced her button nose and then snatched his hand back, scowling. Being a dragon had its draw backs at times. They had a penchant for coveting attractive things that they crossed paths with. His eyes lingered far longer than they should have upon her face.

He *should* have been tracking down Old Mother's cohorts and discovering more information about the diamonds. Logically, Damien knew he could have left her with any healer, but he just couldn't do it. Dragons were beings of honor. It didn't feel right to hand her over to someone else. It was his responsibility to care for her.

Damien focused on her injury and pushed his attraction to the woman to the back of his mind. He flushed out her wound, surprised that she didn't rouse. No doubt it hurt something fierce.

She's strong.

And he liked it.

He pressed the paste into her shoulder and dressed it. He

mixed the rest of the paste into a cup of water and trickled it down her throat. It was a slow-going process, but he didn't mind. It had been a long time since he'd cared for anyone other than himself and his kin. There was a certain type of peace that came with it.

Finished, he cleaned up his supplies then spread one of his cloaks across the floor. He gently lifted the female from her spot, leaving the back of her tunic and shirt on the floor and placed her atop his cloak. Damien covered her with half of his cloak and reached beneath her to pull away the rest of her soiled shirt. His nose wrinkled as his fingers caught on what he assumed was a breast band. Why females wore the torture contraptions, he'd never know.

Gathering up the bandit's old cloak and the rest of her tunic, he tossed those into the fire as well. The woman shivered, causing him to frown. Maybe she needed something more. He pulled out another one of the cloaks he kept in a wooden storage box, hidden at the very far end of the cave. It was made of far thicker, more luxuriant material, and was large enough to swamp the woman in its folds three or four times over.

Far more efficient as a blanket for such a lovely creature.

He rested it over her shivering form and then crawled behind her to hold her close to his body. It was a relief when she stopped shaking and slipped into a deeper sleep. Damien knew he should move, but he found he didn't want to. He gritted his teeth and slowly pulled away, but not before pushing a lock of hair from her cheek. She'd bewitched him, and it was a problem. He didn't have time for alluring damsels. Tempest had given him a mission, and justice needed to be served for the attack on his cousin. The sheriff needed to be caught and *punished.*

With a growl, he jumped to his feet and paced to the back of the cavern. It was time he shifted. If he didn't have arms, he couldn't be tempted to touch her. And maybe, just maybe, he delighted in the idea of the woman waking up and discovering a gargantuan dragon staring back at her.

Chapter Nine

Robyn

She was dreaming again.

For a bleary second, Robyn wondered how she could be aware she was dreaming, and what it was she was hiding from inside her head instead of facing up to it in real life. There was something... Something urgent. Something life-threatening that she had to deal with.

But try as she might, Robyn couldn't wake up. She was dreaming, and there was nothing she could do about it, so she accepted it and moved on. At first there was nothing to be seen in the dream. The edges of the landscape glimmered and shifted, impossible to focus on. All around Robyn the air was warm—pleasantly so—but it was dark and full of absolute nothingness.

Then, just as Robyn was about to give up that there was anything of interest to appeal to her in her dream, a familiar figure appeared on the horizon. The figure limped in her direction, stooping slightly as he always had.

"Papa!" Robyn called out, immediately forgetting she was in a dream in favor of chasing after her beloved father. Her heart pounded as she reached him, and she turned to stand in front of him. She reached out for his hands, but he kept them firmly clasped together in his long sleeves. "Oh, how I missed you so. I didn't mean to run away—you must know that—and if we just sit down, I can explain everything."

But her father refused to look at her. Lord Lochslee appeared to simply see right through her. It was as if Robyn didn't exist. Her stomach dropped, and she clutched at his broad sleeve.

"Papa, look at me," she pleaded. "I did what I had to for the sake of the family. If I didn't leave, if I didn't fight, then you would have had to... And I couldn't bear that. Please look at me. Please."

He ignored her, his gaze distant. "You have dishonored me."

Robyn gasped and dropped his sleeve. She fell to her knees before him as flashes of memory appeared around her, giving her the highlights and lowlights of her life so far. The moments that made her realize her family had to depend on her, and her alone. Her sickly twin brother, taken from this world despite his bright attitude and kind heart. Tears burned in her eyes, and she cried out as John smiled at her, his image wavering next to her father. John had really taken after their papa in this regard, especially with how he treated the smallfolk. Robyn had sought to emulate him in every aspect of her life, especially in the tragic months after his death.

"I miss you," she whispered.

And then, all of a sudden, Robyn's mother materialized in front of her, except it was not the poorly woman she currently was. Not the sickly, ill Lady Lochslee, who had never recovered from the destructive kick to the head she'd suffered at the hands of a nervous war horse. Not the mother and wife who, more often than not, did not recognize her husband nor her children.

No, this was the Lady Lochslee of Robyn's younger years: beautiful, carefree, and easy with her smiles. Robyn had loved her so. Loved her still, though there were hardly any traces of the incredible woman she had once been upon her face in the present day, when Robyn was not dreaming.

Her hand shook as she reached out and hesitantly touched the hem of her mum's sumptuous blue gown. "Mama! Mama, it's your daughter, Robyn. Do you know me? I have finally come home," she whispered.

Lady Lochslee, unlike her husband, allowed Robyn to touch her. She held out her hand to Robyn and pulled her into an embrace. "Hello, my beautiful daughter."

She pressed her face into her mother's straight black hair and cried. When was the last time her mum had recognized her? It felt like ages. She was warm against Robyn's skin—too warm, in reality—and Robyn nuzzled against her. It felt as if she had been starved of such heat for months now. Years.

"I love you," she murmured.

"And I you," her mother replied. She broke away and cupped Robyn's cheeks, intelligence in her gaze instead of the chaotic madness Robyn had grown accustomed to. She frowned as her mother choked, her eyes going wide.

"What is it?" Robyn cried.

Her mum gasped for air, hand going to her throat and clawing at the skin there as if something was desperately trying to make its way out. Her gaze blanked a second later.

"Mother!" Robyn screamed, when the woman collapsed in her arms, dead in an instant, her body cold to the touch. The woman was too hot and growing hotter still. Hotter than burning coals. Hotter than firewood set ablaze. She hissed but didn't let go, for how could she? This was her mother.

"Do something!" she bellowed at her father.

That was when Lord Lochslee finally acknowledged Robyn's presence, face contorted in fury at the sight that lay in front of his eyes. A ring of fire sprung up around them. Robyn flinched away from the blaze. Without a word, he grabbed her by the collar of her dress, ripped her mother's body from her arms, and tossed Robyn into the flames.

Flames.

They closed in on her from every direction. She choked on the smoke and tried to claw her way out of the fire, but there was no relief. She was burning and screaming, screaming and burning. It was agony. Robyn's skin, pricked by a thousand white-hot needles, blackened and cracked like a pig roasting on a spit. She was going to die. She was—

Robyn gasped, her eyes flying open.

For a few wild, manic seconds, she could not see, nor hear, nor feel anything. Except for heat and pain, but they felt like old friends to her now. She clawed at her chest, finding nothing but uncharred fabric. A sob wracked her chest as she ran a hand over her unscorched face. The dream had felt *so* real. Even in sleep, she couldn't escape pain. Was this to be her lot in life?

Calm down. You're okay.

She laid her left arm over her eyes and tried to steady her breathing. It was just a nightmare, nothing more. Her mother and father were fine. John was gone. None of it was real.

64

What was very real though, was the throbbing pain in her shoulder and her aching throat and lungs. It was as if she'd swallowed a handful of nails. She tried to focus on what happened before she passed out, but her memories were a mess; she could hardly remember a thing. A snippet of men chasing her, pain, and floating feline eyes. She huffed out a tight breath. Her fever-induced hallucinations were something else.

A frown wrinkled her brow as she registered the rich smell of burning wood. She lifted her arms the tiniest bit and squinted. Flickering orange light came from her left, along with the gentle crackle of a fire. Her fire had been decent before the attack, but it should have dwindled down to ashes by now. She pulled her sweaty arm from her face and gently laid it down beside her. Her whole body was sweat-slicked from her fever, but it was more than that. She wasn't bone-chilled anymore, and she could hear the patter of the rain.

Something wasn't right.

Her brain niggled at her to figure it out.

Robyn blinked at the sky, her eyes slowly focusing. It wasn't the sky at all. Shadowy stalactites hung from the stone ceiling high above, barely visible. A cave? How in the blazes had she gotten to a cave? She strained to hear any movement around her. Nothing but the fire. Had she run here in a fever-induced delirium?

Focus.

She rubbed at her head with her left hand and tested whether she could sit up. It hurt but didn't cause the world to tilt and blur, so that was something. Her stomach growled, and she swallowed hard against her parched throat. When was the last time she'd drank anything?

65

Robyn ignored that to focus on her surroundings. A huge bonfire sat to her left, in the middle of the gigantic cave. The cave was so large she could not see the other side of it; the fire could not illuminate its darkest recesses. To her right, the entrance to the cave was mostly obscured by vines and snow.

Her attention moved back to the flames.

For a moment, all Robyn focused on was the fire, its flickering and dancing emulating her last moments in her dream. Her nightmare. She shivered violently and made to pull her clothes in tighter against her body.

Only to realize she was wearing nothing at all.

She blanched. A cloak lay over her in place of a blanket, but there were no clothes whatsoever to be found. Blinking furiously to bring further vision back to her eyes, Robyn peered around her immediate vicinity, desperate to find something—anything—that she could wear.

There was nothing.

Where were her clothes?

Panic blossomed in her chest as rational thought started to filter back in. There was no way she'd be able to create a fire like that in a fevered state. The rocks placed around it were too symmetrical. Plus, there was the matter of the cloak. It was enormous and clearly a man's cloak.

Clutching the cloak to her body, she unceremoniously got to her hands and knees to look for her bag, for her weapons. Clearly, she'd not made it there alone. Who had brought her? Were they friend or foe? Where were her bloody clothes?

Her shoulder ached viciously and sweat beaded on her brow. Exhausted, she plopped back down and pulled the blanket-cloak around her and yanked up the hood. Rather than overloading herself with unanswered question upon question, it was much better for her to take stock of what she *could* understand about her present situation. Under the cover of her cloak, she used her left hand to search the ground for a loose rock or anything that she could use as a weapon. Her fingers curled around a sharp, fist-sized stone.

Weapon secured. Now it was time to take stock of her body.

Robyn was on fire with fever, yes, but the acute pain in her shoulder had considerably lessened. She released the rock and pushed aside the cloak so she could see her injury. It was uncovered. Her eyes widened. It had been cleaned, stitched, and bound. Tenderly, she lifted the fingers of her left hand to touch the wound. Gone were all signs of poison. It was ugly, to be sure, but it no longer looked life-threatening.

Whoever had taken her didn't want her dead. They wanted her healed and lucid.

She didn't know if that was a good or bad thing. To be honest, she found no great comfort in the fact that she was not dead yet. For all Robyn knew, she was now in even greater trouble than she'd been in with the bandits before.

When the back of her neck prickled, Robyn stiffened.

You are being watched.

How had she missed that?

She forced herself to relax and lowered her lashes so she could peek around the cavern without looking like she was snooping. Nothing. It was too dark, but make no mistake, she was sure someone was watching her from the left in the comfort of the darkness.

Trying to move as little as possible so that the watcher did not realize she had suspected them, Robyn dropped her left hand to the sharp rock. Her fingers found purchase on the makeshift weapon. She clutched it with all the strength she had, tightened the cloak around her as much as she could to protect her modesty, and forced herself to stand. There was no way she'd face a threat while sitting down.

At first Robyn wobbled dangerously—just how long had she been unconscious?—but then she straightened her stance and turned to face the gaze of whoever it was who had saved her life. She lifted her arm to block the firelight from her eyes and braced herself.

"I know you're there," she called, hating how weak her voice sounded even to her own ears. "You went through a lot of trouble keeping me alive. Why not come out and say hello?"

For a second, nothing happened. She held her breath as she heard a snort of humor before a large shadow moved in the darkness. Her jaw dropped as the enormous figure crept forward.

Her brain had not been lying to her before she had fallen unconscious in the woods. The eyes were feline shaped. Vibrant emerald-green with slits for pupils.

Not feline.

Dragon's eyes.

Yes, this situation was definitely worse than bandits chasing her in the woods.

Out of the fire and into the frying pan.

Chapter Ten

Damien

Damien must have dozed off, for when he blinked open his eyes, the barest filtering of light and shift in temperature from the entrance of the cave informed him that it was deep into the night. A dull, constant rainfall had begun outside, just as Damien had predicted from the smell upon the air that day. A shuffling from the direction of the woman told him that she was beginning to stir.

He flicked his tail in delicious anticipation and relief.

It had been three days since he'd brought her into his den. Three long days of waiting and coaxing herbs and broth down her throat.

Damien forced himself to hold still.

What would she think when she took stock of the situation? Would she yell and attack like she did with the bandits? The idea was appealing. Or would she fall to her knees and beg for her life? That was a bit more distasteful.

He hoped it wasn't the latter. A female should never have to beg for her life.

He made sure not to move even an inch as he watched the woman. The shadows in the cave obscured him from her sight—as long as he kept his eyes angled away from the fire so as not to reflect its light.

After growing accustomed to her surroundings, the first thing the woman did when she eased herself into a sitting position and assured herself that she was, in fact, still alive, was look for her clothes.

A thread of amusement wound through his chest as she cursed and clutched the cloak tighter to her bosom. As if anyone would be able to sort through all the cloth to discover her naked body. It humored Damien to no end how concerned humans were with wearing clothes. They hated to be naked, especially in front of others.

Unnatural.

Personally, Damien hated clothing. The fabric itched his skin, no matter if it was made of the finest silk or the roughest-spun cotton. It caught on his scales. It restricted the movement of his muscles. They were annoying and confining and, most importantly, hid the true beauty of a creature.

The woman in front of him was a living, breathing example of this.

The light of the fire was more than sufficient to allow Damien to fully soak in the woman as she searched the cave for her clothes—and her weapons, he realized with glee. She really was tiny. Fairy-like, almost. Delicate and fine-featured, yet incredibly feminine despite the barest suggestion of curves upon her slim frame. Damien usually went for curvier women, but there was something about this one he couldn't quite place...

Desire.

It had been a long time since he'd desired a female. A tight knot formed in his chest. Sure, he wanted to possess or collect beautiful women. He'd always *adored* the fairer sex, but he also knew them to be wily. It was one thing to admire a pretty possession, and another to desire one. Desire easily morphed into other emotions. Emotions were dangerous for his kind. Dragons mated for life, and humans...

A chuff escaped him.

Most didn't keep to their vows and left their mates. It was horrific. Unthinkable.

The woman stilled on the spot, and her scent became tinged with fear. He could taste it on the air. His mood soured. He had quite enjoyed her natural scent once he'd cleaned the muck from her body. But when it was mixed with fear? It disgusted him. He trapped a growl that threatened to spill from his throat. She had clearly noticed him—had realized something or someone was occupying the space inside the cave, and that something was not human.

He picked up the sound of stone against stone a second before the female stood. Excitement burned through his distaste. His little human had picked up a rock. Presumably to use as a weapon. He liked this turn of events.

Just how would she react to his dragon form?

He moved just an inch, but it was enough for the woman to turn and stare directly at him.

The expression on her face as she realized what was watching her was priceless.

That's right, little dove. Time to face the dragon.

Chapter Eleven

Robyn

This was a cruel joke.

To have survived everything life had thrown at her thus far only to fall into the clutches of a dragon? Robyn was quite certain she must have been a terrible person in her past life. A genocidal maniac, perhaps, or the one who birthed Lord Merjeri's bloodline into the world. A consort to the devil would have worked, too.

Couldn't she catch a bloody break? Robyn didn't deserve this based on her own actions. She knew she didn't. This was unfair.

It was happening anyway.

"Just eat me and be done with it," she said, her voice cracked and croaking from disuse. Her throat was parched. Yet, despite this, her words came out booming, echoing off the walls of the gargantuan cave the dragon had taken her to until it sounded as if she were shouting *eat me, eat me, eat me.*

She winced. Hopefully it would be a quick process.

Robyn braced herself and stared the beast down.

The dragon did nothing. Didn't move, didn't blink, didn't even appear to breathe. She blinked at the creature, her fingers tightening against the rock in her hand. What was it waiting for? She'd *invited* it to eat her.

If it wanted you dead, you'd be dead.

The thought struck her as funny. Dragons were intelligent animals, but not that smart. Perhaps he had a human master? It would make the cloak and fire more understandable.

"Do you have a master?" she asked.

The dragon growled, and she flinched. Apparently, he didn't like that. Was it the tone of her voice or the question?

He can't understand you, idiot.

She sighed and decided to stay silent for the time being.

Having now adjusted to the darkness of the cave, Robyn peered through the dim firelight to get a better idea of the dragon's appearance. The flames glanced off its scales and awe filled her, despite the situation. His scales were stunning: every hue of green imaginable. Emerald. Grass. Viridian. The deep, sultry green of the pine trees found in the middle of the forest, so dark it was almost black. In other places, it was the complete opposite: almost gold. Even in such poor lighting, the dragon was magnificent to behold.

And its size…

This dragon was no rangy lizard from the mountains. There was meat on the creature, and muscle. It was perhaps the largest beast Robyn had ever laid her eyes on. Robyn understood, then, why the cave she had been taken to was so large. Her captor needed a large space for his dragon companion.

"Wow," she whispered, unable to help herself.

Her gaze ran over the creature, and her breath hitched as the dragon chuffed, which sounded more like a purr. Its maw caught the light of the fire. Beneath its otherworldly, venomous green eyes, she spied a set of fearsome, wicked, needle-sharp teeth.

The dragon was terrifying. Even in its current state of inaction, every inch of Robyn screamed *danger* in the face of this monster. A danger she couldn't afford. Time was wasting. So, if it was going to eat her, it might as well get it over with. She was tired of this limbo, the same limbo she had been stuck in for days now; she wanted to either know for certain she was going to survive and make it back to her family and her village, or die. She was too exhausted for anything else.

"Go on," she said, trying to goad the dragon into activity. The rock in her hand felt useless against such a huge beast, but her fingers curled tighter around it, nonetheless. "Do something. Smash me beneath your feet. Crush me in your jaws. Do *something*, or else I'll walk out of this cave right now, and you shall never see me again. I'm tired of being at the mercy of everyone else. I refuse to be your plaything!" she shouted, her voice echoing in the cave.

She gasped for breath and steeled herself against what the dragon would do in response to such an outrageous comment, but all the beast did was creep a little closer toward her. Its belly snaked across the cave floor, whisper-quiet, allowing her a better look at the dragon's face, now that the fire was a mere three strides from it.

Its emerald eyes were slits, unblinking, seemingly never

losing sight of her. Robyn moved a little to the left, and then to the right, and those eyes shifted almost imperceptibly to keep her in their sights. It was unnerving.

They reminded Robyn of something, but when she tried to grasp at the memory, a twinge of pain in her shoulder and the delirium of her fever forced her away from it.

Though the dragon had come closer, it still insisted on doing nothing. At the end of her patience—and sanity, perhaps—Robyn shook the rock in her hand at the beast. It didn't move an inch.

"Dotae be good," she cried, feeling hysterical but too far gone to care. "I run into a dragon only for it to be seemingly made of stone? Why won't you do anything? Why did you take me here? Where did you find me?" She paced back and forth, panic rising in her throat like bile. "Why didn't you let me die? I had *accepted* it. That was my end, so why...?"

She ran out of things to say. There was nothing left *to* say, at least, not to the dragon. Exhausted from the trials and trauma of the past few days, she collapsed against the side of the cave where she'd first awoken and adjusted the enormous cloak around her so she could sit with some dignity.

Not that she had any left, considering her state of nakedness beneath the finely made garment. Who left such a fine garment with a stranger anyhow? It could fetch a good price on the black market. Her lip curled. Perhaps the owner of the cloak had taken her bow and left the garment as trade. Or...

Her gaze darted back to the dragon in horror. She scanned the cave once again. What if her savior had set up their camp in the dragon's lair and it had eaten him?

"Did you eat him?" she demanded.

The dragon just stared back at her.

Great. Now she was talking to animals like they could understand her.

On the bright side, if the dragon had eaten the person who'd rescued Robyn, surely the beast wouldn't be hungry so soon? But what did she know of dragons? Heimserya was known for the beasties, but she knew they kept to their icy mountains and rarely ventured any farther unless it was a very lean year. Dragons were practically fairytales.

She leaned her head back against the wall and focused on calming her heart rate with the thought that if the dragon was going to continue to do nothing then she may as well relax. No use wearing herself out worrying. It was either going to leave her in peace or it would eat her. Plain and simple.

The barest flicker of movement caught Robyn's drowsy attention and she jerked as the dragon retreated into the darkness. What was that about?

"Hey!" she called. "Where are you—" She choked on her words as a man stepped out from the darkness.

A naked man.

A behemoth of a man.

He was massive—bigger even than any male she'd ever seen. He smiled, revealing wicked-looking canines, and brushed wavy, dark-green hair from his face, his eyes twinkling. She didn't even have the decency to blush at his nudity. She was too scared. However, the faint pattern of scales along his pale skin intrigued her. Her attention darted back to his eyes. They were familiar. They'd haunted Robyn's consciousness before she fell asleep for what she had believed would be the final time, before she'd woken in the cave.

Robyn flew to her feet and lobbed the rock she still held at him before she could stop herself. But the man easily caught it in midair and tossed it carelessly away. He took a few easy, assured steps toward her, the fire illuminating his strange features in greater detail with every step.

Her stomach bottomed out as realization dawned. He was the dragon. He was Talagan. A shifter. For of course he had to be a shifter, and he was taller than any man Robyn had ever met before and broader even than the hulking figure of her village's blacksmith, or the Hounds who had come through her village on more than one occasion for business with Lord Merjeri. That soothed one of her worries. She knew he wouldn't eat her, so that was something.

"Two legged predators are just as dangerous," Madam Jada's voice echoed in her mind.

Robyn was utterly thankful to the older woman for the advice and the medicine she'd passed Robyn's way. The advice had kept her safe more than once, and the medicine dampened her natural scent in case she stumbled upon any Talagans. None of them would catch her scent and decide to keep her for their mate against her will. Madam Jada said it was rare for that to happen, but it was better to be safe than sorry. Robyn didn't want to take any chances.

She lifted the cloak from the ground to give her more mobility should the need to run arise. His hair was as green as his inhuman eyes and, just as Robyn had observed in the forest, his skin was dusted with scales. They were most prominent on his forearms and legs—though Robyn tried her best to avoid looking below the line of the man's hips. His facial features were surprisingly fine and well-boned.

Noble-looking. Highborn.

"Like what you see, my lovely?" he crooned, his deep rumbly tone causing goosebumps to rise along her arms. His voice was cultured and crisp with a slight accent that she'd never heard before.

She didn't know what to think. Sure, he struck a handsome figure, but that didn't matter. Robyn pressed her lips together to keep from retorting something rude. She didn't need to sour their tentative connection when he had the ability to change into a monster of legend.

He swaggered closer, a devilish smirk on his lips. "Stunned silent by my beauty. Why am I not surprised?" he purred, his voice a low growl that Robyn could feel in her very soul. He tapped his ear and cocked his head. "Even now, I can hear your heart flutter for me. That is unexpected but not unwelcome, although you are not in any shape to pursue such games, are you?"

He thought her heart was beating faster because she was attracted to him.

A snort escaped Robyn before she could shut it down. She arched a brow at him. "I don't take monsters to my bed, thank you very much." *Shut up.*

The dragon shifter smiled. "I love a good challenge. Shall we make a deal, my lovely?"

Chapter Twelve

Robyn

She'd be making no deals with the devil today.

Despite everything that had occurred so far—and the fact Robyn should have been terrified by her captor—the dragon shifter's comment sent nothing but pure outrage through her. Robyn picked up another rock and flung it at the strange, hulking man, for all the good it would do. His smile widened, making her even angrier as he swaggered closer in all his naked glory. Not that she was looking, but it was hard not to gape when he was so *big.*

"You are bold," the shifter said, amusement plain as day on his unusual face. "Not many women would stare so openly at a naked man."

"You're not a man," Robyn spat out even as her cheeks heated. She'd been raised with a brother and had been around men her whole life. Not to mention her time in the army. Her lips curled. She'd never be able to unsee some things she'd been exposed to. Men were *gross.*

"How right you are, little dove," he murmured. "I'm not *just* a man."

The hint of a smile danced across the dragon shifter's lips. Robyn didn't like the look of that smirk one bit. It told her the shifter knew he was the one in control of the situation, and he was confident everything would work out the way he wanted it to. He was sadly mistaken. Whatever the lout wanted from her, he wasn't going to get it.

She averted her eyes, still completely aware of his attention upon her. If the shifter was going to continue making assumptions about her staring, then she was going to make sure she never looked at him again. From how he'd swaggered from the darkness, she had a feeling he was a vain creature. She could use that to get under his skin.

Out of the corner of her eye, Robyn realized the man had turned his back on her and moved farther into the cave from where he'd been watching her in his dragon form. A hinge creaked, and then the rustle of fabric followed. Just what was back there? Perhaps her clothes and weapons? Her breath hitched as she spotted the shifter purposefully striding toward her from beneath her lashes. Keeping her eyes off him wouldn't work. One never turned their back to a predator. Robyn widened her stance and faced off with him.

To her relief, he had tied a cloak around his shoulders; it fell to his feet, obscuring his body from view. At least, that was one less thing she'd have to worry about. Bodies didn't make her uncomfortable, but the unknown intentions of the male she was essentially trapped with did.

Her gaze dropped to the enormous cloak covering her own frame and back to the shifter's garment. Who owned three luxurious cloaks? Plus, the size... It must have taken meters upon meters of fabric to create just one.

He arched a brow at her. "Like what you see?"

She schooled her expression and shrugged. "Just noting how much fabric went into creating the cloaks. They're fine garments."

"It's not the clothes but the man who wears them," he purred.

Robyn snorted and inwardly danced at how his smirk faded. "If you say so."

When the dragon shifter took another step toward her, attempting to get closer than he had been before, she held up a hand. She had her space, and he had the rest of the cave. They didn't need to get any closer than they already were.

"Stay right where you are," she ordered, using her refined, lady-of-the-house voice her parents had taught her when she was young. None of them ever used such voices with their folk; it was a tone implemented solely for the benefit of Lord Merjeri and his odious son, to make them believe the Lochslees were their idea of highborn, instead of siding far more with the lowborn people of their land. It wasn't a voice Robyn had used in a long time, given that she'd been living as her brother for the past few months and was now on the run, but it returned to her as easily as breathing.

"Such an imperious tone." The shifter clicked his tongue. "How rude."

Still with that outrageous smirk on his face, the man pulled out a bundle of cloth from underneath his cloak and tossed it at Robyn. She caught a glimpse of his naked body beneath as he did so, which somehow felt more salacious than seeing his full-frontal nakedness a mere minute before.

Trying desperately to ignore the hot flush that spread

across her cheeks, Robyn assessed the material that she had caught on instinct. It was a dress—finely made, with expensive stitching, but perhaps a little big for her. Where had he gotten the clothes? A lover? Another captive? Either way, it didn't matter. She wouldn't be wearing them.

She shook her head. "I need men's clothes."

"That hardly seems appropriate," the dragon demurred. "You are a highborn lady. If the dress is not to your taste, I can fetch another dress."

Robyn flinched at the assertion. He was sharp, that much she was certain of. "A dress will put a target on my back," she said, fighting to keep her tone level and calm.

It was important that she told the man as little as possible about her situation, lest he use that to his advantage. Plus, kindness usually won over a person, not ungratefulness and insolence. The dragon shifter had given her clothes to wear, which suggested he had nothing improper in mind. Although, the appreciative gleam in his eyes as he watched her was anything but innocent. She pursed her lips. What exactly did he want with her? No one else was around, so he had clearly been the one who saved her from the bandits and healed her wounds. Now, Robyn was reasonably certain he didn't mean to kill her, so that meant she had to explore other options. The dragon *wanted* something from her. She had to work out what it was—and then get out of there.

"Please," she added, batting her lashes for good measure.

"It is improper," the shifter insisted with a shrug. "Take the dress or remain naked. We'll see how far you get outside the confines of this cave with no clothes on your back."

Robyn glared at the dragon, who stared smugly back at her. Clearly, she was not going to win this battle with her own resolve, but that didn't mean she wanted to give in so easily. But she *was* naked, and then there was the way the dragon's eyes had raked over her body that highly suggested to remain improperly dressed was dangerous. Clothing was just one more layer of protection. She clutched the dress to her chest and lifted her chin haughtily.

"Turn around," she demanded. *That wasn't very diplomatic.*

The dragon chuckled very softly, a sound like water over gravel. He clearly had no problem working out where Robyn's thoughts had gone. "If you think I would ravish a wounded woman, you are sorely mistaken. I prefer my women with a little fight to them, not sickly and scared."

"I'm not scared," she muttered. *Well, much.*

He studied her face. "You don't need to be. I will not hurt you. *Ever.*"

With that, he turned from Robyn, giving her just about as much privacy as she imagined he was capable of giving for her to dress. She gazed at his back. What did he mean by ever? It wasn't like they were going to stay in each other's company for long now that she'd woken.

Counting her privacy as a win, Robyn gave him her back.

She didn't know why it mattered to her so much to be on something of an even footing with the strange, mysterious shifter. Perhaps it was because he had saved her life, and she didn't like owing anyone for anything. What would he expect in payment for his kindness? Some of the soldiers she'd camped with expected certain *concessions* from the women they were nice to or protected. It made her sick. A person couldn't be considered good or generous if they expected payment for kindness.

You were lucky your regiment never discovered you were a female.

Robyn bit her bottom lip to stop that horrible train of thought. She'd gotten out. That's all that mattered.

As quickly as she could, she pulled the dress up and over her hips. Fabric rustled, and she glanced over her shoulder, making sure the dragon wasn't peeking. Her shoulder arched as she slipped her arms through the sleeves. Once she'd adjusted the top so her chest was covered modestly, she reached her arm back to do up the buttons that snaked along the spine of the dress. Though she fumbled to do one or two, there were several that her injured shoulder prevented her from being able to reach. The cloak would cover the open back at least, and the tight sleeves would make it impossible for the bodice to slip. As if sensing her discomfort, the dragon shifter turned around and raised an eyebrow.

"Do you require my assistance?" he rumbled happily. "I would be most pleased to help."

"I could still have been dressing."

He rolled his eyes and tugged on his ear. "Dragon hearing, remember?"

He had a fair point.

"I don't think so. This will do."

Robyn gave up on doing the buttons and merely tied the cloak that she had previously been using as a blanket over her neck and back, protecting her from the dragon's eyes as well as the bitter wind whistling through gaps in the cave's entrance. It was far too big to serve as a useful cloak for moving about, given that it swamped her narrow frame, but she doubted she would be able to get very far right now. So

84

long as the dragon shifter didn't plan on touching her in any way, shape, or form, she was content to take advantage of the protection his hideaway afforded her until she was recovered from her injuries.

For now, at least.

She eyed the dragon, and they went back to their standoff. Robyn was quite determined not to be the one who broke the silence that had fallen between them. Well...maybe if she got him talking, he'd reveal what his game was so she could formulate her escape.

What if you're not a captive? Perhaps he means no ill will.

She stuffed down her mirth at the errant thought. If there was one thing that the last few months had taught her, it was that no one was perfect, innocent, or blameless.

You're jaded.

Now, that was the truth. Life had been hard for a long time. She barely remembered her childhood these days. She turned her focus back to the shifter. He clearly preferred it when women had some fight to them. Well, Robyn had enough fight in her for an army, but the dragon was not going to find himself happy that this was the case.

If he had nefarious plans, he was in for a world of hurt.

Chapter Thirteen

Damien

She didn't trust him.

Smart woman.

His nameless, helpless rescue had claws, it seemed. For a woman to be so bold as to throw a rock at him in such an injured state riled Damien up in all the best ways. She had spirit and lacked even the inkling of surrender. She even dared to call him a degenerate for his decidedly naked state.

Maybe you can change her mind about that given time. Though it would be better if she fell into degeneracy with *you.*

Now the woman stood in front of him, her eyes never leaving his hulking frame, and he felt like preening. It had been a long time since he'd had the pleasure of female company. A woman's mind was an interesting place, and they made for intriguing companions for debate on almost any subject. He watched as the little female crossed her arms and eyed him from head to toe. It wasn't in the way of finding someone attractive but more of assessing how much of a threat someone was. She was analyzing him.

What an intelligent creature.

He already knew she was smart by how she dealt with the bandits, but he had a feeling so much more lurked beneath the surface.

Just what else is she hiding behind that fair face?

It was clear she didn't want to be the one to break the silence between them. Damien was all for a standoff but, for the sake of knowing more about the woman, he decided to relent.

Just this once.

"Won't you sit?" he said, indicating to the hay-lined area the woman had been sleeping in before. "It cannot be comfortable standing here like this, injured and starving. I can only assume you're hungry?"

"That would be a reasonable conclusion," she replied carefully. Her eyes were still trailing Damien's figure from the top of his head to his feet, seemingly without being aware of it. Her cheeks never went paler than rose-colored. Damien didn't bother smothering his grin. She may not want to find him appealing, but her body language said something else altogether.

"The way you're looking at me is disgraceful, noblewoman," he teased.

The woman bristled, as he'd known she would. "That's because you're a degenerate who stands around wearing nothing at all!"

"What is this, then?" Damien asked, holding out a length of his cloak to emphasize his point—and exposing part of his leg in the process. With a flourish, he let the material fall back into place, but only after the woman had hidden her face behind her hands in outrage. "A cloak is a piece of clothing."

"Hardly!" she cried, peeking between her fingers. "You are a scoundrel, through and through."

"What an astute observation. How did you know that was my middle name, noblewoman?" he crooned, batting his lashes.

"Don't call me that."

"Then what should I call you?" He kept his expression casual, although his chest tightened in anticipation. He wanted—no, *needed*—to know who she was.

The woman thought about this for a moment. Damien assumed she was considering whether to give him a fake name, then clearly decided against it. Her shoulders slumped. "Robyn," she said simply.

"Robyn," he said, tasting the name on his tongue. "I like it." The name Robyn suited her well.

"It's a boy's name," she challenged

"Why does that matter? It's pretty, and I like it." Damien shrugged. "Is there a family name to go with that?"

"Not one you can be privy to." A pause. Robyn faltered on the spot, betraying how feverish she currently was. If she didn't sit down soon, Damien would have to *make* her. Stubborn female. "And what about you?" she asked. "What's your name?"

Damien was tempted not to give it just to rile her up further. But then he inclined his head—almost politely—and said, "Damien."

To his surprise, Robyn softened at the name. As if she expected Damien not to have given her a name at all. The instance of genuine honesty had apparently taken her aback.

Damien noted that for later. It would likely come in useful. His little female didn't like lies.

"Sit," he insisted when she swayed on the spot once more. "Sit, and I shall cook for you."

In truth, Damien had already cooked for Robyn while she had slept. He had felled a young doe in the forest and trapped several rabbits, then cooked them over the bonfire until the meat was tender and crispy-skinned. Then he had cut the meat into perfectly edible chunks and stored them in a box lined with snow. He would have preferred his meat raw, but those of Heimseryan blood usually were squeamish about such things.

He felt her gaze upon him as he went about getting dinner ready. He took these chunks of meat out now and slid them onto skewers he had fashioned from stripped, narrow branches. Then Damien staked the skewers into the rocks surrounding the fire for them to heat up. Once finished, he wiped his hands on his cloak, sat on a rock near the fire, and smiled at his guest. She slowly sank down onto the nest he'd made for her, mirroring his action. Amusement filled him. She'd waited for Damien to make the first move at every turn, even though it was clear she needed to rest.

They lapsed into silence as the meat began to heat up. He watched her, and she gazed back passively. If he went by her heartbeat, she wasn't as calm as she was pretending.

"Do you have to stare?" she finally said.

"I like looking at you." He did. There was no shame in it.

"Well, stop it." A pause. "What do you want from me?"

"If you think I will slip up and tell you what my intentions are," he murmured, stoking the fire after a few minutes of silence, "you're sadly mistaken."

"That's what all men think," she replied. "Until they fall into their own trap like the rock lickers they are."

He burst out laughing and shook his head. She said the most outrageous things. She stiffened beneath the gargantuan cloak and turned away from him. Maybe she had no sense of humor? Or she thought he was laughing at her?

Damien wiped his eyes. "Is that something you learned while in the guise of a boy?" he asked.

Robyn said nothing. Her silence spoke volumes.

But then, she asked, "How long was I out?"

"Three days, give or take a few hours. Would have been better for you if you slept longer." While it had driven him nuts that she'd slept for so long, the dark bags beneath her eyes told him she still wasn't quite up to scratch.

"Given the circumstances," she murmured, glancing warily at Damien out of the corner of her eye, "I'd say I woke up right on time."

"I can't fault that logic, Lady Robyn."

"Robyn is fine, or nothing at all."

"Why do you dislike mention of your status so much, *Robyn*? You're highborn, are you not?" If she wasn't, he'd gnaw on his own tail. Her words were way too crisp.

"And what does it matter to you if I am?"

"I'm simply getting your measure. Isn't that what you expected me to do?"

She said nothing, and Damien concluded he had hit the jackpot once more. But for all that Robyn and her reactions were easy to figure out, there seemed to be an impenetrable barrier between the two of them. A mystery that he couldn't figure out.

Just why does she intrigue you so?

90

Sure, she was beautiful, but lovely women came and went.

The cloak slipped from Robyn's injured shoulder, and Damien grew very, very still. Though he had cleaned and bound the wound on her shoulder, without the cloak to protect it Damien could smell Robyn's blood.

You should have insisted on buttoning up that dress—for her own good.

His dragon rolled beneath the surface, and he gritted his teeth. Damien leaned forward before he could stop himself, though because Robyn was turned mostly away from him. The meat was sizzling, and something was burning, but he found he didn't care. Not when a far more irresistible sight and smell lay before him. He wanted to press into her space and run his nose along the column of her neck. He wanted to—

"It smells like the meat may be burning," Robyn said, finally turning back around to peer into the fire.

He gritted his teeth and focused on the skewers, so it didn't look like he was leering over her like the degenerate she'd accused him of being. His heat-resistant fingers pulled the skewers one by one from the white-hot rocks with practiced deftness. What was wrong with him? Control was one of the first virtues a young dragon learned. Without control, people got hurt.

Exhaling heavily, he tossed two skewers of meat in Robyn's direction, not trusting himself to get any closer.

"*Ow!*" Robyn growled, shifting the skewers from hand to hand before letting them fall into the swathes of cloak that covered her lap. She glared at Damien through the flames of the bonfire. "You did that on purpose."

"Would you believe me if I said I didn't?" Damien

countered, holding on to his own skewers as if they were as cool as ice. He was an idiot. Why would he throw hot skewers at her?

Because you're losing your mind.

"Probably not."

"Then it makes no matter what I say."

He ripped into the venison and rabbit with slightly too much gusto, but if Robyn noticed a change in his demeanor, or the fact she had managed to set him off-balance, she did not show it. Instead, she daintily picked up one of her skewers from both ends, blowing on the steaming meat before breathing in the scent of the food deeply. Her belly rumbled, but he ignored it. In his experience, females didn't like it when someone pointed that out.

A contented smile crossed her lips, and she closed her eyes. Even her shoulders relaxed. "Thank you," Robyn said, her tone begrudgingly sincere. "I have not eaten properly in...well, in a long time."

"You're most welcome," Damien said after a long, lingering moment where all he did was breathe in the very essence of the woman in front of him. He hated that a fire sat before them, churning out smoke that mixed and muddied her muted scent. "Eat all you'd like."

"This is more than enough," she answered. "Did it come from your stores?"

He hid his smile at her probing question. She'd have to do better than that to get information out of him. "I hunted it."

Her plush lips thinned adorably, and he found himself wanting to touch them. Were they as soft as they looked?

Get yourself together, man.

He didn't understand. Damien gnawed on his second

skewer simply to have something to do that wasn't absently staring at Robyn, trying to figure her out. He'd had consorts over the years. Female companions who did nothing but cook and read to him. Even powerful women like Tempest stood at his side in battle as friend and comrade. So why was this woman who had been masquerading as a man, on the run from Dotae-knows-what, invading his senses and setting his instincts ablaze like fire whiskey incarnate? It was pure madness.

"This is good," Robyn said around a mouthful of meat.

Damien blinked slowly and gently threw the final skewer at her. "Eat your fill. You need to build your strength back up." She needed some more meat on her bones.

The smallest of smiles quirked her lips in the dim light of the cave, enticing and addictive to behold. Damien wanted to see her smile for him—and only him—forever.

He squashed that thought and turned his scowl on the fire. She didn't smell completely like a mate. Why was he acting like a newly bonded male? Sure, dragons tended to obsess over treasure, but this was something else. He didn't like it one bit.

"What for? To fight you?" she murmured.

"If that's what you want."

"Is that what *you* want?"

"Nice try, Not-a-Noblewoman Robyn." Damien chuckled. A flash of disappointment crossed her face, though Damien rather thought that it was all part of the show she was putting on to lower his defenses. To make him tell her more than he wanted to.

Clever dove.

She knew how to get a man to talk.

"It was worth a shot," she replied. "Clearly you are a more challenging opponent than I'm used to."

She was piling on the flattery now, and Damien knew it was working. He was a dragon, after all; he basked in flattery. From her grin, she knew he liked it. Blast her. Every movement, every word, every glance from her was calculated, the little minx.

She was a highborn noblewoman practiced in the art of appeasing odious dukes and lecherous lords if ever there was one. Robyn couldn't hide that part of her, no matter how short her hair was cut or how much grime stuck to her skin.

"The bow," Damien said, changing the subject. He pointed toward the back of the cave where he was storing it. Where she couldn't reach it unless Damien willingly let her. "Is it yours?"

"Of course! It's *mine*."

Now that was dragon-like possessiveness if he ever heard it.

"Do you believe I stole it?" she asked.

"Not stole it, no. Perhaps borrowed it from a brother or father." It seemed a bit big for her.

"It is mine." Her eyes were blazing as hot as the fire. Damien wanted to burn in them. "It is mine, and I know how to use it well."

A veiled threat. How delightful.

"I know. I witnessed first-hand how talented you are with it," he soothed. "Even on death's door, with fever and poison clouding your eyes and shaking your hands, your arrows did not miss. It was truly impressive."

Now it was Damien's turn to see how Robyn responded to flattery—genuine flattery, at that. He meant every word of it.

94

He'd warred with many a man who couldn't shoot as true as she had, even when they were under better circumstances.

Damien expected her to blush, or protest, or insist he was making fun of her. Again, she surprised him.

She bowed her head, her shoulder-length black hair obscuring her face from him. "My talent wasn't enough to save my life."

"That does not make it useless."

"No, but it *does* mean I need to get stronger. Better. Faster."

A woman after his own heart.

"Then eat, and drink, and sleep," he said, taking a long draught from a skin of watered-down wine and wiping the back of his hand across his mouth, then throwing the water skin over for Robyn to drink from. She eyed it with suspicion, then, upon seeing Damien raise a challenging eyebrow at her, took a sizeable gulp from the liquid.

When she was finished, she corked the skin and set it aside, then rested against the wall of the cave. "Providing a dragon doesn't intend to devour me, I will," she said. "Only..."

"Only?"

A lost, pained expression crossed Robyn's face when she focused her gaze on the fire. It made Damien want to embrace her—to protect her from whatever ghosts were haunting her.

"I do not wish to sleep."

"Why?"

"Too many times I have fallen asleep not knowing if I'd wake up," she admitted softly.

Mine.

It was an easy decision to decide he'd look after her. After all, he'd become the patron of many people before her. He'd take care of his little sheriff and diamond problem and then she'd be his.

This is different, and you know it.

He cleared his throat. The prickly, raven-haired beauty would be the death of him. "I'll watch over you."

"Comforting," she quipped sardonically. She sighed. "It's going to be a long night."

"It doesn't have to be," he said, offering her as gentle a smile as a dragon could ever muster. "We can talk instead. Tell me what you want to know, and if I can—or want to—tell you, I will."

"No lies?"

He nodded. "No lies."

She grinned, and he knew he'd stepped into a trap of some sort but didn't find it too worrisome.

"Ask away, my dove."

Chapter Fourteen

Robyn

"Do you breathe fire?" Robyn blurted.

The dragon sniggered. "I have many talents I assure you, but breathing fire isn't one of them. I'm a physical being just like you. Nobody can breathe fire. Such a feat would be magical, and magic, my dear, does not exist."

She rolled her eyes at his imperious tone. "Well, *excuse* me. It was a logical question. I've been told the tales of dragons burning villages and stealing livestock. Plus, you can handle extremely hot items with your bare hands."

Damien pointed to the pale-green scales on the backs of his hands. "Some of my scales are so tiny they're not visible to the eye. It gives me an extra layer of protection, if you will."

"So, fire doesn't bother you... What about swords?" she asked.

He gave her a droll look. "Are you planning on stabbing me?"

"No." As long as he didn't try anything funny. She nibbled at her charred meat. "So, you're highborn, I take it?"

His gaze sharpened upon her. "What makes you think that?"

That wasn't a no…

Robyn shrugged, her shoulder pulling the tiniest bit. "Fine cloaks, fine dress, and your speech pattern speaks of old money." A shiver ran down her spine as he gave her a lazy smile and butterflies took flight in her stomach. She had a feeling this dragon was a bit of a rake.

"Dragons do like gold," he mused.

Time to needle him. "I'm surprised you know how to cook." She paused for emphasis and then wrinkled her nose as she tossed a burnt hunk of meat into the fire. "*Cook* is generous." She hid her smile as he bristled at the comment.

One point for Robyn.

"Be grateful I cooked it at all," Damien retorted, letting out a huff of air, apparently to show exactly what he thought about cooking. "It was a bloody waste of meat."

Robyn blanched. "You normally eat it *raw*?"

"I'm a dragon; of course, I can eat meat raw. It's quite excellent." He smacked his lips together. "You should try it some time."

"I quite literally do not have the stomach for it," Robyn said, settling into the folds of the gigantic cloak that wrapped her in its embrace. It was warmer than any blanket she'd ever donned and perhaps more finely made, too.

The faintest whiff of sage and something else caught her attention. Surreptitiously, she sniffed the cloak. Sage and citrus. Though she hadn't been close enough to Damien while conscious to know what he smelled like, some deep, hidden part of her brain knew his scent by heart from when he invariably carried her through the woods, toward the cave.

Robyn scowled at herself. She didn't have any business sniffing the dragon's cloak. What the devil was wrong with her? A morbid curiosity. That's all it could be.

She bit her lip and focused on the matter at hand. She needed information, and Damien was a bloody dragon. When did anyone speak to or see such beings anymore? She needed to make the most of it.

"Tell me about dragons," she said. "Tell me about your kind."

"Do you really want to know?" He arched a dark green brow.

"Would I be asking if I didn't?"

"I don't know. Would you?"

A question for a question. They were going to get nowhere speaking like this.

Robyn peered at Damien through the fire, simultaneously grateful for the protection it gave her from his far keener eyesight and irritated because its existence stopped her from observing him properly. There was not a single man in all of the province of Merjeri that Robyn had ever met with whom she could verbally spar like this without disguising herself as a man first—and, even then, verbal spars invariably ended up as fistfights, much to her parents' chagrin. She hosted one too many scars to be considered ladylike anymore.

But Damien was different.

The dragon shifter hadn't once belittled Robyn for being a woman. Hadn't told her that her skills with a bow were good 'for a woman.' Though he had made his desire for her obvious, and clearly had no intention to hide such a fact, he did not seem to think himself superior to her.

It was refreshing in the most infuriating way.

"Yes," Robyn finally said after a silence that was far too long stretched out between them. "Tell me about dragons. I'd like to know what is true and what is not from the fairytales."

A slow smile moved across Damien's face as he stretched his enormous body in kind across the cave floor, relaxed as if he were lying on top of a pile of silken cushions instead of the hard, cold surface of a cave floor.

"Your wish is my command, my lady," he said, most likely to try and get a rise out of Robyn. "Well," he continued, when it was clear she was not going to form a rebuttal, "dragons do not have their own kingdom—taken over by Heimserya or otherwise. Not like the Talagan shifters, or the Mers to the south, or the Giants to the east."

"You have no home?" she asked. That made her sad.

"I didn't say that."

"So where do you...come from?"

Damien shrugged almost lazily. "Who knows? We live long enough lives that none of our kind really care. We're nomads, content to spend our considerable time in this world going where we wish, meeting who we wish, fighting who we wish, and seduc—"

"I get it," Robyn interrupted, a flush crossing her face at the realization of what Damien was going to say.

A wicked, filthy grin crossed his face. "Do you?"

"Where do *you* specifically come from?" Robyn asked instead, getting back onto the subject at hand.

"I'm from the Dread Mountains," Damien said.

It was Robyn's turn to be surprised. "I wouldn't have known! You're so—" She waved toward Damien rather uselessly.

"Well fed?" he ventured, cackling. "Large? Well-endowed?"

Robyn ignored that last one. "The dragons of the mountains are...well, certainly smaller than you. Rangier. The prey up there is hardly plentiful."

"Hence my point about dragons being nomads. The Dread Mountains are our *kingdom*, so to speak, so it follows that the less adventurous of my kind choose to dwell near there, despite the slim pickings."

She frowned, leaning forward despite herself. Robyn had always thrived when learning something new, and learning about dragons *from* a dragon? It was truly a rare opportunity. She didn't want to squander it. "I thought you just told me you don't know where dragons came from?"

"That's where we congregate now, but if we originated from the Dread Mountains, then nobody knows that for sure. What's the point of saying where we come from if I don't know it for certain? Lying is pointless."

"Yes, I'm beginning to realize that," she murmured. "Are all dragons shifters?"

He snorted. "Are all kitsunes in the forest Talagans?"

She grimaced. She'd walked right into that one. "Fair point." It certainly didn't seem like a single word out of Damien's mouth had been a lie. But whether that meant he'd avoided telling Robyn the truths she actually wanted to know was another thing entirely. "So..." she continued, "you have a kingdom that has no borders. Then does that mean dragons have a monarchy? Do you have a king? Or a queen?"

Was it just Robyn, or did Damien still for one tiny moment in response to her question?

"We have one," he said, holding her gaze, "but it is not nearly as interesting or treacherous as your own human throne. If a dragon has royal blood within their last two generations, then they can vie for the throne. That's about as exciting as it gets."

"Of course, it is," Robyn said, not believing for a second that this was all there was to it. When it came to ruling, people were vicious. Dragon or not, she didn't think it was as simple as he said. Plus, the way he explained it all seemed rehearsed, as if he himself had been taught that truth at a very young age.

Just as Damien had worked out that Robyn was highborn, so too could she tell the same about him. His high cheekbones, strong jaw, and slanted brow spoke of good breeding; Robyn had no doubt about it. If Damien was not royal himself, he was at least of highborn blood within his kind.

"Dragon princes and princesses," she muttered. "Do you know any?"

He smiled, but it was sharp, knowing, and...*pleased*?

"History is so dull," he groaned.

It was clear he was not going to tell her about that.

Birds of a feather. She would not tell him about her background, and he would not tell her about his. A true stalemate. Just what was this dragon hiding?

Privacy is not an excuse to be suspicious.

She scoffed but kept her thoughts to herself.

After a few seconds of silence, Damien let out a gargantuan yawn. "I am tired," he murmured, visibly sleepy, "and in need of relieving myself. So, if you do not mind…" He leapt to his feet and indicated toward the entrance of the cave.

"Go ahead," Robyn said, curious and somewhat suspicious that he would risk leaving her on her own. Maybe he believed himself impervious to any attack she might launch on him. Stabbing him was out in any case. His scales took that option off the table. What about poison?

You're twisted. He hasn't made any move to harm you.

Until he proved without a doubt that his intentions were innocent, she'd keep her guard up. Speaking of which… She glanced at the darkest part of the cave where he'd indicated her weapons were. If she was really quiet, she could sneak back and collect them. And if he caught her, well, then she'd really get a pulse on where his mind was and how far out his advanced hearing extended.

The moment she lost sight of Damien through the vines that obscured the cave's entrance, she wasted no time in stumbling upright and rushing into the darkest corner of the cave. Her toes curled against the freezing stone, and she grinned as she reached a cache of treasures.

Not only were Robyn's bow, quiver, daggers, and satchel there, but she also found a plethora of other boxes, materials, and supplies. Knowing she hardly had any time, Robyn grabbed the first set of men's clothes she found—they were almost certainly too large for her but were better than the half-undone dress she was currently wearing—as well as her own belongings.

Stealing from a dragon?

She hesitated for a moment. All the stories said that dragons were obsessed with treasure and that they went to the ends of the earth to capture thieves. Well…was it stealing if the objects weren't leaving his cave? Her mother would be appalled by her loose morals. Robyn scowled, tucked the filched items beneath her cloak, and then fled back to where she had been sitting. She sat on the clothes and arranged her things beneath the cloak.

She laced her fingers and waited.

He said he was tired. No doubt he wouldn't sleep a wink if she didn't. Her lips curled into a secret smile. Good thing she had mastered the art of pretend sleeping long ago to fool her parents so she and John could stay up late reading. If she were to 'fall asleep,' then the dragon might follow suit. It would give her time to escape.

She'd come to peace with the fact that she may have to remain within the relative safety of the cave for a few days to recover, if need be, but she would likely not have an opportunity like this again. She was still feverish, yes, and her shoulder still hurt, but Robyn knew she was out of the proverbial woods. She would live. She had been in a worse condition when she had been fleeing through the forest in the first place. Robyn could still make her way back home—as long as she had a few hours to get ahead of Damien. His dragon form could still be a problem, but if she kept to heavily wooded areas, he wouldn't be able to get to her.

That's if he wanted to keep you in the first place.

She wasn't sticking around to find out.

And, so, Robyn settled down as if she were going to sleep, closed her eyes and focused on slowing her breathing and her heartbeat. At the sound of Damien's footsteps—surprisingly soft and light for someone so large—re-entering the cave, she lay as still as she could. He sighed, and she fought to keep her breathing even as he approached. She peeked at him from beneath her lashes as he stared down at her.

"Poor sweetfire," he whispered. "You'll feel better soon."

He padded to the other side of the fire and added more wood to the blaze. Damien folded himself onto the cave floor where he'd been sitting before. For a while, Robyn was quite certain that all he was doing was watching her sleep. It should have made her feel uneasy, but for some reason Robyn felt almost...safe. She was a ninny, through and through.

Of course you're safe from other dangers with a blasted dragon watching over you. It means nothing.

Over the course of several long, drawn-out minutes, Robyn heard Damien lie down and rearrange himself into a more comfortable position for sleep. Eventually, she risked a glance over at the dragon shifter through slitted eyes and was gratified to see he was asleep. Just a few more minutes. Rushing would get her nothing but caught. She'd lay there for hours if that was what it took.

Time stretched on, and the fire burned lower.

She deliberately shifted loudly and moaned. Damien didn't stir, just continued to breathe heavily. Robyn waited for another few minutes, fighting against her own tiredness.

Once she was sure that Damien was not liable to rouse any time soon, she very, very quietly gathered her belongings, stood up, and crept toward the entrance to the cave. Her cloak trailed on the ground behind her, and she gritted her teeth, praying that it wouldn't wake him. Her pulse picked up speed as she pushed through the vines covering the exit. She looked over her shoulder at the low-burning fire and spared a final glance at the dragon. The glim firelight lined his emerald hair in gold, casting a shimmering edge to the scales of his forearm where it lay, exposed to the cold, outside of his cloak.

Beautiful.

And he was. Part of her was saddened to leave such a rare person behind, but she was no man's plaything, and her family needed her now more than ever.

She faced forward and eyed the starry night sky that peeked out in patches behind the clouds. Thankfully, it had stopped raining. Spotting the East's Star, she pinpointed the direction in which she needed to go. She inhaled deeply, savoring the scent of pine, earth, and smoke.

Robyn rolled her neck and pulled the hood over her hair. She strode into the woods and hated the guilt that churned in her belly, leaving her uneasy. Leaving without thanking someone for their hospitality was terrible.

Getting home is all that matters.

With that thought in mind, she steeled herself for the journey and whispered, "Thank you," to the still night forest, hoping that somehow the dragon would hear her appreciation.

Chapter Fifteen

Damien

She'd left him.

How carefully Robyn had crept from this cave. How agilely. How silently.

He stared at the swaying vines.

Damien had borne witness to her entire escape. He had *let* her escape. *Allowed* her to escape.

"Just what will you do, my lovely?" Damien growled, the sound low and reverberating around the cave once he was certain Robyn was well out of earshot. He chuckled and ran a hand through his hair. It was wildly humorous that the woman had genuinely believed she could escape from a dragon without him first allowing it.

As if he'd have left her alone long enough to collect her belongings and steal *his* clothes to keep up her disguise. Although part of him purred at the idea of his scent all over her. At least it would keep any predators at bay, animal or shifter.

He shook his head as he remembered her sleeping act.

Sure, she was good, but her scent had changed as soon as she'd made for the exit. Damien chuckled again.

As if he'd have fallen for her sleeping act and then fallen asleep himself. She had no idea just how long dragons could go without sleep; Damien could have stayed awake for two weeks if it meant never taking his eyes off his quarry.

You let her go.

He'd been doing that lately. First with Tempest and now with Robyn.

Just what type of dragon was he? Pining after women? His cousin would laugh at him.

Damien's hands itched toward the entrance to the cave. A longing to chase after Robyn filled every inch of his body, urging him to capture her once more. But he had responsibilities. The man who'd hurt his kin was still out in the world. He needed to be punished. Pyre and Tempest needed Damien's help as well.

There would be time to track down his little female and see what she was up to—who she truly was—but it would have to wait.

He smiled. Chasing her now would be no fun. She'd barely have a head start.

And besides, Robyn was wearing Damien's scent, whether she was aware of it or not. It enveloped her. Marked her for what she was.

Mine.

There was nowhere Robyn could run that he would not find her.

He would take care of his duties and then begin the courting of his female.

Robyn wouldn't know what had hit her.

Chapter Sixteen

Robyn

Two tense, miserable days was all it took Robyn to return to the province of Merjeri, running on pure adrenaline and the overwhelming urge to see her parents once again. She skirted around familiar farms and landmarks that were a sight for sore eyes. The dragon's cave had been close to home, so that was a blessing in and of itself. A few times, she felt as if someone was watching her, but no one ever appeared. It was probably just her imagination, but her heart skipped a beat each time she thought it might be Damien.

The fear she felt on this journey through the woods was an entirely different kind of fear to the one she felt when she had first fled. For she did not consider her life to be in danger—not in the way it had been when she was running from the battlefield before anyone realized she was, in fact, alive, or when the bandits poisoned her. But Robyn knew her life was on the line in an entirely different way. If Damien caught her...

Something told Robyn he would not let her go a second time.

She didn't want to be the belonging of a dragon. A plaything. Not that Robyn knew that's what he wanted from her, of course, but as she ran farther and farther from the cave, it was the best and only conclusion Robyn could reach. She was thankful for the rain on the second day, which fell in seemingly never-ending cascades for the last six hours of her journey, for it helped cover her tracks and obscure her scent. Given that all shifters had a keener sense of smell than humans did, she didn't want to discover just how good a *dragon's* sense of smell was right now.

She swept through the forest, only stopping to eat and drink. Her eyes felt gritty from the lack of sleep, but she couldn't risk resting, even to aid her recovery. Aside from her personal safety, too much was at stake. To her relief on that front, Robyn quickly deduced that whatever Damien had given her to ease the poison in her system and reduce her fever was long-acting.

By the time she came upon the outskirts of the city of Merjeri—her hometown—her fever had completely abated, despite the days of running hard and fast in the rain and wet cold of spring. It was amazing how the foliage had changed in her journey southeast. Grass and flowers pushed up from the sodden forest floor, and all the trees had bloomed out.

She rolled her shoulder, nose wrinkling. Though her injury still hurt, it was the dull kind of ache that told Robyn her wound was healing. The worst was over. All she had to do was reach her family home, then she could give herself the rest she properly needed to ensure there was no lasting damage to her shoulder and back muscles.

The lasting damage to her mental state, however…

No. Don't think about it. You went to war because you had to. Everything will be all right. Nobody will ever discover you were the one fighting. 'John' died on the battlefield and now, if anyone were to come upon the Lochslee house, they will discover that the man you were impersonating is indeed dead. Nobody will ever know what you did in the name of your family.

No one could ever know. It would be the end of her and the family.

Robyn was fairly certain the bandits who'd attacked her hadn't known who she *truly* was, and indeed merely believed her to be a young man of decent social standing at the beginning. All they had seen was a person of clearly noble lineage, carrying an expensive bow and traveling solo through the woods. They'd been desperate. She had seen it in their gaunt faces when she'd traded with them. People were hungry and destitute around these parts. Even though they had almost killed her, Robyn could not find it in herself to blame them for what they had done. People were capable of great feats and destruction when backed into a corner.

Picking her way through the muddy spots, freezing liquid seeped through the makeshift shoes she made from the bottom half of the cloak. It was a travesty to cut up such a pretty cloak, but necessary. A sense of urgency filled her as she moved through the trees at the very edge of town. The familiar smells of the village were beginning to fill her frozen nostrils: woodsmoke, horse manure, beer from the tavern. She heard a woman chastise her children. A donkey brayed and hooves clattered upon the cobbled streets.

Butter and cinnamon teased the air, and her belly

growled. When was the last time she'd had a pastry? It felt like years. She veered toward the bakery but hesitated in the tree line. She had no money to pay for such goods, and she had a feeling the baker wouldn't welcome her inside looking like a grubby, drowned rat.

She spied a well-dressed woman through the alley. A child held her dirty little hand out, and the woman sneered and kicked muddy water at the wee one. "Get away from me!"

The child cringed back against the building, icy water soaking into her thin clothes. Anger exploded within Robyn's chest. The woman clearly had plenty, and the child none. Why act in such a way?

She was moving and halfway down the alley before she knew it. At her approach, the little girl turned her huge watery eyes on Robyn.

"There, there," she murmured, holding her hands out. "I'm not going to hurt you." She pulled the cloak from her shoulders and held it out to the little one. When the girl hesitated, Robyn took a step closer. "Take it. It's for you."

The little one shook her head. "Too fine for me. Someone will think I stole it."

Robyn pursed her lips, and then an idea came to her. She pulled her dagger out and cut away more fabric from the bottom of it until the length would fit the child. Shaking it out, she smiled at the girl. "Now it looks more like your size. Plus, if you smear a little mud along the back, no one will suspect a thing." She held it out once again.

The little one took it hesitantly, hugging it to her chest. "Thank you."

"You're welcome," Robyn said sadly. She pulled a dried piece of venison from her bag. Food she'd stolen from

Damien. She held it out.

The girl's eyes widened, and she snatched the meat from Robyn's hand with a toothy smile. "Thank you!"

"Your mum around?" Robyn asked, eyeing the road for any more people. It wouldn't do being seen like this.

"Nope. She died. But Gran is out doing washing for the lord."

"What is your name?" She turned her attention back to the girl who'd wrapped herself in the cloak.

"Aria," she answered, gnawing on the meat happily.

"It was nice to meet you." Robyn wrapped the leftover fabric around her neck to cover her neck and ears. "Keep your head down and take care of yourself. Now, scurry on home."

Aria nodded and skipped from the alley, bare feet slashing through the mud.

Robyn's lips thinned as she scanned the road one last time and retreated down the alley and into the forest. The rich kept on getting richer while the poor kept getting poorer. It wasn't fair. If only the Merjeris cared more for their people than themselves. If only there was someone who could make them honest...or even distribute some of their wealth among the masses, things would get better.

You could be that person.

She snorted.

Becoming a bandit who robbed the rich was ridiculous.

As her mother used to remind her, Robyn was a lady of status, whether she liked it or not. She couldn't risk her position by doing something so stupid. She could, however, use her position to defend the smallfolk far better than she could if she were a thief. Robyn had done her duty protecting her father by going off to war in his place. Now it was time for her to take her real place.

To be Marian Robyn Lochslee. Not her deceased brother. Not a thief.

Not a dragon's plaything.

As she observed the people of the village from the safety of the trees, she noticed just how haggard everyone and everything looked. When she left for war, things hadn't been great, to be sure, but now it looked as if the state of the village had taken a turn for the worst. A lone wolfdog, barely skin and bones with its patchy fur falling out in clumps, morosely swept through the main street of the town looking for scraps. At one point, he'd surely been a beautiful creature. Her heart clenched at the sight of a single beggar in the nearest alley.

She pulled the fabric up over her head and wrapped it around her face and neck until all was covered but her eyes. She once again left the safety of the trees and approached the beggar. Robyn browsed through her bag, locating what was left of the food she had managed to steal from Damien's cave which she hadn't spared herself time to eat on her journey— her stomach growled horribly at the sight of it—before holding it out to an older man.

She blanched as his familiar blue eyes met her own. It was the candlemaker Norman.

"M-many thanks, sir!" Norman cried, when he gently took the chunk of venison into his hands. "May you be blessed."

"How did you come to be here?" she murmured softly. Norman had always been a generous, kind man.

The candlemaker's smile dimmed. "You haven't heard?"

"Just returning from the war."

"The younger Lord Merjeri had a gathering and in his drunken state knocked over several lanterns and candles that I had provided for the event." Sadness and grief lined his face. "Two highborn died and part of the property was destroyed. It was ruled my fault, and my business was seized, my family sold into indentured service."

"No," she breathed. "That's not right, Norman. How could they do such a thing?" she rasped. "It's unthinkable."

His gaze sharpened. Recognition flooded his blue eyes as he studied the small part of Robyn's face he could see. "My lady, you should not be here," he hissed. His gaze took in her appearance. "It is too dangerous." A pause. "But it is good to see you back from the convent. The village will be all the better with you back."

"It is imperative that you keep my identity to yourself," she said firmly.

He nodded. "I would never betray your family. Your father has been so good to us."

She handed him the rest of the food except the leftovers of a rabbit. "For you."

"Bless you," he whispered.

"And you as well," she murmured back.

Robyn spotted the mangy wolfdog eyeing the goods she'd given Norman. She pulled out the final chunk of rabbit and tossed it to the skin-and-bones animal who had followed her every movement since she'd stepped into the alley. He lunged forward and snapped up the food. She held up her hands as he moved closer and nudged her back with his nose.

"I'm sorry, lovely," she told the dog. "I have nothing more to give."

He wagged his tail hopefully for more food and bumped her thigh with his nose, amber eyes staring up at her.

"I'm sorry." She backed away and moved into the forest once more. She paused and glanced over her shoulder. The wolfdog was following her. Robyn rolled her eyes and patted her leg. "Well, don't lurk about."

She pretended to ignore him as she once again observed the town and made her way toward Lochslee Keep.

During the previous winter, everyone in the village had come together to keep all of the streets clear of snow to allow horses and carriages and merchants alike free passage through the village. It ensured the market square remained busy and that people from outside—traders from Dotae and, sometimes, from farther afield—would visit the place. At least that had not changed, but the stillness of the town set her on edge. Where there had been much noise and life, now it was as still as a graveyard.

Something was clearly wrong with the village. Aside from the beggars, none of the locals were out and about, every door locked and every window shuttered. No slivers of light showed through the shutters, either.

What happened here?

She startled when the wolfdog licked her palm. She eyed the beastie. "I hope that was a kiss, not a taste. I'm not your dinner, you know." Carefully, she reached a hand out and let the animal decide if it would like a scratch from her. He pressed his muzzle into her palm, and she gave him an affectionate rub. "It's time to go home."

She quickened her pace, making sure to keep to the forest.

By the time Robyn came within sight of the keep, she could barely stand. She was exhausted, and her final burst of energy through the village had used up all the adrenaline Robyn had left in her system. She felt as if she could sleep for days and days on end. Plus, her toes had gone numb a long time ago. In fact, she couldn't even feel the bite of the wind.

In a haze of exhaustion, she almost wished to be back at that spot in the cave by the bonfire, Damien's imposing presence watching over her and ensuring she stayed safe.

Do not think that. Do not think of him.

Then Robyn spotted a figure whose presence extinguished all signs of exhaustion from her body.

His slightly stooped shoulders and distinctive limp carried him through the grounds of the estate. He stopped to smell a pale winter rose before talking with the stable master Andrei about the horses. A rush of warmth filled Robyn's body even though the air was freezing and her clothes were soaked through from the two-day torrent of rain. Tears filled her eyes as she stumbled from the forest and began running through the winter wheat.

"Papa," she yelled. And then, louder, "Papa!"

Andrei and her father turned at the sound of her voice. They wore shocked expressions on their faces—mouths open, eyes wide.

Robyn broke through the winter wheat and tore off her scarf. She stumbled in her haste to reach her father, and all but fell into his arms. The man stumbled under the weight of her, but Robyn was quick to rebalance herself and then him. She sobbed.

"I can't believe I made it," she blubbered. She hugged her papa fiercely, noting that he was much thinner. Had the keep fallen under lean time, too? *Just what happened while she was gone?* "I'm so happy to be home."

"Home? My girl, I think you may be confused," her papa said to the top of her head.

She froze, stunned to silence. What was the meaning of this? Gently, she extricated herself from the man's arms and looked up to meet his gaze. "What is going on, Father?"

His face was all bland, polite surprise, curious at the appearance of the young woman with the short hair and bloodied, mud-soaked skin who still clung to him. He cocked his head when Robyn did not respond, patiently waiting for an answer.

Her father did not recognize her. Robyn could see it in his eyes.

Sweet poison, she was going to be sick.

Chapter Seventeen

Robyn

Her nightmare had come to life.

Two shallow, empty eyes stared at her from within her father's face, and he clearly did not recognize her. Did not recognize Robyn as his daughter.

All that was missing were the flames consuming her body and soul.

She was going to be sick.

"R-Robyn!" Andrei cried, as Robyn began to shake.

Andrei's excitement at recognizing her through the filth covering her was palpable; he yanked her into a hug, his familiar scent of hay and horses pulling her from the nightmare, threatening to swallow her whole. She clung to him, her heart feeling like it had been torn to ribbons. Andrei dropped a kiss to the top of her head and pulled away, clasping her shoulders in his massive hands. A large smile stretched across his face, exposing crooked teeth.

"Hello," she rasped. Andrei had been John's best friend,

and now that she stood in front of him, it was just another reminder of what she'd lost.

"How are you alive?" he demanded.

"Later, Andrei," Robyn said, trying not to cry at the way her father continued to look through her, like from her dream. She pushed her hair from her face, hoping that it might spark her father's memory if he could get a good look at her face. "What's...what's wrong with Papa?"

Andrei bowed his head and lowered his voice. "His memory has been slowly going. In truth, it was getting worse *before* you left, Robyn, but ever since you disappeared, he's taken a huge turn. But...he's never forgotten *you* before."

That was troubling and heartbreaking.

Her papa painted a kind smile to his face. "Do you need help, young lady?" he asked Robyn.

She shrugged out of Andrei's hold and took her father's hands in her own. "I know this is a shock and that I don't look like the girl you raised right now, but, Papa, it's me. Your daughter, Marian Robyn Lochslee. I'm sorry I left. I swear I won't do it again. Please remember me." She squeezed his fingers gently.

A moment of horrible silence passed, during which Robyn could see her father painfully trying to parse what it was the young woman in front of him had said. Her toes dug into the mud as she tried to ground herself. Was this how it ended? With her father forgetting his last remaining child?

Tears flooded her eyes as her father's gaze narrowed, scrutinizing her face. A spark of recognition flared in his eyes, and his mouth gaped open with a wheeze.

"Marian?" he whispered, using her formal name. "My dear little Robyn, is that you?"

"Yes!" she whispered. "I'm home."

He stared at their hands and dropped them. Her heart clenched as she thought he was going to step away. Instead, he pulled her into a tight hug, his body shaking.

Robyn clutched him close, her fingers holding the long, black duster coat he always preferred in the colder months. She pressed her face to his shoulder and murmured, "I am so sorry I left! I can explain it all. I can—"

"I do not care, child," he murmured, speaking the words into Robyn's hair. The warmth of his breath against her scalp caused Robyn to finally relax, her shoulders slumping as all the tension left her body. "I do not care. You are back, and that's all that matters. You are *alive.*"

Lord Lochslee began to shudder with silent sobs, and the dam of emotion inside Robyn finally broke. She wept openly for all that she'd lost, for all the horrors she'd experienced in the last few months, and with relief of being home once again. She didn't care that Andrei was watching; after all, he had witnessed firsthand their grief when John had passed away.

"My dear sweet girl," her father choked out. "I can't believe you're in my arms. How are you here? We were told you were *dead.*" His voice broke on the last word. Her papa pulled back, his weathered face crinkled in concern. "How are you *alive?*"

"It's a long story." Out of the corner of her eye, she saw the stablemaster wring his hands, clearly troubled by something. She forced a trembling smile onto her face and gently pushed away from her father. "One I'd like to speak to you about in length once I'm dry."

Her papa finally took in her apparel and scowled. "You're

soaked through, pale as a ghost, and you've no shoes!"

"I know." She nodded toward the house. "Papa, why don't you head back inside for now, and I shall clean myself up so we can talk? The weather is far too wet and cold for you to be wandering the grounds."

He opened his mouth to protest. A bit of rain and snow had never stopped him from keeping charge of his estate and conversing with his people, after all. He huffed. "You've been back a total of five minutes, and you're already looking after your old man." He smiled softly and reached for her arm, squeezing it once. "I'll have Maya prepare a bath for you."

"Thank you, Papa."

He hesitated a moment, and she swallowed hard as the thoughts in his mind were visible upon his face.

"I promise I'll not disappear again. I'll see you soon."

He nodded and slowly moved back to the keep, glancing over his shoulder several times before he disappeared inside the manor, bellowing orders. If he kept that up, the whole village would know she'd returned home in the next hour.

Only once Robyn was sure her father was out of earshot did she turn to Andrei and hugged him again. "I'm sorry I left," she said. "I'm sorry I left without telling you, or Pavel, or Will—"

"There will be time enough for apologies later, Robyn," Andrei cut in, squeezing his arms around Robyn before coughing and letting her go. "You smell awful, by the way. How much of this is mud and how much of it is blood? You look like death barely warmed over!"

She quirked her lips, trying to work past the surreal feeling of being home. "There were times I wished I was dead."

His smile fell. "It was that bad?"

Robyn swallowed hard and glanced away from the concern in his gaze. "What is done, is done."

He pursed his lips. "You don't need to speak about it now, lassie, but you can't stuff it away. Things like these have a way of festering."

Andrei wasn't wrong, but she didn't know if she'd ever be able to speak about everything she'd experienced and witnessed. "I—"

"It's true!" a familiar voice interrupted. "You're back!"

Robyn flinched and turned at the sound of the voice. It was Pavel, who worked at the village orphanage with his father and had been John's other best friend. Where Andrei was tall, gangly, smooth-faced, and covered in freckles, Pavel was a brute of a man with an impressive beard to match. The only thing the two young men had in common was red hair— auburn curls upon Andrei's head, and wiry, and fire-red hair upon Pavel's.

Pavel was skilled with a great sword, but he hadn't been drafted because he'd had an older brother. Had Robyn told him about her plan to go in her father's place, she had absolutely no doubt in her mind that Pavel would have joined her.

Which was exactly why she hadn't told him, nor Andrei, nor Will.

Especially not Will.

Pavel thundered toward her, and she grinned at the sight of him.

"Hello, stranger," she said. "Did you miss me?"

"I won't give you the satisfaction of an answer," Pavel said before grabbing Robyn and encircling her in a bone-crushing hug. "But where have you been?" He practically shouted in her ear.

She wound her arms around his shoulders and let him hold her for a moment that was longer than proper. He'd always given the best hugs. She squeaked as he hugged her tighter.

"Can't breathe," she teased.

He released her and set Robyn on her feet gently. It was one of the things about him that she loved. While Pavel was a beast with any weapon in his massive hands, he was a gentle giant. He'd always possessed a kind soul, like her brother John.

She stepped back from her friend and ran a dirty hand through her tangled hair. When she'd cut it months ago, it had been beneath her chin. Now, it fell to her shoulders—far too short for a lady. She had grown used to it being short, though, and wondered whether she'd ever have it long again.

Not likely, if she could get away with it.

Pavel crossed his arms and eyed her. "Where have you been?" His gaze ran up and down her figure, lips turning downward. "Clearly, not in a convent as everyone has been saying."

She snorted. As if. "War," Robyn explained to her friends. "You know they drafted John; news of his death clearly hadn't reached anyone of importance yet. If John couldn't go, then it would have fallen to my father. I couldn't let that happen." Her father was a proud warrior, but he would have gotten himself killed on the battlefield. Even now, she didn't understand how she survived.

To her chagrin, only Pavel looked surprised. Andrei shoved his hands into the pockets of his canvas trousers and sighed heavily. "I figured as much when we received news yesterday that John had died in battle." He glanced away, clearly fighting deep emotion. "I never thought we'd see you again."

If she hadn't been poisoned and captured by the dragon, Robyn would have made it back before the courier arrived.

Be fair. He helped you.

Blaming Damien was wrong, and she knew it. Had it not been for the dragon, she'd have died three days ago.

"And Papa… He took that at face value, didn't he?" Robyn asked, venturing a guess based on how his memory had been getting worse.

Andrei nodded sadly. "He wouldn't listen to us when we tried to explain that John died months ago. Perhaps, now that you are home, he will settle. He's been a mess since you disappeared."

Guilt churned in her belly. Had she caused his forgetfulness to get worse by her actions?

"You really went off to fight?" Pavel cut in, regarding Robyn with approval. "You should have told me. I'd have—"

"Gone with me, I know. I couldn't have that on my conscience. That goes for *both* of you," Robyn added on, when it looked as if Andrei agreed with Pavel. "I care for you both. How could I drag you into something so dangerous?"

"But what about Will?" Andrei said with censure. "You should have let him know."

Robyn's stomach twisted uncomfortably. She knew fully well she should have told Will. She cast her gaze in the direction of the local forge. "I couldn't. He's worked so hard to get to where he is. I couldn't ask him to risk all that for a fool's errand."

"You wouldn't have had to ask. He'd have simply done it."

"Which is precisely the problem."

"Dotae be good, Robyn," Pavel said, scratching his beard. "You've always held the weight of the world on your shoulders. Why do you insist doing it on your own when you have friends who are capable and willing to help you shoulder them?" She grimaced. He wasn't wrong. "You're more stubborn than your brother ever was, do you know that?"

"I may have had an inkling." A soft smile curled her lips. "In any case, it's clear I did not, in fact, die on the battlefield while masquerading as John. I am back in one piece." That wasn't completely true. Part of her soul had been destroyed with part of her hope in humanity. She shifted and rolled her neck, her wound aching.

Andrei touched her shoulder but frowned as she winced. "You sure you're in one piece? You don't need a doctor?"

"I'm healing. Trust me." Her tone brooked no argument. *Don't ask questions.*

Andrei and Pavel didn't look entirely satisfied by Robyn's answer, but they were used to her insisting that she look after herself.

"Make sure to see Will once you've caught up with your father," Pavel said, fidgeting with his cloak as he prepared to leave for the orphanage. "It would kill him to hear it secondhand. And you know he won't be able to get away from the forge until sundown, what with all the weapons Lord Merjeri is having him make."

That was news to her. "Ruslan is making him do what now?"

The two men looked at each other uncomfortably.

"That's a conversation to have with your father," Andrei said. "Or with my parents; they can inform you better of the situation. Speaking of which, my mother will be complaining about your bathwater getting cold if you dally much longer. Be off with you or you'll catch your death. We'll catch up properly later."

Pavel grinned. "Yes, you can regale us with your war stories, and tell us how many men were bested by a tiny demon of a woman without ever knowing she was female!"

Robyn sniggered, even though her heart wasn't in it. "You can bet on it." A pause, then: "It is good to see you both. Truly. There were times when I didn't know if I..." She swallowed the words down, not wanting to give them any more power over her.

"Do not dwell on it." Andrei pushed on her back—avoiding her injured shoulder—encouraging her toward the Lochslee residence. "Off with you. And tell my father he needs to purchase more grain for the horses!"

Andrei's father, Danil, was the estate man for the Lochslee residence, and he was married to Maya, the housekeeper. They were more like Robyn's aunt and uncle than they were staff; she couldn't wait to see them.

Robyn crossed the bailey and wandered slowly up the stairs to the manor. She spared her friends one last glance over her shoulder. They watched her in silence, too much worry on their faces. They obviously hadn't bought her platitudes.

Smart men.

She waved and braced herself as she pushed the door open to the keep and stepped inside. No sooner had she set foot in the house when Danil—the elder version of his son, only twenty years older—came rushing toward her, enveloping her in an embrace far stronger than her father's had been.

"Welcome back," he said. "It is so good to see you, dear. We've been so worried." He released her and then indicated up the stairs toward the bathing quarters. "Don't keep my wife waiting. I can catch you up on the affairs of the house once you are rested." He gave her a warm smile.

"I appreciate it, Danil," Robyn said, meaning every word of it. The man had never tried to lie or soften things for Robyn, preferring to be straight and upfront with her. But, equally, he was a kind and loving man and knew when and where it was acceptable to talk about specific matters. Her belly gurgled, and she winced.

"Food first?" Danil asked.

"I'm just going to grab something from the kitchens before I head up to Maya."

"I can do it."

She waved him away and padded down the hallway, conscious of the mud she was leaving in her wake. She'd need to clean this up. Danil nodded, and she felt his scrutiny on her until she turned the corner. It was odd to be back in her home after being gone. Everything was the same and yet felt different.

When she reached the kitchen and entered, Herbert the cook gasped at her in surprise and delight upon noticing Robyn's presence.

"My lady!" he said loudly. "The master said you were home, but I said I wouldn't believe it until I saw you with my own eyes."

"It's good to see you, Herbert," she said loudly as he

cocked his right ear toward her. He'd lost most of his hearing in the same war where her father had damaged his leg.

The cook gestured to the fresh buns and the small bowl of butter. "Take what you'd like, and I'll have someone bring up a bowl of stew to warm you up." His eyes narrowed. "You look too thin, lass."

"Too much time running," she muttered. She gave him a bright smile and took one of the rolls, deciding to forgo the butter. If the rest of the village was starving—so starving that previously well-fed, housed, and happy people were now beggars on the street—Robyn doubted the Lochslee estate had escaped unscathed. She wandered to the larder and peeked inside. Her stomach dropped and her lips thinned. The keep was still working from last year's supply of salted beef and venison. Robyn would know; she'd hunted down the deer herself. And if they were using what was left of last year's haul...

That means not enough was caught in the run-up to winter this year.

That wasn't good news.

She didn't linger long in the kitchen, because the smell of meat was setting Robyn's stomach grumbling and also reminded her of the venison the dragon had cooked for her.

Charred, more like.

She munched on the roll as she took the servant's staircase to the family wing. When Robyn opened the door to the bathroom, she was met by the sight of Maya. Her salt-and-pepper hair was damp from the steam as she fussed over adding various oils to the bathwater. Maya straightened and fixed a critical expression to her face.

"Well, aren't you a mess," she mused, as Robyn dropped

her bag, bow and quiver to the floor. She unwrapped her makeshift scarf and hood, dropping the soiled fabric on the stone floor. "I shan't be hugging you until every ounce of grime has been wiped clean off you. Get in the bath, dearest, before you catch your death." The older woman tsked. "You're soaked to the bone."

Robyn grinned at the brusque words and Maya smiled back, her eyes twinkling. The older woman rushed across the bathroom and hugged Robyn.

"Daughter of my heart, how good it is to have you home."

Once again, Robyn's eyes misted. "I missed you, too."

"Let's get you cleaned up." Maya pulled back and moved to the tub, once again fussing with the oils. "Do you need help getting out of those rags?"

"No. I can do it," she said, wincing as she sloughed out of the too-large men's clothes she'd stolen from Damien. The dress he had given her was folded away in her bag, though it was heavy and had slowed Robyn's journey back home because of its weight. But she couldn't throw it out.

Why was that again?

She had tried to reason that to throw it out would be a slap in the face of the dragon's hospitality, when in reality...she didn't want to forget about him.

Stop thinking of him!

Unwinding the bandage over her shoulder, she gritted her teeth through the pain. A sharp breath pulled Robyn from her thoughts. She glanced up at Maya. The old woman's gaze latched on to the injury. "It's nothing," she soothed.

Maya rushed over, tenderly taking the bandage from Robyn's fingers. She unwound the rest of it.

"Dotae be good," the woman gasped upon catching sight

of Robyn's shoulder. "Just what exactly happened to you? We must clean and re-dress this at once!"

Without another word, Robyn was bundled into the bath—the water so hot it made her skin feel like it was on fire, though she quickly grew accustomed to it and welcomed its searing heat. Maya set to work washing her and cleaning out Robyn's wound with various salves and a generous dose of mimkia.

As the drug set in, Robyn felt a pleasant wave of drowsiness wash over her, though she blinked away the urge to sleep. "My mother," she said to Maya when the bathwater was dark with grime and blood. Robyn was, in turn, clean and pale as snow once more. "How is she? Can I see her?"

"Don't go today," Maya replied softly. She helped Robyn out of the tub and eased her into a thick cotton robe. "She had a bad night. Better to give her a day or two to recover."

Robyn's heart twisted painfully. She missed her mother, even more so after her terrible nightmare. All she wanted was to see her mum's face—if not well, then at least alive. But that was selfish, and she knew it.

Her desire to see her mother could wait until Lady Lochslee knew she was being visited by her daughter in the first place. It had been hard enough coming face-to-face with her father when he did not know her.

Robyn would sleep first, then tomorrow she would face everything she had missed.

Chapter Eighteen

Robyn

A rustle to her left caused Robyn to silently lift her bow and aim an arrow. Giving the rabbit no time to react, she loosed the arrow and prayed it flew true. To Robyn's abject relief, it did, and the creature landed on its side with the barest of thumps. She wasted no time in retrieving the rabbit; given the chill and lack of bigger prey within the forest, there were likely to be foxes, wolves, and other predators lurking nearby, ready to steal away Robyn's quarry before she had it in her grasp.

She bowed her head in thanks, bled the rabbit properly, and then pulled the arrow from the animal. With quick sure movements, she cleaned and hung it from her game bag.

Robyn eyed the quiet forest and stood, brushing her hands on her leather pants.

She only wished there were *more* kills in her grasp.

Despite how dog-tired she'd been upon arriving home,

and how she'd sworn to herself she'd rest to give her shoulder time to heal, the reality of what she had come back to meant rest was impossible. She had to hunt. Her family, as well as the villagers, depended on what was stored in the larder, and it was slim pickings. Thank the stars she'd come home when she did. An extra pair of hands would be greatly welcomed.

She sighed.

Her father had gotten rid of most of their staff while she was away. He hadn't been able to afford to keep them because of tax demands from Duke Merjeri. Her lip curled. The duke was as cruel as he was devious and intelligent. He'd taxed the people into poverty, and that's where he kept them, under his thumb. Robyn leaned against a nearby tree and stared up at the budding branches. His son Lord Merjeri wasn't much better. If anything, he was worse.

Last night, she had fallen asleep straight after her scrub— she suspected Maya laced her bath with a sedative to ensure she went straight to bed—and so she was yet to talk to her father and Danil about what was going on in the village, and in the Merjeri province in general. When she'd woken that morning, she'd not known where she was. The longer she stayed inside, the more suffocated she felt. She had quickly dressed in her old clothing and crept from the keep with a soft word to Danil about where she was going. But this delay in talking to them was a good thing: it gave Robyn a chance to think about things clearly.

For there was someone else she should talk to about such things first, before she was given the 'official' explanation her father might give her, someone who would give a from-the-ground explanation.

She needed to talk to Will Scarlet.

The forge wasn't far from the Lochslee woods—it made sense for it to be close to its supply of firewood—so after managing to fell another rabbit and, miraculously, a frail-looking doe, Robyn hauled the spoils of her hunt across her shoulders and headed over to see Will.

Her shoulder smarted as the legs of the small doe hit against it, but whatever Maya had slathered over the wound, on top of the treatment Damien had given her, meant her shoulder was in much better shape than it had been the previous morning. She had her suspicion that it would always ache, but that was better than death.

As she walked along the carefully dug-out road to the forge, her nerves sang. Will was the most tempestuous of her friends. His emotions always burned right beneath the surface. How would he react when she showed up? For that matter, what would she say to Will when she saw him? Andrei's and Pavel's comments lingered in her head, making her feel like she should run home instead. Her footsteps slowed.

Don't be a coward.

She gritted her teeth and pressed forward. She could face Will today. Robyn had to.

The smell of molten iron filled her nostrils before she turned the corner and was met with the sight of Will's forge. He had purchased it all on his own, after her papa took him under his wing when he was a young boy. Some time spent fighting for the Crown three years ago—on top of apprenticing at a weapon forge in the capital—had allowed Will to save up the money required to buy it. He was fiercely proud of the place, and Robyn was just as proud of Will for having achieved his dream. He was a self-made man.

The large door to the forge was open, and she stepped inside and scanned the walls covered in tools and a few well-crafted weapons.

"Just a moment!" Will called out, sensing the presence of another person nearby, despite the clanging of metal against metal making it impossible for him to hear Robyn's approach. His shirt was rolled up to his shoulders, revealing umber-colored skin crisscrossed with scars and burns from his years as a soldier and weapons-maker. His left hand was missing two fingers. Robyn still remembered the day that happened. It was the same day she had first met him. He'd escaped the Pack of Betraz but lost his fingers in exchange for that freedom.

Her heart galloped in her chest when he lifted the visor which protected his eyes from any sparks flying off the metal he was working with. Robyn spied a sizeable drop of sweat fall from beneath his curly black hair and down his forehead.

"Take your time," Robyn said over the clamor, smiling despite herself. It was exciting to see Will again. She had missed him dearly, and the sight of him working in his element filled her with happiness. If he could forgive her for running off to fight without telling him—*and* forget about what had occurred the evening before Robyn ran away—then she would be even happier.

A clean slate. That's all she wanted.

Will blinked slowly and stiffened as he realized who had spoken, then stood up straight to regard Robyn. A flash of something Robyn couldn't name crossed his face, but then he scowled. He tossed his tools down and crossed his thick arms. "You're back, then."

"I take it Pavel told you," Robyn said, taking a few careful steps toward him. Weren't they the ones who told her to tell him herself? The snitches. "Or Andrei."

He snorted. "The whole village knows you're back. Why come back at all when you fled the first time?"

Robyn would have put her hands on her hips if she didn't need them to balance the kills she was carrying over her shoulders. "You and I both know I didn't run away."

"There were rumors all over the village," Will said. "But your father was quick to squash them by lying to everyone."

"How did you know he was lying?"

He arched a black brow. "There is no way he would ever send you to a convent, nor would you ever tolerate such a thing. Give me more credit than that."

She gave him a hesitant smile. "You know me well."

"I thought I did," he shot back. "The girl I knew would have never left her family behind and worried them sick."

Robyn shifted on her feet. "I know you're angry...but please listen to what I have to say."

"I've already heard it. Pavel told me yesterday why you left. You shouldn't have left the way you did—sneaking off like a thief in the night."

"And what good would that have done? If I had been caught, anyone with knowledge of what I'd done would forfeit their lives as well. I couldn't do that to you."

"You chose for me."

"No. I made a choice for myself to protect my family." She glanced around the forge. "Look what you've built. How could I jeopardize the life you worked so hard for?"

"And how could you leave me to think the worst!" he bellowed. Will dropped his head and placed his hands on his hips. "I worried for you every single day. When I went to bed each night, I wondered if I would know if you died"—he touched his heart—"in here."

"I'm sorry," she whispered. "I truly am."

Will lifted his head and met her gaze. "And yet you wouldn't change things, would you?"

She kept silent.

He chuckled lowly and tossed his hands in the air. "Same old Robyn. Taking everything upon herself and letting no one in."

"That's not it and you know it," she retorted, her anger rising.

"After John's death, you shut everyone out."

"Shut up," she hissed.

"What would your brother say if he were here? Do you think he'd condone what you've done? Do you think he'd be happy with the way you've been working yourself into the ground for the last few years?"

"You know nothing!" Robyn cried.

He took a step closer, anger and pain creasing his handsome face. "You're wrong. I know what it's like to grieve so deeply that you feel you will die from it."

She bit her bottom lip and glanced away. How could she say such things when Will had not only lost John but also his wife and child three years earlier?

"I shouldn't have said that," she uttered lowly.

"It's okay. I've been where you are. I just don't want you to make the same mistakes that I did."

She nodded and lifted her gaze back to one of her oldest friends. "Friends?"

He rolled his eyes and gave her a fleeting smile. "Always."

Her shoulders slumped in relief. The two of them had always burned hot. She and Will were much alike in many ways. He cleared his throat and straightened his apron.

"There is one other thing we need to address," he rasped.

She squeezed her eyes shut, knowing what he was referring to. A few days before Robyn decided she had to run off to war, she and the boys had drunk a little summer wine, and Will had kissed her. Robyn had kissed him back, caught up in the moment, but in the morning, she knew it was a mistake. She loved Will dearly, but only as a friend.

"That night," Will began.

Robyn held up her hand. "You don't need to make any explanations to me. You were seeking comfort, and I was happy to help."

Will's brown eyes searched her face. "I haven't ruined us?"

"You could never," she said gently.

His whole body seemed to sag with relief. "I felt so guilty. I took liberties and… I just wanted you to know that I would take you as my wife if you wished it."

"Over a little kiss because you were missing your Ina?" she said, but not unkindly. "I will kindly say no. Not only for you, but for myself. We would be an ill match."

Will grinned at that. "Your temper is something to behold."

She rolled her eyes. "Says the pot to the kettle." Robyn set the doe down, pulled a rabbit from her game bag, and held it out to him. "Here," she said. "An apology for not telling you where I was going."

Her friend waved a dismissive hand at the offering. "Give it to someone who really needs it. You've caught more from the forest in one morning than most of the villagers have managed to find in a week."

"That's not good. Though it leads me to ask: just what is going on, Will? There's no food, no game, no money..." The village looked terrible.

"That's obvious. The duke raised taxes again."

"*Again?*" She tucked the rabbit away and shook her head. "But he raised them at the beginning of winter!"

"When has that ever stopped him from doing what he wants?"

Robyn cast a glance over her shoulder to make sure no one else was around. "Then...why is his son having you forge new weapons even though the war is over?" she whispered.

At this, a feral grin crossed Will's face. "I'm working on finding that out. The axes and bows at least I know about; Merjeri's been pillaging the forest of its beasts and its trees."

Robyn gasped in outrage. "He can't do that! That's Lochslee land. What has my father—"

"Your father can do nothing but allow it to happen. The duke isn't just taxing the lowborn but the highborn in the province as well," Will said.

That explained the dismissed staff and the quiet wood. They were clearly over-hunting the area. She scowled. The Duke of Merjeri had set his sights on the Lochslee land years ago. "Do you think it's another ploy to get my father to sell the land?"

"Possibly." Will gave her a look that set her on edge. "I think it's something more than that. This amount of weapons..." He trailed off and winced. "If all he wanted was Lochslee, he would need way less weapons."

So, the duke had grander plans, ones that undoubtedly

involved war. "How has it been here since the queen's appointment?"

"Things have gotten worse," Will said solemnly. "The duke doesn't like her. I have a sneaking suspicion that's what all of this is about." He indicated toward a stack of swords and spears. They were made for fighting men, not hunting animals or chopping down trees.

"Civil war." Stars, no one needed that. Robyn set the doe on the floor.

He nodded. "Those are my thoughts as well. No one comes into or out of the province without the duke's say so."

"Let's pray his ambitions are not that lofty." She wiped at her forehead. "I best return home and discuss these issues with my father," Robyn said, nodding at Will. "But I'll be sure to tell him of your concerns. If he has any information that you could use, I'll send it along."

Will closed the gap between them in a moment and clasped his hand around Robyn's forearm. He wasn't nearly as tall as Pavel—and had nothing on Damien—but still, he was taller than Robyn. She looked up to meet his eyes.

"I missed you," Will said, voice low and full of barely contained emotion.

Robyn swallowed the lump in her throat that meant she was about to cry. "I know. I missed you, too. And about what hap—"

"I know," Will said, echoing her words. "Let's not dwell on the past. You know I'm always here for you. How could I not be? You saved my life, remember?"

"Taking an injured drifter to my housekeeper to clean up your poor hand hardly counts as saving a life, Will," Robyn whispered, brushing her own hand against where he was missing two fingers.

His grip on her arm tightened slightly. "You don't value your kindness enough, Robyn. But I do. I'll follow you anywhere you need to go. Your family helped me escape my old life in Betraz. What do you need me to do? Just say the word."

Robyn hugged him before he plucked the doe from the floor and helped her set it about her shoulders. She smiled gratefully at him. "We'll get to the bottom of Duke Merjeri's mischief."

"Together," he said firmly, squeezing her forearm once.

"Together."

Then Will let go of her arm, and she swiftly exited the forge. Tears of relief filled her eyes, and her soul felt lighter. They were friends and always would be. She was happy about this; it was the best she could have expected.

By the time Robyn returned to the Lochslee estate, the sun was shining, and winter wheat shimmered like liquid gold. She waved to Andrei.

"Your father is waiting for you. He's been pacing about in the garden," the horse master called.

"Thanks!"

She kicked the door to the kitchen three times and waited.

"I'm coming," Herbert bellowed, yanking open the door. His eyes widened, and he gave her a toothy smile. "Gifts of game already?"

"From me to you," she shouted back, stepping into the kitchen.

"Put it on the table." Herbert helped her place the doe on the large, bare kitchen table that dominated the middle of the room.

"I already cleaned it out," she said loudly.

The cook waved a hand at her. "You've done enough, lass. I'll take it from here."

Robyn dropped the game onto the table and exited the kitchen the same way she'd come in. A smile lifted her lips as Herbert began to talk to himself as she closed the door. She made her way to the white gravel-pathed garden that lay to the back of the house. It had been her mother's favorite place to be, before her accident, and her father was still dedicated to keeping it in perfect condition for her, should Lady Lochslee ever be fit enough to appreciate the garden again.

As expected, Robyn's father was washing his hands in the narrow stream that ran through the garden. The stained pair of shears by his side let Robyn know that he'd been pruning the lilacs and winter roses.

"Father," she said, and discomfort filled her when he jumped in shock at the sound of her voice. But then he relaxed and moved over to sit on the carved wooden bench that overlooked the garden. He patted beside him for Robyn to sit, so she did so.

"You were gone when I awoke." It wasn't quite an accusation.

"I'm sorry, but I was restless. I saw the larder."

Her father nodded and stared down at his hands. "It's been a lean winter."

"I see." She brushed her hands along her trousers. "I spoke with Will. Duke Merjeri has raised taxes again?"

Lord Lochslee sighed heavily. To Robyn's relief, he looked lucid and capable today, like the man she had always known and loved. Sharp and clever, but kind and compassionate.

"Yes," he said. "I'm sure Will told you about what they've

been doing to our forest, too?" When Robyn nodded, he continued: "I'd rather the woods than our people, though at this rate, there soon won't be a single creature left beneath the trees. The duke's men don't understand that the forest needs rest in winter, to allow new life to come forth in spring."

"And yet it is our people who are suffering, not his men." Robyn kicked a stone across the path. "But it is not only food that is scarce, nor money. There's something else wrong with the smallfolk. They look...haunted."

"As perceptive as ever, my beautiful daughter." Her father smiled, causing his eyes to crinkle. Robyn's heart wept with fondness. "Yes, something else is awry. There's a new drug going through the province."

Robyn turned her head sharply to face her father. "A *drug*? I thought Queen Ansette drove away all the poisoned mimkia from the villages surrounding the woods?"

"Alas, the queen is not yet aware of the problem. Anyone I've sent to Dotae to inform her about the problem conveniently ends up dead enroute or disappears. I imagine a similar fate befalls any messengers coming from any other region that might also be having this problem. We're quite cut off."

A chill ran down her spine. "So, you believe this is being orchestrated by the duke?"

"And the nobles still loyal to her father."

A grave accusation. "Not drugs again..." Robyn muttered. She hated drugs. Lord Lochslee had sought out all manner of drugs to aid in the healing of her brother, but it had all been to no avail. Even the drugs that did good—such as the healing properties of mimkia, rather than the evil, tainted

144

version of the plant which King Destin had used to enslave the Talagan shifter villages—could do little for John.

"Wolves have been spotted along the edge of our forest," he said softly.

Robyn frowned. "Wolves?" They'd never been a problem before. "Is it because the game is scarce?"

Her papa shook his head, frowning. "Not woodland wolves, *Old Mother's* wolves."

A chill ran down her spine. "But they don't leave their territory in Betraz."

"The old witch's enterprises are expanding."

The duke. "That blasted codger made a deal with her?"

Her papa shrugged. "Old Mother's wolves have been seen on the duke's land. Whatever they are up to, they've kept it quiet."

Lovely. She squeezed her eyes closed. Things just kept getting worse. Why would the duke get into business with the likes of the wolf version of the Dark Court? Were they running drugs for him? Or were they purely mercenaries? Either way, it didn't bode well for the people.

"I am sorry I did not recognize you yesterday, Robyn," her father said quietly, bringing her out of her head. "My memory is a fickle thing. My old age is catching up to me."

She opened her eyes. "That isn't true," she insisted, even though he merely shook his head. "You're not old at all."

"How kind you are to me, daughter." He touched his wrinkled face. "We have to prepare for the day I can no longer manage this family accordingly." A change in his tone of voice told Robyn they were moving on to business matters now. She straightened, then cocked her head to listen to every word. "When you disappeared, I had the rumor passed around that you had been sent to a convent—to give you time to come back without suspicion, wherever you may have gone. But the moment you returned, I had Danil, Pavel, and Andrei spread the news that you were back."

She groaned. "Why, Papa?"

"You know why, dearest. John's death had already reached us. Lochslee Keep was vulnerable without an heir here."

"Heir? Women can't inherit, remember?" she said bitterly.

"I know, but there may be a way that we can control what happens to us." He reached inside his jacket and pulled out a missive with a seal she knew all too well.

Duke Merjeri.

"It seems that the duke and his son will be visiting within the week to welcome you back."

Lead settled in her stomach. It concerned Robyn greatly that her father felt it necessary to do all of this so quickly to ease his own descent into infirmity, though she understood why he had to do it. It was the right and proper thing to do. She only wished it didn't involve her having to stomach a visit from Ruslan Merjeri and his father.

Robyn knew what they were *really* visiting for. They didn't care about Robyn or her family at all; there was only one thing the Lochslees possessed of interest to the Duke of Merjeri.

Their land.

The woods.

And Robyn was how they were going to get it.

Over my dead body.

Chapter Nineteen

Robyn

"You will do well, my dear." Lord Lochslee reassured his daughter, though he didn't look happy about this. "You know how to handle Ruslan, and we both know he controls the Merjeri family, not his father. Just...try to keep out of trouble. I'll keep Duke Merjeri busy, and you should try not to set off Ruslan's temper." Her father narrowed his eyes at her.

"I will make no such promises," Robyn said, holding her hands up. She bowed to her father and vacated his study before he could critique her manners anymore. They'd thought the Merjeris would give Robyn at least a week before they visited, but it was not to be. The greedy louts were coming today. Only three days had passed since she'd arrived home.

Her pulse thundered as she ran down the steps of the service stairway.

The Duke of Merjeri and his son were due any minute now, alongside their usual retinue. Robyn was determined that they should not bully the smallfolk for their own pleasure, as they usually did when they came to the village. Ensuring that neither Maya nor Danil noticed her do so, Robyn escaped the house and bounded in the direction of the winter crops.

Andrei paused in his brushing of Nibbles, their gray mare. He arched a brow as if saying, *Running away already?*

Robyn mirrored his look and smiled in a way that said, *What are you going to do about it?*

He rolled his eyes and waved a hand at her. "Don't let them run roughshod over you," he tossed over his shoulder as he continued his brushing.

"Never!" she called back, grinning. Nobody was going to be subjected to Ruslan Merjeri's torment today, not if she could help it.

Before the war, Robyn had often helped the field workers with their crops whenever she wasn't aiding the school or the weavers. Since it was too cold—and folk were too poor— to send their children out to learn or to make clothing, that left only the workers in the field for her to protect from Ruslan.

"Lady Marian, so it is really true you've returned!" Lucy— one of the workers whom Robyn was fond of—beamed when she saw her. She brushed her silvery-brown hair from her face.

Lucy was a Talagan from a long line of gray wolves, or so Robyn was told. She'd yet to see the young woman in a full shift.

Robyn shook her head in amused resignation. "I've told you to call me 'Robyn' at least a thousand times, Lucy."

"You shall have to ask me a thousand times more before

I'll even dare to consider it." The woman wiped mud-soaked sweat from her brow. Though the air was cold, working in the fields was hard, physical work. Lucy was only two years older than Robyn, but already she had three mouths to feed. Thanks to the mimkia epidemic perpetrated by King Destin, she had lost her husband to addiction early the previous year.

She had it tough, but Robyn admired how Lucy kept working. Her three children were her everything, and it would take more than what had been thrown at her to break her spirit.

"Tell me what I can help with," Robyn said, rolling up the sleeves of the servants' clothes she'd 'borrowed' from the Lochslee estate. Her father hadn't approved of her choosing this clothing for meeting with the duke, but she didn't care. They were the ones who had invited themselves to the Lochslee estate without invitation. They could take her as she was. She wasn't dressing up for the pompous corrupt lords so they could leer at her. Especially Ruslan. Robyn shoved down the urge to growl. Ruslan had always been a pretty man with foul manners and an even fouler temper.

"You can help me bundle this wheat for the men to stack in the cart," Lucy replied, pulling Robyn from her thoughts. The young woman indicated to the finished bundles neatly stacked and tied by her feet, waiting for said cart to return from the grain store to collect. She eyed Robyn cautiously as they began working together. "He's coming today, isn't he?"

Robyn feigned ignorance, concentrating on weaving rough twine around a bundle of sickly-looking wheat; the winter harvest was pitiful this year, to say the least. "Whatever do you mean?"

"You always make sure you're nearby to protect us whenever Lord Merjeri is visiting," Lucy said, hitting the proverbial nail on the head. "He's a menace, to be sure."

Robyn made a face. "He should be here any minute. He and his rotten father."

"Oh, I wouldn't be so sure about that."

"What do you mean?" Robyn asked, glancing at Lucy.

"The Duke of Merjeri has been unwell as of late," Lucy explained, frowning at Robyn. She finished tying up a bundle of wheat and began gathering more crops for the next. "You didn't know?"

"Father made no mention of it." It wasn't surprising, though. Such news would spread like a wildfire. Duke Merjeri had made many enemies over the years, Robyn imagined. A weakness would be like waving a red flag in front of a bull.

"Perhaps he forgot." Lucy blanched at her careless speech. "Oh, Lady Marian, forgive me! I should not say such callous things!"

Though Lucy's words pained her, they were true and not meant unkindly. Gently, Robyn touched the woman's shoulder and gave her a reassuring smile. "I am glad for your candor. It is indeed likely he has forgotten. Thank you for letting me know."

For a while, the two women worked side-by-side in perfect harmony and perked up when they heard the sound of wheels approaching.

"That'll be the cart," Lucy said, getting up from where she was kneeling on the frozen ground to begin loading the vehicle. "I'll—*oh!*"

It wasn't the cart; it was the sheriff of Merjeri, leading up the front of the duke's retinue. Lucy barely rolled out of the way before the rat-faced man's enormous black stallion crashed its hooves into the muddy ground where Lucy had been sitting mere moments before.

"What do you think you're doing?" Robyn yelled up at the sheriff, getting to her feet to stand in front of his horse. The cretin of a man leered at her from his position above her. He was the unfortunate sidekick to Lord Merjeri, and somehow, even nastier. He'd even been a horrid child. She'd always tried to steer clear of him.

"You dare speak in such a way to your sheriff?" he said, blowing a strand of greasy black hair out of his eyes.

"If you insist on trampling the people of this village, then yes, I dare." Not to mention she outranked the vile man. "You dare to speak to a lady in such a manner?"

"Claiming to be above your station is a punishable crime." His eyes darkened, and his grip tightened on his whip. "So now you shall pay the price for your insolence."

Robyn bolted.

Away from Lucy and the rest of the frightened crop-workers, she fled, determined to lead the sheriff and Merjeri's men as far away from them as possible. But Robyn could not outrun the man's warhorse, even though she cut corners and leaped over fallen trees as if the wind itself carried her away.

When Robyn knew the sheriff was mere feet behind her, she rounded on the man and his horse, catching the wicked flick of his shining black whip mere moments before it would have sliced her face open. Instead, it tore open the palm of her right hand, and Robyn cursed aloud at both the pain and the fact she should have used her left.

Blast it all.

Despite the pain, she kept hold of the whip and refused to let go. Hot, pulsing blood leaked from her fist, steaming the air around her hand as it met the frozen ground.

The sheriff stared at Robyn as if he couldn't believe she would dare to catch his whip instead of taking the punishment. He sneered as she refused to let the weapon go. If he had the chance, no doubt he'd strike her again.

"You will hang for this, wretch." He glowered, taking advantage of the stature of his warhorse to tower over Robyn.

She bared her teeth. "I'd like to see you try—"

"Lady Marian?"

A voice Robyn had not heard for months—not since before she fled for war—interrupted her goading. These words caused the sheriff to freeze, his expression changing when he realized just who he'd attacked.

That's right, you blighter.

Robyn gave the sheriff a nasty look and turned her attention to Lord Ruslan Merjeri. He trotted forward on his black warhorse almost lazily. From his height, he was clearly taking in the scene. Robyn inclined her head politely and studied the younger lord. He was classically handsome— sharp jawline, haughty nose, full lips. A prettier man couldn't be found. But in his gaze, the cruel tilt to his lips, and the blackness in his soul made him ugly.

A pretty monster.

"Lord Merjeri," she said, still not letting go of the whip even as the sheriff tugged it slightly. "It has been quite some time since I last saw you. You look well."

"And you look as if you've seen better days, I must admit."

The sharp-eyed man flicked his attention to the sheriff, then back again. "Let go of his whip so you might direct my men to the Lochslee estate, if you'd be so kind."

Robyn didn't want to let go. She wanted to pull the weapon out of the sheriff's greasy hands and flay his back open. Instead, she did as she was told and promptly hid her hand in one of the deep pockets of her rough canvas dress before Ruslan could see how badly she was bleeding. Robyn had learned a long time ago not to display any form of weakness in front of the man.

"If you'll follow me, my lord and Gustav," Robyn said, glaring at the not-at-all-apologetic sheriff before taking the long way back to her house—as far from the fields as she could manage. The sheriff's true name was Gustav, but he'd long since abandoned it since he'd become Ruslan's right-hand.

Though Ruslan Merjeri looked every inch the gentleman, with his dark eyes, black wavy hair, regal face, and handsome figure, he made no attempt whatsoever to offer Robyn a place on his horse so that she might escape walking through the slush-and-mud street—not that she would have accepted. He was a haughty and entitled man by nature, and also calculating to a fault: by refusing to offer Robyn his horse, he was letting her know exactly where her place was.

Beneath him. Serving him.

It had always been this way with Ruslan Merjeri.

And she was fine with letting him think she was below him. It would be easy to pull the wool over his head when the need arose. And it would. She fought a shiver and kept her head high as she felt the sheriff's attention on her. While Ruslan was a problem, he was the devil she knew. He was cruel with a purpose. The sheriff, on the other hand... He *enjoyed* inflicting pain. He'd been that way since he'd been a boy, always hovering at Ruslan's side. What bothered Robyn the most was how much the sheriff looked like Ruslan. They could have been brothers. She was inclined to believe that Gustav was one of the duke's many ill-begotten children, but surely Ruslan wouldn't have been stupid enough to keep a bastard sibling so close in age around?

"What interesting apparel and hair," Ruslan commented from her right. "Has Lochslee fallen into such hard times that you can't afford to dress to your station?"

He was criticizing her already. Shocking. "Not at all, my lord. Why ruin nice gowns in the field?"

"Why work in the field at all when you have workers?" he countered. "It's below you."

"I choose to do it. Therefore, it is not below me," she replied easily, managing to keep the bite from her tone. Barely.

"As you say."

In other words: *you're a simpleton.*

By the time they returned to the Lochslee residence, Robyn was positively bubbling with fury. Her hand ached, and the blood from the wound was drying sticky and thick to both her skin and the inside of her pocket.

Danil descended the stairs and bowed. "Welcome, my lords."

He caught Robyn's eye and nodded toward the keep. She sighed and trudged up the stairs, leaving Danil to attend to Lord Merjeri and his retinue for the time being. Robyn fled up to her room where Maya was, as expected, waiting for her.

"Just this once, you could have stayed here to be presentable for him," she muttered disapprovingly, but there was no malice in Maya's words. She knew why Robyn went out to defend the smallfolk.

Robyn removed her hand from the pocket and held it out. "And this is what I have to show for it."

Maya hissed, her face turning red as she hustled to Robyn's side. "Who did this to you?"

"The sheriff. He mistook me for a worker."

"That blackguard," Maya growled under her breath. "I'll dope his tea, so he'll have to sit on the privy for the next two days. That'll teach him for striking women."

Robyn hid her smile as she moved to her washbasin and began cleaning the stinking wound. It would be a wretch to heal.

"There we go. Now, time for your gown. The dress with the long sleeves will do, I think," Maya said, rushing to Robyn's ornate, porcelain-and-hazelwood closet while Robyn cleaned her hand and the rest of her skin as well as she could in the large bowl of warm water the housekeeper had fortuitously prepared. Thank the stars that Robyn had had the foresight to at least pin her hair back that morning.

Robyn allowed Maya to dress the wound on her hand and ease her into a pale pink dress embroidered with gold scrollwork. The sleeves were long and wide, providing Robyn with a perfect excuse to obscure her hand from view.

Lastly, Maya removed the kerchief from Robyn's hair and readjusted the pins, added a pink blossom comb behind her right ear, and dusted her cheeks with the barest hint of rouge.

"You're lucky you're so naturally beautiful." Maya tutted.

"Otherwise, this wouldn't be nearly enough to please Lord Merjeri."

Robyn said nothing. That she held beauty in her features was all thanks to her mother and father and absolutely nothing to do with Robyn herself; all she'd learned to do with it was wield it like a weapon.

Like armor.

"We'll see how pleased he is when he sees how short my hair is," she muttered dryly.

Only men wore their hair as short as hers.

Though her heart was beating frantically with unquenchable anger over what the sheriff had done, Robyn was the epitome of serene grace when she joined Lord Merjeri, the greasy-haired sheriff, and her father in the tearoom.

"You took your time," Ruslan said without looking up. Then, upon glancing at Robyn and taking in her appearance, added, "Though, it was clearly time well spent. You look radiant, Lady Marian."

Once upon a time, Robyn might have blushed at the compliment, and indeed she did so now simply to flatter Ruslan. He had made his desire for her clear on several occasions after she came of age, but she learned early on that he was more interested in her land and her ability to gift him handsome children than he was about her, specifically.

His gaze lingered on her hair. "What an interesting hairstyle." His tone was bland.

She smiled demurely, knowing he hated it, and touched a lock of her hair. "Thank you, my lord. It's become all the rage in the queen's court."

His lips pressed thin at the mention of the queen.

"Indeed."

"Thank you for waiting," Robyn said, folding down gracefully opposite the sheriff and between Lord Merjeri and her father, ever careful to obscure her hand. Thank goodness, she didn't have to serve the tea. That would have been a nightmare. She smiled as Maya entered the room with a tea tray, and poured the aromatic, steaming liquid into everyone's cups.

For a while, the four of them awkwardly conversed and drank, though Robyn was uncomfortably aware of the sleazy way the sheriff kept looking at her. He wasn't even trying to hide it; clearly his friendship with Ruslan made him believe himself immune to any retribution for his behavior. It had been that way since they were children. Gustav had killed all manner of pets, broke other children's arms, and had a vengeful streak leagues deep. Ruslan always made excuses for him and blamed the victims. It was disgusting.

"You really should stop your daughter from fraternizing with the smallfolk," Ruslan said after thirty minutes had passed, directing his attention not at Robyn but at her father. "It isn't seemly that Lady Marian should spend her mornings dressed in rags and stacking wheat."

Robyn bristled, as did her father, but he placed a gentle hand on her knee beneath the low table to stop her from doing anything. "My apologies, my lord," he said. "We shall endeavor to behave as befits our status in the future."

Lord Lochslee said this every time Ruslan or his father came visiting, and every time it was a lie. Still, the words appeased Lord Merjeri, so he smiled at Robyn.

"Since your father is inclined to agree with me, I hope I do not again find you in such circumstances as I did this morning."

"Seconded," the sheriff added, in a manner that suggested he would love nothing more than to chase her down once more and have his whip hit true. If he ever took another swing at her, he'd regret the consequences. "What happened this morning could have had dire consequences."

Robyn couldn't stand it; she could barely contain how much she was shaking.

"If you could please excuse my daughter," her father said suddenly, squeezing her knee before letting go. "She is still not completely recovered from her journey home. I should like for her to have some peace and quiet. This morning was taxing on her."

Ruslan and the sheriff both wore expressions that told Robyn all she needed to know about their views: *Women are weak. Hit them once and they cower at your feet.*

Even though she hadn't cowered. Even though she had been ready to fight.

Not wishing to insult her father's good grace, Robyn bid farewell as elegantly as any highborn lady could, then left the tearoom for her mother's favorite place in the back garden. A well-carved swing hung from an ancient oak tree overlooking the ornate garden lake, big enough to accommodate two people.

Robyn collapsed onto the swing and sighed heavily, holding her hand to her chest and wishing she could *do something.* Anything. When she was fighting in the war, she had felt useful, purposeful, powerful. Even when fleeing the bandits and staying in the cave with Damien, she had felt as if her choices mattered. That her decisions would have an impact.

Damien would burn Ruslan Merjeri and the sheriff to ashes.

"Robyn."

Her papa's voice cut through Robyn's inner rage and dragon-fueled thoughts like a knife, though he spoke her name gently and barely louder than the wind.

She blinked. "Have they left already?" How long had she'd been out here?

"Lord Ruslan only came to see *you*, my dear," he said, sitting on the swing beside her. "He has no interest in talking to an old man such as myself."

"Then he is a fool, and a boring one at that." One she wished would jump off a cliff.

Her father pursed his lips. He only did that whenever he needed to say something that he didn't like.

Robyn's stomach twisted horribly. "Out with it, Papa, and let me face whatever he told you head-on."

A pause and then a heavy sigh. "Ruslan has announced his intentions to court and marry you."

No.

She exhaled heavily, and bile burned the back of her throat. She had expected this. Had always expected this. There were only so many times she could politely decline him before he exerted his authority as the future Duke of Merjeri to claim her hand. But even though she expected the news, Robyn still felt like throwing up. The idea of marrying Ruslan—kissing Ruslan, embracing Ruslan, lying in *bed* with Ruslan—was more than she could bear.

"You do not have to accept," her father insisted, his sad face lined with love and concern in equal measure.

Just when did he age so? When did he get so frail? Had she done that to him?

Tracing the deep lines on her father's face with her gaze, she gave him a weak smile. "You know that would go badly for our family and for our people."

Her father's face morphed into righteous anger. "I'll not send you off with the cretin."

"The world doesn't work that way, Papa."

"Then we change the world." He took her hand in his and swallowed hard. "You could spirit yourself away, like...like you did before. I would be happy knowing you're safe and content somewhere else."

"No," Robyn said, stony-faced and resolute. "No. I won't run from my family—or my people—again. I *can't*. Marrying Lord Merjeri is the right and proper thing to do. It is my duty as Lady Marian Lochslee and heir to your estate."

It was clear Robyn's dedication broke her father's heart. Here was a daughter who would impersonate her dead brother and go to war just to save her father. Here was a daughter who would marry a man she despised to protect her people from the worst of his selfish desires.

Here was a daughter who would never be happy.

But Robyn would do it, regardless; if it would provide safety and prosperity for the people under her family's care, she would marry Ruslan Merjeri. Unprompted, she thought of Damien and what he would say if he knew she had accepted such a proposal.

Stop it. You knew the dragon for a day. Why do you keep thinking of him? He was a degenerate.

The tinkling of a bell informed Robyn that a messenger had arrived via the front gate. Barely a minute passed before a man came rushing to greet her and her father.

"What news do you have?" Robyn asked, her senses

sharpening when she realized the messenger was dressed in the garb of the Merjeri household.

The man was panting; clearly, he had run all the way to the Lochslee residence. "Lord Lochslee. The duke... the Duke of Merjeri is dead! His son now takes his place as Duke of Merjeri."

And so it begins.

Ruslan would be relentless now. A man's first priority was to secure an heir for his estate. Her stomach tumbled, but she steeled herself, resolute even in the face of her sickening nerves. The new Duke of Merjeri now held all the power in his hands. He held the fate of her family and people within his grasp. Nothing stood in his way.

Except Robyn.

All she had to do was give herself up in return.

Chapter Twenty

Scarlet

There was something about the woods that called to her.

Perhaps it was because it reminded Scarlet of her father, or that she was finally out from beneath the thumb of her horrid stepmother, or maybe just because the forest gave her peace of mind.

Scarlet peered up at the immense pines and inhaled deeply, savoring the crispy, sharp scent of the trees. For a moment, she felt safe, free, and whole.

A branch snapped in the distance shattering her fantasy world.

Nothing in the province of Betraz was safe or free.

She stiffened as she spotted a red wolf weave through the trees not forty paces out. Scarlet's hand slipped to the poisoned dagger at her hip. She never went anywhere without it. She pushed her blood red hood from her blond hair and scanned the woods once more for the errant wolf.

It was Tarros.

The shifter had been pushing Scarlet's boundaries in the recent weeks, getting bolder and bolder with each turn that he didn't get caught and punished by the Alpha or otherwise known as Old Mother – Scarlet's stepmother.

She picked up the edge of her long red cloak that marked her as the Alpha's property and began hiking toward the river. The manor was closer, but she'd encounter more wolves along the way, and many would look the other way if Tarros caught her before she made it back home. Scarlet made sure to keep a sedate speed so as not to tip off her pursuer of her intentions. There were several huge rocks in the middle of the river that would offer her the refuge she sought. Tarros couldn't swim. Scarlet would stay there until her stepmother sent Bright for her. She'd be punished severely for being late, but it was better than whatever the red wolf had planned.

Scarlet struggled to keep her emotions in check as she spotted the river. Wolves were sensitive beings when it came to scents. If Tarros scented her fear, it would all be over. Scarlet reached the water's edge and waded in slowly, the frigid water biting at her skin. She bent low as if looking for pretty stones and caught a flash of red fur from her right.

Time to move.

She launched herself forward into the deeper water just as a growl ripped through the air. Scarlet pumped her legs and arms as fast as she could through the icy water, her long cloak dragging behind her.

Almost to the boulder.

"Not so fast little rabbit," Tarros crooned from behind her.

Scarlet glanced over her shoulder as the shifted wolf caught the end of her cloak and yanked. She sputtered as it dug into her throat. If he got his hands on her... panic threatened to drown Scarlet. She tore at the clasp, ripping a few of her fingernails off. The pain barely phased her. The clasp popped open, and she swam for all she was worth, the current pulling her a little farther down before she reached the boulder. She clung to the stone, shivering in the water as she looked back at Tarros who now held her abandoned cloak in his clawed hands.

He bared his teeth at her and growled low. "You really think that will stop me?" As quick as it came, his anger vanished, replaced by glee. Tarros lifted her cloak and ran his cheek over it before rubbing it against the rest of his body.

He'd scent marked it.

That was stupid.

Her stepmother didn't tolerate anyone touching her possessions which included Scarlet.

Her teeth began to chatter, and she forced her muscles to work as she clambered on top of the rock. Her breath sawed in and out of her chest as she watched the bloody wolf smile back at her.

He draped her cloak over his shoulder. "So this is how it's going to be?"

Scarlet just stared back at him. He wanted her to fight, to fear him. She'd give him neither.

"Cat got your tongue?" He cocked his head, eyes narrowing. "You think you're something special because you were the daughter of the duke? Do you think you're too good for a Talagan male?"

This was the special side of Tarros that he kept hidden from everyone but the women he accosted. His father was one of Old Mother's Betas and that's why Tarros got away with his crimes.

She methodically rung out her simple dress while watching the wolf watch her. He slogged out of the water and paced the shore. Now it was a waiting game. Eventually Bright – her stepmother's second in power – would come looking for her. The sun was setting and now the challenge would be staying warm. Scarlet wrapped her arms around her body and tucked her hands into her armpits, shivers wracking her body.

"Poor little human with no fur. Come to me and I'll warm you right up," Tarros heckled.

She ground her teeth and stared right over his head like the wolf wasn't there. He didn't like that. A feral snarl emerged from him and the hair along her arms rose.

Tarros tossed her cloak on the ground and crossed his arms. "Just remember I wanted to do this the easy way."

Scarlet blinked slowly at him and watched as he disappeared into the trees. Nothing was ever that simple with him. Ice ran down her spine as he returned a few minutes later, dragging a long log.

No.

From the looks of it, the log would be able to reach her rock.

Scarlet stood on shaking legs and Tarros flashed her a triumphant smile.

"Already anticipating my arrival, Red?" he taunted.

She yanked two daggers from her sleeves and backed to the edge of the boulder as the wolf hefted the log up into the air and then down onto the boulder. Scarlet had two options. One, fight Tarros and lose. The poison acted quickly, but not before Tarros damaged her beyond repair. Or two, jump into the river and swim for as long as she could manage.

The wolf sprinted across the log and the vicious look on his face was enough for her to jump.

A large hand wrapped around her waist.

"NO!" she screamed, stabbing with all her might.

Tarros bellowed and released her for a second and she leapt. The wolf grabbed a handful of her dress and toppled into the water after her. The current snagged her away from him and threatened to pull her into the depths below. Scarlet fought against the panic and didn't fight against the river. She opened her eyes under the water and reached for the nearest roots, her lungs burning. It slipped between her fingers a moment before she slammed into a rock. Her ribs screamed and she dropped her daggers. Scarlet clung to it despite the pain, breaking the surface.

She gasped for air and oriented herself. She wasn't far from the bank. Leaning her head against the rock, she took several deep calming breaths. She could do this.

Scarlet released her rock and struggled toward the shore. Her bare feet touched sand and she slogged to the bank, falling on her hands and knees. The hair at the nape of her neck rose and she stiffened. Glancing over her shoulder, Scarlet spotted Tarros perched on top of a rock not too far away. Why would he not go away.

She scanned the other rocks. If he played his cards right, he'd be able just to leap to the shore.

Tarros grinned and pointed a clawed finger at her. "I'm coming for you."

Scarlet ripped the bottom of her dress away and got to her feet, running through the last bit of water. Her feet touched forest floor and she made it four steps before Tarros knocked her to the ground. She spun onto her back, yanking a garrote from her bracelet. A green blur launched from the trees and knocked Tarros down. Scarlet skuttled backward on her hands and feet, blinking the water out of her eyes.

Was that a man?

Said man grabbed Tarros by the throat and lifted him like he was a twig. He gave the wolf a good shake, his green scales shimmering in the fading light.

"You think to harm a female? Have you no honor?" the shifter hissed. He slammed Tarros against the nearest tree, rendering him unconscious. The shifter dropped the wolf on the ground and gave him a good kick in the ribs.

Scarlet trembled as she clutched her garrote to her chest. She stood silently and took one step back, her eyes glued to the shifter's back.

"Are you alright?" he asked, not looking in her direction, placing his hands on his hips.

She nodded and then cleared her throat when she realized he couldn't see her. "Yes," she rasped.

"You shouldn't be out here by yourself."

"You and I both agree on that." Was he a snake shifter?

He inhaled deeply. "You're from the town near here?"

"Yes."

"You're one of Old Mother's?"

She gritted her teeth and forced out another, "Yes."

"Perfect." The shifter faced her, his shocking emerald eyes locking on her. "I'm looking for a man. He calls himself the sheriff, have you heard of him?"

Oh, how Scarlet wished she hadn't. He made her skin want to crawl. "Why do you want to know?"

The shifter grinned, flashing two wicked looking fangs. "That is my business."

"I don't make it a habit to speak to strangers." Her stepmother punished her for just looking in a stranger's direction in the past.

"We're not strangers any longer. I just saved your life."

Her attention darted to Tarros. But for how long? He'd be even more merciless after today. The shifter followed her gaze.

"I can make him disappear."

Scarlet blinked. "What?"

"You heard me, lovely. I can make the big, bad wolf disappear."

"Forever?" she whispered.

"Indeed. Just tell me what I need to know."

She stared hard at Tarros. It would be so easy to say yes, but did that make her any better than her stepmother? The shifter was clearly speaking about killing the wolf. "No, it wouldn't be right." The words were difficult to say.

The shifter scoffed. "What wasn't right was the way he was hunting you. That was not fun sport between the two of you. You *wreaked* of terror." His upper lip curled. "Even if you don't give me the information I seek, I will not harm you, nor will I let this worthless male go without punishment."

"No one gives something for nothing."

He smiled. "You're not wrong, but I'll make an exception this time."

Scarlet's gaze darted to Tarros and then back to the shifter. He'd done her a service and while he wasn't requiring payment, she didn't want to be in his debt. Secrets were the currency in her world, she could part with one as repayment.

"You won't find the sheriff here. He's in the province of Merjeri – he's employed by the duke's son."

The shifter smiled but it was scary. "Thank you, lovely. I will not forget our encounter. Do you need assistance home?"

She shook her head no. "I'll be fine."

"Then get home. This is no place for a lady."

He didn't have to tell her twice. She ran for the river, using the rocks to help her cross. As she reached the other side, Scarlet hesitated, glancing back at the mysterious shifter as he grabbed Tarros by the ankle. "What do you plan to do with him?"

"Make sure he can never harm a female again."

"You won't kill him?" She couldn't have that on her conscious. While Tarros was a bad egg, his family wasn't. She couldn't do that to them.

"No." The shifter looked put out. "But he'll wish he was dead."

"Thank you," she murmured.

"The only thanks I need is your silence. Can I trust you?"

"You can." She was a collector of secrets. What was one more? "Safe travels."

"Know that I have your scent memorized." The shifter dipped his head. "And that I hate liars."

A threat. She wasn't even offended.

"I'll keep that in mind," Scarlet called back as she trudged away from the river.

She'd managed to escape Tarros unscathed, but would she survive her stepmother's wrath?

Chapter Twenty-One

Robyn

The next four days passed in a blur and before Robyn was quite prepared for it, her first official outing with Ruslan Merjeri was upon her.

After polite greetings and an appreciation from Ruslan for Robyn 'dressing for the occasion', she was helped into the back of Ruslan's carriage to sit opposite him for an afternoon journey across his family's land. It had taken all her willpower to put on one of her nicest gowns to meet the new Duke of Merjeri. Though, it was also one of convenience, for it had large sleeves that obscured her many weapons. The new duke was impeccably dressed in a deep-blue coat trimmed in silver, which perfectly offset his wavy black hair and pale skin. Together with black, velvet trousers and black, leather knee-high boots, he looked every inch the perfect nobleman.

But appearances were deceiving.

While he looked like every girl's version of a fairytale

prince, that's where his perfections ended. The man was a venomous serpent, and she was stuck in a confined space with him. Maya slipped her foot beneath Robyn's dress and pressed on her toes.

She barely kept from groaning. It was time to make nice with the pompous donkey.

"Your land is well-kept," Robyn said, offering a compliment for the sake of easing the awkward silence inside the carriage. She glanced a look Maya's way, hoping the older woman would be pleased, but she was looking out her window, seeming oblivious.

Robyn coughed behind her gloved hand to cover her laughter. Maya was very much listening despite her play acting.

"We keep a tight ship, as it were, within the Merjeri province. I'd shudder to have a hair out of place," Ruslan replied, pulling Robyn from her musings.

That much was true, both about the man and his land. The roads were perfectly maintained, with straight-edged hedgerows and identical poplar trees lining the fields. The rain from the last few days had washed away what was left of the snow—with no small help from the people who worked the land, Robyn knew—leaving the view a breathtaking wash of green and yellow and orange fields, all perfect squares lined in a row. In the distance was Lord Merjeri's manor, a handsome building built three centuries ago. Robyn had been to it once, when she was very small, and did not remember much of it.

"Your father did much to it in his life," she commented.

Ruslan's expression tightened. "He did. I plan to surpass it."

"I'm sure you will."

They both fell into silence, and Ruslan seemed to disappear into his own mind as he stared out the window. Robyn frowned. Why had he insisted on them meeting today? His father hadn't even had a proper funeral yet. How could he stand to be among anyone? Robyn would have been beside herself with grief if either of her parents passed away.

Maybe he didn't care for his father.

"I must give my condolences on the death of your father. He ruled your land a long time. I'm sure you miss him dearly," she murmured. "I know right now must be so difficult. I am happy to shorten our outing if need be." It was the polite thing to say. The proper thing to say.

Ruslan Merjeri did not look aggrieved in the slightest at the mention of his father's so recent death. In fact, he appeared most displeased that, of all things Robyn had said, she'd chosen to bring up the man. "His reign was long," he muttered. "*Too* long. At this point, we were all waiting for the old codger to die." He smiled at her. "Plus, it is not a burden to be here with you."

"Are you quite sure?" she pressed. Maybe she could go home early.

He waved a hand at her. "You are graciousness itself, but the servants have everything well in hand, as does Gustav."

Her injured hand burned at the sheriff's name. "He is arranging the service?"

"He has a great many talents."

"Indeed," she replied, turning her attention to the outside. What sort of man didn't preside over his father's funeral? And why was the sheriff taking care of it? As far as she knew, the former duke hated Gustav.

Her attention once again landed on the manor. It wasn't the prettiest of buildings. While grand, it was built for a siege. Her eyes narrowed as she spotted a new addition to the mammoth stone building.

"Is your home under new construction?" she said lightly, even though she had heard the story from the candlemaker.

"It's tragic, really. One of our serfs sold us lanterns of poor quality. Because of that, part of our home burned down. It was devastating that part of our history went up in smoke."

She covered her mouth like she was in shock, although all she wanted to do was retch. Ruslan wasn't just a bully but a liar as well. "I'm sorry to hear that."

"I dealt with it." His tone held relish. "No one will try something like that ever again, I assure you." He looked gleeful that he'd sabotaged a whole family.

Bootlicker.

How would he react if she actually called him that to his face? It was an intriguing idea. She forced herself to keep her breathing slow as Maya tapped the tip of her right boot once again—a warning to keep calm.

Robyn watched as they passed the houses of the people who *worked* within the province. They were all the same— compact but watertight, with whitewashed stone and slate roofs. Plain and pretty, made from local materials. These houses Robyn knew had been constructed over a hundred years ago, and so had absolutely nothing to do with Ruslan himself. Going by the state of the people maintaining the land, if it were up to him, they would not have nearly so sturdy lodgings.

For within the perfect square fields, and trimming the trees, and watching the roads, were people in various states of exhaustion. Their haggard, gray faces and bony bodies stood out like a sore thumb against the beautiful backdrop of the Merjeri province. How hard did he work them? Were they not provided food?

They look more akin to slaves than they do servants. He might pay them, but it is clear he keeps such a tight hand on everything else that there is no way they could leave.

Suddenly, the pretty little houses seemed far more like a means to blackmail these people into living on the land. She was doubtful they'd receive lodgings like these anywhere else. Not straight after the war—not just after the country was ravaged by mimkia.

The thought of mimkia reminded Robyn of what her father had said. *There is a new drug going through Merjeri province. Does Ruslan have anything to do with it?* Going by the fact he was commissioning Will to make weapons, it was beginning to look that way.

Equipping thugs to dispatch envoys to the capital and protecting the drugs from thieves. Clever, if it was true.

Clever but wicked. Robyn figured that described Ruslan rather succinctly.

"Your workers look thin," she said, not able to keep herself from needling him. People were suffering. She couldn't stay quiet.

"It has been a lean year," he replied, completely at ease.

Only because he and his father had taxed the people into destitution.

"Oh?" She arched a brow at Ruslan. "I thought Merjeri lands were plentiful?" Let him get out of that one.

The new duke stiffened and gave her a thin smile. "They are, my lady, I assure you. We are broadening our horizons."

"Indeed," she sniffed and ignored Maya's incessant tapping. Ruslan may have the position to push his intention of courting her, but she didn't have to be nice. He certainly wasn't, so why should she?

"Lady Marian, are you all right?" he asked slowly, his full attention on her. "You're flushed." A frown of suspicion shadowed his brow.

"The rocking of the carriage," Robyn lied, wincing convincingly. "It unsettles my stomach somewhat. It has always been this way."

Ruslan sniffed disapprovingly and stretched his long legs out, so the toes of his boots pressed against the hem of her skirt. She scooted her legs farther back, not wanting any part of him touching her.

"We will have to do something about that. It isn't befitting a lady of your stature to go around walking on your own feet, like you were doing a few days ago with the commoners." Another sniff of displeasure. "I will never allow my wife to degrade herself in such a way."

Oh no, he didn't.

Bristling, Robyn replied, "I find it helps me identify what needs doing on the Lochslee land if I talk to the people who live and work upon it. It is why we've always done well even in times of harsh winters and war. The people are who our lands are built upon, would you not agree?"

He sniggered into his perfectly manicured hand. "Forgive me, Lady Marian, I do not mean to laugh at you"—he clearly did—"but it is not your place to find out what the commoners need. They are working your land for *you*. If *they* have issue with something, then it is *their* responsibility to come to you and tell you about it. You should never have to go to them. It is beneath someone of your station to go galivanting among the rabble."

She was going to punch him in the nose.

The way he emphasized his words as if Robyn were a simpleton, was an utter gas. She'd probably read more books than he could ever fathom and knew how to run his land better than he did.

"We must agree to disagree, my lord," she replied tightly. "I do not think we will find a common ground here."

A spark of interest flared in Ruslan's eyes. That right there was why she tried to present herself as a demure young lady. Any time he saw a hint of her temper, it excited him. He wanted her to fight. Ruslan clearly relished breaking the spirits of those around him.

He's not getting yours.

She blinked innocently at him as he studied her. What was he looking for, exactly? Robyn dropped her gaze to her hands and glanced up at him through her lashes. Ruslan was a problem to be sure, but his vanity was easily manipulated. If she chose to marry him, it wouldn't be the most difficult thing in the world to slowly usurp his power. She just had to figure out a way around the sheriff. The new duke could be manipulated...but his pet viper was a different story.

"Speaking of things about grounds," Ruslan drawled, "and on the topic of what's making this winter so difficult..." With the way his features sharpened, it was clear he had been waiting to get onto this point of conversation from the very beginning of their excursion. "I have heard tales of wolves scouring your woods. Of stealing game and coin alike, and timber, too. Your father had not mentioned this to me; I had to find out from one of my men. Why is that, do you think?"

Because you're the one doing the pillaging and stealing.

"I am not my father, my lord. I think it wise for you to bring it up with him since I am just newly home." She gave him a pretty smile and batted her lashes. "I have been assured that the matter will be dealt with swiftly and is under control."

Make of that what you will.

The thieving wasn't under control at all, but she wanted to mess with Ruslan. Maybe he'd pull his men from the Lochslee forest if he believed a raid would be coming soon.

"Clearly," Ruslan murmured, his voice dripping with sarcasm and piety. "In any case, through our union I can protect the land more than you currently can. It is of huge benefit to you and your *people*"—Ruslan almost spat out the word—"that we marry."

"My people?" she said softly. Maya clutched her knee, and Ruslan did not miss the gesture. "What do you mean by that?"

"Just that you seem to have an unholy fascination with those beneath your station and with the Talagans."

"We are not better than those we serve," she said, reciting one of her father's lessons.

"That is where you're wrong, and I look forward to educating you on the matter after our marriage," he said, as if she'd already accepted his hand.

Do not slap him. Do not stab him. Do not throw him from the carriage.

"My lord," Maya said, censure clear in her voice. "You are much too forward with your words."

Ruslan smirked but nodded. "My apologies, I meant no impropriety. I am a man in love. It makes me a little crazy."

He was crazy all right. But he didn't love her. He wanted to possess and control her.

This is his first mistake.

"And my lands have nothing to do with it?"

He grinned. "That is just an added bonus, my lady. We can reinforce the strength of the Merjeri province in the face of our new monarchy. The queen means well—and is smart, for her sex—but the kingdom is in a state of flux right now. Better that we protect what's ours with our own two hands and provide for ourselves with no external help."

That was a very pretty way for Ruslan to say he wanted to make his own money *his* way and defy the queen in the process. Robyn already knew she had to be careful around him, and this only made her more certain of it. If he wasn't planning treason, she'd eat her own hat. Now just how did she prove it?

"Did your father feel the same way?" she asked.

Ruslan laughed, the sound hollow and dead. "My father was a man of many interests, but he thought small. I have plans to make Merjeri something great."

A horrible shiver ran down Robyn's spine. It told her that the late Lord of Merjeri's death might not have been as natural as she had heard it from the messenger. A heart attack was easily induced by external substances.

If that was the case and she decided to marry him, she'd be signing her life over to a murderer.

Is it worth it for the good of the people? Yes.

"To be clear, Lady Marian. Robyn." Ruslan's eyes glinted with the unearned usage of her informal name. "Courting you at this point is a formality. One day soon, I *will* marry you, you can be sure of it. But let's put on a gracious show for your family and your people, yes? The last thing we want is for any doubt to be cast regarding our affection for each other."

Chapter Twenty-Two

Robyn

The audacity of this man.

Robyn couldn't believe what she was hearing. She seethed beneath her calm façade as Ruslan scrutinized her expression for mutiny. She was so furious at his assertion of marriage as an inevitably that she felt the overwhelming urge to kill something. He knew exactly what corner he'd backed her into. He wanted her land. He had the power to devour it like locusts *or* he could secure her hand. If she turned him down, her people would suffer. Ruslan was known to be ruthless when it came to acquiring what he set his sights on.

If only she had a dragon to gobble him up…

Robyn brushed aside the radical idea. She wouldn't stoop to that level. Becoming a murderess would make her just as bad as the Merjeris. But the look on Ruslan's face if a dragon showed up would be *priceless.*

"I hope that you allow me to enjoy our period of courting,

nonetheless," Robyn allowed, proud that she kept her tone even. The idea of tethering her life to the duke was about as palatable as eating a pile of horse dung. She smiled even though she wanted to scream.

"Lovely," he replied, looking like the cat who ate the canary. "I'm glad we can come to an understanding."

"Not quite."

He frowned at her. "What do you mean?"

Robyn painted on her damsel in distress face. "Your man, the sheriff, he scares me. During our courtship, I have no desire to look upon his face."

Ruslan cocked his head. "Gustav would never harm a highborn maiden."

Her hand throbbed in reminder. The sheriff had no qualms about hurting a woman.

"I cannot abide him, my lord."

He pursed his lips and then nodded. "I will do this for you while we are courting. Once we're married, you'll have to get used to him."

"Thank you," she said, staring at him like he'd hung the moon in the sky.

A little simpering, and he thought he'd won. Even after he had witnessed Robyn fighting against the sheriff and had seen her countless times helping her people and getting her hands dirty, it was clear he still fully believed Robyn to roll over.

Fool.

Plus, there were the three times in the last four years that she'd rejected him. The weasel had finally found a way to trap her into matrimony, but the joke was on him. She'd let him be blinded by his desire and ambition, and she'd take his birthright from him. It was only fair.

Ruslan leaned forward on his seat to point through the right-hand window. His hand very purposefully brushed against Robyn's knee in the process, and she held still. If he wanted to play it that way, she wouldn't balk.

"Would you like to see the manor?" the new duke asked her. "How could you not? The décor has just been updated. Especially in the bedrooms—"

"Unfortunately, my father is expecting me," Robyn cut in, appalled by the brazen suggestion that had clearly been on the tip of Ruslan's tongue. As if she'd entertain ideas of him in the bedroom. "You must forgive me, Your Grace," Robyn tacked on at the irritated expression on his face, "but I have not been back long from the...convent. My father is loath to be parted from me after being absent for so long. You can surely understand?"

His lips thinned, but he waved a haughty hand at her, ignoring Robyn's rebuff of his not-at-all subtle invitation to his bed, pre-marriage. Like she would ever consider such a thing.

"It pleases me you haven't changed in that way," he said. "Even when we were children, you were always so devoted to your family, to John."

She flinched at the mention of her brother's name.

"It's a good quality in a woman," he crooned.

Like men didn't need to be loyal to their families.

"Thank you," she said woodenly.

"Most highborn women only think of themselves and are empty headed, but not you. You're an oddity."

Not only had he brought her brother into it, but he had complimented Robyn while insulting every other woman. In almost every case, the highborn ladies she knew were far smarter than their husbands and fathers—they simply had no opportunity or position to use their intelligence.

Maya cleared her throat.

"I shall take you back then," Ruslan continued cheerily, seeming to know his barb had dug deep, "so that you may do your duty. I shall call on you after my father's service is completed. I hope that you will not deem it appropriate to arrange to talk to your father on the same day. Though I can't imagine you would, given that you're so keen for me to court you," he said dryly.

As if she'd ever be keen about doing anything with him other than strangling him to death.

Her smile was brittle as he smirked at her. Either Ruslan was aware of it and was testing her or he was so full of himself that he genuinely believed she should clear all future engagements from her calendar simply to see him. Regardless of why he'd said it, she'd play along if it got her what she wanted in the end.

"I would not dream of it, Your Grace."

Unlike Ruslan having the audacity to use Robyn's informal name without her consent, he did not tell Robyn to use *his* name. He enjoyed her deferring to him. Serving him. Pleasing him. She'd let him play his little games, but while he was so focused at trying to possess her and pilfer her lands legally, she would pull the wool over his eyes and steal his own estate.

It was with some relief that Robyn made it back to the Lochslee estate without once insulting the Duke of Merjeri or in some other way spoiling his mood. He'd known her since she was a child, and they'd never gotten along. She would needle him where she could, but all in all, she'd be the obedient highborn woman until she'd secured *his* land.

She schooled her expression as he helped her out of the carriage and even let him kiss the back of her hand.

"Until we meet again," Ruslan said, more an order than anything that sounded excited by the prospect.

She curtseyed and then turned her back on him, Maya hot on her heels. The new duke chuckled before climbing back into the carriage. The door clicked closed and she heard him ordering the carriage around. The wheels creaked as the carriage began swiftly moving down the lane. Robyn stormed through the bailey and into the entryway of her home.

"That odious, privileged *peacock*!" Robyn seethed the moment she was within the safety of the Lochslee walls. She stepped out of the outer layer of her dress in the hallway, the speedy appearance of Maya the only thing that saved the garment from being tossed to the floor. "That self-entitled, evil little—"

"What is wrong, Robyn?" her father said, appearing in the doorway of his study at an alarming speed considering his age. "What happened?"

"Nothing, nothing at all," Robyn said, flapping her hands in dismay. She knew she sounded hysterical, but she was close to bursting. "Everything is fine, except for the fact that Ruslan Merjeri is a degenerate of the first order."

Her father stiffened. "Did he try anything improper?"

She shook her head, even as Maya harumphed in disagreement beside her. "He was his typical self. Nothing that I can't handle. Now if you'll excuse me," she said tightly. "I need a few moments to myself." She gave her father a strained smile, and though she was a full-grown woman and had not done so since she was a small child, she stormed up the stairs and slammed the door of her bedroom behind her in order to rage and rampage alone. She leaned heavily against the door and stared at her room.

Before long she would be *all* alone, save for the snake who would share her bed.

But being in her bedroom did nothing to help Robyn's mood. Glancing out of her window toward the woods, she decided that going on a hunt was perhaps a better way to vent her anger. The walls of her room felt like they were closing in on her. She needed to be outside.

Hands shaking with rage as she changed out of her gown into far more practical hunting garb—her injured hand protesting against being used at all—she wasted no time in equipping herself with her short sword, and bow and quiver, before bounding back down the stairs toward the front door.

"Robyn, if you could wait a moment," Danil said, holding out a hand as if to stop her but knowing he couldn't. "Your father said he received some overwhelmingly good news while you were out with the Duke of Merjeri. If you could just—"

"Is it a matter of life and death?" Robyn asked, slipping on her boots.

"It is not," Danil replied.

"Then it can wait until I calm down and get my temper in check."

"A wise choice, my lady." Danil bowed and disappeared into the library that also functioned as his study.

"Thank you."

"It's nothing," Danil called back.

She pulled up the hood over her hair and exited the manor, closing the door behind her. Robyn headed to the stable for her piebald mare, Blossom, on impulse. She wanted speed today—to get as far away from her problems as possible, and to investigate the usual hunting trails through the forest. Perhaps she'd be able to sneak up on Ruslan's men and suss out the damage they were doing to the forest.

Maybe you could stop it.

Anything so Robyn would feel useful.

"I take it things went well with the new Duke of Merjeri?" Andrei said as he approached the stall, passing Blossom's bridle over to Robyn the moment he spotted her. Clearly, he'd had a notion Robyn would want to go out upon her return; for this prediction, she was sorely grateful.

"Swimmingly," she said, and then: "He's even worse than I thought."

Andrei's nose twitched. "How is that possible? He was horrid even as a child."

"Trust me, it's worse."

"Do you want any company?"

"No."

"Then be careful, Robyn," Andrei said, genuine concern filling his freckled face. "You know as well as I do that it's dangerous to hunt in a foul mood."

At this, Robyn softened. "I know. I'll calm down soon enough. I just need some space."

She swung onto her mare's back and was off, every muted clip-clop of Blossom's hooves upon the muddy road helping settle Robyn's temper more than any other sound could. The wind had picked up since the morning, whipping the hood from Robyn's head and her hair around her face as she entered the forest. It stung her lips and made her eyes water with how cold it was.

Robyn relished every sensation.

It was only then she realized she was crying. Hot, angry, bitter tears, which the wind knocked off their straight path down her cheeks.

"How stupid," she muttered, wiping the tears away as she powered deeper into the woods, having to fight to remember that she needed to keep her horse's steps light and silent instead of the pounding tirade she had taken to reach this point. There was little point in scaring prey away—not when it was in such dangerously low supply.

Calm down. Feel the wind. Feel your horse beneath you. Center yourself.

It was something her mum would tell her every time she got close to losing her temper as a child. It still helped as an adult, it seemed. Her pulse slowed and the tension leaked from her body.

Eventually, she came across a small clearing beneath the boughs of a group of ancient alder trees. Robyn dismounted in order to gather her thoughts within the relative silence and safety of their looming branches. Her horse nibbled the mostly dead undergrowth of the woods, content to allow Robyn to hug her tightly around the neck until she was ready to move on.

"It isn't fair, my love," Robyn cooed at Blossom, stroking the mare's nose absentmindedly. It was something Robyn would never say aloud to her father—or anyone else, for that matter. She had tried so hard thus far to do everything herself. She could get through her problem with Ruslan

Merjeri on her own, just like every other obstacle she'd faced. Couldn't she?

It was beginning to feel like he was, perhaps, a trap she could not escape from.

Robyn stood by her horse, took a deep breath with her eyes closed, and prepared to survey the most common hunting trails in the woods. The trail to the south seemed the most likely place to find Ruslan's men. At this time of year, there was usually more prey to be found in that part of the forest.

Just as she mounted Blossom once more and set off, a ruckus from the *north* caught Robyn's attention. Then a child cried out, clearly terrified and in *pain*. The sound cut through her, and she headed in the direction of the noise before she could stop herself. Just what was going on?

Careful to keep quiet, she wound through the trees, squinting her keen eyes until she could perceive what was happening some distance in front of her. She recognized the blue uniform of the duke's men immediately. She scowled as she spotted the family they were clearly harassing. Going by their ragged clothes and generally poor disposition, she could only conclude that the family was traveling through the forest in search of a kinder place to live. The last few years had been tough on everyone.

She hissed when one of Ruslan's men stabbed at the tallest member of the group—a man who stood in front of the rest of his family to protect them. An unarmed man. Before her eyes, the man turned into a stag, pawing at the ground and shaking his impressive antlers at them.

Talagans.

The stag's rack tangled with a spear, and he was knocked

mercilessly to the side.

Her gaze snapped to the little ones, hiding in their mother's skirts as the duke's men pressed closer, holding them at sword-point.

Chapter Twenty-Three

Robyn

The duke's men were robbing a shifter family. Within the confines of the forest. Lochslee land.

Robyn squared her shoulders.

This was her land. They would rue the day that they stepped foot on it.

"Over my rotting corpse," she growled, knowing she didn't have long to decide what to do and how to do it before it would be too late. The shifter family had two young children—fawns, by the size of their eyes and the shapes of their ears—but Robyn knew the duke's men didn't care about avoiding violence around children. The smallfolk were beneath them, after all; not even their children's lives mattered.

But they mattered to Robyn.

They should matter to everyone

The stag reverted to his human form when he toppled to the forest floor, the spear which the first of seven—no, eight—of the duke's men had thrown at his antlers having cut his head open and fallen to the ground. The shifter groaned in pain, blood running down his forehead and into his eyes.

Robyn needed to do something *now*. She urged Blossom forward, keeping to the denser trees. Charging in would get them nowhere.

Behind the stag, two women who looked like sisters, along with the two children, cowered in the face of the duke's men, with their shining swords all pointed at them. Gleaming, shiny, and untarnished by use.

New swords.

Weapons Will had designed, no doubt.

That settled sourly in her stomach. Ruslan was using her friend to create weapons to attack innocent people. The assumption that they were also used as part of the new drug business going through Merjeri province seemed more and more likely by the second.

The lead man laughed at the shifters. "Pitiful. This is what you get when you walk through Duke Merjeri's land without permission. If you are on his land, you pay his taxes!"

Not his land.

One of the shifter women fell to her knees, weeping. She kept glancing at the fallen stag shifter.

Without medical attention soon, he was likely to die.

"We mean no harm!" the shifter woman cried. "We are simply passing through. I beg you, do not harm us, and have mercy. I have to help Frederick, otherwise—"

"You can help your *Frederick*," the duke's man cut in, spitting at the stag shifter. He did not respond, but instead grew motionless. "When you have paid your dues."

"But we do not—we have nothing, sir! That is why we are searching for a better home. Perhaps fortune might favor us in Dotae, now that Queen Ansette reigns."

At this, all the duke's men laughed uproariously.

"You hear that?" one of them said. "The child queen will save them when she can't even take care of herself."

Such talk was treason.

The first man thrust his sword beneath the shifter woman's chin. To her credit, she did not shy away, though her tears fell harder. "Give us everything you have of value. If you have nothing, we will take payment in... kind." His lecherous gaze fell over the kneeling woman and then her sister, who gently pushed the fawn children behind her as if hiding them from sight would somehow protect them.

That was the last straw.

Robyn considered her options. If she went in there, high and mighty as Lady Marian, then the soldiers would have no choice but to back off... but then word of what she'd done would filter back to the duke. She couldn't risk it. He would not take her interference kindly. Plus, if he thought she'd caught wind of his operation, Ruslan would just become sneakier. At least, she knew where to look for the problem now. That left her with one option.

Being someone other than herself.

One woman against eight? What could go wrong?

Thanking the stars that she'd changed into all of her proper hunting garb, Robyn tied a scarf around the bottom half of her face and pulled up her hood. Then she strung her bow, nocked an arrow at the leading duke's man—her injured hand protested violently, but the bandages held tight, and Robyn didn't feel the cut beneath it open up again—and urged Blossom forward. They broke into the small meadow, and she released the first arrow.

"What the devil?!" one of the men yelled the moment Robyn's arrow pierced through his commander's shoulder, sending him to his knees. They all scrambled to turn their attention to the person rushing at them upon horseback, screaming and yelling like they were mad.

Perhaps Robyn *was* mad. There were seven men left, and they were all trained Merjeri soldiers. Luckily for her, she knew that they were lazy. They'd rather benefit off the backs of others and cut corners than put in the hard work. By all accounts, it would be easier than dealing with the bandits. This time, she didn't have a mortal wound, nor was she poisoned. She could handle the injury in her hand. If she could just loose enough arrows...

Another of the men fell. Two. Three.

Four down, four to go.

Robyn swung Blossom around to aim and charge at the men once more.

Dispel them. Prevent them from regrouping. Remember all your training, her father's voice whispered in her mind.

She caught the eye of the woman who had bowed down on her hands and knees, her mouth hanging open in shock and fear.

"Get to safety and help your man!" Robyn hollered at the shifters, who were watching the fight with a stunned, incredulous, terrified fervor. The two fawns looked at Robyn with their big eyes as if she were an angel.

She slung her bow over her back when it became clear she could no longer do the most damage with her arrows. She pulled out her short sword instead, wishing it were longer, before deciding on chopping down a path to the spear that had been used to fell the stag. The soldiers circled her as best they could, jabbing at Blossom with their own spears to try and back Robyn and her horse into a corner.

"As if I'd let that happen," Robyn muttered, reaching down to grab the spear before—

The flat of a sword slammed against her left side as she leaned down over her right, and she toppled off Blossom. On instinct, she slapped the mare's closest leg to urge her out of the fray; the horse obediently ran toward the shifter family.

Robyn barely had half a second to get back to her feet, grab the discarded spear, and face her opponents. To her dismay, they had used her dismount as an opportunity to regroup, forming a sharp porcupine of spearheads and swords against Robyn.

Her grip tightened on the stolen spear she'd picked up, and she hissed through her teeth. The gash on her palm had fully split open, soaking through the bandages Maya had so carefully wrapped around Robyn's hand and soaked in mimkia. The shaft of the spear grew slick and slippery and almost impossible to grip.

"You thought it wise to attack the Duke of Merjeri's men, *boy*?" one of the men—second in command, going by the way the other three looked to him for guidance and orders— leered at Robyn. "That was brave, I'll give you that. But stupid. So utterly stupid."

At least they believe you to be a boy.

The man cackled when he caught sight of the blade. "You think you can best all four of us with that tiny blade, and an injured hand that can barely hold a spear? Surrender now, and I will vouch for a quick death at the hands of the duke. If not...I'm sure we'll all enjoy ripping you to pieces *slowly*."

Robyn had no intention of surrendering, nor of dying. She had been through too much to die at the hands of these idiots. If they'd had any skill, they would have already taken her out.

Taking a deep breath, she dropped the spear, seized the dagger from her waist, and struck the nearest soldier in the gullet. She spun on her heel and sprinted away, cloak billowing behind her. The men yelled and gave chase.

Robyn knew she wouldn't get far. Knew that running would barely give her a few seconds to work with. She knew these woods better than anyone, but the men still had longer legs. She ripped through the trees in the opposite direction of the shifter family—and her horse—as fast as her legs could carry her. If the Talagans were smart, they'd take the opportunity to disappear. Her lungs burned, and she gulped down cold air, pumping her legs and arms harder as the sound of cursing came nearer.

Bloody Ruslan always causing problems.

"Gotcha!" a male voice growled a moment before a hand yanked on her hood and knocked Robyn to the ground. She swiped blindly at her attacker with her sword. He bellowed as it sank into something soft. "Blighter!"

That was the only warning she got before the sword was torn from her fingers and then, barely giving her an opportunity to breathe, steel-toed boots began kicking her in the stomach in earnest. She curled in on herself to protect her head and organs.

Why do you always get yourself into situations like this?

Think through the pain. Her papa's voice rang in her ears.

Rocks dug into her side. She clawed the ground and seized

a fist-sized rock and lobbed it at the soldier hovering over her. He yelped as it hit him squarely in the face. He cupped his nose, and she rolled in his direction away from the other man kicking her. Robyn popped to her feet, her ribs screaming in protest.

She pulled out her remaining dagger from her belt, and the other soldier rushed her. She ducked under his arm as he swung at her with a hook. She punched him squarely in the kidney before kicking in the back of his left knee. As he fell, Robyn slammed his head against the nearest tree, knocking him out.

Breathing hard, she eyed the other man who was a sniveling bloody mess and picked up her sword.

"You broke my nose and my teeth," he slurred.

"You deserved it," she spat. And a whole lot more.

"Are you going to kill me?"

"No," she snarled. "But death is what you deserve. Change your ways, or I'll be coming for you." Not really, but it was entertaining to see the panic on his face.

Robyn left him crying on the moss-covered forest floor and limped back toward the clearing. She tucked her dagger away and wrapped her left arm around her aching ribs. Her fingers tightened around the hilt of her short sword as two more men crashed through the trees in her direction.

Two more down. Two to go.

Chapter Twenty-Four

Robyn

"Come here, you sniveling upstart!" the commander bellowed. "I'm going to beat you into the ground, boy!"

She bared her teeth at him in a grisly smile. She was no *boy*. Soon, he'd know he'd been bested by a *woman*.

Don't lose your head. Keep your identity hidden.

"Come and get me," she growled lowly. "Your shoulder hurting much?"

"We will have your head for interfering with the duke's business," he yelled again, clutching his shoulder where she'd shot him. "This is treason."

The revelation that she should have really thought things through before jumping in to defend the shifter family washed over Robyn like a bucket of ice water. So many more lives were at stake than hers; if she were dead, she could do nothing to help them or anyone else. Yet Robyn knew, instinctively, that had she been given the choice once more, she would still decide to help the family—every single time.

She couldn't sit around and do nothing. With privilege came responsibly. She had to help those who could not defend themselves.

You're pretty beat up yourself.

Robyn pointed her short sword at the other soldier who was trying to edge around her. "I don't think so."

His eyes narrowed on her, but his hands shook as he clutched his spear closely to his chest. She eyed him from beneath her hood. He looked like a boy of fourteen winters.

The commander rushed at Robyn, and she parried his attack, her boot sliding in the mud as he pressed closer. She gritted her teeth. She couldn't give him any more ground. The young soldier darted in, and Robyn managed to break away from the commander. She panted hard as she faced off with both soldiers. Her ribs screamed as she lifted her sword and eyed each of the men.

"You can walk away," she rasped. "We can forget this even happened." No more violence needed to occur.

The commander's eyes filled with malice. "I'll drop dead before I'll let you go."

So stubborn.

So be it.

She spat blood onto the forest floor and dropped into a defensive stance as the younger soldier twirled his spear. Robyn almost rolled her eyes. It wasn't a bloody baton. Hadn't anyone ever told him not to play with weapons? A flicker of movement to her left caught her eye. Another soldier limped through the trees, and he didn't look happy.

Great. Three against one. Could nothing ever be easy?

A low rumble coursed through the earth.

The hair at the nape of her neck rose as the sound rolled

through her body. The three soldiers froze, and she blinked at them. An earthquake? She glanced around. Nothing lurched or moved. The wind whipped her hood from her face, and the pine trees swayed as a large shadow passed above.

No. It's not possible.

A second rumble, closer this time, unsettled the leaves littered on the forest floor, and it took Robyn an exorbitant amount of effort to keep standing. She clutched her side. One of those blighters may have broken several of her ribs. The soldiers were ignoring her, their attention pinned to the sky.

This was her opportunity to disappear.

Robyn took a step backward while they were distracted.

"What was—*oh my*—" one of the men bit out when a shadow crept over them, and a gigantic shape came swooping down.

Gigantic, winged, and green.

She staggered, and her heart leapt in her chest.

A dragon.

Damien.

She could scarcely believe it. Here, now, in her hour of need, the dragon shifter had appeared as if he'd read her mind. But Robyn didn't have the time to simply watch as the magnificent creature snapped a spear in two and knocked the closest man—the one Robyn had stabbed in the ankle— against a tree.

"It's a dragon!" the commander screeched. He dropped his spear and sprinted through the trees without his remaining men.

Robyn blinked slowly. What a coward.

The young soldier picked up the abandoned spear, one

weapon in each of his hands and stood tall, waving them about, despite how he trembled. "I will slay the beast!"

Loyal and stupid to a fault.

She considered disappearing into the trees, but that would make her as much of a coward as the commander. Robyn couldn't leave the boy to the dragon, any more than she could run from Damien. She spat more blood from her mouth as she raced toward him to try and pull a spear from his grasp.

"What are you doing?" he cried.

"No need to die for a lord who cares nothing for you," she yelled back.

But it seemed as if the boy was not as unskilled in battle as he was stupid. He twirled away from Robyn's grasp and slashed at her with one of his spears.

She barely ducked in time to get out of the way. The mud beneath her feet was slippery, so she used this to her advantage to slide toward the man once more and sweep him off his feet. She doubled over in pain from the movement, her ribs aching. But Robyn couldn't dwell on the pain; she knelt upon his left spear, yanked the other one from the boy's grasp, and tossed it out of his reach.

A branch snapped to her right, and she locked gazes with the other soldier. He used the nearest tree for support as he watched her. He lifted a crossbow, and her pulse thundered in her ears. Where in the blazes had he gotten that?

"Goodbye," he whispered and lifted the bow.

"Damien!" she shouted. "Help me!"

The earth shuddered as the dragon dropped into the space between Robyn and the soldier with the crossbow, his tail curling around her like a shield. The boy screamed, and she punched him in the face, knocking him out. Robyn shook as she slowly pulled herself up onto her feet. Ice trickled down her spine as the dragon released a menacing growl that made her want to hide. She forced herself to crawl over his tail. His scales were surprisingly warm. Robyn dropped to the ground and edged around the dragon. Damien had the soldier pinned to the spot. She paled as the dragon snapped his forearm-length teeth inches away from the man's face. The soldier trembled in fright, the crossbow dangling from his hand, apparently forgotten.

"You thought to touch what is mine?" the dragon rumbled, his voice like nothing she'd ever heard.

The soldier whimpered.

"Pathetic male," the dragon hissed. He lunged, and the soldier jerked back, cracking his head against the tree. His eyes rolled up, and he dropped to the forest floor like a sack of potatoes.

For a long while, Robyn simply glanced between the unconscious men and the dragon. What was she supposed to do now? Surely, they'd tell Ruslan about what happened here. Reprobates working for Ruslan Merjeri, yes, and they had been serving under his orders. What separated them from the destitute and homeless in Robyn's village was merely a stroke of luck and change in circumstance.

She eyed Damien as he swiveled his neck her way, his emerald eyes locked on her. She gingerly set her sword down and held her hands out as she took a step away from him. He growled softly, and she stiffened. Her eyebrows slashed low as she glared at him.

"Don't you take that attitude with me," she hissed. She ignored his sharp perusal as she moved to the soldier he'd taken care of. She ran her hands over his body and rolled her eyes as the dragon hissed in displeasure behind her as she stole his gold. "What are you doing here, Damien?" she questioned, eyeing the fancy crossbow. Robyn only hesitated a second before she plucked it from the forest floor and slung it over her good shoulder.

Damien stayed silent, just watching her.

"I know you can speak in this form," she said.

Still, he said nothing.

She didn't have time for this.

Quickly, she moved back to the boy and relieved him of anything of value, including his weapons. She adjusted his limbs, so he was somewhat comfortable.

"I'm sorry it had to be this way," she whispered to the boy and then walked in the direction of where she'd last seen the shifter family.

Robyn crossed paths with another of the duke's unconscious men. She searched him for anything useful, too. Her breath stuttered when she found two whole bags of gold, mimkia, as well as a glass vial of liquid. She held it to the light and studied the black potion. Was this the drug her papa had been speaking of? She pocketed it, hating how aware she was of Damien's eyes on her.

Stop it. Pretend he's not here.

She snatched up the man's sword and eyed the fine craftsmanship. It was one of Will's, to be sure. What would her friend think if she showed up and gave it back to him?

He'd demand to know what you've been up to.

That wasn't a conversation she was ready to have.

After freeing the unconscious men of all their useful belongings, ripping away the expensive white cotton of one of their shirts for the stag's head in the process—there's no way he'd be going anywhere fast—Robyn followed her horse's tracks until she came upon the shifter family.

At the sound of her footsteps, the woman who had begged on her knees cried out in fright. "Please don't hurt us! Please—oh. *Oh.*" Her eyes grew wide when she realized it was Robyn, not the duke's men, who had come after them.

"It's just me," Robyn said softly. "I mean no harm."

The doe-eyed woman stared in stunned amazement at Robyn, then seemed to remember her manners and rushed into a bow. "Thank you for defending us!"

Robyn could only smile, though she was sure it came out as more of a wince. "Please don't thank me for such a small courtesy. Any decent person would have helped you."

"I think you hold too much faith in others," the injured stag shifter murmured.

Not enough these days.

Her smile felt brittle as she dropped to her knees beside the fallen stag shifter and pulled out the mimkia she had stolen from the duke's men. She held out the salve. "This should help you."

The man eyed her. "I can't afford such a thing."

Robyn placed it in his palm and curled his fingers around it. "Consider the salve a gift."

"Thank you." He frowned. "Don't you need it for yourself?"

She waved a hand at him. "Not badly. I shall be all right."

The man handed the salve to his wife, who quickly dipped into it with her fingers and began to dress his wound. Robyn gave the little fawns a smile and groaned as she sat down on the ground, setting down her loot around her. "I hope you don't mind a spot of company."

The man's gaze drifted over her shoulder. "As long as your dragon is not hungry."

Robyn peeked over her shoulder at Damien. He hadn't moved a muscle. Just watched. She turned back to the stag shifter. "Don't worry about him."

The man arched a brow. "Your mate?"

"No."

"Hmmm," he murmured.

"What are your names?" Robyn asked.

"It is better not to ask, my lady. Names can be dangerous."

He wasn't wrong.

She blinked as realization dawned. "My lady?" she questioned.

His wife paused in her ministrations and touched the tip of her nose. "Talagans are keen to scents. You are clearly feminine." She studied Robyn for a moment. "Why dress in trousers and cut your hair?"

"As you well know, the forest is not as safe as it used to be." She pressed her lips together but forced herself to continue. "Life is safer as a man. Women are always a target."

"It's not right," the man said, brushing his white hair from his face.

"No, it is not," she murmured, "but it is the way of the world."

She caught the little fawns watching her from behind the other woman who'd stayed silent, content, it seemed, to listen. Robyn winked, and the little girl giggled. The sound lightened the weariness in Robyn's soul.

"May I give a gift to your children?" she asked softly.

The parents nodded, and she slowly got to her feet. She padded over to the other young woman and dug into her cloak, peeking at the fawns from behind her tangled hair.

"Do you like shiny things?" she asked.

The little girl released the other woman's skirt and darted forward, her threadbare skirts floating above her ankles. "I do." Her brother followed behind, shyer.

"I'm so glad, because I have a bag of shiny things for the both of you." She produced the bags of gold and gave one to each of the children.

The other woman gasped and shook her head. "We cannot accept that."

"You can." Robyn glanced back at the parents who'd frozen at the sight of the gold she'd just given to their children.

The male shifter met her gaze solemnly. "This is too much."

"It's not enough. Take the money, take the mimkia, and take *these*." Robyn gestured to the weapons she'd collected. "And get as far from here as you can. The Merjeri province is not safe right now. Can you walk?" She nodded at the stag.

"I can."

"Good. Then leave now before the duke has time to retaliate. His temper is fierce."

"We can. But how could we ever thank you?" the wife whispered, tears gathering in her eyes.

"You don't need to thank me."

For a moment, it looked as if the family might hug her, but then they thought better of it.

The wife helped her husband to stand. He held Robyn's gaze and bowed deeply. "I will never forget this. I know I said names are dangerous, but it you ever need a helping hand, feel free to call upon the House of Pine. Ask for Frederick.

Someone will find me, and I will come."

"I will keep that in mind." She held her hand out, and he shook it. "Not all of Merjeri is bad. I've heard the Lochslees are a decent lot for the highborn."

Frederick's eyes twinkled. "I will not forget. May the wind be with you, Lady of the Forest." With that, he slung his arm over his wife's shoulders, and they began their journey. Their steps were slow and labored as they retreated north, but Robyn made sure to stay exactly where she was to watch them until she was certain they were gone with no further trouble.

She tipped her head back and closed her eyes.

Today she'd done some *good*.

Blossom whinnied from her right, and she opened her eyes to watch as her horse ventured from the trees, munching on nettles. She butted Robyn in the chest. Robyn wrapped her arms around her horse and patted the mare on her neck.

"I'm fine, Blossom," she said, before rubbing the mare's muzzle absentmindedly, trying to process the last few minutes felt like walking through sludge. Was it just a few hours ago that she'd been riding with Ruslan?

Her mare shied away, tossing her head. Robyn shushed Blossom and looked over her shoulder. Damien stood a few paces away, his cloak draped over his large shoulders. He'd shifted, and she hadn't heard a thing.

He picked at his claws like he wasn't the least bit interested in Robyn, but his attention on her felt like a physical touch. He really came looking for her and saved her life again. What did he want?

Robyn knew there was only one way to find that out for

herself.

Ask.

Hating the painful thumping of her heart and the way her thoughts flitted, unbidden, to the memory of the dragon shifter standing before her, naked and confident and perfectly at ease within the cave, she turned around to face her dragon.

"Why are you here?"

"Hello, Robyn," Damien said, his voice low and lilting, as he brushed imaginary wrinkles from his cloak. "Or, should I say, Lady Marian Lochslee?"

Robyn gulped. "So, you investigated me after I escaped?"

"Escaped? Is that what you think you did?" A mischievous smile curled his lips.

It took her too long to chew this over. Robyn blamed it on her potentially cracked ribs, splitting headache, and bloody hand. She chose her next words very carefully. "You mean to tell me you let me go? Let me believe I could escape?"

Damien's smile became a sharp-toothed grin. "That's an excellent way of putting it."

"Thank you for your help," she rushed out. "But it's time for me to go."

"You dare run from me now? I thought you had more backbone than that. Will you stand your ground and face me as the woman of nobility we both know you are?"

That piqued Robyn's interest. *He has deemed something about who I am to be useful. I wonder what it is he's hoping I can do. Or is this merely part of his cat-and-mouse game?*

Regardless, Robyn knew she was too involved with the dragon shifter to flee now. And given everything that had occurred over the last few days that Robyn *did* want to run from—all of it leading back to Ruslan Merjeri—she discovered, upon matching Damien's glinting, emerald stare, that she had no inclination whatsoever to take a single step away from him.

Instead, she took a step toward him.

Chapter Twenty-Five

Damien

Damien had spent days apart from Robyn, hunting down leads in Betraz. It hadn't taken him long to get the info he sought. The man he was looking for was indeed in Merjeri. Not only that, but he was the new duke's right-hand man.

Color him surprised, when he'd snuck past Old Mother's wolves along the border and into the Merjeri province through the Lochslee forest, stumbling across Robyn's scent a day prior. Luck had been smiling down upon him. It had been easy to suss out who she was from there. He'd followed the trail back to the manor and had listened to the cook gossip with a woman called Maya. Damien had learned a great deal about who Robyn was.

Lady Marian Robyn Lochslee was the only daughter of Lord Lochslee. He'd spotted the elderly man hobbling about his garden the evening before, and several things became very clear. One, Robyn loved her father very much. Damien knew of the former king's draft for the war, and the lord was in no state to fight. Two, Robyn's soldier uniform made sense now. She must have impersonated her brother and taken her father's place. And three, there was a mystery to be solved that surrounded Robyn's brother John. If he hadn't been fighting in the war, where was he? Four, the puzzle around the raven-haired woman was intriguing.

To top it all off and find Robyn in a similar position to when he first found her—teeth bared, covered in blood, outnumbered, and staring death in the face—was more than he could take.

She was vicious. She was fearless. She defended what was hers.

Well, Damien did that too, and it just so happened that Robyn was *his*. He could not possibly let the men of the Duke of Merjeri touch a single hair on her head.

He enjoyed circling overhead, descending farther and farther in circles in order to intimidate the men. He could smell their fear; Robyn, on the other hand, was not frightened at all. *Knowing her, she is looking for a way to turn this distraction to her advantage.* The notion only made Damien like her more.

When eventually he dived into the forest, pine trees scratching uselessly past his scales like feathers, he chased down the man standing closest to Robyn. Out of the corner of his eye, he noted one of the remaining two fleeing for his life—*sensible man*—while the final man decided to remain and fight Robyn.

Damien had no doubt he would live to regret that.

When he snapped his prey's spear in two and tossed it to the side, the man tried crawling away to avoid the same fate, all sense of dignity lost in the face of his imminent demise.

But it was not Damien's place to kill him. If Robyn wanted these men dead, then that was up to her.

With a swing of his heavy tail, Damien sent the man straight into unconsciousness. Sparing a second to confirm he was really out cold, Damien grabbed his quarry's sword between his teeth and threw it in the direction of his broken spear...just in case the man was to rouse in the next few moments. Damien doubted he'd awaken for several hours, given the blow he'd taken to his head. Such delicate beings humans could be.

"Damien!" Robyn cried from behind him. "Help me!"

He turned to help her immediately, taking in the sight of her pinning the duke's thug's spears to the ground beneath her knees with pride. She'd had no weapons left against a man wielding a bow and shield, yet still she had gained the upper hand. He loomed over the man, growling into his face.

"You thought to touch what is mine?" he rumbled.

The soldier whimpered.

"Pathetic male."

After retreating a few steps, Damien then stood, still in his dragon form, and watched Robyn catch her breath, intrigued by what she would do next—what she would *say* next.

She said nothing. She barely acknowledged Damien existed.

Irritation pricked him. She couldn't just pretend he wasn't there.

He growled lowly and wondered what it was Robyn was thinking about with such intensity that a frown shadowed her beautiful eyes.

"Don't take that attitude with me. What are you doing here, Damien? I know you can speak in this form."

He chose to stay silent. If she wanted to be prickly, so could he.

She staggered to her feet. Damien had to resist the urge to shift and help her maintain her balance, knowing Robyn would swat his help away. If she needed his help, she'd ask for it.

For a long moment, Robyn looked from one unconscious man to the other, and Damien realized she was trying to decide whether to kill them. But then the moment passed, and instead Robyn took the men's swords and... robbed them of all their possessions.

Damien almost laughed. Almost, but a stirring in his chest as he watched Robyn rob the men for some unknown purpose gave him pause. He knew, instinctively, that she was robbing them for a good reason.

And he liked that very much indeed.

Still without speaking to him, Robyn walked through the woods in the direction of the strong smell of blood. Damien could only assume the fight had started there. He gave Robyn almost fifteen minutes to do whatever it was she was doing, then he gave into boredom and curiosity and prowled through the forest after her. Despite his size, he managed to do this with very little disturbance to the forest around him, his body sliding between trees with a flexibility nobody ever expected him to possess.

It was in this way that he witnessed Robyn help a deer shifter family with their injured stag, before gifting them the swords from the fallen duke's men, along with all their gold and the mimkia. The fact that the men had possessed the addictive version of the drug was something Damien had immediately noted going by the smell of it; before the night was through, he had to get a messenger to Tempest to inform her of this.

Drugs and diamonds. The female Hound would be happy, indeed. Only after the shifter family had disappeared and Robyn had reunited with her horse—a very pretty mare who suited her master perfectly—did Damien shift into a man, wrap himself in the cloak he always traveled with to cover his nakedness for shy humans, and take a step toward her. Though it was clear she was aware of his presence, still the woman ignored Damien.

He didn't know *anyone* who'd keep their back turned to a dragon for so long...let alone ignore the King of Dragons. It was a bold move. Damien wasn't sure if it was brave or stupid.

"Why are you here?"

"Hello, Robyn," he said, conversationally, when she finally deigned to turn around and face him. She was just as lovely as he remembered, even covered in mud and leaves and the blood of the duke's fallen men. "Or, should I say, Lady Marian Lochslee?"

For the first time, he saw an inkling of fear cross Robyn's countenance. With a gulp, she asked, "So, you investigated me after I escaped?"

"Escaped? Is that what you think you did?"

Robyn spent a short while mulling it over. Damien could tell she was wondering how she hadn't come to this conclusion on her own already. Her eyes narrowed. "You mean to tell me you let me go? Let me believe I could escape?"

Damien grinned at her, all sharp teeth that would have been menacing to anyone else, but Robyn seemed to see them as a challenge by the way she glared at him. "That's an excellent way of putting it," he said.

"Thank you for your help," she rushed out. "But it's time for me to go."

He wasn't going to make it that easy. "You dare run from me now? I thought you had more backbone than that. Will you stand your ground and face me as the woman of nobility we both know you are?"

Damien watched with interest to see what Robyn would do next. *Will she flee? Will she argue? Will she try to make a deal with me?*

Robyn took a step toward Damien. Then another, and another. She didn't stop until she was almost within touching distance of the dragon's long reach.

It was in this way that Damien smelled more than the blood of the duke's men on Robyn. The stench of her own blood was concentrated and heavy on her hand.

His upper lip curled as he scowled.

"You're hurt," Damien seethed, seeing red as he grabbed Robyn's arms before she could think to back away. She yelped in surprise, trying to pull her hand back, but to no avail.

"Let me go!" Robyn exclaimed, looking anywhere but at Damien: his cloak had flown open during his surge of movement, but he didn't care. "Damien, of course I'm hurt, I—"

"No sword or spear did this," he growled, examining the deep welt that crossed Robyn's palm. He turned her hand around and saw the curling tail of a bruise, and the red marks that indicated the woman's hand had been bound and bandaged for some time before the fight. "Somebody else did this to you." That person would die. "Who was it?"

Robyn still wasn't looking at him. "It was nothing. I can handle it. My injury is none of your concern."

"Of course, it's my concern," Damien bit back, shocking even himself with the certainty of his words. They were clearly of surprise to Robyn, too, for finally she got over her stupid human modesty to look at Damien. His anger softened for the briefest of moments when her sage green eyes focused on his, wide and curious in the face of his statement.

"It was Gustav," Robyn eventually said, quietly. "With a horse whip. He mistook me for a commoner." And though he hadn't seen it before, Damien could see it clear as day on her face *now*: Robyn was furious about this injury. About how it had happened, and why.

However angry Robyn was, Damien was infinitely more so. Nobody harmed a woman, especially not one under his protection. This man would pay for his life for such an infraction.

"Damien... Hold on, Damien," Robyn said, holding her hands out as if to keep him from leaving. "Why are you looking like you're about to murder someone? The sheriff will get what is coming to him."

He froze. "The sheriff?" he asked softly.

Robyn shivered. "Yes," she said slowly.

"You know the sheriff?"

"Since I was a child. What's wrong? Damien?"

He could hardly hear her through his rage. He was on the verge of shifting and hunting down the bloody man that very instant; all that held him back was Robyn's hand still held within his own. The sheriff of Merjeri had attacked Luca and Thorn, and had hurt a female under Damien's protection?

Death was too good for the blackguard.

"Damien, you're holding my hand too tightly. Calm down."

It took all his willpower to focus on Robyn once more. His hand shook where it gripped onto her; his claws were beginning to extend from his fingers as he readied for a fight. He loosened his grip, and she pulled away before taking his trembling hand in her own.

"*Damien*," Robyn said, firmer this time. She did not look frightened in the least by his no-doubt terrifying appearance. Instead, Robyn almost seemed concerned. She risked brushing her hand over his knuckles—the most intimate touch he'd experienced in a long time. "What's wrong? Calm down...please."

Finally, after several tense seconds, he exhaled heavily, his shoulders drooping. He blinked repeatedly, as if to remove the red haze from his eyes. His anger wouldn't dissipate any time soon, but he could at least soothe his female.

"I am calm," he said, in a voice that was a touch too growly even to his own ears.

"Very convincing. Can you let me go now? I must collect my weapons from wherever they dropped."

He blinked again, only then noticing that his left arm had snaked around her waist at some point.

You need to get yourself under control.

When was the last time he'd acted so rashly? What was it about this female that made him lose his mind?

Robyn emphasized the word 'dropped' in a way that Damien immediately understood to mean 'from wherever they injured the duke's men.' And so, though it took every ounce of strength within him to do so, he let Robyn go and allowed her to search around the forest until she found two daggers, a short sword, a bow, and a quiver of arrows. She winced as she moved, which told him that she had likely been injured internally during the fight.

"You are so eager to kill yourself," he muttered. Robyn had fetched her belongings and attached them to her horse's saddle in lieu of carrying them herself. She had also taken other swords from the men which she hadn't given to the shifter family, as well as their spears bundled and tied together; these she also attached to the saddle.

Damien wondered why she took them all.

She glanced at him as if she hadn't heard him. "What did you say?"

"I said you are eager to kill yourself."

"I'm not."

"The physical evidence speaks for itself." This was the second time he'd saved her life. How did she get into these situations in the first place? Did she like danger?

Robyn made a face. "I cannot stand by and let others suffer."

"You are helping nobody if you're dead," he countered, feeling anger well up in him once more. "At least tell me you've kept some of the mimkia to treat your wounds."

To his relief, she nodded. "Our village supply of mimkia is low, so I gave the shifter family only a portion of it."

"Good. You don't have a *complete* death wish, then."

An awkward silence fell between them.

Robyn gave him a brittle smile and then a curtsey. "Once again, it was an interesting experience to be in your company. Thank you for your help, and good day." She took hold of Blossom's reins and started walking away.

Damien gaped at her back. Did she think to leave him here? She wasn't getting away that easy.

"Blasted female," he muttered beneath his breath.

He caught up to her quickly, his cloak brushing against the forest floor. She glared at him.

"What are you doing?" she demanded.

"I think it obvious."

"Spell it out."

"I'm accompanying you home."

Robyn rolled her eyes. "I don't need an escort. I can make it on my own."

He snorted. "Clearly."

She paused and set her jaw. "What is that supposed to mean?"

Damien leaned down so their noses almost touched. "It means that you would have died if I hadn't shown up. You are a formidable warrior, but you can't take on everyone by yourself. Robyn, you're going to get yourself killed."

"I'll be fine."

He clenched his jaw as she skirted by him and stomped forward.

"Will you?" he said, sticking to her side like a burr.

"Yes. And if you insist on following me, you could at least do it in silence."

Damien snarled but kept quiet. If she wanted silence, he'd give it to her. Maybe it would give her time to think on his words and her reckless actions.

As the two began hiking back through the forest toward Robyn's village, the woman's horse whickered at the smell of blood upon her mistress. Damien felt an overwhelming urge to shadow each and every one of Robyn's footsteps. As determined as she was to court death, Damien knew it was only a matter of time before she finally faced a challenge she could not best.

Damien couldn't let that happen. He felt a possessiveness toward Lady Marian Lochslee that he'd never experienced before. That he hadn't thought *possible.*

Is this how Pyre felt when he first met Tempest?

The kitsune had reacted viciously when Damien had merely flirted with the Lady Hound. Then there was Luca with Thorn... His cousin had almost beaten him into the floor when Luca had discovered that Damien had taken Thorn back to her village.

How did they manage to contain such feelings—to keep them at bay so they weren't overwhelmed by them?

At this, Damien almost chuckled. Pyre and Luca hadn't contained their feelings at all. They had embraced them and, in doing so, embraced the women they so dearly loved.

Is that what I'm feeling? Love?

The notion seemed ridiculous to him. One could not simply fall in love just because their bodies were compatible.

But, as he watched Robyn gently soothe her horse and change her gait into that of a lady of nobility the closer they got to her home, Damien concluded that he couldn't discount the possibility that he was overly attached to the pretty female. Her ferocity and gentleness were intoxicating.

It wasn't love, but it was *something.*

More like obsession.

Damien huffed out a breath. That was probably more accurate than anything. Dragons were known for their compulsive obsessions.

No matter the reason, he couldn't stand the idea of Robyn

being so close to death once more. If that meant he had to be by her side at all times to prevent her falling upon some wretched man's sword, then so be it.

Chapter Twenty-Six

Robyn

Even though Robyn was walking ahead of Damien, she was painfully aware of his murderous gaze on her back, sizing up her injuries and plotting his revenge. She had no doubt he would cut down the sheriff the moment he set eyes upon him.

At this point, her moral code wasn't even stopping her from indulging such a thought.

He is dangerous for making you entertain another human's death. Check yourself.

She should have felt ashamed for such unladylike desires, but, instead, they filled her stomach with fire.

She wanted to set the corrupt ablaze.

"You *are* aware," Damien eventually said, after almost twenty minutes of silence as they wandered through the woods. Robyn and Blossom paused until he was on their right, then continued, side-by-side. The bloody dragon couldn't be silenced. It did not escape her attention that

Damien's hand twitched toward her own, bloodied hand; she resisted the urge to hide it within her cloak.

"I'm aware of what?" Robyn asked, when Damien let his sentence hang, unfinished, between them.

He huffed out a breath—a cloud of frosty air that almost looked like smoke—then said, "The shifter family. You know you just killed them, right?"

A horrible chill ran down Robyn's spine, but the fire in her belly was stronger. "What do you mean?"

"The goods you handed over to them will be traced directly to them."

"What would you have had me do? Nothing?" she demanded. "They were destitute! If I didn't give them anything—not least to afford a doctor to help the stag—then they would be sure to starve!"

"That is true."

Then what was his bloody point?

"Then what *can* I do?" She ran a hand over her face, at the end of her patience—with her current circumstances and those of her people, rather than with Damien. But the dragon was beside her, and she could vent at him. She couldn't vent at the idea of poverty. "What would you do?"

"I'm a dragon." He shrugged. "I don't get involved with human conflicts."

She narrowed her eyes at him as a memory sparked in her mind. "You're a liar."

He narrowed his eyes back. "Excuse me?"

"I knew I had seen you before." She smiled sharply. "You were on the battlefield with the Dark Court."

He arched a brow. "So?"

"You joined the battle."

"Because it affected shifters."

"Then why did you help me twice?"

He smiled. "Because you are pretty, and I want to add you to my hoard."

Robyn gave him a droll look. "I think part of you believes that."

"It's the truth."

She was getting nowhere with him. "Hypothetically, if you had been in my position, what would you have done? Leave them or give them the goods?"

"Neither," Damien replied, shrugging as if it didn't matter to him. "I'd have sold the goods and redistributed the gold to the people."

"Oh, so it's that easy?"

"Yes. If you know how to do it."

Robyn chuckled. She was beginning to gain an inkling into how Damien's mind worked—and how that translated into what he said. "Is that your way of saying you do that?"

"And if I did?"

"If you did, would you teach me how to do it? Or *help* me do it?" What was she doing? Why would she ask him that? She was already in way over her head.

The smallest smile hung upon Damien's lips. It was a welcome change from his murderous glare; Robyn found herself staring at his handsome face before she could gather the wits to remind herself not to. But if Damien was aware of her attention—she was sure he was—he did not comment on it. He was prettier than she was.

"Just what is it you want to do, Lady Marian?" Damien asked, batting his lashes. Robyn knew fully well he could see where her brain was going. If he hadn't, he'd never have told her about selling the duke's ill-gotten goods, after all.

"Don't call me Lady Marian if you want to retain the ability to speak," Robyn threatened without heat, more to see how Damien would respond than anything else.

She wanted his smile to grow larger.

Instead, his eyes grew intense, and a dangerous flash of *something* crossed his face. "Don't flirt with me if you want to return home rather than be flown directly to my keep," he murmured, a shocking challenge that Robyn had not expected.

Her face flushed crimson at the outrageous, outspoken remark. "I— We're getting off-topic," she said, turning her attention to the forest floor as if she needed to watch where she was stepping so she wouldn't trip, even though she knew these paths like the back of her hand. Blast it all. She was attracted to the vain, snarky dragon who wanted nothing to do with humans. It was just her luck.

"I see you didn't refute the *flirting* part," Damien teased, easy-going once more. He chuckled, a low and throaty sound that sent pleasant shivers down Robyn's spine.

She ignored the shivers, just as she ignored Damien's pointed attempt to get her to admit to more than she knew was wise to. "I want to help my people," she said, forcing them back to the subject at hand. "I want to help those who come to Merjeri province seeking aid, and shelter, and a new life. I want to protect the weak from the strong. I don't want anyone to starve through another winter. *That's* what I want to do."

"Oh? Is that all?" Damien laughed. "That is no small feat, for one person alone."

A singular glance at Damien out of the corner of her eye.

"Who said I'd be doing it alone?"

"You have back-up? Where was this back-up today, pray tell?" He held his arms out.

"Busy," Robyn lied, because she doubted Damien would like it if she explained that she went into the woods alone to fight off the rage Ruslan Merjeri had instilled in her with his selfish attempts to *court* her.

It was funny. Since Damien had showed up, the idea of Ruslan had seemed...smaller. More manageable. As if he wasn't worth thinking or worrying about.

Her steps slowed as they got closer and closer to the edge of the trees next to the village border.

Robyn wondered why that was, even though she knew perfectly well it was related to the presence of the dragon shifter who had twice now saved her life. True, she didn't know Damien well, but despite her misgivings, she trusted him.

"Busy isn't good enough, Robyn," Damien criticized, his tone unexpectedly serious. It was gratifying to know he *was* taking her and her fledgling plan seriously, though, rather than dismissing her out-of-hand like many of the men she knew did.

Then again, Damien wasn't a man.

"They won't be *busy* if we have a proper plan," she retorted. "If we have a plan then we can, you know, *plan ahead.* But I need to know if you'll teach me how to redistribute stolen goods."

"Ah, so we're stealing, is that it? How immoral." Damien looked as if he didn't care about the morality of it in the slightest.

Robyn risked knocking into his side in an almost playful

manner. "Only from the wealthy. The *immorally* wealthy. The ones who stole it in the first place. So, we can give it back to those who need it. I mean, they're not the ones who are supposed to possess it, anyway. In reality, I'm merely giving back what's rightfully theirs."

Damien hummed his approval. "Good. I was afraid you'd be too upstanding to do such a thing."

"And how could you possibly know enough about me to be worried over such a thing?"

A wickedness lifted his lips into a heated smile. "Is that an invitation to get to know you better?"

Though Robyn's face felt like it was burning, she forced herself not to look away. If she did, then she lost this game of *I dare you to look away* which Damien had been playing with her from the beginning—with his bawdiness, with his actions, with his words. She enjoyed his wit, but she couldn't afford to get attached.

She ran a hand through her filthy hair. Every inch of her needed a wash, and she was aching, but she still felt better than she had when dressed in her silken gown, clean and primped for the enjoyment of Ruslan Merjeri.

"Teach me what it is I need to know and *perhaps* you'll learn a thing or two about me in return," Robyn offered, careful with her wording. Something told her that if she promised Damien too much by mistake, he would take her verbatim on her word, and there would be no getting out of it.

"I can't teach you," Damien said, eliciting an unexpected sigh of disappointment from Robyn. But then he added, "Or, rather, I won't. The people involved in such a thing as redistributing stolen goods... They aren't people you should be seen consorting with."

She narrowed her eyes at him. "Which means...?"

"That I'll help you with your plan instead. But..." He cast his gaze over Robyn from her head down to her feet, for once apparently critical instead of approving. Robyn fought the urge to cover her chest self-consciously with her arms when his eyes lingered there.

"But what?" Robyn demanded, impatient to know.

Damien waved toward her clothes. "But you can't be dressed like that for this to work."

Understanding dawned on Robyn as she stared down at herself. Though she was in her hunting garb, it was still obvious that she was both highborn *and* a woman. She needed new clothes.

A disguise.

An almost feral grin spread across Robyn's face; Damien matched it with a delicious smile all his own.

"Good thing I'm a veteran at pretending to be someone else."

Chapter Twenty-Seven

Robyn

It didn't take long for Robyn to root out John's old clothes from the eaves of the house. She had separated them—what felt like a lifetime ago—into formalwear, traveling gear, and fighting garb before she went off to war in his place. Robyn had wanted to keep John's clothes in her room after her twin had died, but her father wouldn't allow it. Aside from John's ceremonial armor and the robe he was supposed to wear if he'd ever lived long enough to marry, Lord Lochslee in his grief had wanted all of John's clothes removed from the house.

So, Robyn had, naturally, moved them to the attic.

She was sincerely grateful to her past self for having organized the piles of clothes already—it made her current job of rooting out appropriate garb so much easier.

Damien was currently waiting in the forest for Robyn's return, setting up a camp along with Blossom and the weapons Robyn had stripped from the duke's men. He hadn't told Robyn *where* the camp would be, instead trusting that she'd be able to track him down.

The confidence he had in Robyn's abilities filled her with a comfortable warmth her life had been lacking for so long that she eagerly let it wash over her.

Thanking Dotae that both Maya and Danil had taken her father to the village hall to help distribute food to the smallfolk, Robyn ran back to her room with her arms laden with John's clothes. She didn't have much time to get cleaned up and dress her wounds. She rang a bell to call a servant to her door. When the servant arrived, Robyn did not open the door, but instead asked through the wood, "Could you bring a pail of hot water and leave it outside, please?"

Whilst Robyn waited for the water, she stripped out of her blood-and-mud-soaked clothes as quickly as she dared. An ugly bruise was beginning to bloom over the bottom left of her ribcage; gingerly, she touched the tender skin, pressing her fingertips in deeper to test the extent of the injury.

She sighed in relief.

Not broken. Just bruised. Which leaves your hand.

"Lady Marian," a muffled voice said through the door. "Your water is here."

"Thank you," Robyn called back. "That will be all. Actually, wait, it isn't. Hold on a minute."

Though she was rushing about her room naked, bleeding, and dirty, Robyn knew the order she had to do things in. Opening a handsome mahogany writing table, she pulled out a small slip of parchment and grabbed a quill.

Gather Pavel and Will and meet me at the shooting range behind the forge, Robyn wrote, biting back a gasp when the length of the quill rubbed against the open wound on her right palm. But she persevered, as she always did.

When she was done, Robyn went over to her door and slipped the note beneath it. "Take this to Andrei and tell nobody else about it. Tell him they aren't to be seen, if possible."

A pause. "Yes, Lady Marian," came the reply, followed by the sound of retreating footsteps. Only once Robyn was sure they had truly gone did she open the door and haul the pail of hot water into her room.

Grabbing a cotton hand towel from her closet, Robyn washed all the grime from her skin and hair, sloughing the dirty water out of her window. The chilled air that entered her room when she opened it set her teeth on edge. She couldn't wait for full spring. The winter had been too long.

Once she was as clean as she could manage, Robyn focused on her hand, cleaning and treating the wound with a generous—stolen—quantity of mimkia. The substance caused her to gasp in pain. It burned right through her nerves, but after a few seconds, the burning left and was replaced with a calming numbness. Before her very eyes, the deep lash began to close.

"This is the really good stuff," Robyn murmured, impressed and discomfited in equal measure by the speed with which the drug took effect.

Dotae-level quality. The Hounds-level quality.

Just where on earth had the duke's men—and, by extension, Ruslan Merjeri—gotten his hands on such potent mimkia? The stuff costed a fortune. Only the royalty and the Hounds had access to it. Had the soldiers stolen it? And if the healing salve was this strong, just how dangerous was the addictive, lethal version of the drug that he'd begun peddling throughout the province, killing anyone who spoke out about it?

Robyn shook her head. She would have time to ponder such things with her friends later. And with Damien. She had a sneaking suspicion he wasn't in her forest by chance. The dragon was up to something.

It hadn't escaped her notice that he'd taken some of the addictive mimkia into his possession. Robyn doubted he used the stuff—nor distributed it—which meant he had other reasons for taking it. Was he investigating it? Was that why her being Lady Marian might be of use to him?

What if he saved you in the forest because of the mimkia?

She rubbed at her temples. There were too many what-ifs.

"Focus on getting dressed, fool," Robyn chastised herself, finishing dressing her hand in a fresh roll of bandages before smoothing the rest of the mimkia over her bruised ribs. Then she bound her chest in more bandages—a trick she'd learned to hide her shape during the war—and pulled on a simple shirt, leather waistcoat, and dark-brown breeches with matching brown boots from the stock of John's old clothes.

Robyn's heart twanged painfully when she breathed in the scent of the shirt; it still smelled faintly of him.

"You would choose to do this, too," she whispered to her brother's clothes. "You would do what needs to be done."

Lastly, Robyn braided her hair against her scalp in a similar way to some of the men she'd fought with during the war, then picked up a forest-green headscarf she often wore in summer to keep her hair back when the weather was hot. But instead of tying it on her head, she tied it around the bottom half of her face, then swept a plain, inexpensive cloak over her shoulders and lifted the hood up.

"There," Robyn said, standing in front of her mirror to inspect her reflection. "I'm someone new."

She doubted anyone would easily recognize her; Robyn herself barely saw her reflection as someone she knew.

She had to be careful not to be seen as she exited the Lochslee estate. If she looked like an intruder, she'd be forced to reveal her identity, and then the disguise would be useless.

I should make sure the disguise is sound by walking through the village.

She tested how sure and steady she could make her footsteps now that the mimkia had taken effect. After a few uncertain strides, she became more confident, then settled into the masculine walk she had adopted when masquerading as her brother during the war.

To her satisfaction, what few folks were out and about viewed Robyn with suspicion. They did not recognize her— did not know her.

Perfect.

Now it was time to blend in. She didn't want word to reach the sheriff of a new drifter in town.

By the time she reached the shooting ground behind the forge, Andrei, Pavel and Will were hanging around waiting for her. She grinned as they watched a stranger approach them, recognition flashing across their faces only at the very last moment.

"You look like—well, you don't look like yourself," Will said, shocked beyond reason.

Andrei laughed softly. "It's no wonder you got away with fighting in the war for so long. Just how did you—you know—" he coughed, "*flatten* everything?"

Pavel punched him in the arm, but Robyn snorted at the question.

"A woman has her ways," she teased. Painful ways. "But I'll keep them to myself. Did anyone see you come over here?"

"No," Will said, shaking his head, "but there are a couple of men from the edge of the village on their way to the shooting range soon. They always show up for the last hour before sundown."

"Sounds suspicious," Pavel said.

Robyn agreed. "We'll check in on that. But first... I need your help."

This garnered even more shock than the way Robyn looked. Instinctively, all three men took a step closer to her.

Will crossed his arms and eyed her. "Help? Since when do you ask for help?"

She sighed. "Really, Will? Now?"

"Yes, now. You hold us at arm's length and suddenly you need us? What changed?"

"Me," she murmured. Robyn squeezed her eyes shut. "My whole life my papa had me live for John and myself. I had the expectations of being the future lord and lady of the manor on my shoulders. Then when John died..." She hiccupped and opened her eyes as Pavel laid his huge hand on her slim shoulder. "It shattered me. The only way to survive was to bury myself in work. Then with the draft... I saw things that will haunt me 'til I die." She shuddered and met Will's eyes. "Our people can't go on like this, we can't go on like this, I can't go on like this. Something has to change, and it won't unless we do something. I can't do it by myself. I need you."

Will nodded. "Okay."

"That's it?" she asked, wiping at her damp eyes.

"Yeah. We're with you. Right, guys?" Will asked.

"Yes!" Pavel and Andrei said in unison.

"Don't be hasty," Robyn warned. "If we get caught, you'll lose everything and so will your families."

Andrei snorted. "If we don't do anything, our families are already lost. The Merjeris are slowly killing us."

"What's your plan?" Will questioned in an undertone.

"We bring the duke to his knees, obviously," Pavel teased.

"Is that all?" Will deadpanned. He arched a brow. "But seriously, how are we going to do this? We have no army and no money."

"I can help with the last one," Robyn said.

Andrei toed his boot in the dirt. "I don't mean to be indelicate, but Lochslee Keep is not what it used to be. The former duke has taxed everyone into poverty."

"I know. I didn't mean family money," she replied.

Will frowned. "Then what do you propose? Did you find a dragon hoard while you were with the army?"

Robyn smiled. If only he knew.

"No, but I have information that will get us the funds we need. The duke has been running his men through the Lochslee forest. He has them robbing anyone traveling through the woods looking for a better place to live, as well as taking anything they want from the people of the province." Robyn glanced at Will. "They're decked out in all the weapons Ruslan has been making you forge."

Will crossed his arms, suspicion plain as day in his expression. "And you would know this *how*, exactly?"

"I may have stopped them in their tracks earlier today."

"*Robyn!*" all three men cried in unison.

She sheepishly smiled at her friends.

"Tell me you didn't do something so foolish," Will begged. "Come on, Robyn. You know better than this. What if they'd recognized you? What if they told the duke? Or, even worse, what if they'd *killed* you?"

"Luckily for me, none of those things happened. I had help."

"Help?" Pavel raised a quizzical eyebrow.

"Yes, help," Robyn replied. She waved toward the forest. "And he's waiting for us now, if you'll follow me to introduce you."

"*He?*"

Robyn didn't miss the way Will's voice hitched half an octave, though he was quick to bring it down.

"And where, pray tell, did you meet this man?"

Not a man. "You'll find out soon. Only—"

"Shh, hide, those two men are approaching," Pavel cut in, ushering them to the side of the forge, out of sight of anyone using the shooting range. The two men were dressed far better than most of the villagers Robyn had seen recently, and their quivers were full of well-fletched arrows. Their silver hair stood out against their golden complexion. Unusual.

"Who are they?" Robyn whispered to nobody in particular.

"Rumor has it they're cousins of that bastard Merjeri, moved up from the south for some purpose or other," Will muttered, dark eyes glowering as he spoke. "Which is code for 'spying.' Why would they move *here* for any other reason?"

One of the men paused and glanced in their direction, his head cocked as if he heard Will's voice. A shiver went down her spine at the feral gleam in his gaze. There was no way he could hear Will unless...

Wolves.

Robyn thought of what Ruslan had said—about how someone had been telling him about the goings-on of the village.

Spies and mercenaries, then.

She'd have to be more careful in the future. It would be too easy to get caught plotting treason.

The wolf caught up to his partner as they arrived at the range. Robyn listened intently as the two spies nocked arrows to their bows and aimed at the closest target. They barely made the outer ring of the target.

"The duke wants us to take four of his soldiers to intercept a carriage leaving the province tonight, then track and take down some shifters he's reported got away today."

"How'd they get away?!" the second wolf with lighter silver hair asked, incredulous. "How many of 'em were there, a small army?"

The first wolf shrugged. "With how competent his men are, I suspect the opposite." He spat on the ground. "Bloody humans." His friend grumbled. "Dotae be good, I can't wait until we can go home. I *hate* the blighted stench of this place. I miss our woods."

"Me, too. But we have our orders from the Matriarch—"

"Yeah, yeah, the Merjeri family is to be protected. The duke is an investment of Old Mother."

Will stiffened, his fingers clenching into fists. Robyn laid a hand on his arm in comfort and a reminder to keep calm.

They couldn't risk discovery.

The first wolf chuckled. "What family? He is only the new duke now that his father passed."

"You forget about the tarte he is courting. Did you get a good look at her earlier today? I caught a glimpse of her and she's a delicate beauty. Ruslan will destroy her in no time."

"Hopefully he'll get an heir from her beforehand."

Bile burned at the back of her throat, and she could practically feel the animosity radiating off her friends.

Both men cackled. The lighter haired wolf rolled his neck. "Ugh, I can't be bothered with this today," he said, after loosing a second arrow at a target farther away and hitting it way off the mark. The first wolf had already aimed an arrow there with similar results. "Should we see what beer the tavern has and get a pint in us before the job?"

"Sounds good to me."

Their silver-headed figures retreated, speaking complaint after complaint, until eventually Robyn couldn't see nor hear them.

"Well, that makes our first job easy, then," Robyn said matter-of-factly, wiping dust off her trousers from where she'd been leaning against the forge. She smiled weakly as her friends glared down at her.

"When were you going to tell us that Ruslan is courting you?" Will demanded.

Robyn winced. "He only came today."

"That degenerate," Pavel swore, tugging on his red beard.

"It's not the end of the world."

"How do you figure?" Andrei asked softly. "He's always wanted you. Now that his father is gone, he's going to press the issue. Ruslan is not a good man. You need to be careful,

Robyn. Don't ever allow yourself to be alone with him."

"Noted, and I will make sure not to put myself in that position."

"This may be a good thing," Will said.

Pavel glared at him. "How can you say such a thing? He's despicable."

"But he will be distracted chasing Robyn. Plus, we'll know his whereabouts."

"My thoughts exactly." She shared a smile with Will, his white teeth bright against his swarthy face. "But we can come back to this. Our first assignment just fell into our laps."

"And how do you figure that?" Pavel asked, evidently curious and suspicious in equal measure.

Robyn pulled down the scarf that covered her mouth and grinned. In that moment, she knew the men saw the shadow of her carefree brother then, not her, which she hoped would encourage them to agree to help.

"We're going to intercept the interceptors," she said. "That carriage must be able to leave the province."

Andrei was unconvinced. "Why?"

"Because if Ruslan wants it stopped then that's good enough reason to stop *him*. And those shifters the wolves were talking about... they're the ones I saved today. The head of the family is badly injured; if the mercenaries find them, they won't survive a second attack. We must stop them."

"And then what?" Will asked.

"We rob them, of course."

"We rob them, just like that?"

"Yes."

Between the five of them, there was barely a scratch on
them—Will had a shallow cut on his cheek where a sword
skimmed him, and Pavel had taken an ineffectual kick to
gut. Nobody looking at them would have thought they'd
osted a group of trained Merjeri soldiers and robbed
m blind.

Except they had.

"We can do this, Robyn," Will said, when they reached
ir base camp and sorted through the stolen goods for
mien to sell and 'redistribute.' He smeared blood from the
on his cheek across his mouth. It looked like a wicked,
hteous grin. "We can really do this."

"Revenge for everything Merjeri has done," Pavel added

Andrei nodded in agreement, but they all startled when
byn shook her head.

"Not revenge," she said, slowly, though she grinned as
idely as the bloody one on Will's face. "Never revenge. Only
stice."

"Yes, justice," Damien said, lowering his hood so that
obyn could fully see the fervor in his venomous eyes. She
as quite sure they reflected the way she felt. "The sheriff is
ine."

Robyn eyed the dragon. "Once this is all through, you can
ave him, but not a moment before. Ruslan has been friends
vith Gustav since they were children. His disappearance
vould cause hell to rain down on the province."

Damien scowled. "You'd make me wait?"

"Patience is a virtue," she retorted.

The dragon mulled it over. "Once this is through, he's
nine?"

"And then...?"

"And then, my new *friend* comes into the equation,"
Robyn said, still grinning even though Will, Pavel, and Andrei
were growing more confused by the minute.

But then Will pointed at the arrows the duke's cousins
had fired. "Hit each of them, right through the middle, then
hit the bullseye on the farthest target. If you do that, I'll do
whatever you say."

Robyn rolled her eyes when Pavel and Andrei agreed with
him.

"Boys," Robyn chided, though it humored her greatly that
Will thought this might be a challenge to her. Taking a few
steps toward the edge of the shooting range, she strung her
bow, barely spent a moment aiming her first arrow, then
fired. She let off another three arrows in close succession,
then a final arrow for the bullseye.

Every one of her arrows hit their marks fair and square.

Andrei let out a low whistle. "Color me impressed. Fine,
consider me in."

"Me, too," Pavel said.

Will smiled at Robyn as if he'd have said yes even if she'd
missed. "Where's this friend of yours, then?"

Robyn waved toward the forest. "This way. He'll be
getting impatient, I bet."

"What, do we not want to make him impatient?"

"Probably not." Robyn chuckled, thinking of Damien
sitting on a log in the woods with her horse, twiddling his
thumbs as she took her sweet time to return. It was unlikely
he was doing such a thing, but still. The image was fun.

It took them almost an hour to reach Damien's camp,
during which time Will, Andrei, and Pavel had all but

exhausted their numerous questions about Robyn's 'friend.' And perhaps Damien had heard them. She sighed as she spotted him. Of course, he couldn't have met her friends like a regular person.

He cracked one giant reptilian eye.

"Is that a— Dotae be good, it is!" Andrei said, his hand over his eyes as he peered at the gigantic green dragon curled around one half of the small meadow.

"Bloody hell," Pavel muttered, face paling, causing his freckles to stand out starkly.

Damien smiled in his dragon form, showing all his huge, sharp teeth.

Robyn rolled her eyes. The dragon knew exactly what he was doing.

Will stared at Robyn instead of the dragon. "Your friend is…a dragon?"

"Shifter," she muttered. Her eyes widened as the dragon's face contorted and his body began to change shape. Robyn blanched and spun around to look the opposite way as Pavel, Will, and Andrei stared in morbid fascination. She knew what came after the shift, and she'd seen enough bare dragon flesh for a lifetime.

"My dove, it's just skin," Damien called.

She shook her head, keeping her gaze averted. "Cover it up. No one here wants to see it."

"I think he's pouting," Pavel whispered.

"Dragons do not pout," Damien called.

"Super hearing," Andrei muttered. "Must be nice."

"It is," Damien said, the sound of his voice drawing closer. "I'm covered, darling."

"She's not your darling," Will said.

Robyn turned around to see Damien and W[ ] other up and down in distaste. She wasn't goin[ ] of that. "I brought help."

"So, I see," Damien commented, not taking h[ ] Will. "Although, we'll see how much help they re[ ]

"What's that supposed to mean?" Will ground[ ]

Robyn took a step closer to her friend and la[ ] on his chest. Damien stiffened, and a growl escap[ ] he could stuff it. Sure, they were bonded becau[ ] experiences, but she'd only known him a short p[ ] had been her friend for years.

"He's just trying to get underneath your skin[ ] attention to him. I don't."

Will smiled at her. "You have a way with words[ ]

"I always have," she retorted with a grin. Roby[ ] at Damien who was watching the interaction wi[ ] lips. "This is Will, Pavel, and Andrei. Introduc[ ] happen later. For now, we have a job to do."

Damien's eyes gleamed with interest. "Busin[ ] then. Lead the way."

With three men and a dragon on her side, the [ ] worked far better than it had when Robyn acted on [ ] Ruslan's men barely had a chance to pull out their [ ] before they were knocked down, tied up, and robb[ ] their gold and clearly stolen belongings from the d[ ] souls who lived in the province. They, too, had the a[ ] drug version of mimkia on their person, which [ ] placed inside a satchel to do with it whatever it [ ] needed to do.

"Please take him far from our province," Pavel muttered. "He's worse than Ruslan."

A shiver ran down Robyn's spine at the dark smile on Damien's face.

"Oh, he will pay for his crimes. That, I promise."

Chapter Twenty-Eight

Robyn

One Month Later

Sweet poison, she was truly going to do this.

Here goes nothing.

Robyn tossed her bow over the zip line and jumped from the tree. Her stomach did summersaults as she flew through the trees at a dizzying speed as one of the duke's carriages thundered through the forest toward the western border of Merjeri. She gritted her teeth and let go, freefalling. Her heart pounded as she landed in a crouch on the top of the carriage, her legs like jelly beneath her.

She'd done it and managed not to kill herself in the process.

Shouts went up and she dropped to her belly, an arrow whistling past her head.

Hurry up, boys.

This was all part of the plan. She was to be the distraction while her men took out the sheriff's men, one by one.

She yelped as a hand grabbed her by the ankle and yanked her backward. Robyn spun around and slammed her other foot into the soldier at the back of the carriage. He released her and fell off the carriage. She blanched as she caught the eye of the sheriff, who just ran right over his soldier with his war horse. The sheriff gave her a nasty smile and loosed an arrow, three other men flanking him.

She slammed back against the carriage as the arrow missed its mark.

Winter's bite. The sheriff wasn't supposed to be here.

Besides herself, he was one of the best archers in the province. She needed to find cover now.

The carriage swerved to the left, and she scrambled to hold on to the roof, praying she didn't get tossed from the vehicle.

A shrill whistle cut through the air, and her shoulders sagged.

Her men were here.

Robyn lifted her head the tiniest bit. The sheriff had gained ground, his greasy hair whipping through the wind as he drew up beside the right side of the carriage.

Blast it.

She swung her bow like a staff and slammed it against his bow and fingers, causing his arrow to miss and almost unseating him in the process. He hissed and tried to right himself, his horse slowing down. Robyn swallowed hard when he lifted his head and stared her down, his dark eyes holding a promise of pain. It was time to go.

Robyn scrambled to her feet and bolted for the front of the carriage. She dropped over the edge to the driver's seat as several more arrows embedded themselves in the top of the roof.

"What took you so long?" Andrei yelled from the driver's seat, urging the horses of the carriage to move faster.

She clung to the seat as he swerved to the left. "Some unexpected company." The ground whooshed past them, and she tried not to think about falling. "You sure you know how to drive this thing?"

Andrei laughed. "You don't like my driving?"

"You almost tossed me off the roof!" She peeked around the side and whipped back as another arrow flew past. "Where are the rest of the men?" Robyn nocked an arrow and twisted in the seat toward the carriage.

"Our honorable sheriff had a few surprises for us. Will and Damien are dealing with them."

"Lovely."

She took a deep breath, ignoring her pulse beating in her ears and the sounds around her. Robyn carefully crouched on the seat and peeked over the top of the carriage. A volley of arrows flew overhead as she ducked and then popped back up. Robyn hit one of the soldiers in the shoulder, knocking him clean off his horse. Her eyes widened as she spotted four more soldiers join the fray, their silver hair a beacon in the dark forest.

Wolves.

The carriage lurched, and Robyn lost her balance. Her eyes widened as she fell. Andrei bellowed and reached for her, missing Robyn by an inch.

She caught the corner of the carriage with one hand. She grunted as her body slammed against the side of the carriage, her shoulder screaming from the jarring fall. Robyn slipped her bow down her arm and grabbed the edge of the carriage with her other hand, her feet dangling below her. She pushed through the pain and scrambled to find purchase for her feet but there was nothing.

The sound of galloping caught her attention.

Robyn glanced over her shoulder to spot one of the mercenaries. Her jaw dropped as he shifted atop of the great war horse into a silver wolf.

Devil take it.

She scrambled closer to the front of the carriage and wrapped her right hand around the top rail, bracing her feet against the side just as the wolf leapt for her.

Please let this work. Don't let go.

She swung her legs and let her body's momentum carry her. Robyn's booted feet slammed into the wolf's face, knocking it to the ground. The beast yelped, and the whole carriage lurched as the wheel went right over the wolf.

Shaking, she managed to climb back to the driver's seat, Andrei's face devoid of color.

He grabbed her by the cloak and hauled her against his side. "Sweet poison, Robyn! That was too bloody close."

"We ran over a wolf," she murmured, wanting to wretch.

"Just a little farther."

A howl cut through the air, and the hair along her arms rose.

"We need to move faster!" She caught movement from the left and shot an arrow at the wolf trying to sneak up on them. It snarled and darted out of the way into the foliage.

"Almost there!" Andrei shouted. He urged the horses even faster and veered to the right.

Robyn spotted Will with a lit torch a moment before they passed him in the carriage. She turned around and hefted herself carefully to stand on the driver's seat, her fingers curling around the bar tightly. She grinned as the flames raced along the oil-filled trench Robyn and her men had dug. It formed a large, perfect circle around the sheriff, his men, and the wolves, trapping them.

The sheriff's horse reared as he pressed closer to the ring of flames, his gaze locked on her. He lifted his bow and shot an arrow. Robyn ducked, and the entire carriage shuddered. She peeked over the edge to find Damien crouched on top holding the arrow in his palm.

He'd caught the bloody thing midair.

The dragon stood slowly and walked to the edge of the carriage, his black robe billowing in the wind, and pointed the arrow at the sheriff in challenge.

"You will die by my hand for your crimes," Damien growled lowly.

She straightened as the sheriff's face turned ugly with his rage.

"You won't be able to do this forever," he spat. "I'm coming for you, Hood!"

It was sooner than she would have liked.

Robyn stood in the town square the next day, clinging to her father's arm for dear life as the sheriff nailed a wanted poster of the Hood to the gallows.

The sheriff turned to face the crowd. "This man is not a hero. He is a criminal! The duke has generously offered a reward of one hundred gold coins for anyone who has information about the Hood."

She sucked in a sharp breath. That kind of coin could feed

a family for years. She glanced at the crowd from beneath her lashes, spotting some of her men among the crowd. She'd managed to band together many from their community against the sheriff and the duke, but that kind of money was tempting for anyone.

Her papa squeezed her arm, and she turned her attention toward the gallows once again. She jerked as she spotted the candlemaker being led up onto the dais.

The sheriff's gaze scanned the crowd, resting on her for a moment before moving on. "And any who are found consorting with the Hood and his men will be put to death for treason." A dark smile curled his lips. "Anyone found with stolen gold will also face the noose."

Panic fluttered in her chest, and she took one step forward. Her papa pulled her back to his side, his grip like iron.

"My dear, do not interfere."

"I cannot just stand here and do nothing," she hissed.

Norman stood proudly as they slipped the rope over his head and then tightened it around his throat. Robyn shot a look in Will's direction. He caught her eye and shook his head, his face like stone. Her heart sank. He wasn't going to do anything, either. The candlemaker was going to die.

Heat permeated her back, along with the familiar scent of citrus and sage.

"Calm yourself," Damien whispered in her left ear. "Trust me."

And then he was gone.

"Do you have any last words?" the sheriff asked.

"Long live the Queen and may the Hood bring you to your knees!" the candlemaker shouted.

Cheers erupted from the crowd.

The sheriff gave a nod, and the wolves began to descend into the group of people with clubs. Screams ripped through the air. The sheriff strode to the lever and pulled it, and Norman dropped. Robyn yelled and pushed forward, her father's grip tearing her sleeve.

A roar rose above the chaos, and Damien in his dragon form crashed into the square, destroying the gallows. She froze as her people cried out and surged away from the dragon. She stood stunned as Damien tucked Norman into his immense paw and spread his wings.

"Kill it!" the sheriff bellowed.

The wolves abandoned the people and sprinted toward Damien. Arrows pelted his scales but bounced off uselessly.

"We have to go!" her papa yelled, grabbing her arm and towing her backward away from Damien. "We have to get our people out of here."

She stumbled after him, turning her attention to the trampled or injured people. They managed to get everyone out as Damien took to the skies, with Norman in his grasp. Her papa hustled them down the main road as Ruslan made an appearance with his men.

He spotted them and paused, his horse prancing in place. "I'm so glad you made it out. Go home where it is safe."

"What of the people?" she asked.

"They can care for themselves if they were stupid enough to get hurt." He smiled. "There are more important matters. We have a dragon to hunt." He nodded and then urged his mount forward, his men following him.

Robyn stared after him in disgust.

"I suggest you wipe that look off your face right now,

before you get us both killed," her papa said softly, but firmly.

She schooled her expression. "He doesn't care," she seethed, taking her papa's arm. Somewhere along the mayhem, he'd lost his cane.

"A dragon attacked our city. He has a duty."

Robyn snorted. "That dragon did nothing but save Norman."

They entered the woods, and her father paused. "Dragons? Revolts? The Hood? Change is coming, but I fear it's nothing good."

"How can you say that? The Hood is helping our people."

"Lower your voice," her papa chastised. "You speak treason."

"No, I speak up for the good of our people. How can you stand by?"

His face turned red. "Stand by? Is that what you think I've been doing? I'm trying to keep our people safe." He exhaled heavily. "While the Hood is galivanting around, stirring up trouble, I'm making sure we all have crops to grow this summer."

"What do crops matter if we're all dead?" She felt sick. While her father didn't know she was the Hood, he thought she was a troublemaker. "Our people are suffering and being taxed to death for Ruslan's greed. The Hood is trying to stop him."

Her papa sighed. "Dearest, do you think I don't know what happens on my own land? I know that vigilante is hiding in our forest. It's why he leaves little gifts."

"Then why do you hate him so?"

"I don't hate him."

"Will you turn him in?" she asked, heart pounding.

Her papa stared deep into the forest. "No."

"Why?"

"He and I just have different paths to the same goal." He patted her arm, and they began walking once again. "Mark my words. Times are going to get harder. Be prepared for war."

"War?" she whispered. She didn't want to go to war. She wanted to oust the corrupt.

"It will be the small folk against the duke and his army of mercenaries. Who do you think will win in that scenario?"

"I think you're underestimating the masses."

He pressed his lips together. "I hope you're right."

So did she.

Chapter Twenty-Nine

Robyn

Two Months Later

The only thing Ruslan Merjeri had going for himself was his baker.

Robyn daintily dabbed at her mouth with the linen napkin before placing it in her lap and savoring another bite of the lemon tarte. It had just the right amount of sweet and sour. She'd die a happy woman if she could weasel the recipe from the baker.

You're going to marry the man. You can ask for them whenever you want.

The thought soured her joy and she set her fork down.

She took a small sip from her goblet of wine and eyed the table. Much to her chagrin, the sheriff had joined them and sat straight across from her. Her father to her right and the duke to her left at the head of the table. He took a deep draught from his own goblet and eyed her father in a way

Robyn didn't like.

"I hear you've been having problems in your forest," Ruslan drawled lazily.

He was the one causing said problems.

"Nothing we can't handle, your grace," her father answered.

The duke nodded and leaned back in his chair. "Of that I'm assured, but we are soon to be more intimately related," Robyn schooled her expression, her fingers tightened on her cup, "your misfortune and hardship is mine. I'd like to assist."

Her stomach dropped. *Tell him no.*

Her papa placed a hand on her knee and squeezed discreetly as if to say, keep calm.

"Your grace is too kind."

"Not at all." Ruslan smiled. "We're to be family, are we not?" He placed his hand over the fingers of her left hand and she had to fight not to pull away.

Robyn wrestled with her distain, feeling the sheriff studying her from across the table. She arched a brow at the duke, playfully removed her hand, and shook her finger at him like he was a naughty schoolboy.

"You, my lord, are awfully presumptuous."

Ruslan smirked. "I am told it's all the rage in court."

"I know nothing of such things. I'm a simple country girl."

The sheriff snorted. "If only."

"Something to say, Gustav?" Ruslan asked.

Robyn met the sheriff's gaze evenly as an ugly smile played about his mouth.

"Our Marian is the farthest thing from simple. Even as a child, she was always better at her sums than either you or

I."

Our Marian. The way he said it made her want to bathe.

Ruslan chuckled. "What a lucky man I am indeed to be courting the most beautiful and clever woman in the province."

"Your praise is too much," Robyn demurred, almost gagging on the words.

"Nonsense," the sheriff commented, holding her gaze. "You are resourceful for a woman. In fact, it's the talk of the town how you help those less fortunate than yourself."

"It is my duty," she replied calmly, even as her heart began to pound.

"They're very loyal to you." A pause. "But not as much as they are to that miscreant the Hood."

She took another slow sip from the wine, hardly tasting it. "The Hood? You mean the vigilante causing mischief?" Her father squeezed her knee once again. A warning to tread carefully.

The sheriff swirled his wine around in his goblet before setting it on the table. "Mischief? I had you pegged as a sympathizer, my lady."

Robyn frowned. "Why would you think such a thing?"

"Because you always seem to side with those who are your lesser."

"Just because I take pride in caring for my people does not mean I condone the actions of a criminal," she bit out, hoping he'd buy her act. "The Hood – whoever he is – is only causing more harm than good."

"My thoughts exactly," Ruslan cut in. "What do you think, Lord Lochslee?"

"I don't agree with his actions. Perhaps he believes his

actions are pure, but our people will suffer for his actions," her father said.

"So you don't sympathize with his goals?" the sheriff asked carefully.

Robyn blinked slowly. This wasn't a dinner. It was an interrogation. The duke wanted to know their family's view on the Hood.

"No. He is no friend of mine," her father replied.

It was like he'd punched her in the stomach.

"Good, then we are of like minds," Ruslan said.

"Are you close to apprehending him?" Robyn asked, unable to help herself.

"We are." The sheriff smiled again. "No doubt you noticed some of our new hires."

Robyn nodded, her gaze flickering to one of the silent wolves in the corner who watched them with glittering amber eyes.

"The Hood can't hide forever. Soon he'll get what he deserves."

"Such morose talk." Robyn gently placed her cup and napkin on the table, scooted back and stood. "I'll leave such topics to the men and excuse myself to freshen up."

Ruslan stood and took her hand, placing a kiss on the back of it. "Do you need an escort, my love?"

"No, thank you." She smiled. "I know the way."

Ruslan had become pushier in his pursuit of her in the last few weeks. In fact, this was the second time, Robyn and her father had dined at Merjeri Manor that very week. While she didn't want to spend anymore time in his presence, the duke's invitations gave her the chance to poke around.

Her father smiled. "Maya is in the solar. I'll fetch you when it's time to leave."

Robyn curtseyed and then sedately left the room. She kept her false smile in place as she glided down the silent hallway lined with flickering lanterns and still guards. Her deep green velvet gown rustled around her feet as she approached the powder room to her right. Robyn slipped inside and locked the door behind her.

She only had about thirty minutes before her father came for her.

Robyn hustled to the left wall and ran her fingers along the edge of a gaudy painting of one of the old dukes. Her fingers discovered a depression and she pushed. The hidden door swung open without sound.

Thank the stars for oiled hinges.

She picked up the bottom of her dress and kicked off her heeled slippers. Bare footed, Robyn ran down the secret hallway, thankful for Will's spy inside Merjeri Manor. She turned left at where two hidden corridors intersected and sprinted down the next one until she reached the dead end.

Robyn took a slow breath and placed her hands on the wall. If Will's information was accurate, the door led to Ruslan's personal study.

She strained her ears for any sound. Nothing.

That didn't mean there weren't wolves on the other side.

Carefully, she pulled a small pouch from the pocket of her dress and opened it, scooping up some of the powder that Damien had gifted her. It didn't affect humans, but it knocked a Talagan unconscious in just a few seconds.

Prepared as she could be, Robyn pushed open the door and slipped into the dark study.

Her shoulders sagged.

It was blessedly empty.

Robyn dropped the powder back into the pouch and placed it in her pocket. She snuck farther into the room and smiled at the open window. Moonlight poured in, giving her enough light to see. She stopped at his desk and rifled through the duke's correspondence. There were invitations for events, notations of the crops, and lists for household items.

She opened one drawer after another looking for any information on the movements of his shipments.

Nothing.

Frowning, she opened the last drawer and blanched.

It held a suggestive art piece of her.

That disgusting degenerate.

If she took it; he'd know someone had been snooping around.

It took all her self-control to close the drawer.

Robyn ran a hand through her hair and moved to the opposite wall, finding the next hidden door and stepping through. If Ruslan didn't have the information she sought, the sheriff did.

She ran down the corridor, little holes in the wall filtered light into the space enough that she could navigate. Robyn turned left and reached the next door. According to Will's spy, this door led to an alcove covered by a hanging tapestry.

The door swung open, and she stepped into the alcove, on high alert for any sound. Robyn peeked out from behind the heavy tapestry. There was only one guard within five feet of her space. His silver hair shone in the light.

A wolf.

All you have to do is reach him. Then the dust coating your fingers will do the rest.

Robyn gathered up her dress once again and slipped from the alcove, thankful for the thick carpet that masked the sound of her steps. Her pulse roared in her ears as she reached the wolf and jumped on his back, the dust covered fingers of her right hand covering his mouth and nose.

He growled only once before he dropped to his knees with her clinging to his back, before toppling backward to the floor. Robyn wheezed as his unconscious form threatened to squash her body. She yanked her hand away from his mouth, blew the hair from her eyes, and began wiggling out from under the Talagan. Sweat beaded her brow as she finally escaped. Robyn panted softly, kneeling next to the massive wolf.

What was she supposed to do with him now?

There was no way she could leave him out in the open, but he was too big to drag. Her attention darted to the hidden alcove, and she smiled. No one would find him there.

Robyn rolled the shifter under the heavy tapestry, her muscles screaming. Once he was sufficiently hidden, she stood and brushed her hand down her dress, smearing streaks of dust along the velvet. Maya was going to be irked at the state of Robyn's dress, but there was nothing to be done for it.

She slipped down the hallway, avoiding the puddles of moonlight along the way. She made it almost to the end of the hallway when she heard the rumble of voices. Her heart clenched and for one moment, Robyn froze. Should she make a run for the alcove?

The voices neared from behind her.

There wasn't time to go back.

Robyn sprinted to the corner and peeked around.

No guards. At least luck was on her side.

She rounded the corner to the right and snuck forward, only to stop in her tracks. Robyn darted behind a tall suit of armor, her pulse thundering in her ears. The sheriff was not thirty paces down the hallway, walking in her direction with his head down.

The voices from the other corridor grew louder.

This was how it all ended. There was no way the sheriff would believe anything she said when he discovered her.

A hand covered her mouth.

Her eyes widened as a masculine arm wrapped around her waist and yanked her into the darkness. Robyn raked her nails down her captor's arm.

"Dove." It was the barest of whispers.

Damien.

Robyn stilled and tried to regulate her breathing as he pulled his hand slowly away from her mouth. She blinked repeatedly until her vision acclimated. Decorative lattice woodwork was only a handsbreadth away from her face. Damien pulled her deeper into the darkness and pressed her against the wall. Robyn turned her head to the right so her face wouldn't be plastered to the dragon's chest. She stared through the lattice, able to see a little bit of the hallway.

She stilled as the sheriff came into view. His steps slowed until he stopped just outside their hiding spot. He glanced around and sniffed the air. The hair along her arms rose. Was the sheriff a Talagan? He'd never exhibited any traits when they were children. Could he have been hiding it all these years?

The former duke hated shifters.

A shiver ran down her spine. If the sheriff was hiding his heritage and gifts, Robyn needed to be more careful around him. He was more dangerous than he put on. And that was saying something.

"What are you doing here?" the sheriff barked.

"Just making our rounds," another man answered, just out of sight.

The sheriff sneered. "You're not needed here. Get out of my sight."

"Yes, sir," two male voices echoed, followed by hasty steps.

The sheriff glared down the hallway before he muttered underneath his breath and slunk in the opposite direction. His steps faded away, and Robyn registered Damien's breath tickling her left temple and the way his heart pounded against hers. His body put off so much heat.

Robyn tipped her head back and stared at Damien's jawline. He glared at the lattice, his jaw tight. As if noticing her attention, he slowly peered down at her, fire in his eyes.

"What are you doing *here*?" he hissed.

That wasn't the reception she was expecting. "I take it that it's safe to speak?"

He growled. "For now. The other wolves are out of earshot. Now answer the question."

"For dinner of course and a bit of spying."

Damien's unique eyes narrowed. "And was this a spur of the moment sort of thing?"

"No."

"Why wasn't I told?"

She blinked at the bite in his tone. "Because you are not privy to all my plans." Robyn frowned. "And neither am I

261

aware of all your plans. What exactly are you doing here?"

The dragon leaned closer. "That is my own concern. Not that it matters now."

Her brows furrowed. Had she ruined his spying or... She eyed how he seemed to vibrate with rage. His visit wasn't for the cause it was for something much more personal.

He was here for the sheriff.

"You promised," she accused.

"I didn't break my promise," he countered, between clenched teeth.

"And if I hadn't been here?" Robyn challenged.

Damien placed both of his hands on the wall on either side of her and ducked low so that he could stare her straight in the eye. "I am a dragon of honor. I am not seeking his life this night."

"Then why are you here?"

"Because I don't trust the duke and because I wanted to look after you."

Her jaw dropped. "I don't need a nursemaid."

He snorted. "Clearly."

Robyn pushed at his chest, but he didn't move. "I'm not made of porcelain."

"But you are precious!"

"What?"

Damien's nose brushed hers and she realized they were breathing the same air. His intense gaze burned into hers as she felt his hand cup the back of her head, his fingers weaving through her hair. Butterflies erupted in her belly.

"You drive me mad," he rasped. "Always running headfirst into danger. You're as fierce as a dragoness and worth more than the largest horde by a hundredfold. You don't see it, but

I do."

She opened her mouth to reply when he closed the tiny distance between them. The first touch of his mouth was soft and gentle, coaxing her to trust and give. She sighed against his lips, and he deepened the kiss.

"You're precious," he whispered against her mouth.

Robyn didn't argue. She was lost to the touch and taste of him. She nipped his bottom lip, and he made a growling noise, causing her to shiver. It was as if that one little action caused him to snap. Damien swiped his tongue against hers and kissed her with the desperation of a man drowning.

Her eyes closed and she pressed up to the tips of her toes and threaded her fingers into his hair, hanging on for dear life. The dragon didn't just kiss. He possessed. There was nothing tender left about it, only raw desire and frustration.

He pulled away, trailing kisses along her cheek and down her neck before his mouth crashed back against hers in a kiss so hungry that it stole her breath.

A little bell went off in the back of her mind and Robyn pulled back, her brows furrowing. Damien followed her, pressing kisses to the corner of her mouth and down the other side of her neck, his chest rumbling.

What in the blazes was she doing?

"Damien."

He lifted his head as she released his hair. His pupils where so dilated they almost looked humanly round instead of their normal slits. She swallowed hard at the emotion she spotted swirling in his gaze. There was desire and lust, but affection... and devotion too.

He frowned. "Dove?"

"We can't do this," she whispered, her voice cracking.

Emotion rippled across his face. "I can see you over thinking this."

"We're friends."

"We are, but we are more than that and you know it."

His soft declaration rang of truth, but she'd seen how he was with all women. He loved and cherished the female sex. While she knew he cared for her, they couldn't pursue any feelings they might share. Too much was at stake. "We don't have time for this." Robyn pressed against his chest and this time he stepped back to give her some breathing room. "I need to go."

"You and I are inevitable," he said resolutely.

Robyn turned her back to him and hovered at the lattice, gathering her wits. She couldn't afford an attachment to the dragon. Her future was already set in stone. It involved marrying the Duke of Merjeri.

"I'm not the one for you." It tasted like a lie.

Damien chuckled, causing goosebumps to break out across her skin. "That is where you're wrong, dove. You're mine."

She stiffened. "No one owns me."

"That's not what I meant."

"Isn't it? You told me yourself that dragons live to collect precious items." Heat pressed at the back of her eyes. She needed to get back to the powder room *now*. "Is it safe to leave?"

A beat of silence.

"If you hurry, you can make it back to the alcove."

"How did you know..."

"Like I said. You're precious to me."

She bit her bottom lip and pressed on the hidden door.

"Oh, and make sure you stay away from any wolves. My scent is all over you."

Robyn shot a glance over her shoulder at the smug looking dragon. "We're going to pretend this never happened."

Damien gave her a slow smile. "We'll see."

Chapter Thirty

Damien

Three Months Later

In under three months, Robyn had managed to do what most men in power Damien knew personally couldn't do in four times as long: she'd created an entire character for people to fear...or admire.

The Hood.

When Damien was first introduced to Robyn's friends—not at all surprised that they were all men, for what other highborn ladies could possibly be involved in so daring a venture as robbing the rich to give to the poor?—Damien had been unsure whether they would really be up to the task at hand. But after the first ambush, then the second, then the third, Damien realized that Robyn's friends were good and true and completely trustworthy.

More than that, they were excellent fighters in completely different ways.

Though Andrei wasn't anything more than average with a

sword, spear, or arrow on foot, when the man was put on horseback he was as fearsome as any cavalry-seasoned knight Damien had ever met. He had a way with horses that meant his steed seemed to know on instinct what it needed to do with little to no direction from Andrei himself. It made him ideal to lead their forest ambushes—to direct and corral their targets without them even knowing what was going on.

Pavel was an absolute brute with a sword in his hand. He was a mere three inches shorter than Damien—no small feat when Damien was huge...and a dragon shifter. The man could overcome almost any opponent with little effort on his part and was an expert at close combat.

But it was Will Scarlet whom Damien was most impressed by out of the three of them. Cautious, quiet, and lethal in equal measure, Damien had more than half a mind to tell Pyre about the man so he could be trained as an assassin for the Dark Court.

No doubt he already knows about him, considering how many stolen goods I've been filtering through him.

It didn't escape his notice how Will occasionally looked at Robyn. It was clear he loved her, but Damien wasn't quite sure what kind of love Will felt for her. He was territorial and protective, but so were all of Robyn's friends. The fact that Will kept whatever feelings he had to himself and never made Robyn uncomfortable indicated to Damien that the man had no immediate designs on her. Plus, not once had Damien smelled desire on him.

It was a good thing too. Amongst Damien's people, male suitors battled for the chance to court a female. He wasn't quite sure what he'd do if he had to fight Will for Robyn. It was bad enough that the bloody duke was coming around more often.

He glanced at the woman in question, admiring the determination in her expression as she surveyed their next mark.

Under the mantle of responsibility as the head of her little crew, Robyn became truly alive, and an illuminating sight to behold. Now her crew was not so small, spreading across the entire province but all under Robyn's tight instruction. Being a diminutive highborn lady who did as she was told did not suit her in the slightest, though Damien now knew from experience that Robyn excelled at pretending to be exactly that. If she hadn't been, then Damien suspected their group would have long since been discovered and, more importantly, Robyn's life would have come to an end.

But so long as Robyn remained faceless and nameless, she remained safe. The moniker of the Hood was her armor.

And Damien was her shield.

No sword could touch her. No arrow could pierce her. No challenge was too much for her.

Damien made sure of it.

The longer he spent with Robyn, the harder it was to leave her. He always wanted the woman beside him, no matter what they were doing: fighting, eating, planning, spying. Whenever she left for the Lochslee estate or to attend to her duties as Lady Marian, Damien felt a keen sense of loss by her absence. It was bothersome.

He'd formed a blasted attachment to her.

It's more than that.

Admiration? Yes. Love? He didn't know.

It felt different from the lust he'd experienced for women before. The desire to possess. The desire to *have*.

Damien wanted Robyn to *want* him in return. He'd never felt that kind of intense reciprocal desire in his entire life. He found himself mentally begging her to smile at him or look his way. One thing had become abundantly clear: Damien had no idea how Luca or Pyre didn't go mad while waiting for their females to get on the same page as them.

At this, Damien chuckled. Pyre and Luca *hadn't* done nothing—but then, neither had their mates. Their pining had been mutual.

Where Robyn was concerned, Damien had no idea how she felt. She treated him like everyone else despite how he flirted and courted. It was as if they had never kissed. He inhaled and exhaled slowly, Robyn's scent teasing his senses pleasantly. At least the mystery of her essence was solved. After spending so much time together, he'd noticed she'd been taking a draught each day. Upon further inspection, he'd discovered it was a scent-dampening agent. That's why it kept confusing him.

She was a match to him, but she knowingly dampened it. At first, he'd gotten irrationally angry that she would do such a thing. But Damien came to his senses. Robyn didn't know what she was to him. She wasn't Talagan. It was an excellent safety measure against others of his race that didn't have moral guidelines when it came to the fair sex. And it kept Merjeri's wolves from paying too much attention to her.

"Damien?" Robyn whispered, pulling him out of his head. He stared at her lovely eyes above the line of the scarf she used to obscure much of her face and, with it, her identity, for a moment or two, simply to drink her in. He had long since become enamored by those eyes, and the scent of the woman that all the bandages and hoods could not hide from him.

Damien nodded. "I'm listening."

"Will your contact in the Dark Court be here soon?" she asked, shifting on the spot behind the ramparts they'd crept up onto. "If we don't move soon—"

"They'll be here," he reassured her, then returned his gaze to the group of men sorting through a pile of goods upon a stone courtyard far below them. The stronghold was one of the Duke of Merjeri's lesser-known estates for storing gold and items ill-gotten from 'taxes' Robyn and her group had since discovered. Damien had no doubt they were *storing* prisoners, too, though they hadn't managed to breach the stronghold yet to confirm whether this was true.

Lately, the duke's men had become tetchy and on-edge; news of the Hood traveled fast, and though it was clear Ruslan Merjeri was attempting to quash rumors that a small group of bandits were destroying his hold on the province, his own men took such rumors seriously. Too many in their number had been knocked out and robbed, after all.

The Hood was a real threat. The Hood was something they had to defend against at all costs.

A slow grin crept across Damien's face as he identified a weakness in their defense formation around the pile of stolen goods. With a twist of his hand, he signaled for Pavel, who was on the rightmost rampart, to begin his descent.

"You and Will should sneak down with the rest of the men while I make a distraction," Damien murmured, knowing Robyn was about to suggest the exact same thing.

If she hadn't been wearing a scarf over her mouth, Damien would have sworn that Robyn had smiled at their shared decision. "Andrei can hold back and ready the horses and wait for your contact," she said. "Will your *other form* be making an appearance as said distraction?" She'd been very edgy about him using his dragon form after saving Norman a month prior.

He now had a warrant and reward out for his arrest, too. Not that he minded. As if the duke and his sheriff could ever bring him down.

Damien was tempted to wink at Robyn or do something else as equally foolish. Instead, he said, "You'll have to wait and find out," before Robyn slid from her position in the shadows to take aim at the men below with her bow. On the southern rampart, the barest flash of movement visible only to Damien's keen eyes told him that Will was moving into position.

Time for me to move.

He spared a final glance at Robyn before leaping from the ramparts and shifting form. It was midnight, and moonless, so nobody would be able to discern much from his dragon form that would identify who he was. All they'd know was that Damien was large, and intimidating...

And a dragon.

He kept to the darkest parts of the night, swooping and soaring above the keep just often enough to attract the attention of the duke's men. At first, they dismissed the movements of the night as mere illusions—they'd been working too hard, or they were hungover—but as Damien increased the frequency of his rapid dives and ascents, they could no longer ignore him.

"Sheriff, looks like that dragon wants trouble," Damien heard one of the soldiers call out, uneasy and clearly in desperate want of cover from the gargantuan beast flying overhead. "We should call it a night and—"

"And what? Hand over all this gold to him?" the sheriff scolded. "Merjeri would have our heads if we—"

"*We'll* have your heads, if it's all the same," Pavel growled. All the men turned to him, swords out and ready for a fight immediately. Damien circled overhead to observe, a sense of pride slithering down his spine when Robyn fired three arrows in quick succession to the knees of three men. They collapsed to the ground, crying in pain and surprise, allowing Pavel to knock them unconscious with the flat of his blade.

That left ten men.

And the sheriff.

He was like a rat.

The man would never die.

No, eight, Damien amended, because Will had crept from the shadows to cover the mouths of two men with a cloth full of a cloying, mind-numbing drug. When Robyn let loose another two arrows that number went down to six. Then five.

Easy. I won't have to move.

He spotted the sheriff hiding beneath a set of stairs and allowed himself to smile, baring all of his fangs. Today the vermin would pay for his crimes against Damien's kin.

From his position, he caught movement from the corner of his eyes. He focused on the petite hooded figure and watched Robyn adjust her position, ready to fire another arrow into a man's hamstring. But then movement to her right on the ramparts pulled Damien's attention. He tensed, but when he recognized the man responsible for the movement as the one he was waiting for from the Dark

Court, the dragon relaxed once more. When Robyn spotted the man, she drew her sword and prepared to fight—an understandable reaction—and only lowered her weapon when the stranger made a complicated signal with his hands that Damien had taught her to recognize as a sign of the Dark Court.

Robyn relaxed just as Damien tensed again.

It was *last* month's signal. Something wasn't right.

The sheriff would have to wait.

Blast.

At that moment, a wave of more than a dozen men erupted onto the courtyard from the keep. Damien swept down to help Pavel and Will immediately, knocking the men out one after another with his tail, his head, his claws. When his sheer size became a hindrance, Damien shifted back into the form of a man and began simply punching assailants into unconsciousness. It was easy, considering they were shocked by his brazenly naked and inhuman appearance.

"There were never supposed to be this many guards!" Will called over to Damien, furiously stabbing at soldiers with his double daggers in non-lethal positions. "If we could just kill—"

"Robyn said no killing!" Pavel cut in. "That can't be what we're known for—these men have families!"

It was clear Will agreed with him, though it didn't make their job any easier. Damien also agreed with them...within reason. No sense in killing and making a situation more complicated, after all.

As with all things, there were exceptions. Especially when the silver-haired wolves sauntered in. Blast it.

"Deal with the rest of these men," Damien growled,

kicking an unsuspecting guard directly at the knee so that he buckled to the ground, then backhanding his skull so that he fell into unconsciousness. "I'm going to help Robyn."

Will's eyes grew wide with alarm. "Is there someone up there with her?"

Damien simply shifted and flew toward her, which was answer enough for Will's question. When he reached the ramparts, Robyn was screaming at the traitorous Dark Court spy, who had used her temporary trust of him to pin her to the ground. Her sword and bow had skittered across the flagstones; the dagger in her boot was unreachable. She grappled with the wolf to try to reach the second dagger attached to her belt, but the blackguard tightened his grip on her wrist and pulled out her dagger to use against Robyn instead.

"The Hood comes to an end tonight," the wolf hissed triumphantly, holding the dagger to her face, ripping into her scarf, "and I get a pretty pay day."

"I think not," Damien thundered, swiping the lout off Robyn as if he was made of air rather than flesh and bone.

He went crashing across the floor but rolled back to his feet. He wiped blood from the corner of his mouth and shook his head. "You'll pay for that."

"We'll see," Damien retorted.

The wolf rushed him, and he slammed his head into the mercenary's face, knocking him out. That was easy at least.

Robyn stared up at him with a shocked expression. The spy had managed to cut away her scarf, which meant he'd seen her face. A cut across her jaw that had clearly been meant for her throat turned Damien's blood cold.

She had been too trusting of the spy. Damien had

emphasized time and time again how important it was to keep up to date with the signals used by the Dark Court, but Robyn had fallen for an old one. She'd almost died.

Damien didn't know if he wanted to shake bloody sense into her or grab the front of Robyn's cloak to pull her lips against his, so relieved he was that she was still alive.

"Damien...?" Robyn breathed, when he made no motion to move from his position looming over her.

He had too tenuous a hold over his emotions to risk touching her, so Damien stood aside to allow Robyn to rise to her feet. "This was a planned ambush." He glared at the Dark Court spy.

"Well, we're alive, which gives us the advantage," Robyn murmured, touching the blood on her cheeks and shaking out her shoulders as if she was completely unperturbed by how close she'd been to death and discovery. She cut part of her tunic away and wrapped it around the lower part of her face.

Damien was about to say something about it when Will called up, "You're going to want to see what they have down here!"

Damien pushed passed Robyn and grabbed the spy. He needed to move. Storming to the stairs, he dragged the mercenary down them, making sure to bump the devil hard with each step as he descended from one of the rampart towers. Robyn wasted no time in following him down to the courtyard. All the guards had been knocked unconscious and were injured in various non-lethal ways. Considering how close Robyn had come to death, Damien was tempted to raze them all to the ground.

Will and Pavel were breathing heavily, but thankfully

uninjured. They opened up two of the chests which stood in the pile of stolen goods. Inside was not gold, as expected, but diamonds and countless vials of addictive mimkia.

This was what Tempest and Pyre were searching for. A direct connection between the Pack of Betraz and the Duke of Merjeri. He looked down at the spy still within his grasp.

And this wretch meant to betray them—and us—for a cut of the profits.

He shook the unconscious mercenary. "This won't be the associate we were meant to wait for. Likely the man *we* want will be outside with Andrei and the horses already. Load our cart with every vial of mimkia. Don't let any of it go unaccounted for."

Will and Pavel nodded, then Will turned to Robyn and asked, "Are you all right? What happened up there?"

"What happened was that she nearly got herself killed," Damien growled, staring at Robyn only to find her avoiding his gaze.

"I didn't realize his signal was wrong until too late," she said, defensive. "It's hard to remember everything to do with the Dark Court on top of everything I have to do as Lady Marian. In the heat of battle, not everything is clear."

"You *must* remember these things!" Damien exploded, rounding on her. "If you don't, then it isn't just your head that's on the line!" Right now, he only cared about hers, though. Just what did he have to do to make her understand? He could barely breathe thinking about what could have happened. His stomach churned. Was he going to be sick?

He tossed the traitorous spy to the ground and tied his feet and hands behind his back. "I'm taking him with me. I'll be in contact tomorrow."

Now, finally, Robyn dared a look at Damien. A pained expression crossed her face. "What are you going to do with him? You can't kill him, Damien."

"And why not? He meant to at best expose you, and at worst kill you! This scum does not deserve your mercy. Do you think he would have shown you mercy?"

"It doesn't matter."

"It does," Damien snapped. Without thought, he caught her around the waist and pulled her against his chest. He dropped his head and like a bloody beast, he kissed his mate savagely. He consumed her before he jerked back, breathing hard. Damien stared down into her glittering green eyes. "He is not worth the dirt beneath your feet."

"And that's the type of thinking that makes elitist dictators," she volleyed back, pushing out of his arms.

He stiffened. "What are you saying?"

"That you're wrong, Damien, and I won't ever agree with you on this."

"You're a hypocrite." Robyn gasped, but he continued. "You have blood on your hands. What makes him different to all those you've dispatched in the past?" he demanded, desperate to poke holes in Robyn's logic. Why couldn't she see why Damien was so furious?

But Robyn shook her head. "That was different." she insisted. "I would have died—"

"*He would have killed you!*"

"We are not savages, Damien!" Robyn bit out, hackles firmly raised. She straightened herself out, and when she spoke again, he saw Lady Marian speaking to him just as much as he saw the Hood. Righteous and honorable. "We have to have a code of honor, a code of justice, a sense of right or wrong. Otherwise, we cannot call ourselves human."

"Then it is a good thing I'm not human." Damien shifted into a dragon, clasped his claws around the wolf and shook him for good measure as he pushed off the ground. "I'm a beast."

If Robyn had anything to say in return, Damien didn't hear it. *Wouldn't* hear it. For if he did, and he listened to her, then that meant he had to admit to his feelings, and how they were changing how he acted.

That was unconscionable to the King of Dragons.

Chapter Thirty-One

Pyre

He kicked his feet up onto the long stone table of his war room and watched his mate, who flicked an annoyed glance his way before going back to the intel from one of her spies. Her fingers tightened on the wrinkled parchment when Pyre smacked his lips noisily. He loved needling her. Tempest like to pretend she was immune to his little games, but eventually she'd break.

Pyre knocked his boots together and leaned back in his chair. His wife blew a periwinkle strand of hair from her cheek and then sighed. Slowly, she lowered the paper to the table.

Gotcha.

She turned in his direction and arched a brow. "Something on your mind?"

"Not at all," he crooned.

Her grey eyes narrowed, and her cheeks pinked with anger. "Then why the theatrics?"

"Because I wanted to admire your pretty face."

She snorted. "You're ridiculous." Tempest gestured to the bruise on her right cheek. "Briggs caught me unawares." She cocked her head and scanned him from head to toe. Pyre preened for his mate. "Did you get *more* new clothes?"

He grinned and ran his hands down his new orange velvet coat. "It's nice of you to notice."

"Sweet poison, is this why you've been bugging me for the last half hour? Because you got a new coat and I hadn't noticed yet?"

"I would never," he drawled, winking at her.

"You're the worst."

He dropped his feet to the floor. "I am the best," he growled, pushing from his chair and advancing on Tempest.

She scooted back and stood as he got to her. Pyre wrapped his hands around his mate's waist and sat her on the edge of the table before stepping between her legs. She draped her arms about his shoulders and smiled up at him.

"What a needy creature you are," she teased, pulling his top hat from his head and plopping it on her own.

He brushed his knuckle along her left cheek, completely enamored with his mate. She was one in a million. "I need only you." And it was the truth. She was his anchor.

His breath caught when she pressed a sweet kiss to his lips, making him long for more.

"Do you need affection?" she whispered.

"Always."

Tempest snatched the parchment off the table and held it between them. "This is what's kept me busy. Maybe if you helped me, we could go back to our rooms sooner."

He flashed her a wicked smile. "Are you trying to bargain

with me?"

"I would never," she said with a silly grin.

Pyre sank his fingers into her hair, tipping his hat from her head and pressed closer. "I'm always willing to negotiate—"

The doors to the war room slammed open, and he growled underneath his breath and pressed his face into the crook of his wife's neck. There was only one person who'd dare enter this room like that.

He groaned. "Say the devil hasn't arrived."

Tempest patted his shoulder. "Indeed, he has, and with a guest."

A guest?

"Is he dressed at least?"

"He is, husband," Tempest said wryly.

The degenerate liked to prance around in the nude too much.

Pyre schooled his expression and straightened, stepping away from Tempest. He impassively watched as Damien stormed into the room. The dragon king tossed a bound man onto the floor between them, Damien's expression contorted with rage.

How interesting.

He held his hand out to Tempest and helped her from the large table. Pyre arched a brow at Damien. "What have you brought me? A gift, I hope?"

"A traitor."

Pyre's eyes narrowed. "What do you mean?"

His friend's eyes turned to slits. "Exactly what I said. You sent him to us, and he almost got *my* woman killed."

Well, well, well... Damien had a woman? Intriguing in the

least.

Tempest took a step toward the hooded man on the floor. "Is he dead?"

"No." Damien's jaw flexed. "She didn't wish it."

"Who exactly, if you don't mind me asking?" Pyre asked delicately. Damien rarely took others' opinions into consideration. Especially if there was justice to be meted out.

The dragon bared his teeth. "No one."

"You're awfully worked up over *no one.*"

"Pyre, stop messing with him," Tempest chastised as she approached the unconscious man. "He's worked up. Leave the poor man alone." She bent low and yanked the hood off the man. His mate cursed and straightened, her attention on Damien. "He is one of my own. Are you sure he betrayed you?"

Damien hissed, his whole-body trembling in anger. "Yes! This is the link between the Dark Court and the Pack of Betraz that you're looking for."

Pyre took a step closer to his mate, and the dragon's attention snapped to him.

"I'm not going to hurt her," Damien snapped.

"Forgive me if I want to be near my mate when you're a second away from shifting and destroying my war room." He glared back at his friend. "You need to calm down."

"Don't tell me to calm down! I almost lost my mate!" Damien thundered. "If I had been even a moment slower, she would have died."

Pyre stepped up to Tempest's side but didn't push her behind him like he wanted to do. She was his partner, not his damsel. "Mate?"

Damien ran his hands through his green hair and began

to pace. "I'm not sure."

"You just claimed her," Pyre pointed out, watching his friend.

"She hasn't claimed me." The dragon stopped and dropped his head. "After the way I left... I don't think she wants to see me."

"I take it, you said some things you shouldn't have?" Tempest asked gently.

"I lost my temper. And on top of that, I lost my chance at that weasel of a sheriff."

Tempest whistled. "Did you scare her?"

Damien snorted and lifted his head. "Nothing seems to scare her. I...hurt her...with my words."

"Well, there's an easy fix for that. Apologize."

The dragon's jaw flexed. "I hate apologizing."

"Get in line," Tempest muttered. "But it is a necessity of life being as we're imperfect beings."

Pyre dropped a kiss onto her head. "Speak for yourself."

His wife elbowed him in the ribs before focusing on Damien once again. "Why did you bring him to us?"

"I didn't want to," Damien rasped. "I wanted to do a great many things, but she wouldn't have wanted it. Even now, I want to drop him from the highest mountain into lion-infested territory. Her feelings are what stayed my hand."

"Thank you," Tempest murmured. "Perhaps we'll get some useful information from him."

"Oh?"

Pyre's lips thinned. "Two more of our spies have shown up dead in Merjeri with Old Mother's signature on them."

"That blasted wretch," Damien growled. "She needs to be eliminated."

"She's like a hydra. You cut off one head, five more grow in its place," Tempest muttered. "We need to root her out and then burn her operation to the ground."

"I can go into Betraz again," the dragon volunteered.

Pyre shook his head. "You're doing good work where you are. The duke is losing business because of the heists, and you're keeping the wolves at bay. Old Mother hasn't been able to move farther into Merjeri because of your actions. We can't allow her to gain any more ground."

Damien crossed his arms. "What now?"

Tempest clapped her hands together. "You go back to your mate, and we deal with this spy."

"What if she won't see me?" the dragon asked in an uncharacteristic show of vulnerability.

"Then you grovel and make it right," Pyre replied.

Damien nodded once. "I'll do what's necessary." His gaze dropped to the unconscious man. "He will be handled? He's seen her face."

Pyre shared a dark smile with his friend. "I'll personally take care of it."

"See that you do." Damien bowed to Tempest and then spun on his heel and left just as quickly as he came.

"She certainly has him riled," Tempest commented, humor coloring her tone.

"Mates certainly have that effect." Pyre had just about lost his mind when Tempest had almost married the king.

"I'm concerned."

Pyre met his wife's gaze. "For Damien?"

She shook her head. "Nothing about the situation in Merjeri and Betraz sits right with me. This is more than just drugs. The new duke isn't that intelligent. Old Mother is pulling the strings. The question is why the drugs are more valuable to her than the diamonds?"

He turned her toward him and embraced his mate, resting his chin on top of her head. "This is a game of chess. Soon we'll discover her strategy." He smiled. "One thing is for sure; she doesn't tolerate mistakes. The Hood and her merry men have seized a sizable amount of the duke's diamonds and Old Mother's drugs. Who do you think she's going to blame?"

"The duke."

Pyre grinned. "Exactly. She'll put pressure on him, and he'll get emotional and make a bigger mistake that will cost him everything. Give him enough rope and he'll hang himself."

And he couldn't wait.

Chapter Thirty-Two

Robyn

Of course, Robyn was angry with Damien. She was outraged. Furious.

He'd kissed her.

Again.

She wanted to batter her fists on his chest and scream at him for putting her in this position.

More than that, she wanted to understand him. Wanted to know *why* it was so important for him to enact his version of justice on the traitor spy, no matter what Robyn said against him.

You thought you mattered to him. You thought your opinion *mattered to him.*

That's what really rankled. Over the last few months, they'd grown really close. Sure, Damien was as vain as a peacock and had no sense of propriety, but she found herself unable to dislike him. He made her laugh and lighten up when she felt like she was drowning under a sea of responsibilities. She'd grown to trust and respect him, and she'd thought he felt the same way. Turns out, he didn't.

And it hurt. More than she wanted to admit.

She was attached to him, and that was a problem. It would only lead them down a road that would bring them both pain. Damien went where the wind took him and Robyn was as rooted as a person could get.

Robyn brushed loose strands of hair from her face and winced when she realized they were coated in blood. That wasn't good; Ruslan was having dinner with Robyn and her father in the Lochslee residence that evening, and she would now have to wash her hair for it. She sent a glare up at the empty sky as if it would reach Damien. He would have to be dealt with later.

Robyn couldn't afford the time to dwell upon it.

"The drugs," she muttered, then louder for Will to hear. "The drugs. We have to get them out. We have no time to lose."

"Are you… Is everything—"

"I'm fine," Robyn snapped, not meaning to take out her anger on Will or Pavel but unable to stop it. Though the last two months had gone by in a flash of successful heists, ambushes, and robberies, with the stolen goods sold off and the gold redistributed throughout Merjeri without the Hood and her crew once getting caught, the act of living a double life was beginning to wear Robyn down.

Now that Damien had blown up at her—Damien, who was always on her side, who had taught Robyn everything she needed to know to defend her people, who had fast become the highlight of her day after spending drawn-out hours with Ruslan—she was close to a breaking point. Most days, she wasn't sure who she was anymore. When would she get to just be herself and not play a part? Those were questions for another time.

She had to keep it together. For everyone's sakes.

They gathered the mimkia and diamonds and carried them to where Andrei was waiting with the horses and their carriage. Robyn, Will, and Pavel were met with an unfamiliar woman who signed the *correct* signal when she saw them.

Her stomach churned.

Damien was right. She'd been stupid. She should have known the spy's signal was wrong. He drilled it into her so many times that it changed every few weeks.

"I'm so glad everyone is unhurt," Andrei said, visibly relieved. "When Damien swooped in from the ramparts— When I heard the screaming—"

"It's all fine," Robyn said with a forced smile. She had to get a grip of herself. "It's nothing we couldn't handle. Are you here for the mimkia?" Robyn directed at the woman.

She was dressed in black, a slight figure with white hair and wide, owlish eyes, with a scarf wrapped around the bottom half of her face. It seemed Robyn wasn't the only one who wanted to keep her identity hidden. The woman nodded. "I was told I could borrow your carriage and horses once you're back in your village," she said, indicating toward Andrei.

"It's the quickest way to get the drugs out of our hands," Andrei said. "Plus, that way, she can take the rest of the goods off our hands, too. We can't chance getting caught by the wolves with it."

"I agree," Robyn said, "though we must be quick in returning. I am late for a meeting."

Her friends all knew what that meant, but the woman didn't have to know. It wouldn't be difficult to work out who Robyn was if she possessed such information.

"The horses are well-rested, since we didn't have to use them to fight," Andrei said. "We'll reach the edge of the woods in no time."

"Are we going to speak about Damien?" Pavel asked.

"No," she replied tightly.

"It's not going to make it go away," Will added.

She glared at her friend. "Not now."

He held her gaze. "He was scared Robyn. For you."

Robyn clenched her jaw. "He was out of line."

Will arched a black brow. "That man cares for you as do all of us. Today could have gone very differently if it weren't for him."

"Are you saying I'm wrong?"

"Not exactly, but you should grant him some slack. That's what friends do." A pause. "That's what we do for those we love."

She blanched. "We don't love each other."

Will chuckled. "Keep lying to yourself."

They finished loading the carriage before departing for the village in absolute darkness, with no lanterns or torches betraying their silent journey. Even the horses seemed to know not to whinny and wicker; Andrei truly was a genius when it came to the beasts.

Robyn barely acknowledged the goodbyes her friends gave her when they reached the village and she departed for the Lochslee estate. As had become part of her usual routine, Robyn scaled the ivy-covered wall outside her bedroom window and tumbled inside, then used the pail of water she'd had a servant bring in hours earlier to wash the blood and sweat from her skin. It was freezing cold; though the season had turned toward spring, the evenings were still bitter.

Only once Robyn was quite sure she was clean and dressed in a pale green gown that looked striking against her skin and hair, did she call for Maya to help her braid her hair into a delicate twist at the base of her neck.

"It has gotten longer," Maya remarked, gently combing through Robyn's thick locks the same way Robyn remembered her mother used to. "Soon nobody will even know it was ever cut so short."

Robyn knew what she was insinuating: soon, there would be no traces of the man Robyn had pretended to be to defend her father and her family. Soon, no suspicion could fall over the Lochslees regarding who had gone to war for them.

She stared at herself in the ornate round mirror hanging on the wall. Robyn didn't recognize the woman staring back at her. Her lips were thinned, and the glint in her eyes a little too dark. She exhaled slowly and arranged her face into a pleasant expression.

"You don't have to do that, dear," Maya murmured, meeting Robyn's gaze in the mirror. "You don't have to wear a mask around me."

A lump of emotion rose in her throat, and Robyn swallowed thickly. She gave Maya a small smile. If only the housekeeper knew what Robyn was up to now as the Hood. These days, all she knew how to do was wear a mask.

Maya patted her shoulder and then fixed a jade butterfly into the twist of Robyn's hair. "Very beautiful."

"Beauty," Robyn murmured, dropping her gaze to her lap.

"It means nothing."

"It's okay to accept a compliment," Maya said, setting her hands on Robyn's shoulders.

She chuckled and patted the housekeeper's right hand before standing from the stool in front of her vanity. "I'm sorry. It's just that I've heard enough flattery about my looks for a lifetime."

"Oh, sweet girl." Maya cupped Robyn's cheeks gently. "Don't let the duke take your joy."

Robyn hugged Maya. "Never." She glided from her room and made sure to compose herself as she walked down the corridor. It was time to be Lady Marian and erase any traces of the Hood. The wellbeing of their people hinged on her performance.

No one but her inner circle could ever find out what she'd become.

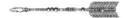

When Robyn entered the dining hall, both Ruslan and her father were already sitting down, enjoying a bottle of peach liquor that Robyn knew was very expensive. Daintily, she bowed before sitting down opposite the duke and accepting a small cup of the liquid.

"My apologies if I am late," she said. "I was having trouble with my hair."

Ruslan's sharp eyes took in her appearance, looking for the slightest thing to criticize. Finding nothing, he said, "You look lovely."

How nice it is that he can only compliment someone once he can no longer find personal fault with them. That was a first that he didn't complain about your hair.

Robyn plastered a beaming smile to her face to hide her irritation.

"Robyn, the duke was just discussing how the smallfolk seem to be doing much better these days," her father said, so calmly anyone else would not have known his words were a warning.

"It is always this way once winter turns to spring," Robyn said, knowing exactly what to say. "It is a time of rebirth."

"It is more than that," Ruslan said. "They are all paying their taxes."

Robyn raised an eyebrow. "And this is a bad thing? Surely, it is only for the benefit of the province if the smallfolk can pay their taxes?"

Go on, say it. Say the money you robbed from the people has been robbed back and then some. Say that you know how and why the smallfolk are paying your ridiculous taxes.

Ruslan stayed silent. Whatever information he was hoping to get from Robyn or her father, it was clear he hadn't gotten it.

"The weather is getting warmer when the sun is up," he said, changing the subject when the servants brought in a veritable buffet of food Robyn knew very well her father could not afford. She'd have to find a way to pay it off without him knowing where the gold came from.

"It is indeed getting pleasant in the afternoons," Robyn agreed. "Isn't it, Papa? Soon, my mother might be able to go outside and enjoy the garden once more."

Her father smiled kindly at this, though they both knew Robyn's mother was still unable to recognize Robyn even though she'd been home for over two months now. "Perhaps," he said, "when the blossoms are out."

"Which leads me to my point," Ruslan said, clearly irritated that he'd been interrupted but not wishing to look anything but gracious to Lord Lochslee. "I—"

"My apologies, Your Grace, Lord Lochslee, Lady Marian," came the voice of a servant as they knocked on the screen door. They slid it open and knelt in front of Robyn. In their outstretched hands was a note. "This just came for you. It seems urgent."

Careful to hide the contents of the note from anyone's eyes but her own, Robyn read the elegant scrawl on the thick paper.

Damien's handwriting.

I'm outside. You're needed.

Robyn rose gracefully with a secret smile as Ruslan studied her. She batted her eyes. "I must see to this immediately."

"What matters could be so pressing that you must leave me?" Ruslan demanded.

She bit her lip and glanced at the floor. "It is woman business, my lord."

Ruslan shifted uncomfortably and glanced away, waving a hand at her. "Well, then. Begone, my lady."

Robyn curtseyed, making sure to keep her gaze averted so he couldn't see the contempt in her eyes. As if she needed his permission to do anything in her own home. It was difficult not to rush from the room, but she managed slow gentle steps until the door closed behind her. The smile dropped off her face, and she grabbed two handfuls of her dress before silently running down the hall.

It took Robyn almost ten full minutes of rushing about the gardens—wishing she had brought a cloak to chase away the chill of the evening—before she caught sight of Damien.

He was sitting on the swing her mother loved, the moonlight casting an ethereal glow on the faint outline of the scales on his face. Blowing gently in the breeze, his hair was almost silver against the dark blanket of night.

Much to Robyn's relief, Damien was wearing a white shirt and leather trousers, though by now, his frequent nakedness no longer scandalized her as it once had.

But she was glad he was clothed, all the same.

"Why are you here?" she barked, anger suffusing her words. Now was not the time to be admiring his ethereal beauty.

"I needed to see you," Damien said simply. Robyn believed it; it was very like him to show up just because he wanted to.

She flung her hand out toward the manor. "This is reckless, and you know it! You need to leave."

Damien didn't move. "I couldn't wait."

Bloody dragon. "The duke is inside," she hissed.

He stiffened in the swing, his eyes narrowing. "Are you in such a hurry to run back to him?"

What the devil did that mean? She took a slow breath, trying to rein in her temper. "You know I want nothing to do with him. What I want to talk about is why you're here."

"Am I not welcome?" he asked sharply.

"That's not what I said." Robyn rubbed her temples. This was such a mess. Considering what he'd said and done earlier—and what he'd interrupted—now was the worst occasion for Damien to have shown up because he wanted to. They never had time to speak—just the two of them—anymore, and now that they did, they were fighting?

He hurt you.

Robyn folded her arms over her chest, feeling vulnerable. "What did you do with the spy?"

"Do you have so little faith in me, Robyn?"

She stared at him just as Damien did the same thing. Though he sat, immobile, upon the swing, it was clear he wanted Robyn to come to his side.

You shouldn't. He's dangerous.

"You know I trust you with my life," she answered, deflating some as her anger rapidly dissipated in the face of something—someone—she so badly wanted herself.

His jaw flexed. "It didn't seem like it today."

"That's because you vexed me." He always knew which buttons to push. "I need to know, Damien."

"I took the traitor to Tempest. The stars know she has better judgment when it comes to things like this."

"The Lady Hound?" Robyn asked.

"Yes, she's infuriatingly black and white."

"That's not always a bad thing."

"So I've learned." The corner of his lips lifted into a roguish grin. "Are you going to stand there and glare at me all night?" He patted the swing in invitation.

Just this once.

"No," she said, closing the distance between them. A pause, an inhalation of breath, and Robyn fed a wild impulse and hugged him. With Damien sitting on the swing, his head rested perfectly beneath her chin. She expected him to freeze in surprise, but Damien's arms were quick to wrap around Robyn and squeeze her tightly. He was warm— impossibly so. Robyn craved that heat with every fiber of her being.

She wanted it to consume her.

"You cannot be here," she whispered into Damien's hair. It was unexpectedly soft and silky against her lips. "You know you can't. It's too dangerous."

Damien huffed out a laugh, which was largely muffled against Robyn's chest. Her face flushed as she realized this. "I'd like to see anyone try to take on the two of us and emerge victorious."

"You know what I mean, Damien."

"I know. But I couldn't leave things the way they were earlier." A pause and a low growl. "I just needed to see you."

Needed. He came here not because he wanted to, but because he needed to.

The heat in her body grew unbearable.

She pulled out of their embrace. "Then I am glad you came here. Truly." She cast her gaze away, then looked at Damien through her eyelashes. His face was flush with desire and an emotion she didn't want to put a name to. It wouldn't do either of them any good. "But, still, you must leave. We can work this out tomorrow."

Damien sighed, then got to his feet. Once more, he towered over Robyn, intimidating and impressive in equal measure. "I know. Though it pains me to leave you alone, I know I must." His hand grazed against Robyn's. "Sleep sweet, my dove."

Her eyes closed as he pressed a kiss to her temple. Her heart clenched when she opened her eyes and he walked into the woods that lined the back of the Lochslee estate and melted away between dark pines and heavy oaks.

It took Robyn far too long to return to the house, choosing instead to sit upon the swing and revel in the lingering warmth within the wooden seat from where Damien had been.

She wanted him. She wanted Damien more than anyone or anything she'd ever met. But she couldn't take the chance on letting him know.

Robyn knew she could never have him. Not when she was Lady Marian Lochslee. Not when she had people to protect. Marriage to Ruslan was in her future whether she liked it or not.

On silent feet, she reached her house, padding over the ornate veranda with the hope that she'd managed to miss the entirety of her dinner with Ruslan.

"Once we're married," an icy voice hissed, "there will be no other men. If it weren't for your land and your good looks, I'd be treating you like the whore you clearly are. Do you understand me?"

Robyn froze. On her left was Ruslan Merjeri himself, leaning against the wall...with a perfect view of the swing in the garden.

"Y-Your Grace," she stammered, "I wasn't—"

"Do not make me look like a fool, Robyn. You will regret it." Ruslan's dark eyes gleamed, filled with a wicked intent that had her wishing she could flee from his sight. But she forced herself to stand her ground; if she made one wrong move now, it would not only be her who would pay dearly for it.

"You do not need to worry, Your Grace. I know where my place is." The words tasted like ash upon her tongue.

"Do you?"

She didn't trust her voice. She nodded her head. Let him think she was a trembling maiden in the face of his threats. But that's all they were. Ruslan wanted to possess her too much to actually do anything now.

Until you're married.

Well, even then...hopefully she'd have usurped his duchy right out from beneath him. *He* was the one who should have been worried.

This seemed to appease Ruslan. "Good," he said, taking her hand and raising it to his lips. He kissed her fingers one by one, never once taking his dangerous gaze away from her eyes.

Looking for proof that I might betray him.

Robyn knew she was standing on a precipitous edge. Ruslan was a viper, and he suspected too much. And so, swallowing her disgust, she stood on her tiptoes and replaced her hand against Ruslan's mouth with her lips. Barely a kiss, but it was enough to elicit a rumbling of desire from the back of the Duke of Merjeri's throat.

"Who else could I hope to serve but you?" she whispered into his mouth, before pulling away. She bowed her head politely. "It is late, Your Grace, and I am tired. I will retire to my room, if that doesn't displease you."

When Ruslan reached out a hand to grab Robyn's sleeve, she feared the worst: that he would demand she come back to his estate—and his bed—with him. But then he pulled his hand back and breathed deeply through his nose. "You certainly know how to use your considerable charms when you want to, Robyn." A pleased smile lifted his lips. "It's a good quality in a wife." A pause. "I shall see you in three days."

"As you say," she murmured with a curtsey.

Goosebumps ran along her arms as he trailed his fingers across her collarbone and shoulder when he moved past her to leave. She slipped her hand into a hidden pocket of her dress, her fingers clenching around the steel of her dagger. It would be so easy to stab him in the back for his wandering hands.

She rolled her neck and watched as Ruslan stepped into his carriage and left the Lochslee grounds. She had to fight not to vomit. She'd kissed that degenerate. Robyn gagged.

You kissed him. You kissed Ruslan Merjeri, of your own volition!

She dry-heaved again, her eyes watering.

It hadn't even been an intimate kiss, and it affected her so.

Robyn shuddered at how she could possibly go through with spending a night with the man.

Chapter Thirty-Three

Scarlet

"He's an incompetent imbecile!"

She kept her expression placid as her stepmother raged at her cronies. Scarlet scanned the room from beneath the rim of her blood-red hood. All of the loyal wolves bowed their heads in submission. Her stepmother paced beside her long rectangular table, her black crinoline dress rustling in the silence.

"Well, has everyone nothing to say?"

That was a trick question. Scarlet knew it and so did everyone else.

You did not speak unless directed to by the Alpha. Or at least that was one of her titles.

Old Mother.

Alpha.

Duchess of Betraz.

Stepmother.

Monster.

The last one was usually spat out by those who Scarlet's stepmother preyed upon.

A shiver ran through her, and Scarlet dropped her gaze to the floor as her stepmother studied the room full of people. That was another of the rules. Never meet her gaze unless you wanted to challenge her or suffer the consequences.

Scarlet had only done it once.

It was right after her father had died and she'd helped her friend Will escape Betraz. Her stepmother had threatened to hang her for her part in his escape. Scarlet had met her gaze, smiled, and said, "Try it." It had earned her a shattered cheekbone and a nasty scar, but it was worth it to see the smug smile knocked off the wench's face.

That had been years ago when she was only twelve summers. Now she'd never try something like that. Too many lives depended upon Scarlet catering to the whim of her stepmother. Plus, years of public humiliation, beatings, and punishments had left her with a very healthy fear of the Alpha. The ageless woman had a malicious streak leagues deep which was part of the reason Scarlet wore the cursed red cloak. It was to mark her as property of the Alpha, as a slave.

Her stepmother grabbed a handful of raw diamonds from the table and shook her fist. "Someone is stealing my diamonds and my mimkia right out from under that pompous pup of a duke. Who is it? Who is the Hood?" Her attention homed in on her second in command, Bright, a midnight middle-aged wolf with streaks of silver through his hair.

Bright dipped his head. "My lady, we know that the Hood's men are commoners. Most don't seem to have any military training, but our spies have revealed nothing about the Hood's identity."

"Nothing?"

Her stepmother pelted Bright with the diamonds, and Scarlet inwardly winced as one cut him just above the eyebrow. The evil woman grabbed the edge of the table, her long black nails digging into the wood.

"This has gone on long enough! I'm tired of some little common upstart ruining my plans." She dropped her head, her long, silver hair falling over her shoulder to the table. "And the dragon?"

"He's not known to us."

She slapped her hand against the table. "Dragons do not involve themselves in human affairs. Why is he doing so now?" A pregnant pause. "Red."

Scarlet shoved down her fear and clenched her fingers into fists to keep from trembling. Any trace of weakness and she'd be punished before all. She stepped forward from the back wall, making sure to keep her head down as the small crowd parted for her.

"Yes, Alpha," she answered softly, halting beside Bright.

She shivered as her stepmother reached over the table and ran a long nail down her left scarred cheek. "I need you to fix this."

"As you wish."

Her cheek flared with pain when her stepmother pinched the skin a tad too hard. "See that you do. Don't fail me."

"Never, Alpha."

"Be gone from my sight. Your human stench offends me."

Humiliation burned in her cheeks as she backed away from the table, making sure to keep her head down. It was an old insult but effective. Her stepmother was always quick to tear her down for not being Talagan. When she was a child, she'd never seen a difference between those who could shift and those who could not. People were people. But now, she *hated* the fact that she was so weak compared to the wolves around her. No matter how hard she fought back, the shifters always won. Scarlet had heard whispers that humans in other provinces weren't enslaved and deemed as lesser.

She turned on her heel and left the room, walking down the long, dark corridor lined with wolves on guard. She'd always hated how dark her stepmother kept the house. Scarlet wasn't a shifter and didn't have night vision like everyone else. It was a constant reminder that she didn't belong, nor was she welcome in her childhood home.

Squaring her shoulders, she turned her attention to her task. Scarlet needed to find the identity of the Hood. If this person had evaded Bright, then they were good with covering their tracks, but she was better. Scarlet had spent years hiding in plain sight, gathering secrets and hunting down leads to appease her stepmother. All she needed was a trap, and she knew just what to use.

People were predictable. Everyone had a weak spot.

Scarlet's was her people.

And the Hood had someone they'd die for.

She just had to discover who it was.

Chapter Thirty-Four

Robyn

"I come bearing good news."

Robyn looked up from the pair of leather trousers she was repairing. She had to stop herself from indulging the thrill she felt at the sight of Damien and how every part of her wanted to run straight to him; instead, Robyn merely stared him down from where she sat. "And what is this good news? Where exactly have you been?"

After their dangerous liaison by her mother's swing, Robyn hadn't seen Damien in almost a week, even though he had promised he'd see her the following day. Although, considering what Ruslan witnessed and the way she felt toward the dragon, it was for the best she didn't see Damien the next day.

At this, he looked genuinely apologetic. He inclined his head slightly. "I was investigating something."

"For your friend in the Dark Court?" Andrei asked between sips of beer. He, Will, and Pavel were enjoying a cask of dark ale they'd taken back from Ruslan's wolves...unbeknownst to them. It was something Robyn would have disapproved of if it wasn't for the fact that, in reality, they were all in need of a break, and her friends were risking their lives for her justice.

A cask of beer was the least payment they could ask for.

Damien grinned at the comment. "My *friend*, yes."

"Just tell us who it is already," Pavel said.

"We all know it's the Jester," Will threw in.

"Oh, you *all* know?" Damien said, smiling slyly at Robyn. The way he looked at her made her far too excited. "When did you all have this discussion regarding my contacts?"

"We connected the dots," Robyn said, because she agreed with Will's conclusion. "How else could you process so many stolen goods and gold and *mimkia*? It must be the Jester."

"Well, it's hardly my place to confirm or deny it," Damien said, accepting a wooden cup of beer from Andrei when he offered it and joining them by the fire and their small camp in the woods. Right beside Robyn, like it was the most natural thing in the world. "But on the subject of mimkia and diamonds, I do happen to have some news."

"Oh?" Pavel said. "Pray tell." From his work in the orphanage, he had witnessed the drug directly affecting people—children he'd helped out, who were now grown but out of work because of the harsh winter, turned to mimkia in an effort to numb their woes. Robyn knew he was determined to stamp out Ruslan's drug ring, no matter the costs. Her friend was desperate for any news on the matter.

"Our friends in Betraz were quite put out that they did not receive their goods that they paid the duke for. It seems that they're sending a special emissary to meet with Ruslan,"

Damien said.

"Old Mother?" Will asked in a hushed voice. "The Alpha?"

Robyn stared at her friend's stricken face. Even after escaping the Pack of Betraz all those years ago, it still haunted him.

"No. She doesn't leave her province, but someone called Red."

Will's lips thinned, but he didn't comment further.

"Anything else?" Pavel asked.

"Seems with our last raid we really interfered with the spread of mimkia," Damien said, eyes glowing with green fire. "Not just in Merjeri but much farther afield, too."

This caused everyone to perk up.

"Farther afield?" Robyn asked. "How far are we talking?"

"Beyond the borders of Heimserya."

"You're joking!" Andrei cried.

"I am happy to confirm that I'm not joking." Damien chuckled warmly. "And I've just received word about a huge shipment being moved east out of Merjeri's very own estate in three days—all required to reinvigorate the drug ring once more. If we get hold of it before them, not only will we leave the entire business destitute, but we'll bankrupt a good few of the key players in the process. That will bring them out into the light, and your good Queen Ansette can deal with them appropriately."

A blood-thirsty expression crossed Damien's face, made even starker by the flickering firelight. "And then I can exact vengeance on the sheriff."

Robyn should have been frightened by it. She was hopelessly drawn to it.

They all looked at Robyn.

"So, what's the plan?" Will asked.

Luckily for them, Robyn was quick to think on her feet. "I'll confirm the layout of the duke's estate tomorrow and formulate the plan then. It'll have to be just the five of us. Nobody else; we can't risk getting any more people into Ruslan's manor."

It was time to hit Ruslan where it would hurt him most: his pride, his work, and his money.

Some pretty words and admiring of the Duke of Merjeri's decorative taste was all Robyn needed to scope out his house and memorize its layout as best she could. The moment she returned home she committed all she had seen to paper, allowing her to work out how to hit Ruslan's gold as effortlessly as possible.

Still, when the evening came to carry out her plan, Robyn's stomach was filled with sickening nerves.

At least Ruslan himself was in Dotae for "business" with his nobleman friends. Robyn couldn't fathom what would happen if she ran into him, even though he was highly unlikely to recognize her in her disguise as the Hood.

Still, Robyn thought, nodding at her friends one-by-one and then, finally, at Damien, as they crept along the rooftop of the Merjeri residence, *it is better not to take any risks. Ruslan being gone is a good sign.*

They only had tonight to steal the gold and mimkia drug. In the morning, Ruslan would return, and the gold would be moved. Adrenaline coursed through Robyn's veins; if they succeeded tonight, his fledging drug empire would crumble.

I wonder what that will mean for Ruslan and me, she

mused, grateful for the scarf obscuring her face that hid the blush spreading over her cheeks when Damien offered her a wicked grin. *Will he be found responsible for the new mimkia problem? Will Queen Ansette imprison him? Because if she does...*

That meant Robyn would be free of him, and her union with him would no longer be necessary. With Ruslan out of the picture, Robyn could truly help the Merjeri province without having to seduce him into giving her what she wanted. But more than that—even though Robyn knew it wasn't nearly as important as helping her people—was that she would finally no longer feel so guilty every time her heart skipped a beat when Damien looked at her. Touched her. Laughed with her and ate with her and fought the world with her.

She swallowed down the butterflies in her throat. Robyn could ponder such things tomorrow. For now, she had to focus on stealing Ruslan's gold and drugs.

"Andrei, now," Robyn whispered, and the man unlocked a hatch built above the expansive attic of the manor. Robyn knew about it thanks to some choice words and coin exchanged with the maidservants. *Perhaps if Ruslan paid his servants more than a pittance and treated them kindly, they wouldn't have betrayed him so easily,* she mused, as one-by-one they eased down through the hatch.

"The east wing, right?" Damien checked with her, a hand brushing protectively against Robyn's back for a moment as he walked past her. She ached with longing the moment his touch left her.

"Yes," she replied, taking far too long to reply. Damien raised a quizzical eyebrow at her, and, once more, she was glad for the scarf covering her face.

Get it together. You need to be on the top of your game right now, Robyn!

"Does everyone remember what they've got to do?" she asked the group at large, as they crept across the dark and gloomy attic floor. It was a windy evening, which was perfect; it covered the sound of their footsteps creaking over the old floorboards of the manor.

"We're to knock out any guards we see along the escape route, then bring the carriage around," Andrei whispered, pointing at first himself and then at Pavel.

"And I'm dealing with the soldiers outside the vault," Will said, his eyes shining with anticipation. His dangerous sleep-inducing drug sloshed inside a bottle hanging from his belt, alongside his favorite dagger and two rags. Robyn knew he'd grown rather partial to knocking Ruslan's thugs out this way—less blood was far more convenient, and the drug kept them unconscious for almost an hour.

"Which leaves us to break into the vault from above and handle anyone within it," Damien finished, smiling at Robyn.

But she didn't return the smile, remaining serious as she addressed the entire group. "Don't let your guard down. This may well be our final—and biggest—hurdle. We can't afford to mess up here."

"As if you had to remind us," Will said, sliding between two huge traveling trunks in order to pry open one of the trapdoors that led out of the attic. He peered through the inch of light that filtered through the crack he made. "All right, time to move. Come on, Pavel, Andrei, we don't have long."

Once the three of them were out of sight, Robyn turned to

Damien. She exhaled slowly, then reached out and squeezed his hand. Damien's eyes widened at this voluntary touch, then gently—for him—returned the squeeze.

"Let's show them why they're right to fear the Hood," Damien growled.

"And the smallfolk are right to love her," Robyn added, lowering her scarf for a moment so Damien could see her smile. "And when this is over…"

"Yes?"

Robyn let go of his hand and turned for the trapdoor, though she glanced at him over her shoulder. "Let's talk."

The look on Damien's face meant Robyn knew he was well aware of what she meant.

Now all they had to do was pull off their heist without a hitch and ruin Ruslan Merjeri in the process.

Robyn and Damien's route to the vault was different than Will's. She had bribed more servants to give them safe passage to a secret escape route *out* of the vault—all her group of men had to do was break open the door, then unlock the main doors from the inside to let Will, Andrei, and Pavel in once they'd dealt with all of the guards and soldiers.

"You'd think Ruslan would have made this door out of more than wood," Robyn mused, after handing a hefty bag of gold to the maid who showed them through the passageway. "What with it being the back entrance to his stolen fortune and all."

Damien snickered. "The hubris of man cannot be underestimated. The duke no doubt believes nobody would have cause to even *know* of the door, let alone reach it without him there. In any case"—the dragon felt along the edges of the door for a weakness, then let loose his razor-sharp claws to break down the hinges and lock—"it's all to our advantage."

He pulled the door away as easily as if it were made of paper. Robyn watched the rippling muscles of his sizeable forearms as he did so, equal parts of her mesmerized and intimidated.

Damien could break me like a twig without even trying.

It was thrilling to know he never would. Robyn had that much of a hold over him, and she knew it. She was no longer afraid to accept this, nor deny what it meant.

After tonight, she reminded herself, as the two of them padded into the vault on practiced, silent feet. *After tonight, once everything is sorted, we can talk about how we feel.*

But when Damien lit a torch to brighten the dark and cavernous vault they found—

Absolutely nothing at all.

Blast it.

"A trap," he hissed, as the two of them immediately drew together, back-to-back, sword and bow at the ready. But there were no soldiers within the vault. *Outside* it, however...

Robyn rushed to the main door into the vault—a heavyset piece of iron she doubted even Damien could do much damage to—and placed her ear against its cold surface. "There's too much fighting going on out there," she cried, panic-stricken. "Damien, there wasn't supposed to be any fighting!"

"We need to get out of here, Robyn," Damien said, grabbing her arm to pull them back the way they'd come in. But Robyn struggled against his grip.

Her friends were out there. "We can't leave them! They'll die!"

"They won't, and you know it. You think Merjeri set all of this up to kill us?" Damien's eyes glittered dangerously. "This is a trap to catch us. Catch *the Hood.* So long as you evade his grasp, he'll keep your friends as leverage to weed you out. We can break them out. But we must leave *now.*"

"I can't—if we join them fighting, then we can beat the soldiers!" They had to try.

But Damien shook his head and pointed to his ear. "I have far superior hearing than you, Robyn. I can hear no fewer than fifty men out there. I can't shift in such a tight space— I'll only end up trapped and an easy target. We can't fight off that many soldiers when they were prepared for us, and we were not."

Robyn wanted to cry. Wanted to scream. Wanted to tell Damien that he was wrong—that his level-headed, reasonable plan of escape was selfish.

She knew he was right. This was what it meant to lead. Difficult choices had to be made.

"I'll be back for you," she whispered.

Scrubbing away the unshed tears in her eyes, Robyn and Damien ripped back through the passageway the maid had taken them through until they reached the attic, then they fled up through the trapdoor into the night air. Outside, Robyn could hear even more fighting.

Where their horses and carriage were waiting.

"Damien, how are we—" Robyn began, but when she turned to face him, he'd shifted into a dragon, answering her question. Wasting no time, she clambered onto his back— aware that this was the first time she'd even been conscious when flying with him—and Damien deftly leapt off the roof into the sky.

By the grace of the gods and sheer luck, Robyn had escaped. She had escaped, and Damien, too. She spared a glance down at the soldiers and mercenaries swarming around the manor. Her brows furrowed as she spotted a person covered in a blood-red cloak, before Damien flew higher.

She blinked back her tears and faced forward.

None of her friends had made it out.

And it was all her fault.

Chapter Thirty-Five

Robyn

All Robyn could think about were her friends, locked away in Ruslan Merjeri's dungeon. It was her fault they had been captured. *If I'd never enlisted their help in the first place, then they would be safe.*

But Robyn knew Andrei, Pavel, and especially Will would knock her over the head for believing such a thing. They *chose* to fight beside Robyn. They held the same beliefs. They wanted to help people and take down the drug ring that was infecting their home. And if that was their choice...

Then Robyn could do but one thing.

She had to set them free.

In silence, Damien dropped her back off at the Lochslee estate by her mother's swing. It was only once she was safely on the ground that he said, "We'll save them, so get some sleep and we'll talk tomorrow."

Then he was gone. The dragon clearly knew Robyn wasn't in a position to even look at him, let alone respond.

Everything that had occurred tonight felt like her fault, even though if she thought about it seriously, it was clear their group had fallen into a trap.

Someone fed Damien wrong information. Or they believed it was correct, but his source had been fed a lie. And if Damien believed the information to be true...

That meant there was no way Robyn herself could have identified the trap before they'd fallen into it.

It was on numb feet and with an even number brain that Robyn somehow crept back into her room, stripped off her disguise, and fell into bed. She thought she wouldn't be able to sleep; how could she, after everything that had happened?

Instead, Robyn fell into a dead sleep within minutes, exhausted beyond measure.

"...Robyn? Robyn, you must wake up. A messenger from the Duke of Merjeri's estate has arrived announcing the duke's intention to call upon you within the hour."

For a while, Robyn thought Maya's voice drifting through the door was part of a dream, but when the housekeeper repeated her wake-up call, Robyn sat bolt upright in bed, immediately alert.

"Thank you," she managed to rasp, rubbing at her parched throat. "Could you bring me some water, Maya?"

"Of course. A bath has already been prepared for you, if you wish to head straight to the washroom."

Robyn nodded, then thanked Maya out loud. Forcing herself to her feet, Robyn staggered to her mirror to inspect her appearance. Despite the dead sleep she'd had, she still had gray circles beneath her eyes, and her cheeks looked hollow. Everything about her expression screamed *haunted*.

"Get it together, Robyn," she scolded her reflection, slapping her cheeks to restore some color to them. Maya would have to be a little more heavy-handed with the makeup to paint Robyn as the perfectly deferential and lovely Lady Marian that Ruslan had recently become accustomed to.

By the time Robyn was dressed in a robin's-egg-blue gown, her glossy hair braided around her face like a crown and pinned in place with periwinkle flower pins, Ruslan was waiting for her in the dining hall.

It took her far too long to train her face into neutrality before facing the man. He looked positively full of glee when he caught sight of her—and Robyn doubted it was because of her appearance.

"We've caught his men," Ruslan said, in lieu of a *hello* or any other kind of greeting.

Robyn flinched, despite herself. "Whose men?"

"The Hood's, of course!" he replied, a snide smile twisting his handsome features. "We have his men, which means we have *him*."

Ruslan had never once brought up the Hood to Robyn before. She assumed it was because he was trying to play off the problem as inconsequential or beneath him. Now that he had the bandit in his grasp, it was clear he was going to sing of his victory from the rooftops.

He planned the trap himself, which was why he was 'in the capital' yesterday. Which means he has more spies in the Dark Court than Damien and the Jester know about.

"And how do you suppose you have him, if you have his men?" Robyn asked, careful to keep her tone politely interested.

Ruslan's eyes glittered, and he leaned against the wall, cornering Robyn between his body and a handsome mahogany display cabinet. It took every fiber of her being not to shrink away from his sudden closeness.

"Because he doesn't view them as dispensable," Ruslan explained. He laughed haughtily. "A real flaw, if you ask me. I almost respected the man until now. But his loyalty to his followers will be his downfall. Given the coward that he is— hiding behind a hood and a scarf—I'll be generous and give him three weeks to hand himself over before I hang his friends."

Robyn's blood ran cold. She knew Ruslan truly *would* kill Andrei, Pavel, and Will. It would do her no good to beg for clemency on their behalf, though she had no doubt the duke knew the men were from her village and likely knew her.

"You really think it will take him three weeks to come forth?" Robyn asked, playing things as coolly as she could manage even though she wanted to scream.

"That's more for my own convenience," Ruslan said, finally looking at Robyn as if he could actually see her. He shuffled an inch closer to Robyn, as if daring her to retreat. "I have a more important event to organize in that time, you see."

It was in that moment that Robyn knew what was going to come out of Ruslan Merjeri's mouth before he said it.

"It is time for us to marry, Lady Marian."

And that was it. All at once, the noose around Robyn's neck was tightened.

How could I have believed I'd be free of this last night? To have even entertained the notion that Damien and I...

"Robyn?"

Her hesitance was clearly not what Ruslan had expected, nor what he wanted. But she couldn't seem to find her voice. She *wanted* to say no. Of course she did. But she still had to look after her people, not to mention her friends.

If the wedding is before Ruslan plans to hang them, then Damien and I can use the wedding as a distraction to save Andrei, Pavel, and Will. One final plan.

And then the Hood will be no more.

Slowly, very slowly, Robyn forced a smile to her face and looked up at Ruslan through her lashes. "I accept," she said. "I was always going to accept."

A raised eyebrow. "Always?"

"Always," Robyn lied. "I'd be a fool not to."

Seemingly satisfied, Ruslan held out a hand and stroked Robyn's cheek. "Good. We'll hold the ceremony in three weeks, then. Dealing with the Hood after such a day of celebration will be most enjoyable."

Going by the look in his eyes, Robyn was fairly certain the prospect of murdering her friends was more appealing than a wedding.

Once Ruslan left to 'begin the preparations'—Robyn had no doubt he'd had everything organized for months now—she wasted no time in sloughing out of her Lady Marian garb, though it would be many impatient hours before she could fling on her disguise and creep off to the woods. She wanted to meet with Damien and the rest of her men *now*.

They had no time to lose. They had to begin their rescue plans as soon as possible. Still, she forced herself to wait, checking in on her mother, who was sleeping, and her father, who was kindly tending to the horses with Andrei's right-hand man, before the sun finally set.

Then, Robyn dressed as the Hood and slipped into the night.

She felt Will's, Andrei's, and Pavel's absences keenly when she reached their hideout in the woods, though several of the local men who'd joined the fight in the last month were milling around, despondent with the news of their capture. It didn't take long for Robyn to locate Damien sitting by the large fire burning in the center of their hideout, large and impressive as he was.

His face lit up when he saw her, and Robyn's heart shattered into pieces. This was not a conversation she was looking forward to having.

"I almost thought you wouldn't show tonight," Damien said, standing to face Robyn. She didn't want to meet his gaze, but she forced herself to, nonetheless. His green eyes were intense and warm on hers—not at all like Ruslan's cold, venomous stare. "Of course I would," she said. "We have to save my friends." Then, louder, to address everyone: "We must be careful. The Duke of Merjeri set us up in order to bring out the Hood. He plans to execute Will, Andrei, and Pavel in three weeks."

All at once, a roar of outrage passed around the hideout, though Damien was quick to quell this with a raised hand.

"We knew this would happen. What we need is a *distraction* in order to save them."

"I have that sorted already," Robyn said. She bit her lip. *Here goes nothing.* "Ruslan Merjeri asked to marry me. I said yes. The ceremony will be held on his estate the day before my friends are due to be executed."

Silence descended over the camp of her rag tag men.

"No."

It was one word, simply spoken, but it cut through Robyn like a knife.

"Damien, I—"

"*No,*" he repeated, stronger this time. The previous warmth in Damien's eyes had been replaced by a burning, blazing inferno. His entire body was shaking, and before her eyes, he shifted into the form of a dragon. Men dove in all directions as Damien swiped his tail across the ground.

And grabbed Robyn.

"Damien? *Damien!*" she cried, as he leapt from the ground and went past the canopy of the trees. "You can't— Where are you taking me?"

Though Robyn knew Damien could talk in his dragon form, he refused to answer Robyn's demands as he gripped her in his monstrous claws and stole away into the night.

She had no idea where the dragon was taking her—nor what was awaiting her upon her arrival.

Chapter Thirty-Six

Damien

There was a scent upon Robyn that wasn't hers—nor his. Masculine, yet cloyingly full of the idiotic perfumes the excessively wealthy liked to drown themselves in. The idea that another man had touched Robyn, had looked at her, had decided to claim her as their own, was more than Damien could bear.

It was driving him crazy.

What was worse was the knowledge that Robyn had agreed to a union with this man.

The wind whistled past him as he forced himself to fly faster toward his home in the Dread Mountains. All he knew was that he needed to get Robyn there. Everything would be okay if he got her home.

Where she belongs.

When he reached his hoard in the mountains after hours of flying, Damien very gently placed Robyn down upon a pile of furs and blankets. She was freezing, which wasn't surprising. Damien knew he should feel bad.

But all he felt was rage.

"D-Damien, how dare you— What are you doing?" Robyn yelled, when Damien began rubbing his snout all over Robyn. He was desperate to remove the smell of the Duke of Merjeri from her clothes. Her skin.

Her face. He had touched her *face*.

"*Damien!*" Robyn bellowed, slapping at his snout. "That is enough! You need to shift so we can talk. *Now.*"

The anger in her tone was enough to make Damien shift, and he stormed away to pull on some clothes before Robyn could complain. How dare she be angry at *him*! She was the one who was going to marry another. Someone who wasn't her bloody *mate*.

"You're marrying that degenerate," he seethed, pulling on a shirt as Robyn shivered uncontrollably and wrapped herself up in the blankets. Damien set a fire going in the nearby hearth, built right into the stone wall of the opulent cave. His whole body shook as he turned to face her. "Why? *Why*, Robyn?"

"B-because I have to!" Robyn stammered. "How else can I protect my people from Ruslan's c-cruelty? I can't c-continue to be the Hood!"

"And why not? We can still take him down, then you'll be free of him!" Damien would cut him down where he stood if that's what it took.

"How can you know that for sure?" Robyn shook her head, her expression heartbreakingly set as she stared Damien down. "Even you fell for his trap. If Ruslan has spies in the Dark Court, that means he's got a very good network of contacts. If we take him down, someone else will take his place. I have no doubt he'll have someone else named to take over from him should he disappear—someone even worse than him, potentially. He's allowed the wolves of Betraz into our province. They will not leave easily."

Damien wanted to disagree, but he knew he couldn't. If he didn't feel the way he felt about Robyn, he'd have said the same thing. *Cut off the head of the snake and another appears.* There was a reason Pyre, Tempest, and Queen Ansette hadn't managed to bring Destin's previous supporters to heel yet.

Corruption and desire ran too deep to ever fully be stamped out.

A dull silence fell between them. Eventually the chattering of Robyn's teeth stopped, and Damien's vision slowly went from red, to black, then back to normal. He collapsed onto the pile of blankets beside Robyn and pressed his shoulder to hers, needing some connection. He wrapped his hands around the backs of his legs to keep from pulling her into his lap. One thing he'd learned in the last few months was that Robyn needed time to process things. If he pushed her too hard, she'd shut down and lock him out.

"What are you thinking?" she asked, her voice soft and too tender for Damien to bear. When he didn't reply, she said, "You must take me back, Damien. If Ruslan discovers me missing—"

"No." The moment she'd told him the news, his dragon had made a decision. "You're staying in my hoard. It's where you belong."

"I'm not a *thing*, Damien."

"I never said you were." She was his future. Couldn't she see that?

"So, you can't keep me with all your *things*!" Robyn pointed out, waving a hand around to indicate toward Damien's treasures. "And since you told me you don't actually have a home—that you prefer to travel around—I can only assume this is *literally* just a cave of things."

"I have many of these caves all over the world," Damien said simply, knowing they couldn't change the subject, not really, but wishing they could simply talk and argue about banal things like this instead of the far more pressing topic at hand. He couldn't handle the thought of returning Robyn to Ruslan Merjeri. "You could travel between them with me. See the world and all it has to offer you. All *I* have to offer you. You would lack for nothing."

"I don't need material things."

He scoffed. "Everyone does."

"So help me," Robyn hissed, pinching the bridge of her nose. "Why do you have to be so contrary?"

"Why do have to be so obtuse?" he snapped back. "I've been following you around like a lovesick kit for months while you keep me at arm's length. I'm a bloody dragon and yet I'm pining for a human who won't see the truth that's right in front of her."

"And what is that?"

"That I love you!"

Robyn gasped and he stared down at her. Her lovely mouth remained half-open, as if she wasn't sure what to say, but her expression was soft and made Damien want to kiss her.

"And you love me, too," he growled. It was in her eyes. Before he could think about it, Damien reached over and kissed Robyn, his mouth capturing hers in a frenzy of fierce emotions that he could barely restrain. Part of him expected her to pull away.

She didn't.

Bliss and heat roared through him, and he sank his hands into her silky black hair.

Robyn's hand trembled against Damien's cheek, urging him closer and inviting him to deepen the kiss. A burning in his heart desperately wanted to tumble Robyn onto the blankets—to push the moment as far as he possibly could—but Damien knew, instinctively, that Robyn would not reciprocate such an action. While his little dove was wild and free in many ways, she was a proper innocent in this case. He wouldn't tarnish that for anything in the world. Even if it physically hurt not to succumb to his instinct to make her his mate in all ways. "You're my mate, Robyn," Damien breathed against her lips, his chest heaving with desire. It gratified him to see Robyn experiencing a similar reaction. He brought his hand up to curl around hers, squeezing her fingers as hard as he dared. "I've known it from the moment I met you. I love you. You must know that."

The saddest smile Damien had ever seen crossed her kiss-swollen mouth. "I know," she said, her eyes becoming suspiciously shiny. "I love you, too."

Elation filled him as well as satisfaction. They'd hidden their feelings from each other for too long. Today, they could finally move forward. Together. He smiled and brushed a tear away. "Then come away with me! Or stay here forever! We can do whatever you'd like, as long as you allow me to stay by your side."

His smile dropped as he caught a whiff of her scent. Those weren't happy tears, but sad ones.

No. This could not be happening.

"You know there's more than just the two of us, Damien," Robyn said, her voice thick. Gently she kissed him again, then agonizingly broke contact with him. "I have people to look out for. I have a duty as Lady Marian—"

"But that isn't who you are!" Damien insisted, fervently trying to make Robyn understand how easy it would be to give up her old life—one she didn't want—for him. Together, the two of them would be ungovernable, unstoppable, invincible. "You aren't Lady Marian. You're so much more."

And yet Robyn shook her head. "But that's where you're wrong, Damien. Lady Marian *is* just as much a part of me as Robyn is. My duty, my honor—my family's honor—is more important to me than anything. It's the Hood I must let go of once we've saved my friends. And...and—"

She was going to reject him. Reject her mate. He was going to be sick.

"Don't say it. I know you don't mean it." Damien couldn't bear to hear it.

Robyn spoke anyway. "But I have to say it. There can be no room in my life for you, Damien, if I am to keep my people safe."

"No!" Damien cried, leaping to his feet, and bringing Robyn with him. He swept his hand in the direction of the opening to the cave, toward the vast expanse of the rest of the world. "We'll free your men, get back at that blackguard Merjeri, and do things our way. The way it *should* be." How could she not see it?

"You know that won't happen. He's won, Damien. To strike back against Ruslan now will only incite his followers and accomplices to create a civil war. Dotae can't have that.

Can't afford that. Too many people have died already. It is a small price to pay, really, to give up my freedom in exchange for the people."

He swiped a hand down his face. "You're being naïve."

"Don't you dare," she growled. "I'm not ignorant of the situation. Do you think I want this?"

"You're sure not fighting for us."

Robyn looked as if he'd slapped her. "I've done everything within my power to help those around me. I can't live for myself and my wants. They come first."

"I don't agree with that at all."

"I know," Robyn said, tears in her eyes. "Because you're a carefree dragon who is beholden to no one."

"What is that supposed to mean?"

She glanced around his hoard. "You told me you don't get involved with those who need help in Heimserya, because it's not your business. You'd rather sit among your jewels and collect pretty things than truly interact with the world."

"You're not being fair. Have I not helped you with all you've asked?"

"Was there not something in it for you?"

He blinked slowly at her. "I may have started out helping you because I wished to possess you, but that's not why I stayed. Those men have become my family, just as *you* are my family." A sob escaped Robyn, and the sound sent an arrow straight through his heart. "Marrying him is a mistake."

"I've already agreed."

"Doesn't matter," he snarled. "Merjeri cannot have you. You are *mine*."

"You can't own me."

Damien pulled her to him and cupped her cheeks. "You own me, heart, body, and soul."

Robyn squeezed her eyes closed. "I am sorry."

He leaned down and kissed her salty tears away from her face. "Don't do this."

"I have to." She opened her eyes and touched his face once more. "Please, please take me back."

"And why would I do that?" he whispered. "I have you in my home. I could keep you, and eventually your anger would pass. We could move on."

"You won't do that."

He scoffed. She had no idea what he'd do to keep his mate. "What makes you think that?"

"Because you love me." A swallow. "And I love you."

"If I love you, why should I let you go?"

"Because that's the way love works. You can't force or trap love. It will die."

Damien hated Robyn's logic. He hated that she was right. If he were an impartial observer, he'd agree with everything Robyn had concluded. She *did* have to marry the Duke of Merjeri...at least, for now.

But that didn't mean he would allow it to happen.

He'd see the duke dead first.

"Take me home, Damien," Robyn said, cutting through Damien's tumultuous reverie with her quiet, calm words that belied the emotion in her eyes. "Please."

He wanted to say no. With every fiber of his being, Damien wanted to say no. To keep Robyn exactly where she stood, safe from harm and the touch of other men. He'd been selfish all his life; what did it matter if he was selfish once more?

Because I will lose her love. I'll lose the way she's looking at me right now. The way she kissed me.

I'll lose everything.

Slowly, painfully, Damien exhaled and dropped his hands. It hurt not to touch her, so he took one of Robyn's hands. He squeezed it and smiled when she squeezed right back.

"All right," he said. "I'll take you back."

Those six words were the hardest he'd ever had to say. He couldn't believe them even as they came out of his mouth. But he'd said them now, which meant he had to do it.

Damien had always been honorable. He kept his word.

Even if it meant losing the only woman he'd ever truly loved.

Chapter Thirty-Seven

Scarlet

She'd made a mistake.

Scarlet gazed down the stairs that led to the dungeon.

You can't pretend this didn't happen.

Forcing herself down the curved staircase, she made it to the dungeon, her feet moving silently across the stone floor, down the long-curved corridor that held cells on each side. She may not have had shifter skills, but Scarlet had learned a few things over the years.

Stealth was one of them. She could even sneak up on some of the wolves despite their heightened hearing.

Mourne, one of her stepmother's wolves, spotted her from the end of the hallway. Scarlet cocked her head and arched a brow. "Just you?"

"Do you really think they pose any threat now that they are in chains?" Mourne replied, his tone gruff like most of the wolves.

Scarlet flicked a glance to the left, eyeing the three of the

Hood's men they captured – one with a very familiar face. She kept all recognition from her expression and sighed. "No doubt you're right. I do need you to take a break."

Mourne's amber eyes zeroed in on her. "Interrogation so soon?"

"No time like the present," Scarlet answered. "Please station yourself at the top of the stairs."

The wolf's eyes narrowed. He knew the pecking order and she was at the bottom except for times like these.

Scarlet touched her red cloak. "Do you know why the Alpha has gifted me these colors?" she asked softly.

"Because you are her property."

She smiled. "Also to hide the blood." Scarlet pinned him with an intense stare. "Unless you want to interfere with what the Alpha has assigned me to do, I suggest you *leave*."

That got him moving.

Mourne nodded and strode toward the exit.

"Make sure no one interrupts me," Scarlet said softly. "That duke and his sheriff are awfully nosey."

The wolf huffed and then disappeared up the spiral staircase.

Scarlet held completely still and listened for a few minutes to make sure Mourne wasn't listening. Most wolves wouldn't dare mess with orders from her stepmother, but every once in a while, one would start getting a little too independent. Those ones didn't survive very long.

"Are you here to torture us?" a deep masculine voice asked.

She turned her attention to the large man who sported a red beard. "I'm not here for you." Scarlet focused on the man in the middle who gazed at the ceiling with no expression, blood dripping from his black curly hair.

Will.

How many years had it been since she'd seen her friend? Six or seven? He had been a gangly young man the last time Scarlet had laid eyes on him and helped him escape. Now he was a man in his prime. And from the vacant look on his face, he hadn't lost his training. Will knew what her stepmother did with prisoners and deserters.

Scarlet reached for her hood and slowly lowered it, revealing her golden hair. She pressed closer to the bars and held on to them.

"Will," she called, managing to keep the wobble from her voice. He didn't stir. "Will, it's me, Scarlet."

The third man, tall and thin with dark-brown hair, frowned. "How does she know his name?"

"Quiet," the redhead admonished.

The brunette snapped his mouth shut and studied his hands.

That told Scarlet many things.

First, that either the redhead or Will was in charge. Second, they trusted each other. And third, they had prepared for this eventuality.

Smart men.

Scarlet pulled a sheathed dagger from the belt at her hip and tossed it through the bars onto Will's lap. "A gift for an old friend. Please look at me Will." She swallowed. "It's Scarlet. Come back from your vault."

All the wolves were trained to find a vault in their mind where they could hide during interrogations.

Her old friend blinked slowly and dropped his gaze to the dagger on his lap. Slowly, he lifted his head and met her gaze. It was a shock. He'd lost all traces of the boy he'd used to be. A soldier stared back at her. His brows furrowed, and recognition dawned.

"Scarlet? What in the blazes are you doing here?" Will rumbled, his voice deeper than before.

"She's here to interrogate us," the redhead growled.

Will finally looked away from her face and scanned her from head to toe, lingering on her red cloak. His lips thinned and she knew what he saw. A tool of the Alpha.

"I heard stories about Old Mother's red cloak," Will said, his tone hard. "Tell me those weren't about you."

Dread pooled in her gut. She'd been forced into situations over the years that would haunt Scarlet for the rest of her life. "I never got away," she said softly.

Will spat on the ground. "So, you helped her?"

Scarlet held her chin high. "I do it to spare others."

Will laughed. "What are the odds that the same little girl who helped me escape that vile woman would be the one to send me right back to her?"

"I didn't know," Scarlet whispered. "I didn't know you were with the Hood."

"How could you not? Do you think I'd let the Alpha invade Merjeri and enslave others?" Will snapped.

"Lower your voice," she hissed, glancing at the stairwell. "We are surrounded by wolves."

"I know. One is standing right in front of me wearing a red cloak."

That cut deep.

"Don't you dare judge me," she growled squeezing the bars. She gestured to her scarred cheek and then to the cloak. "This was my punishment for helping you. Do you think I want this?"

Will's expression shuttered, and he picked up the dagger. "Why are you here, Scarlet?"

Her heart clenched and heat pressed against the back of her eyes. "Because you were once my friend and my father's friend. You protected me through the first of my stepmother's purges. You held my hand and sang to me while screams cut through the night. Do you think I would ever betray that?"

His expression softened just a touch. "You shouldn't be here."

"No, I shouldn't." It put everything at risk. "Friends never leave friends behind. You told me that, and I don't plan to now." She pulled several vials from her belt and knelt. Scarlet rolled them to Will. "Those should help healing and pain. There is some for all three of you."

"What then?" the redhead asked, running a chained hand over his beard.

"You survive," she whispered. "I'll be sent down every few days for interrogation until the execution. That will give me enough time to figure out a plan to get you out."

"The Hood will get us out," the brunette replied.

Scarlet smiled. "That may be so, but it's always better to have a backup plan, no?"

Will straightened, his eyes narrowing. "Someone is coming."

She pulled her hood over her hair. "Make sure to look

appropriately drugged."

All three men slumped as the sound of footsteps moved swiftly down the stairs.

The sheriff.

Stars, Scarlet disliked the man. There was something off about him. Mourne followed on his heels, his amber gaze looking at anything but her. She brushed her hands off and met the sheriff head on. He eyed her cloak and glanced over her shoulder at Will and the other two men.

"I take it went well?" he asked lightly.

"My methods are effective, but they take time."

"They don't look too bad. I may take a crack at them." The sheriff smiled and went to move around her. "Never send a woman to do a man's work."

She yanked a dagger from her wrist and had it pointed to his jugular. The sheriff froze and glared down at her. "I'll ignore your last comment," Scarlet said softly. "But I warn you that if you touch *my* prisoners, it will be Old Mother you'll be dealing with, not me. I'd think very carefully about going against her wishes."

The sheriff held his hands up. "I beg your forgiveness, my lady," he muttered between clenched teeth.

"It's not me you'll be begging next time," she warned.

He backed away and then turned on his heel, storming out of the dungeon.

"He's going to be a problem," Mourne commented, crossing his arms.

"He's your problem."

Scarlet stashed her weapon and made sure to keep her eyes forward as she left the dungeon.

How the devil was she going to get Will out?

Scarlet sat in the back of the duke's war room, fiddling with the dagger attached to her wrist. Lord Merjeri slammed his hands against the table, but she didn't bat an eye at his childish outburst. She'd seen much worse from her stepmother over the years.

"I want the Hood's head by the wedding!"

The sheriff nodded. "It will be done, my lord."

"See to it Gustav, or I won't be accountable for my actions."

She watched the handsome duke storm from the room from beneath her hood and pursed her lips. The man was beautiful. Too bad his soul was rotted and ugly. Scarlet turned her attention back to the sheriff.

Now the games began.

The sheriff rounded the war table and scanned the room filled with wolves and guards. While the duke was dangerous in his own right, it was the sheriff she was wary of. He was like a serpent waiting to strike.

"We have the Hood's men and yet we've gained no more information on who he is." The sheriff's gaze landed on her and she repressed a shiver. "What say you o famed daughter of Old Mother? Have your interrogations yielded no results?" He gave her a nasty smile. "Or do you need a man to do your job?"

She pushed away from the wall and glided forward, her mask firmly in place. The sheriff thought he was something special by insulting her, but she'd heard it a thousand times. His words wouldn't penetrate her tough skin.

Scarlet pulled the dagger from her waist and tossed it onto the table.

"What is this?"

She nodded at it. "Pick it up."

The sheriff lifted it from the table and eyed the knife. "What of it?"

Scarlet arched a brow. "Can you not see it?"

He glared at her. "Out with it."

"It's a woman's weapon."

The sheriff scoffed. "It looks like any other blade."

"Except for the size of the handle. It's smaller than what you use. It's meant for someone with petite hands."

"You think that the Hood is employing women?" the sheriff laughed. His guards snickered but the wolves were silent. They knew better than to insult the female sex. Their Alpha was more powerful than most men in the kingdom.

Scarlet smiled coldly. "It's possible, but I have a theory of who the Hood is."

"Do share."

"Do you know much about dragons?"

"Enough."

"Good." She cocked her head. "Then you know that dragons are fiercely protective of those under their care and of their mates. When we set our trap, that dragon had ample opportunity to lay waste to you and your men. Yet, he scooped the Hood up and disappeared."

"He?" the sheriff asked softly. "How do you know it was male?"

"The size and horns." Scarlet cocked her head. "But I think you know this already. You recognized the beast. It's why you drew back."

His face turned red. "It was a tactical retreat."

"If you say so," she murmured softly. He was a bloody liar and they both knew it. The dragon had been coming for him. Somehow the sheriff knew the dragon and yet he was hiding it.

"Do you have a point?" he sneered.

"That your Hood? The thief is a *woman*."

Chapter Thirty-Eight

Robyn

The journey back to Merjeri province was largely silent, but not in an awkward way. Rather, it was sad and full of longing.

Even before Damien's feet touched the ground at the edge of the woods and he'd transformed back into a man, Robyn knew something was coming to an end.

"I'll help you save your men," Damien said, brushing his hand against Robyn's for what she knew would be the final time. "But I won't stick around after that. I can't do that to you...and I won't do that to me."

She blinked back her tears. This was her choice. She had to live with it.

"If you choose to disband the Hood and everything you've built beneath it... Well, that's up to you."

"Damien, I..."

He held his hand up. "You don't need to say anything more. I'm barely holding it together. I need you to walk away before I change my mind."

Robyn nodded, not trusting her voice. She was far too close to tears. Damien wouldn't even look at her, clearly afraid that if he did so, his resolve would crack.

It was exactly the same way Robyn felt. "I'm sorry."

He nodded once, his jaw ticking.

And, so, though there were so many things that needed to be said, Robyn turned from Damien and headed home. Each step she took, a part of her soul withered. Once she was sure her dragon could no longer see or hear her, she let her tears free. With silent sobs, she cursed losing her brother, her father's injury, the duke and his machinations, her own stupid honor.

When Lochslee came into view, she picked up speed, only wanting to find her bed and cry for everything she'd lost.

"Robyn!" her father cried the moment she walked through the front door. He embraced her, holding her tightly against his chest, despite how freezing Robyn was. "We have all been so worried. After Ruslan's announcement of the wedding... Well, we all thought you must have run away."

"And with good reason," Maya said. "The man is merciless. He takes who he wants, no matter the law." Her face was pale and gaunt, as was her husband's. It was at this point that Robyn concluded they had discovered Andrei was one of the prisoners being held at the duke's residence.

"I'm sorry," she whispered to Maya.

The housekeeper's bottom lip trembled. "Not your fault, my dear."

Except it was.

Tears fell from Robyn's eyes before she could stop herself. She wept against her father, her chest heaving with guttural sobs that wracked through her entire body.

He held her tighter.

"Do not marry him, dearest," her papa said, believing Robyn's grief to be solely about her impending nuptials. Since she couldn't say anything about what she was really crying about—the friends whose fate *she* was responsible for, the man she couldn't have, and so much more—Robyn allowed her father to stroke her hair until her sobs finally subsided.

"I'll do what I must," Robyn said, pulling out of her father's arms. She wiped her tears away on the edge of her cloak, glad that Damien had given her a far more lady-like, burgundy cloak from his hoard to hide her Hood disguise. She turned to Maya and Danil. "And I'll free your son, and Pavel, and Will. I can guarantee that."

Even if it cost Robyn her life, she would at the very least achieve that.

Danil shook his head. "You need to be careful, my lady. Even becoming the duchess will not save you from Ruslan if you cross him."

"You all are my family," she said vehemently. "I will do this."

"You can't do everything on your own," Danil said, though his eyes were full of gratitude at Robyn's sentiment.

"I can at least do this," she insisted. "Now, if you'll excuse me, I am very tired. And I have a wedding to prepare."

And a break-out to plan.

The next three weeks were full of wedding preparations, interspersed with stilted planning to free her friends. It was clear Damien was doing his best to avoid interacting directly with Robyn, though she knew he was working around the clock to formulate a flawless plan to free Andrei, Pavel, and Will.

Robyn's feeling from three weeks ago was right: that something had come to an end between her and Damien.

Her dragon had accepted her decision and had let her go. While it was what she wanted, it still hurt so much that she could barely breathe at times. She took a few calming breaths before picking up the teapot from the small setting Maya had left on a round table in the garden. "Would you like some tea, Mama?" Robyn asked her mother, who was sitting upon the swing in the garden with her. It was a beautiful, promisingly warm spring day, so she was eager to help her mother outside to enjoy some sun on her face. It may be the last time she was able to do so. Ruslan had been more possessive of her since their run-in at the garden a few weeks prior.

Her mother's expression was blank, but she accepted a cup of steaming chamomile tea, nonetheless. Together, they sipped from their tiled cups in companionable silence, even though Robyn wished for nothing more than conversation. She needed her mother's guidance now more than ever with everything that was to happen.

"I am to be married," Robyn said softly, knowing the words meant nothing to her mother. "I am to be married, and I despise the man I'm to be married to. No... It's more than that. I'm frightened of him." It was an ugly truth. Despite her training, Ruslan terrified her. "And I had to give up the person I *do* love for this—this snake. But I have no choice, if I am to save this family and our people. I'm angry."

There. Robyn had said it. It was the first time she'd

confessed it all out loud to anyone on the Lochslee estate. Though she knew her mother would never reply, Robyn felt like a weight had been lifted from her shoulders simply by speaking the words. They'd weighed her down like rocks.

So, it was with a jolt of shock that Robyn watched her mother turn to her and reply.

"You have always done what is right," Lady Lochslee said, cognizant for the first time since before Robyn went off to war. She wrapped her soft, weak hands around her daughter's. Her hands were reassuringly warm against Robyn's cold skin.

"Mama?" she whispered, not daring to believe this was real.

"You've done what is right, yes," her mother continued, "but always what's wrong for *you,* my lovely daughter. My beautiful daughter." Her dark eyes crinkled with the edge of a smile. "So smart. So kind. So dutiful. But you must live your life for *you,* Robyn. Otherwise, you are not living at all."

Robyn was crying. She didn't care. She couldn't believe her mother was giving her advice. That her mother *knew* her. Really, truly knew her.

"How can I do that, when our people would suffer, Mama?" she asked, desperate for her thoughts.

She patted Robyn's hand. A gentle breeze blew through her long, graying hair, wafting the scents of sandalwood and neroli oil into Robyn's nostrils. Comforting smells that reminded Robyn of kinder days in her childhood, when her family was not broken.

"You'll work out what to do. You always do. But do not give up on love. You're worth more than that, my dear daughter. Don't let anyone bully you into thinking something else."

Robyn wrapped her arms around her mother's frail shoulders, the swing they were sitting on shifting in the breeze. "Thank you, Mama," she whispered into Lady Lochslee's ear. "Thank you for being here. I love you."

"I love you, too, dearest."

For a while, they continued to sit in contented silence until, eventually, Lady Lochslee's eyes began to glaze over, and Robyn knew her miraculous window of time with her mother was over.

She had to hope there would be more in the future.

But, for now, Robyn's mother imparted words that Robyn had desperately needed to hear.

Robyn *would* do the right thing. And although that involved marrying Ruslan Merjeri, that didn't necessarily mean she had to give up on everything else. She had come this far living multiple lives—hiding her true self when necessary to do what needed to be done.

She led her mother back to the keep and then headed to her room.

"Marry the snake, break out your friends, and then do what needs to be done," Robyn muttered to herself, over and over again, as she readied herself for a sleepless night. In the morning, she would be wed to Ruslan, something for which she could never fully prepare.

Whether Damien remained forever out of Robyn's reach was out of her hands. That was something he would have to decide for himself after everything was said and done. She couldn't control him, only herself.

All Robyn could do was hope he could still love a woman who married the Duke of Merjeri, who lay in bed with him for her people, who pretended to *want* a monster for the sake of her friends and family.

Have faith in me, Damien, Robyn begged, hugging her pillow and wishing it were him.

The tiniest flame ignited inside her, beginning to finally chase the cold of the last three weeks away.

Chapter Thirty-Nine

Robyn

For the hundredth time that morning, Robyn smoothed her hands over the non-existent creases in the elaborate skirt of her wedding gown.

This is it. I'm really doing this.

Robyn thought she might vomit if she so much as opened her mouth.

The door swung open and she stiffened as Gustav entered the room, closing the door behind him. She stared at him as he brushed nonexistent lint off his black velvet vest. He slowly lifted his head and smiled, sending chills down her spine.

Robyn gritted her teeth. She didn't need this today.

"What the devil are you doing here?" she said, drawing herself up to her full height.

The sheriff's gaze trailed her from head to toe, making Robyn want to tear out his eyes, and whistled. "What a prize you are."

"You should not be here."

"That's where you are wrong." He sauntered forward and circled her. Robyn followed his movements. He reached out and ran his fingers over the fabric at her hip. She stepped out of his grasp. Gustav smirked. "You and I haven't been able to speak freely in a long time."

"This is hardly the time or the place."

He clapped his hands together, a mean glint entering his eyes. "That is where you are wrong." He leaned back against the dresser behind him. "There's no time like the present and you and I have a few things to discuss."

"Out with it and be gone," she snapped. Where was her father? He should have been there by now.

"You and I find ourselves in quite the predicament. You don't like me but I'm Ruslan's oldest friend, supporter, and adviser." His smile thinned. "I don't like you because you're never where you should be, and you cloud the duke's judgement."

"I am sorry you feel that way. Please leave."

He shook his head. "You know you haven't changed since we were children. Ruslan doesn't see that. All he sees is a woman he wants to conquer and the valuable land she comes with."

"How flattering," she muttered. Where was he going with this?

"But you're so much more aren't you?" Gustav asked. He pushed away from the dresser and circled her again. "As a child I was left out of many things which gave me ample opportunity to study the people around me. You and your brother always fascinated me so." Ice trickled through her veins. "Twins. You both shared the womb and yet... you were

348

so different. John was gentle and quiet where you were wild and outspoken. After a time, it seemed like John started gaining some of *your* qualities."

Robyn shrugged and began to sweat. "It was bound to happen. We were close."

"So close that sometimes you almost seemed like the same person."

He *knew.* She could see it on the sheriff's face.

He has no proof. Keep calm.

"Are you done yet?" she replied icily. "It is my wedding day and I'd rather not reflect on the loss of my brother."

Gustav snapped his fingers and pointed at her. "That right there. You put on a good show." He stepped into her space, and she lifted her chin refusing to back down. "I think you lost John a long time ago and have been playing pretend for quite some time. You know impersonating a solider is a death sentence."

Her jaw dropped and Robyn laughed right in his face. "You think I went to war?"

He reached out and touched the ugly scar along her collarbone. She swatted his hand away.

"How did you come by this scar?"

"An accident on the archery range." A half-truth. "I wasn't paying as much attention as I should have been when I went to retrieve my arrows. Neither was the archer who accidentally shot me."

The sheriff cocked his head and then nodded. "What an excellent lie. Do you want to know what I think happened?"

"Enlighten me," she growled, "so we can be done with each other." Her words were cavalier, but she was anything but.

"Word of your brother's death spread throughout the province, but I did a little digging." Her heart stopped as he gave her a slow grin. "It seems that your brother had deserted and was shot by the captain in the chest. In the same spot, you also have an archery scar. A coincidence? I think not."

"Are you accusing me of something?"

"I think it was you who deserted."

Robyn chuckled and shook her head. "You're right, Gustav. We both have changed little since we were children. You were a delusional liar then and you still are now. You're out of your fool mind."

The sheriff bared his teeth, his face turning red. She'd struck a nerve.

"No, I'm not, but you are if you think I'll let you have any control over Merjeri." He shrugged. "I've always loved games and puzzles, and you're one I can't wait to figure out, layer by layer."

"Gustav, are you done yet?" she sighed as if bored, even though she was quaking on the inside.

"Not by half."

He pulled a scrap of fabric from his pocket and held it out.

Robyn recognized it immediately. It was part of her hood.

She rubbed at her temples and rolled her eyes. "And what is this?"

The sheriff scanned her face. "A noose."

"For whom?"

"The Hood." His gaze dropped to her chest and lingered a moment before moving back to her face. "It will be a pleasure serving you, Robyn. I can't wait to get to know you better." He leaned just a fraction closer. "Don't you know? The duke shares *everything* with me."

Disgusting. "Get out."

The door opened just as the sheriff stepped back to an appropriate distance. Bile burned the back of her throat as her papa entered the room. Gustav bowed deeply.

"Congratulations again, my lady. Welcome to the family." He straightened and walked past her father before leaving the room completely.

Damien needed to move quickly.

Gustav was up to something.

Chapter Forty

The Sheriff

He closed the door to the duke's chambers and watched his highborn half-brother preen in front of the mirror. Sometimes Gustav wished he'd also gotten a portion of Ruslan's beauty but then… handsome looks weren't as useful as brains.

The duke faced him and arched a haughty brow. "Well?"

Gustav fought to keep from glaring at him. He'd always hated how Ruslan could make one word sound like a pompous demand.

Pulling the bit of ripped scarf from his pocket, he tossed it to Ruslan. The duke caught the scrap of fabric and rubbed it in between his fingers.

"It's her." Gustav didn't have any concrete proof but too many things pointed in her direction. She was part of the Hood's merry men or she was the Hood. Either way, Marian was a traitor.

Ruslan pinned him with an angry stare. "Are you sure? Did she confess?"

He laughed and ran a hand through his black hair, the only trait he and the duke shared. "Marian is too smart for that."

"Then how do you know it's her? Because of that hooded freak Old Mother sent?"

"No," he said tightly. "I showed her the fabric."

"And she reacted to it?"

"It was her lack of recognition that makes me believe she's guilty. It was too smooth. Marian has never been that calm and collected. She was *lying*."

Ruslan cursed and tossed the remnants of the scarf into the fire and began pacing the room like a caged tiger. "I cannot believe it."

"You must."

The duke shot a glare his way. "I'm to marry her in less than a half hour."

"You are."

"What am I to do?" Ruslan growled. "I can't hang her, nor would I want to. It would be a waste of flesh and the people would turn her into a martyr."

"You marry her."

"What?" The duke stopped pacing and stared at Gustav. "If what you say is true, she's caused this whole mess."

He smiled at his half-brother. "And what better way to take vengeance upon her and her blasted family than by marrying her? You will essentially *own* her. She will be under your complete control once you threaten those whom she cares for. You will win on all sides. You get your pretty tarte you've coveted for years and an heir, the land the Lochslees took from your family generations ago, and you can punish her for the rest of her miserable life. And once you tire of her... well, people have accidents all the time and die."

Ruslan grinned back at him. "Gustav, you never cease to amaze me."

"I live to serve."

The duke pushed his black hair from his face. "It's time I wed; don't you think?"

Chapter Forty-One

Robyn

Robyn swallowed hard and faced the mirror again, terrified her papa would see everything she was hiding.

"You can still back out, Robyn," her father said, the soft touch of his hand on her back quietly reassuring and grounding. She watched him looking at her in the mirror and forced a smile to her face.

"No," she said, "I'm doing this."

Everything's in place to free Andrei, Pavel, and Will. To back out now would be sending them to their deaths.

It looked like her father was desperate to say something, but he bit his tongue and sighed. "Let's get this over with, then."

Robyn couldn't help but laugh at his honesty. "Yes, let's."

The ceremony went by in a flurry of movement, extravagant decorations, beautiful music, and words spoken from Robyn's own lips that she did not mean. Ruslan had clearly spared no expense with the ceremony, though any admiration Robyn might have had for the classy affair was lost in the face of the knowledge of where the gold that paid for the event came from.

It didn't escape her notice that the place was crawling with wolves disguised as his own soldiers. That would be challenging but nothing less than what she expected.

Ruslan, too, was dressed as well as the marriage hall was, in a beautiful deep-blue tailcoat with matching trousers, a white ruffled shirt, knee-high boots, and a pair of ceremonial rapiers inlaid with silver at each hip. His hair was expertly slicked back from his face, and, for the fawning audience, he looked every inch the excited newlywed husband.

But Robyn knew what was lurking behind his eyes. The calculated nature of every facial expression, every word he spoke, every gesture. It was all a ploy to curry favor. Robyn, after all, knew exactly what kind of man Ruslan Merjeri was, and the one he presented at their wedding was definitely *not* that man.

Still, Robyn had said *I do* and kissed him nonetheless, and when she was sat on his right at the marriage feast, she laughed along with as much false gaiety as she could muster.

Come on, Damien.

Robyn sipped her wine too quickly before remembering she should keep a clear head. But the thought of having to lie with Ruslan in their marriage bed that night was not something Robyn relished doing sober.

Save your friends. Get them out of here. Make this entire charade worth it.

Lord Lochslee, too, was following Robyn's lead and acting jovial with Ruslan, the sheriff, and the other nobles who had come to witness his daughter's union. Her mother, of course, had been excused from joining the ceremony on account of her poor health, though because of her words the day before, Robyn almost felt as if she was sitting with her, holding her hand, and telling her she would do the right thing.

Before Robyn was at all ready for it—not that she imagined she'd *ever* be ready for it—the feast was over, and Ruslan began leading her toward his chambers.

"Careful on the stairs," he said, his face flushed from the wine. Clearly, Ruslan had genuinely been enjoying himself all day, completely ignorant to how insincere Robyn's enjoyment of the event had been. "Many have died upon these flagstones."

Robyn could believe it; the stairs leading to the duke's chambers in the highest tower of the manor were steep and winding, with no rail to support oneself as they ascended the steps. *Or descended,* Robyn mused, carefully placing her slippered feet on the cold stone and urging herself not to trip on the hem of her massive gown.

I cannot imagine descending these stairs every day. How does Ruslan do it?

As if reading her thoughts Ruslan said, "Usually I sleep in my *actual* quarters, on the first floor of the main wing of the manor." He paused on the stairs, glancing over his shoulder toward Robyn. Her stomach lurched at the desirous look on his face. "But a special occasion calls for a special room. I want only the best for you, my wife."

Robyn heard what he was *really* saying loud and clear: *I want to put you in a room you can't escape from.*

Dotae be good, can I honestly do this? Can I let this snake remove my clothes, run his fingertips on my skin and—and—

She bit her lip so hard it almost bled. It wasn't a matter of whether Robyn *could* do it. The tiny vial seemed to burn in the secret pocket of her wedding dress. Tonight, she'd seduce and drug him. Hopefully, in the morning, he'd think they'd actually spent the night together while she was freeing her friends and robbing him blind.

The click of the heavy door closing behind them, after Ruslan let her into their wedding suite, sealed her fate.

"Here," Ruslan said, walking over to a handsomely carved table laden with food and drink positioned in front of a roaring fire to pour Robyn a glass of wine. She eagerly took it, holding the liquid to her lips and relishing in the rich flavor of it.

Small sips. Keep your wits about you.

She gave him a tiny smile and tried to work through the nerves. Her eyes wandered over to the gigantic four-poster bed that took up much of the room. Ruslan followed her gaze with a venomous smirk on his face.

"It's big, I know," he said, trailing his fingers down the length of Robyn's right arm. Her hand twitched when he touched the scar on her palm from the sheriff hitting her with his whip. Ruslan kissed her shoulder, then trailed his lips to Robyn's neck. Robyn felt his other hand exploring the long line of buttons running down her spine—her only protection from Ruslan's touch on her bare skin.

"Seems as if this bed was made for a giant," Robyn murmured. *Or a dragon.*

She couldn't think of Damien right now.

Ruslan began unbuttoning Robyn's wedding dress, and she whistled in a breath through her teeth. She turned in the circle of his arms and faced Ruslan with a forced smile on her face. "Must we move so fast?" she asked. "Can we not take it slowly? Can I offer you a drink, Your Grace?"

But Ruslan shook his head.

Her stomach bottomed out, but she kept her mask in place as a horrible cackle left his mouth, sending shivers down Robyn's half-exposed spine.

"I have moved at a glacial pace thus far for you. I shall wait no more. I plan to take what I've always wanted from you— what you've always denied me, again and again—right now. And besides... you've run out of time, Robyn."

There was no humor left on his face or even desire, just pure maliciousness. Robyn tried to back away, but his hand on the base of her spine was iron.

"W-what do you mean?" she asked, fear painfully apparent in both Robyn's words and her body. She tried to wriggle against Ruslan's grasp, but he only pushed her closer to him.

"I know who you are. I know what you've been doing. And I know exactly how I'm going to punish you for it. Welcome to your new home, my Lady Hood."

Chapter Forty-Two

Robyn

"I don't know what you're talking about," Robyn said, watching Ruslan as a deer might watch a lion when it was slowly backed into a corner. Except Robyn had no corner to back into; she was trapped in Ruslan's dangerous embrace.

"Don't insult my intelligence. I know you're the Hood." Ruslan spat out the title. "Did you really think I wouldn't find out?"

Robyn's entire body felt like ice. It was clear she wouldn't be lying herself out of this one. She could see it on Ruslan's face: he was convinced of his conviction.

"Have you nothing to say, *wife*?" His hold tightened painfully.

If Robyn didn't escape, she would die.

With all the strength she could muster, she twisted and pushed out of Ruslan's arms and ran for the exit. But he yanked at the long train of her dress, stopping Robyn just as she got her hand on the handle. The heavy wooden door barely swung open an inch.

"Oh, you're not getting out of this," Ruslan hissed, snaking an arm around Robyn's waist. He bit her earlobe. "You're mine to do with as I please, and you need to be reminded of your place."

"*Don't touch me,*" Robyn exclaimed, glaring at the duke out of the corner of her eye.

He merely laughed. "After all the hoops you made me jump through—all to give you time to humiliate me, to spurn me, to *rob* me—do you really think I'd let you have your way? After you fell for that trap three weeks ago and my men captured your precious friends, I knew for sure who and what you are."

"You're lying. I don't know what you're talking about!"

Ruslan licked the side of her face. "Stubborn to the bloody end. So, I will have what I've always wanted from you"—Ruslan's hand slipped beneath the fabric of Robyn's dress on her back, fingertips cold on her spine—"and then I'll kill you once I've had my fill and you've borne me an heir."

"Stop this, right now," she said, feeling sick. "We can still salvage this."

He chuckled in her ear; the sound sinister. "You know my father pleaded as you are right before I killed him."

She suspected Ruslan had murdered the former duke but for him to admit it...

He's going to kill you. Run.

"Don't worry, my love. There's a special place for you after death and I'll even be sure to send the rest of your family to you. They won't have a chance to miss their precious daughter. If they have the wits to know your face anymore, that is."

"You *snake,*" Robyn bit out, thrashing in his arms. "You

deign to threaten my family? Do you really think you'll get away with it?"

"It isn't a threat, it's an inevitability. And I've already gotten away with it; who'll question your death when the only witness to such a tragic event is your doting, love-drunk husband?"

Robyn struggled against his touch as Ruslan slid her dress off one shoulder. In a fit of desperation, she viciously bit into his hand, not letting go even when her mouth filled with blood. The man cursed and his grip loosened, so Robyn used his temporary distraction to kick away from him and yank open the door.

She stared at the steep staircase that promised a fall to her death if she ran down the steps. But it was that or Ruslan.

That or...

Robyn looked over her shoulder at the Duke of Merjeri. Ruslan's face was contorted in rage, his hair in disarray as he shook out his bleeding hand and gathered his wits about him to grab Robyn once more.

"I will enjoy taking everything from you," he heaved, his eyes focused on where Robyn's dress was falling from her shoulder, dangerously close to no longer protecting her modesty. "And when I'm done, I'll give you over to Gustav and you'll really wish you were dead."

"You're disgusting," Robyn said, no longer afraid. If she were to die, she'd rather die having said everything she wanted to say. "I rejected you, and you hated that, so you sought to ruin me. Is that how shallow you are? Do you really think this is the way you win?"

"You never knew your place. But you will beg for mercy tonight, Robyn, before the night is up. I can assure you of that."

The rapiers on Ruslan's hips gleamed in the dim firelight of the room, and Robyn knew what she had to do. "I can assure *you*, Your Grace, that I will never beg for anything from you." She turned from the stairs to bend low and lunge for one of the blades just as Ruslan leaped at her—and was met with an empty space where Robyn had been a mere moment ago.

"No!" she yelled, eyes wide as Ruslan tumbled down the stairs with a yell of surprise, followed by a sickening snap that echoed down off the heavy stone walls.

Her heart thundered in her chest, and tears pricked her eyes. She crept to the door, her whole body shaking. No one could have survived that fall.

"Your Grace?" she called.

Dead silence.

Robyn didn't have to go down the steps and see him to know that Ruslan had died. She felt it in her gut. She stumbled and leaned heavily against the door frame. What had she done?

You killed the Duke of Merjeri.

Her teeth began to chatter together as she fell to her knees, her hands slapping against the stone floor. Robyn vomited as she sobbed. Ruslan was a nasty piece of work, but she'd known him since she was a child. She'd wanted justice, for him to spend his life in a prison, not die by her hands.

She wiped her mouth and wrapped her arms around her waist. She'd hang for this.

Run.

"I have to get out of here," she realized, clumsily clambering to her feet. Robyn blankly scanned the room and rocked in place.

Snap out of it and run.

Robyn clenched her jaw and hastily slid her dress back up her shoulder. But she was unable to do up the buttons on her back, and quickly gave up even trying. If she managed to make it out of her lethal marriage chambers, she could worry about more appropriate clothes.

The sound of the door opening way down at the bottom of the stairs set her teeth on edge.

This is it.

Robyn braced for a fight she knew she couldn't win without a weapon. Dimly, she thought of Ruslan's ceremonial rapiers and how she should have armed herself with one while she had the chance.

"Oh my," came a voice from the stairs. A *female* voice. This caught Robyn by surprise. The sound of steps ascending the stairs—passing Ruslan's corpse—filled Robyn's ears. She breathed in and out, in and out, and held herself in a fighting stance, despite her ridiculous dress and lack of weapons.

Robyn snatched a metal vase full of fresh flowers from the table and dumped the flowers on the floor. Next, she picked up a small butter knife. It wasn't much, but it was better than nothing. She rolled her shoulders and prepared for what came next.

When a woman with periwinkle hair in a thick braid appeared in the doorway, Robyn screamed at her and prepared to knock her down the stairs. But the woman held up her hands in surrender.

"I'm here to help!" she cried. "I'm a friend of Damien's!"

"Prove it," Robyn snarled. She'd already been betrayed by the Dark Court before. It wouldn't happen again.

The woman took a slow step inside, making sure to step over the vomit on the floor.

"That's far enough," Robyn commanded.

Shrewd gray eyes met her gaze and the woman nodded. "I'm not going to hurt you. My name is Tempest and I'm a friend."

Tempest. That name rang a bell in the back of her mind. Robyn frowned and forced back her blind panic to focus on the blue-haired woman.

Blue, like the Hounds...

"You're the Lady Hound," Robyn concluded, her brain working on overdrive due to the adrenaline in her system. "You're...the one Damien's been working with on behalf of Queen Ansette?"

Tempest nodded, with a small smile. "And you're Lady Marian. I've heard so much about you."

Robyn cackled, feeling unhinged. She'd just killed the Duke of Merjeri, and now the queen's champion was here speaking with her. "Well, welcome, I guess."

Tempest glanced between the vase and butter knife in Robyn's hands. "You can put your...weapons down."

She blinked at the Lady Hound and lowered her hands. A shiver ran through her body, her wedding dress slipping dangerously low. She tossed the vase on the table and yanked the dress up when all she wanted to do was yank it from her body and toss it into the fire. "I need to leave."

"I assume the duke was your doing?"

Robyn blanched. "He attacked me, and I fought back. It was an accident."

Tempest held a hand up. "You do not need to defend yourself to me." She pursed her lips and then continued.

"Lady Marian, I need you to do something for me."

"Which would be?"

"Stay in here for the next twenty-four hours."

"I can't," Robyn croaked. She needed to leave *now*.

"I know we just met, but you need to trust me. Trust Damien."

She ran a trembling hand over her forehead. Staying in this room all night and the following day would be a nightmare. "Is that it?"

"Don't touch *him*," Tempest said, indicating back down the stairs toward Ruslan's body with obvious distaste. "The guards downstairs have been plied with so much drugged wine, they'll wake up late with killer hangovers and assume the two of you have been happily in bed together all night."

"How does that help? His death will be pinned on me. I'll be hanged for murder."

"Murder?" Tempest barked out a laugh. "From what I see, the man accidentally killed himself. You will not be the one punished on the morrow. Just...try to get some sleep, and I'll come back for you tomorrow. Can you do that?"

She would have to.

"Perhaps not sleep, but I can wait."

Tempest stepped back into the stairwell and paused. "Will you be all right?"

Robyn squared her shoulders. "I have to be."

The Lady Hound gave her a nod of understanding. "I suppose that's all I can hope for. Until tomorrow, Lady Marian."

"It's Robyn."

Tempest smiled. "I'll see you soon, Robyn."

Robyn must have slept, for the next thing she was aware of—after hours of wild overthinking and constantly stopping herself from sneaking down the stairs to look at Ruslan's dead body—was the presence of a handsome, fox-eared shifter wearing a forest-green top hat upon his burnished hair. She bolted upright in the bed. He sat in an armchair by the smoldering remains of the fire, chewing on a chicken leg from the stone-cold, forgotten marriage feast.

"Who the devil are you?" she rasped. It struck her as odd that he was sitting in her room like he owned the place. For some reason, she didn't fear him. Something was wrong with her.

"Afternoon, Robyn," the shifter said, forgoing her formal name as if they had known each other for years. Robyn found that she didn't mind.

She rubbed at her eyes and straightened up on the monstrous bed that she'd found herself collapsed onto at some point in the early hours of the morning. "Are you another friend of Damien's?" she asked. "How'd you get in here?" She'd bolted the door shut.

The man grinned, making him even more handsome. "Indeed. The name's Pyre. We've been working together for a while now, you and I, though you've never known me by name or face. And locks are my...strength, if you know what I mean."

She processed his words and realization dawned. "But I know you by reputation," Robyn said, a small smile flitting across her lips as she worked it out. "You're the Jester."

He'd married the Lady Hound Tempest.

Pyre clapped in approval. "Well met. I have some good news."

"My friends!" Robyn exclaimed, the reality of her situation slamming into her as the blanket of sleep was finally pulled fully away. "Are they—"

"They are free," Pyre said. He removed his top hat and spun it between his hands. "And are eagerly awaiting you. As for your poorly deceased husband... we have a story for him. Poor wretch drunkenly fell down the stairs and broke his neck. On his wedding night, too." Pyre faked wiping a tear from his eye. "But in order to secure your position as Duchess of Merjeri—"

"I'll deal with this, Pyre," Tempest said, heaving herself into the chambers from the window.

Just who were these people?

Get yourself together.

Tempest strode through the window to sit by Robyn's side. She studied the disheveled covers on the bed and Robyn's general state of semi-undress with a critical eye. Robyn reached for her dress and Tempest batted her hand away. "Don't mess up the masterpiece," she said. "You must make sure the guards see you like this. Fake some tears if you can. Now give me your thigh."

"My—my thigh?!" Robyn exclaimed, startled into obedience when Tempest hitched up the expansive skirt of her wedding dress to her thigh.

"Your hand or arms would be too obvious," Tempest remarked, snapping out a tiny knife from her belt before cutting Robyn's skin with practiced efficiency. She pinched the cut until blood welled across it, then gathered the liquid on her fingertips and smeared it on the mattress.

Robyn paled but worked out what was going on, rage suffusing her cheeks. "I will not stand for this! I don't want anyone to think that man touched me!"

"You must. Your people depend on it."

She ran a hand over her face and tried to shove down her emotions. Why would they want others to believe she slept with the duke? Her jaw slackened as it struck Robyn. "You want it to look like I could be carrying his heir," she said flatly.

"It will give Queen Ansette enough time to ensure you keep control of the province. Sorry that you must pretend to have ever lain with such a snake...or that you must now pretend to grieve him."

Robyn wrinkled her nose at this. "I'm good at pretending. Except..."

Except with one person.

His absence was stark and painfully obvious.

She swallowed hard. "Is Damien... is he with you?" Robyn dared to ask, though she already knew the answer.

At this, Pyre smiled sadly and shook his head. "My apologies, Lady Marian. Our dragon friend is entirely unreachable. After we freed your friends last night, he disappeared with the sheriff. Experience tells me not to chase after him."

Her heart shattered, and a lone tear slipped out. Robyn scrubbed it away angrily. Damien had held his end of the deal. She couldn't fault him for leaving after she'd rejected him.

"There's no way to contact him?" she asked, despite herself.

"He is gone," Pyre replied softly, pity in his gaze. "I'm so sorry."

So was she.

And Robyn had no one to blame but herself.

Chapter Forty-Three

Robyn

She'd been summoned to see the queen.

Her palms were sweaty as she approached the double doors flanked by half a dozen guards. A burly man with light blue hair gave her a dashing smile as he stepped away from the wall.

A Hound.

Robyn gave him a weak smile. The crown sent Hounds to fetch traitors.

He opened the door and gestured for her to enter the throne room.

She squared her shoulders and stepped into the massive room with soaring ceilings. The Hound moved to her side and offered his arm. Robyn took it and wished for the hundredth time that Damien was there.

"Take a deep breath," the Hound said in a low, calm voice. Robyn blew out a nervous breath. The man patted her hand. "It's going to be all right."

"So says the executioner," she retorted, before snapping

her mouth shut. Why did she always ramble when she was nervous? Robyn forced herself to focus on the throne at the far end of the room, as her knees began to shake.

The Hound chuckled and led her down the middle of the room, the tall black-and-gold marble columns stood like silent sentinels along the smooth walls.

"Can I at least know your name before you kill me?" she muttered. *Shut up.*

"It's Maxim, my lady, and I promise you that you won't die by my hand today."

Fantastic. He'd said not by his hand, not that she wouldn't die at all.

Her stomach churned as they neared the dais.

Robyn released Maxim's arm and dropped to the floor in the deepest curtsey she could manage and stayed there. Her pulse pounded in her ears at the utter silence.

"Marian Robyn Lochslee. Do you know why you're here?" the soft feminine voice of the queen asked.

"To atone, your majesty," Robyn said, staring at the black-and-white stone floor.

"Rise," the queen commanded.

Robyn rose and lifted her gaze to the queen.

Queen Ansette sat on the edge of her throne examining Robyn from a face that looked far older than her fourteen years, her deep-blue velvet skirts pooling around the throne. Pyre and Tempest stood to her right and a tall foreboding Hound to her left. The queen lifted her chin and arched a brow.

"You have caused quite a stir in the kingdom."

"My apologies, Your Majesty," Robyn said, once again bowing her head. "That wasn't my intention."

"Was it not? You've impersonated a soldier, lied to your commanding officers, started revolts amongst the smallfolk, pillaged and stolen from your duchy, and plotted treason - all which demand your head."

"As you say, Your Majesty." Robyn bowed lower, her eyes closing. And she'd do it all over again for her people.

"And…" Here it came, her death sentence. "You've liberated your people from an abusive duke plotting treason against the crown."

Robyn's eyes snapped open and filled with tears.

Heeled boots clicked against stone, and the Queen's blue dress came into view a moment before a small hand cupped Robyn's right cheek.

"Please stand, my lady." She slowly straightened, meeting Queen Ansette's calm gaze. "Our kingdom owes you a debt for your bravery and valor. I owe you a debt."

A tear spilled over Robyn's cheek. "You owe me nothing, your majesty. My men and women deserve the credit."

"And humble as well. We need more vassals like you in Heimserya. Which brings me to the next topic." Queen Ansette smiled and pulled her hand away. "My spy mistress and master have informed me that there are no heirs to the duchy in your province. The former dukes made sure to kill off any of their family members which leaves me you, the duke's widow." A secret smile played about the queen's lips. "I'm told that the marriage was legitimate, and because you and your father are the highest-ranking highborn in the province, I will leave the duchy in your care from here on."

Robyn's eyes widened. "Your majesty, thank you so much, but I must refuse. I am no duchess." She didn't want to rule the province. All she wanted was to restore equality.

"And that is why you will do well," Queen Ansette said with a smile. "If you weren't so needed in Merjeri, I would be tempted to keep you here as one of my ladies in waiting. I always need someone like you in court."

"I'm honored, My Queen."

Robyn's mouth popped open when Queen Ansette pulled her into a hug. She stared wide-eyed at Pyre and Tempest. The kitsune mimicked hugging and Robyn finally managed to hug the young queen back.

Queen Ansette pulled back. "I have a feeling we are going to be fast friends, you and I."

"I'd be delighted." It felt like a dream. Robyn was just a simple country girl who preferred breeches to dresses.

"That's settled." The queen moved back to her throne and held out a hand to her left.

A soldier dressed all in black prowled from the shadows. His dark-silver eyes assessed Robyn from head to toe as he moved down the stairs like a predator. Without meaning to, Robyn took a step back and fell into a defensive stance. She'd seen men move like that before.

Wolves.

The wolf gave her a half smile and cocked his head, his black hair falling over one eye.

"Your instincts are good," he said, his voice gruff. "I'll give you that much."

"Who are you?" she demanded.

"He's your muscle," Pyre drawled.

Robyn blinked slowly. "Our borders are secure."

"They are," Tempest said. "But not for long. Old Mother does not abide failure or disgrace. She will be back, which is why Brine will accompany you for your protection."

She snorted. "I'll need protection from *him*."

The wolf Brine snorted. "I have no designs on your life, my lady."

"Plus, this is only for a short time, until…a few things iron themselves out," Pyre added.

Robyn took her eyes from the wolf up to the Queen, and then to Pyre and Tempest. "What things?"

The kitsune gave her a slow smile. "Things."

How delightfully vague. "As you command." Robyn could deal with his presence. Stars, it was better than execution. Plus, there was no saying she couldn't lose him on the way to the keep…

Her expression must have given something away, because Brine's silvery eyes narrowed on her. "You're going to be trouble."

Robyn smiled at him. "I would never."

Chapter Forty-Four

Damien

One Month Later

"What are you still doing here?" Luca asked.

Damien ran a hand over his face and tossed his empty goblet onto the pebbled path in front of his bench seat. Being a shifter had its draw backs. Humans could drown their sorrows in spirits but not him. His body burned through it too quickly. He still felt as empty and wretched as when he had stolen one of Luca's bottles of fire whiskey five hours prior.

He stared at the lush flower garden his cousin had planted and sighed. "Trying to forget."

"Your mate or the Sheriff?"

"Do not mention him in my presence," Damien thundered, glaring at Luca to his right. It was enough torment knowing that the sod was alive, let alone speak of him.

His cousin rolled his purple eyes. "Either do something about him or let him go. I don't want him around and neither does Thorn."

"I can't!" he yelled, leaping to his feet. He paced the pathway, feeling uncomfortable in his own skin. Damien had gotten the merry men out almost a month ago and gotten ahold of the sheriff, intending on executing the blackguard who'd hurt his family. When the time came to exact his vengeance, Damien found himself unable to do it. All he could see was his mate's disproving face in his mind. "I can't," he whispered raggedly.

What kind of a dragon was he if he couldn't protect those he loved? If he lacked the strength to do what was necessary? When had he become so soft?

He faced Luca. "Why haven't you done anything?"

"Because Thorn doesn't wish for his death." His cousin frowned. "He's a vile man to be sure, but he was raised by the former duke. He's known nothing but corruption and cruelty since infancy." A pause. "Plus, death would be too good for him. His punishment should fit his crimes."

"He threatened my mate." Even reflecting on it made Damien's blood boil.

Luca smirked, flashing a bit of fang. "Now we get down to the root of it. Why are you here and not with Robyn?"

Damien stiffened. "Because she told me to leave."

That isn't the truth. You left before she could refuse you again.

"She does not want me."

"Is that what she said?" Luca asked, arching a brow.

"Does it matter?"

His cousin scoffed. "This isn't like you to mope around. In the past, when you've spotted something you desired, you worked tirelessly to obtain it."

"She isn't an object," Damien replied softly. "She's everything."

"Then again, I ask you, what are you doing here?"

Damien dropped his head and stared at the ground, before meeting his cousin's gaze. "She's married." The words cut him to the heart. A week prior he'd almost flown back to Merjeri in a moment of weakness and begged her to take him as her lover. It disgusted him. He'd always been a dragon of honor. Vows of marriage were sacred. It didn't matter that his mate didn't love her degenerate of a husband, Robyn would be faithful as was right.

Luca blanched; sympathy painted across his face. "I'm so sorry. Why didn't you say anything before?"

"What is there to say?" Damien replied bitterly. "I failed and I'm to blame." If only he'd taken out the duke and sheriff before the wedding.

She wouldn't have forgiven you.

"Damien..."

He held his hand up. "I can't speak of this any longer." He swallowed down his pain and squared his shoulders. Damien was a bloody dragon king. He needed to act like it. "Something must be done. I can't kill the sheriff, but he must be punished."

Luca sighed and rolled his neck. He stilled and then a slow smile curled his lips as he glanced at Damien. "When is the last time you visited the Dread Mountain mines belonging to Dragoness de Baruette?"

"It's been a very long time." Damien grinned wickedly as an idea formed. The mines were hell on earth. "Do you think the sheriff would fancy a visit?"

His cousin's grin widened. "A permanent stay is in order,

don't you think?"

Two Months Later

"Where is that lazy dragon?" a familiar voice called, his voice echoing down the hallway.

Damien snapped his book shut as Pyre swaggered into Luca's study like a vain peacock. The kitsune pulled his top silk hat from his head and his wool cloak from his shoulders, tossing them onto the large desk dominating the center of the room.

"What are you doing here?" he asked, standing from the window seat.

"Well, that's a fine way to greet one of your oldest friends," Pyre commented, moving to the large fire to warm his hands. "Hello to you too."

Damien snorted and tossed the book onto the widow seat before crossing his arms. He had reread the same page over and over but couldn't remember what it even said. He felt like he was about to lose his mind. A thread of excitement wrapped around his chest. Perhaps the fox had a job for him. Something to keep his mind from Robyn. Or maybe information about his mate.

"It's because I am one of your oldest friends that I know you're not here for a social visit." Pyre hated the bitter cold of the Dread Mountains. Damien strode over to the fireplace and sat in one of the two leather chairs that bracketed the hearth. "Tell me, what brings you to the mountains?"

The kitsune turned from the fire, warming his back. His amber eyes flitted about the room before landing on Damien.

"So this is where you've been holed up? I figured you would have been slumbering away in one of your hordes for the last two months and yet, this is where I find you."

Damien glanced away, feeling like Pyre could see too much. The bloody kitsune was practically a magician when it came to sousing out other's emotions. "It was time I visited my kin. I'd been gone too long."

"And you've been here the entire time?" Pyre questioned, picking at his gaudy vest.

"For the most part."

The fox glanced slyly at him from the corner of his eye. "And the sheriff?"

Damien grinned. "Dealt with." A pause. "And alive."

Pyre blinked slowly and faced him. "How very... unexpected."

"What do you mean by that?" he replied, tone a little too sharp.

"You're even more bloodthirsty than I am, and that's saying something."

Damien stiffened. "I'm not that bad."

The kitsune gave him a droll look, red ears twitching in amusement. "None of your enemies still live."

"Except the sheriff." Because he couldn't do it. Fool that he was.

"The sheriff," Pyre said, his lip curling. "A nasty bit of rubbish. I take it we won't cross paths with him again?"

"Not where I sent him." The sheriff would spend the rest of his life serving Dragoness de Baruette in her mines. Even if the miscreant somehow managed to escape the female dragon, he would never make it out of the mountains alive.

"Good. I'm sure Lady Merjeri will appreciate the news."

It was a punch to the gut. Damien choked on his pain at the mention of Robyn. He'd wanted to ask about her the moment the fox had set foot in the room.

Lady Merjeri.

He hated the sound of it. It should have been *Marian Robyn Firebane – Queen of Dragons.*

"How is she?" he managed to say through clenched teeth.

"Doing well enough."

That was all Pyre was going to say? "I'm glad to hear it." And Damien was.

Even though he was miserable, he didn't want his mate to be suffering. She deserved all the happiness in the world even if she wasn't bound to him.

The kitsune began to slow clap. "You put on a pretty good performance but..." he touched the tip of his nose. "You wreak of rage and sadness. What do you really want to know, friend?"

Damien pushed up from the chair and paced to the window. "Is he treating her well?" Ruslan better be, or he'd rip him limb from limb.

"By he, you mean the duke?"

He closed his eyes and exhaled heavily. "No games, Pyre. Tell me."

"It would be pretty hard for the duke to harm Robyn since he's dead."

Damien froze and a dull ringing began in his ears.

Dead. The duke was dead.

Slowly, he turned to face his friend as his hands began to shake. "He's dead?"

Pyre moved to the desk and plucked his hat from the surface before facing Damien. "He had a mishap with the stairs the night after their wedding."

Two months.

Robyn had been free from the duke for two months.

Red descended over his vision.

One moment he was by the window, the next he had his hand wrapped around Pyre's throat, pinning the fox to the wall to the left of the door. Damien snapped his teeth in front of his friend's face, but the kitsune didn't even flinch.

"Why have you kept this from me?" he snarled.

"In case you need reminding, you disappeared without a word. It's taken me this time to *find* you." Pyre held his gaze. "You have no one to blame but yourself." Damien tightened his hold on the fox, his breath ragged. "You abandoned your mate."

"I would *never* do such a thing." If he had known, Damien would already be back in Merjeri.

"No? She's faced the queen for her crimes on her own. While you what? Languish here?" Pyre's eyes narrowed. "I almost didn't come looking for you, but Tempest convinced me otherwise. You've been stupid."

Damien growled low. "I didn't know."

"So what are you going to do Dragon King?" Pyre asked, his amber eyes hard, the Jester peeking out.

"I'm going to do what I should have two months ago." He released his friend, blinking away the red haze. "I'm going to claim my mate."

The kitsune broke into a grin and slapped him on the shoulder. "There's the Damien I know."

He yanked Pyre into a hug, released him, and rushed out of the study into the hallway and began running, shedding clothing as he went.

Too much time had been wasted.

Did Robyn think he'd forsaken her? He'd only been trying to be honorable even though it almost killed him.

"Don't you dare fly off without me," Pyre bellowed after him. "I am not travelling through these mountains again."

"Then hurry up," Damien called over his shoulder. "Or I'll leave you here."

He wouldn't spend one more minute apart from the love of his life.

I'm coming for you Dove.

Chapter Forty-Five

Robyn

Spring rains washed over her province, and, before Robyn knew it, the inviting heat of summer was upon her.

She had been busy over the last few months.

At first, Robyn had been busy pretending to be a grieving newlywed, torn from the arms of her husband much too quickly. Pyre and Tempest's ruse had worked, with news quickly spreading that the Duke of Merjeri had tragically fallen to his death down the precipitous stairs of his manor after drinking too much wine. Pretending they had lain together gave Robyn the buffer she needed against Ruslan's staunch supporters until Queen Ansette deemed it legal and right that Robyn continued on as the Duchess of Merjeri.

After that, the real work began.

Though Robyn had indeed retired the Hood—what use was the disguise now that she could properly affect change with her own face?—that didn't mean she stopped communicating with Pyre and Tempest, nor indeed did it mean her men stopped rooting out injustice on her behalf.

They managed to push back the wolves into Betraz with the help of the Dark Court and the Hounds.

After that, there were no more ambushes and robberies, of course. No, instead Robyn used her followers to ensure the smallfolk of Merjeri province were returned each and every penny, crop, farm animal, and home that had been unfairly taken from them. The sheriff had been declared missing, not that anyone missed him.

Robyn could not face living in the Duke of Merjeri's estate alone, so with Pavel's help, they turned the manor into both a new orphanage and a halfway house for those who had nowhere else to go—be that because of poverty, abuse...or drugs.

The drugs.

Even now, two months later, Robyn was not sure every trace of the deadly mimkia variant that Ruslan had been peddling was gone. Pyre had headed up the weeding of the substance from the province, and his focus was now on the long arms of the drug trade that had infected other regions, but Robyn knew she had to constantly be on her toes. All it would take would be one of Ruslan's highborn supporters, not convinced by the story of his death, to pick up where the Duke of Merjeri left off. They still hadn't discovered where the mimkia fields were, but Pyre said it was only a matter of time.

And so, Robyn had no time to rest. She had so much to do, and not enough hours in the day to do it all. She wished she had someone by her side to help her through it.

She knew she wanted that 'someone' to be Damien.

There had still been no sight nor sound from him in two months, though that didn't stop her from eagerly awaiting news of him whenever Pyre or Tempest came to update her about the state of their war on mimkia throughout Heimserya. But every time, without fail, they had nothing to tell her.

Robyn didn't want to give up on her feelings for Damien. For why should she? Allowing herself to fall in love with the dragon shifter—allowing herself to *admit* to those feelings, no less—was the most selfish thing she had ever done in her entire life. If she was to take her mother's advice to heart, then she couldn't possibly give up on Damien.

If only she could find him.

"Is that shipment from the south due tomorrow, Robyn?" Pavel asked, heaving a sack of grain onto his shoulder to take into the new orphanage's pantry. "The kids are well in need of new summer clothes, and the refugees from Talaga wish to make them from the linen and silk we have coming in."

Robyn laughed into her hand. "We will have a group of spoiled princes and princesses on our hands before we know it, Pavel. Dresses and shirts of dyed crimson silk! Imagine it."

"May as well put Merjeri's diamonds to good use," Will called out, putting down his axe to take a breath. He and Andrei were busy fronting up the effort to build new houses on the Merjeri estate in the same style as the beautiful houses that littered the province, built a hundred years ago. With more permanent lodgings available, they could house more people coming into the province, and with it, they'd prosper from a larger workforce and bigger skillset.

Already, Robyn had forged new connections with southern provinces for food to help them through the next winter, should it be as bitter as the year before. Ruslan had never deemed such connections necessary—why waste money and time feeding the smallfolk when they should be feeding themselves? Robyn could practically hear him complaining in her head; it satisfied her to no end every time she did the exact opposite thing that her dearly departed husband would have.

But even with all the work to do, and her friends and family around her to help, Robyn was desperately lonely.

"Are you all right, Robyn?" Andrei asked, concern coloring his face as he regarded her. "You're very pale considering it's so hot out."

Pavel and Will had similar looks of concern on their faces.

"I...perhaps I need a break," Robyn said, because in truth she did. With a promise to take care of herself, Robyn retired not to the Merjeri manor, nor to her own house, but to the woods. She always ended up in the abandoned clearing where the Hood had made her base camp with Damien whenever she felt this lonely.

The sun was streaming overhead, warming the mossy ground until it was more comfortable than the most opulent of beds. She lay down upon the springy, green plants, sighing in relief when she closed her eyes against the sun and allowed it to heat her core.

She had not felt truly warm ever since Damien left.

For ten minutes or so, Robyn allowed her mind to wander, close to the edge of dozing, when a shadow crossed over the sun and caused her to shiver. *Odd,* she thought, opening her eyes to investigate the sky. But the shadow was gone as soon as it had appeared, and there were no clouds in the sky.

Resettling, Robyn was once more about to close her eyes when a lightning-quick shape passed over the sun once more.

It glinted green where it caught the light.

Her breath caught. Could it really be?

Robyn bolted to her feet, stumbling with how frantic her heart was beating.

"Is it you?" she called out, her words reverberating all around the clearing. Robyn cupped her hands around her mouth and shouted at the sky: "Do not play with me like this! If you are here, Damien—"

"I'm here, so stop shouting."

The voice came from behind Robyn, so close she yelped, then turned on the spot to see the face of the man who matched the voice.

And there was Damien, as naked as the day Robyn first met him, standing before her with an achingly familiar, arrogant grin on his face.

A sob caught in her throat, and she covered her mouth with her hand. Heat pressed at the back of her eyes. It was her dragon.

She wanted to hit him for disappearing. Wanted to yell at him for leaving before she could talk to him once more. Wanted to be so angry that fire spouted from her throat.

He tossed on a robe and belted it at the waist, then held his arms out. "Come here, my dove."

Robyn ran into his arms and held him as tightly as she could, his familiar scent of sage and citrus surrounding her.

"You're late," she murmured against his chest, tears filling her eyes and threatening to spill down her face. She'd missed him so much.

"I had some things to settle," Damien said, wrapping his huge arms around Robyn and crushing her against him. The feeling was so comforting—so warming—that instead of crying, Robyn felt her tears dry up.

She nuzzled her face against his chest, reveling in the smell of him. "If you had stayed around, I—"

"I know," Damien cut in, though his voice was soft. "I know, but you needed time to settle your *own* things. I did not want to rush you. We've both been through much."

"I should have been the one to decide if I needed time or not," Robyn countered, tilting her head up to look at Damien. "You never gave me the choice by running away."

A throaty chuckle rumbled through the shifter. "How many times do I have to say *I know.* I'm sorry I left that way. But in all fairness, I warned you I would leave."

"I know, but it still hurt. I didn't get to say goodbye," she whispered thickly.

"That was wrong of me. I was angry and hurt, and thought I'd murder everyone around me when you married. After Tempest and Pyre assured me you'd be safe and the men rescued, I fled."

"With the sheriff," she muttered.

"He and I had unfinished business."

Robyn lifted her gaze to Damien's warm green eyes. "Is he gone?"

Damien held her stare. "At first, I planned to torment him for his misdeeds and kill the blighter but when I got him alone...all I could think of was what you'd think. I couldn't do it."

"So, what did you do?"

He smiled sharply, two pointed incisors peeking out. "I put him somewhere he'll never escape and wish he was dead. He'll pay for his crimes for the rest of his life."

"I'm proud of you." She'd never thought Damien would

ever come around to seeing her side of things. "Are you here to stay?"

Damien's expression turned serious. "I can't stay here forever."

Her stomach bottomed out and she tried to push away but he kept her trapped against him.

"Why would you come back? To torment me? Have you changed your mind about me?" A pang of sorrow stabbed her in the chest.

"Never. You're my mate," he growled, brushing his nose against hers. "We will be together forever until death do us part. I love you. I never want to be parted from you from this day forward."

"Neither do I. I love you, you foolish dragon. Why can't you stay?"

"I have responsibilities in the mountains with my people."

Robyn blinked slowly. "What kind of responsibilities?"

"Similar to the ones you now have as duchess."

"So, you're nobility?" she questioned.

He smiled wickedly. "No, I am the king."

Her eyes widened. What the devil? "Tell me you're joking."

Damien's smile grew. "I'm afraid not, my dove. You'll just have to tolerate being a duchess *and* queen."

"I can't do that!" She was a simple girl from the country.

"You'll make an excellent queen." He pressed a kiss to her right cheek. "But we can speak about this later. We have much more pressing matters."

She opened her mouth to retort when Damien's lips on Robyn's turned the rest of her complaint to soft moans and desperate kisses. In that moment, they both perfectly understood each other, and what they meant to each other.

Robyn had chosen Damien above anyone else. She was his mate, just as he was hers.

The dragon had set a fire in Robyn, and she in him, and neither of them had any intention of letting it go out. Together, nobody could get away with injustice without facing them. Together, nobody could interfere with their happiness.

Together, they were unstoppable.

"Will you be mine?" her dragon growled.

"Only if you'll be mine."

"I was yours the day you threw a rock at me in my dragon form." He smiled against her lips. "I do have one request."

"What's that?" she asked, nipping his bottom lip.

"That you must get over your aversion to nudity. I have plans for us."

She tipped her head back and laughed before once again meeting his gaze. "You marry me, and I won't ever complain again."

Damien swept Robyn off her feet with another kiss. "Done. How quickly can we find someone to marry us?"

She rolled her eyes. "This takes planning."

"I have plans. Speak to your father. Marry you. Love you until you're exhausted. Laugh with you until your hair is white and my scales are gray."

"Sounds wonderful," she said.

"It will be, with you by my side."

Chapter Forty-Six

Brine

One Month Later

Brine puffed out a breath, admiring the full moon and savoring the quiet of the night. He leaned against the rampart of Merjeri Manor, the wind ruffling his black hair. He scanned the grounds, his ears twitching atop his head as he heard several childish giggles from the courtyard below.

He moved a few paces so he could see better.

Pavel – the gentle giant – sat on a stone bench with a group of wee ones sitting on the grass at his feet while he read a story by lantern light. A smile lifted Brine's lips as the little ones laughed when Pavel made a silly face. Robyn had made many changes to Merjeri Manor since Brine had joined her. What was once a military compound was quickly turning into a home filled with laughter and joy.

It was a welcome change to the Dark Court.

It had been a long time since he'd enjoyed such peace.